AGE OF VAMPIRES

INFERNAL
CREATURES

CAROLINE PECKHAM
SUSANNE VALENTI

REALM G

THE
BLOOD BANK

REALM F

THE WASTES

REALM E

REALM H

R

United States

Realm G

The Blood Ba

M A

NEW YORK
(BELVEDERE CASTLE)

REALM B

REALM C

New York

Belvedere
Castle

Infernal Creatures
Age of Vampires #3
Copyright © 2019 Caroline Peckham & Susanne Valenti
Cover Art Design by Stella Colorado
Map Design by Fred Kroner

Interior Formatting & Design by Wild Elegance Formatting

Infernal Creatures/Caroline Peckham & Susanne Valenti – 2nd ed.
ISBN-13 - 978-1-914425-92-9

This book is dedicated to worms.
They're just getting on with their business, worming through the ground,
mulching down leaves, and doing other important earthy things. No one
would ever dedicate anything to a worm, they'd have to be crazy.

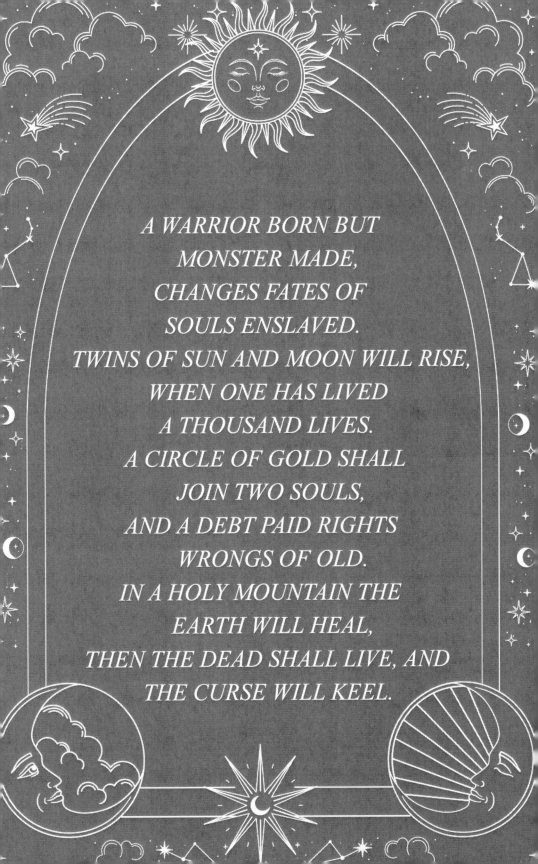

A WARRIOR BORN BUT
MONSTER MADE,
CHANGES FATES OF
SOULS ENSLAVED.
TWINS OF SUN AND MOON WILL RISE,
WHEN ONE HAS LIVED
A THOUSAND LIVES.
A CIRCLE OF GOLD SHALL
JOIN TWO SOULS,
AND A DEBT PAID RIGHTS
WRONGS OF OLD.
IN A HOLY MOUNTAIN THE
EARTH WILL HEAL,
THEN THE DEAD SHALL LIVE, AND
THE CURSE WILL KEEL.

CALLIE

CHAPTER ONE

A voice found me in the pressing darkness. *Sun Child, you have lived a thousand lives. Use their knowledge to guide you now.* I couldn't hold on to the words. They slipped away as quickly as I'd heard them. My mind drifted somewhere between sleep and waking, but no dreams came to me. I was here alone.

I knew pain awaited me when I woke but there was something else too. Something which filled me with a burning purpose I'd never felt before, a path for my feet to follow, a journey for my life to take. I moved towards it and my senses came alive in a way they never had until now.

My eyes fluttered open, and I frowned at the strange room. I was lying on a bed, a heavy duvet draped over me and a musty smell filling my nostrils. Without turning my head, I could tell that someone else was in the room with me. It was like a sixth sense prickling at my skin, informing me that another slayer was close. The fact was reassuring; I wanted my kin near me, but it was disconcerting too, my mind adjusting to this new way of perceiving the world.

I pushed myself onto my elbows, looking around at the large room I found myself in. Wooden furniture lined the dim walls, but it was all covered with a thick layer of dust, making it clear the place hadn't been occupied in a long time. Cobwebs adorned the corners of the space and wooden shutters were closed over the windows. A single candle burned on a desk beside the window, its flickering light the only reason I could see anything at all. My gaze snagged on the details of my surroundings more than usual. A broken corner on the top of the wardrobe. A scuff mark on the wooden floor beneath the mirror. Each thing telling a story of something that had happened here before, hinting at my surroundings and making my senses prickle with awareness.

"You're awake," Magnar rumbled, and I turned to find him sitting in a wooden chair by the door. His gaze was guarded as it fell on me, his face a blank mask, but I could sense his concern.

"How long was I out?" I asked.

My mouth was thick and dry like cotton wool, and my limbs were heavy with fatigue. It felt like I'd been sleeping for a long time. I guessed he'd brought me here from the hilltop after I'd taken my vow and the world had fallen to darkness around me, but I had no idea where here was.

"You collapsed after taking your vow before the sun set yesterday. You have been unconscious for over a day." His tone was clipped, and I frowned as I tried to figure out why he was upset with me.

"Are you pissed at me, Elder?" I shook my head in confusion as the strange word spilled from my mouth. I'd meant to say his name. "I mean Elder...wait, no-"

"Are you having trouble speaking my name?" Magnar asked, pursing his lips. The fact didn't seem to surprise him.

"I don't understand. What's going on?" I curled my legs beneath me and sat upright, trying to align my thoughts. Had I hit my head when I collapsed? Why wouldn't my tongue do what my brain told it to?

"This is what you wanted. You bound yourself to me." He stood and strode towards me, taking my left hand in his and lifting it so I could see the mark on the back of it. The image of a star stood out along my skin, and I blinked as I tried to remember it appearing. He was right. I had wanted this. I could feel a pool of power writhing beneath my skin and it filled me with a sense of the strength I'd been longing for.

Magnar dropped my hand like it offended him and folded his arms as he towered over me next to the bed.

"So what does that have to do with me not being able to say Elder, no I meant-"

"You cannot speak my name until your training is complete and you are released from your bond to me. I am your Elder now. Your mentor."

"But that's ridiculous, surely you don't give a shit about me using your name. Do we seriously have to abide by every little rule?" I shook my head, wondering why I would be following a rule I hadn't even known existed in the first place.

"What I mind or don't is irrelevant. You've taken your vow. You gave up your freedom and bound yourself to the way of our people. The goddess, Idun, will enforce the rules even if you don't wish to follow them," Magnar said icily.

I had to be missing something because I still didn't understand why he was so angry about it. Hadn't he wanted this? Hadn't he been all alone, the last of his kind? So why was he looking at me like I'd just tossed his favourite sword in a swamp?

"But..." I traced my thumb over the star on my skin, a sense of unease filling me.

I'd never asked Magnar about what taking the vow really meant. I knew it would unleash my gifts, but he'd warned me that I'd be relinquishing my freedom too. I clearly hadn't realised quite what that entailed. Though I'd never expected to lose control of my own tongue.

"So I can't say your name? I just call you Elder?" My throat thickened with emotion, heat scoring across my cheeks at the humiliation of having to address him with a name that insinuated respect, regardless of my feelings on it. I'd spent my entire life caged, forced to bow to creatures who had placed themselves above me against my will, and taking the vow had been meant as a way to rise above that, to stop bending to the will of others. But now I simply found myself beneath a different beast, the actions of my own body betraying me and forcing me into submission.

I swallowed down the surge of emotion, forcing back the prickling in my eyes, refusing to allow a single tear to fall over this. I had given all my tears to my grief. I wouldn't spill another.

Elder. The word felt like a chain around my neck. It made me feel like I was something less than him. Like we weren't equals and I was no longer free.

"That's my title, and out of respect, you have to address me that way." Magnar's eyes glinted with steel, fury caged within his gaze, a flash of betrayal there which I didn't understand.

"Don't you want to teach me?" I demanded.

After everything that had driven me to take the vow, I was suddenly beginning to doubt my choice. If Magnar didn't want to take on this position, then what was I supposed to do now?

"When I told you about the vow, you made it clear you didn't want to take it. So I didn't consider teaching you after that," he snarled.

"So what? I changed my mind. Surely you, of all people, can understand the need for vengeance that my father's death caused me to-"

"Vengeance will be the end of your life if you let it control every decision you make!" he yelled, his voice a harsh crash of noise against the silence, making my heart leap and causing me to flinch back against the pillows.

Magnar smacked his hand against the headboard beside me, then turned away from me, stomping across the brittle floorboards and shoving his fingers through his long hair in clear frustration.

The spike of fear had adrenaline surging through my veins, but I refused to cower beneath him like some chastised child. My lips drew back on a snarl of my own.

I shoved the duvet off me and rose in a fluid motion, ready to punch him in his stupid head if that was what it took to force some answers from him. But my legs were shaky beneath me as I tried to take a step, and I had to grasp the bed frame to stop myself from falling. I felt dizzy from a lack of food, but something else was different too. Like my limbs didn't quite move in the way I expected them to anymore, my body responding faster to my desires, my awareness of my surroundings growing as I moved.

I glanced down at myself. My clothes were dirty and torn, and my feet were bare. Mud and blood were still crusted beneath my fingernails from building my father's cairn. I should have felt like shit, but there was a lightness to my body which went against my expectations.

Each movement I made felt different somehow. Like I had to get to know my body again. I crossed the wooden floor with purposeful steps, making no sound as I stalked towards Magnar. It was as easy as breathing. A piece of me wanted to marvel in the changes, but my mind was caught up in what else this had cost me and the most desperate desire to kick Magnar for being such a dick.

I reached for him, meaning to force him around to face me, but he turned before I could grip his arm, catching my wrist in his hand instead, his fingers easily encircling my flesh.

"You wanted this," I accused in reply to the anger in his golden eyes, and he scoffed.

"I have only ever wanted one thing for myself in my entire life," he replied. "Just one. Yet the gods forbade me from claiming it. You think you understand the concept of vengeance but you're just a naïve child when it comes to the world you live in. You know next to nothing about the monsters who have taken ownership of your world, and only an accident of fate set you free of their clutches when you stumbled across my path."

"I escaped the Realm myself," I hissed, jerking my arm free of his hold, and he let me, his lip curling as I tightened my hand into a fist.

"Oh yes," he agreed. "You managed to lead the only people you love in this world out into freedom for all of a few hours before they were hunted down and captured like the weak humans you all are-"

My fist snapped out faster than I expected, endless rage exploding through my core as I launched myself at Magnar, my grief turning to rage, like a wildfire spreading at the turn of the wind.

Memories spilled through me, lessons learned, training which had taken place in other bodies now lending me the knowledge I required. I twisted my body into the movement of the punch, and for a split second, I actually thought I might land it.

But of course, he moved before I could, his head turning just enough to force my strike into a glancing blow which did little more than brush my knuckles across the rough stubble of his jaw.

Magnar batted my arm aside, my second punch deflected just as easily, his arm somehow snaking around my waist as my momentum threw me towards him. He spun me violently, flipping my back to his front, pinning me in his arms.

"You were supposed to leave once you found your family again," he growled in my ear, the rumble of his words vibrating through my chest.

"I haven't found them," I replied, the pain of that truth cutting me far deeper than any savage words from his lips might. "Not all of them. And my dad…"

A sob caught in my chest and I held it there, stamping my lips shut as the grief rose in me once more, the pain too sharp to bear.

Magnar blew out a harsh breath, his hold on me loosening, though he still kept me there, trapped in the cage of his arms.

"You don't understand what you've done," he muttered.

"So explain it to me," I bit back. "You mock me for knowing nothing about the monsters who rule over my kind, but there's only one answer to ignorance, and that's knowledge. I'm asking to know, so give me the answers. Tell me what else the vow will force upon me. What can I do? What can't I?"

Magnar cursed, turning me once again, drawing me around to face the rage which still blazed in his golden eyes. He backed me up against the wall, pressing me against it and placing his arm above my head.

The nearness of him made me blink in surprise as he loomed over me, the weight of his body trapping me against the wall, the immensity of his presence surrounding me as he dipped his head, his lips a single sin away.

"I am your mentor now. Nothing more," he said slowly, the meaning of those words blazing in his eyes, but I didn't understand it.

"What do you mean 'nothing more'?" I breathed, wondering how there was any oxygen for me at all while his aura took up so much space around me.

Magnar laughed, but it was a dark, hollow thing filled with no joy.

"Why don't you kiss me?" he offered, and my eyes widened in surprise. Whatever I'd thought he was going to say, it hadn't been that.

"You want me to kiss you?" I frowned in confusion. "Why the fuck would I do that?"

"Because even when you're furious with me and wanting to spit and curse and strike me, you still can't get the memory of my mouth on your body out of that pretty head of yours. You can't stop thinking about what it might be like if we did that again, or how long you might hold out before you beg me to give you the rest of me."

"Oh please," I sneered. "You'd be begging for it long before I ever would."

"Prove it then," Magnar replied, a wicked dare in his eyes. "Unless you're simply full of shit."

I gave him a hard glare, then pushed up onto my toes, meaning to prove him wrong and have him on his knees for me with nothing more than a damn kiss if that was what it took to wipe that look off his face. I fisted his shirt in my hands, yanking him down, my eyes on his mouth, but instead of feeling his lips against mine, my head turned aside, and my chin collided with his shoulder.

Heat flared in my cheeks as I jerked back. I hadn't meant to turn away, so what the fuck had just happened?

Magnar leaned towards me but didn't try to touch his lips to mine, simply allowing the space between our mouths to become as small as possible, letting me taste the words which fell from his tongue.

"We will be bound by our cause, forfeiting all other ties," he hissed bitterly, quoting the vow. "Thank you for that."

"You mean we can't be together?" I asked, my gut twisting at the thought.

I hadn't even known the words of the vow before I'd spoken them, how could I have realised what I'd been agreeing to when I made my decision?

"No. We can't kiss or fuck or do anything at all inappropriate for an Elder and his novice. The bond between us is one without equal power, and as such, the gods blessed the vow with this protection for you. Perhaps you should thank them for that while you fuck your own hand and dream of me in the dark." He turned and stalked away from me before I could reply, moving to the shuttered window and pulling the wood aside so he could look out into the night.

"Seems like a simple enough price to pay," I snapped even as I felt the loss of his presence like an ache in my gut. But what did I care? It was only sex. Only a physical outlet for my rage and pain. Surely I could claim that through learning to kill the bloodsuckers anyway. Though the tightness in my chest suggested that kind of satisfaction might not be quite the same.

"Perhaps if you'd explained all of this before-" I began, but he cut me off.

"Would your need for vengeance have been any less?" Magnar asked.

"No, Elder." I replied, internally cringing as I used that fucking title again.

"It's done now," he said dismissively, still not looking at me. "Idun continues to test me as always. I never should have thought it would be any different now. A thousand years may have passed but I'm still at her mercy, and she is just as cunning and cruel as ever."

Wind hammered against the window, and I had the strangest feeling that it was in response to his words. He didn't seem worried about offending the goddess though, and he continued to scowl out at the night.

"I still feel the same inside," I muttered.

"I know. Do you think that makes it better or worse?" Before I could answer, Magnar stomped away again. "I brought in some water from a well outside and left it warming by the fire. Go and get cleaned up."

I wanted to protest and ask him more about the vow, but his words fell on me with a command I couldn't resist. My feet turned and walked me out of the room without me telling them to, my body betraying me yet again. It was like I had no option but to do as he said, even as my mind fought against his control. I tried to resist the impulse as I headed down the rickety stairs in the abandoned house, my heart thrashing with panic when my own limbs failed to obey my commands. I caught hold of the banister, stopping my progress for a moment, but after a few seconds, my fingers relinquished their hold on it and I kept going.

Panic built in my chest, and I tried harder to break free of the command, but it was useless. I was trapped inside my body while my limbs worked of their own accord, following his direction and continuing to descend the stairs.

"What the fuck is this?!" I shouted, but Magnar didn't respond, and my pulse pounded in my ears as the silence of the abandoned building surrounded me.

I vaguely took in the large farmhouse as I passed through it, noting the dust, cobwebs and hints of mould which marked the years of emptiness it had endured, but my mind was occupied with trying to break free of Magnar's command.

The light of the fire flickered beneath a doorway on my right, and I moved into the room despite trying to reach for the doorframe to stop myself, but my arm refused to raise at my instruction. I couldn't force my legs to stop walking until I made it to the huge tub of water sitting before the flames.

I sucked in a deep breath as I gripped the edge of the bath, but the command still wasn't finished with me, refusing to let me stop there.

I peeled off my filthy clothes, tossing them to the floor before climbing into the tub with a scream of fury.

The water was warm, as promised, but it did little to ease the weight in my chest while I was left trapped within my body, a witness to its movements, panic threatening to swallow me whole.

I scrubbed at my skin, caught in the hold of Magnar's orders until they were completed and I finally felt the pressure to obey slipping away from me.

A sob forced its way from my throat, my breaths coming in sharp gasps which built them up into a scream of pure rage as my temper fractured into a thousand pieces. What the fuck was this? How could he hold such power over me? He could make me do anything at all now, and I'd be powerless to stop him. I hadn't known I was giving him control over me when I'd spoken the vow. How could I have bound myself so completely to something I didn't even understand?

I'd gone into the blood bank hoping to get my family back, and we should have been together now, heading south towards the sunshine. Instead, I'd found out that Montana was impossibly far away, my father had died, and now I was under the control of a savage who seemed entirely enraged about the situation.

I was more alone than I'd ever been in my life. And to top it all off, I'd traded in my freedom as well. I'd known taking the vow would bind me to a path where either the vampires would die, or I would. But I'd never imagined it would do this to me.

I tried to hold back the tears, but they were like a dam waiting to overflow, unstoppable as the hopelessness of my situation sank down on me.

I broke with another ragged cry, the tears running down my cheeks, mixing with the bath water as I pressed my hands over my face and tried to stave off the rising panic.

I'd been so stupid. So fucking stupid. In seeking revenge for my father's death, I'd managed to lose so much more. Anything I'd had which the vampires hadn't stolen from me already, I'd now lost for myself. And there was no way for me to undo it.

Footsteps sounded beyond the door and I stilled, wrapping my arms over my chest in case Magnar decided to come in. It wasn't like I could do anything to stop him. Hell, he could command me to dance naked around the fire and I'd have no choice but to comply.

Magnar sighed from the other side of the wood. "I shouldn't have done that to you."

"What was that?" Another sob tried to break free of my chest, but I bit down on my lip, forcing myself to hold it together. It was bad enough that I'd done this without me falling apart completely too. I had to find a way to deal with it.

"I won't have this power over you forever. While I'm your mentor, you have to follow my commands, but once your training is complete, you'll be free of the compulsion," he replied.

"And how long will that take?"

"It varies. It took me a little under a year, but it could be as long as five. Once you can fully resist the compulsion, then you'll know your training is finished and you'll be a full slayer. Ready to take responsibility for your own actions."

Something uncoiled in my chest at his words. This wouldn't last forever. I'd be free again.

"But until then, you can make me do anything you want?" I whispered, and I wondered if my voice would even carry to him beyond the door.

"Almost anything. But I have never heard of someone taking their vow the way you just did. Selecting a mentor is something that people spend years deciding. It should be with someone you trust implicitly not to abuse their power over you. Someone you have known your whole life and have spent time learning from in the past," he explained.

"I do trust you," I replied, because even if I hated him sometimes too, I couldn't deny that truth. He had rescued me time and again, fought by my side, helped my father when he was dying. I may not have known him well, and maybe I didn't even like him half the time, but I did trust him.

Magnar released a heavy breath and didn't respond.

"So who did you choose to teach you?" I asked.

"My father was my mentor."

"No issues with wanting to fuck him then, I guess." I cringed as the words escaped me, but I was beyond the point of holding my tongue.

"That rule is in place to protect novices," he explained. "Your mentor has a position of power over you, so the goddess made it impossible for anyone bonded in that way to engage in a physical relationship. I tried to tell you before you could speak the words, but your mind was made up."

"Why would a goddess want to take something like that from us?" I asked.

I couldn't understand what benefit it served to stop me from being with him. Why take away our choice in how we used our own bodies?

"What if I commanded you to fuck me against your will?" Magnar asked. "If this rule wasn't in place, I could force you to be with me even if you didn't want to."

"I don't want to," I said instantly, refusing to allow him to think that that part of this was the problem. It was the violation against my free will which I was balking against, not some forbidden desire to claim him for my own.

There was a long silence while I waited for a response, then his footsteps moved away from the door, leaving me behind.

A chill crept over my skin before sinking down into my bones. I bit back the tears which wanted to fall again, refusing to allow them. This was all my fault. So I'd have to find a way to fix it on my own.

I stared into the flames of the fire for a long time as I forced myself to accept what I'd done. There was a light at the end of this. Magnar had said that I would eventually be able to fight off this compulsion, so I fully intended to do just that. I would resist every impulse that wasn't my own. I'd push back against his will, or the will of the goddess, until I had complete control over my own fate again. I'd learn all I could from him as quickly as I could, and I'd seek out the monster who held my sister before striking him from this world and claiming her from him once more.

I shivered as the water grew cold around me and slid beneath the surface, scrubbing at my hair and washing the tears from my face before clambering out.

Magnar had left a thick towel and clean clothes waiting for me, and I dried myself quickly before dressing again. I wrapped my arms around myself and sank onto the moth-eaten couch as I worked to process what he'd told me.

I didn't even know where to begin with half of it, and I was sure there was much more for me to learn yet. But one thing was for sure. I really hadn't known what I was getting myself into when I'd taken the vow and tied myself to this goddess and her laws. But I wasn't going to just accept my lot and go along with it. If she could fight dirty, then so could I. She'd pushed me into making this decision without understanding it when my grief was at its fullest. And now I intended to use her gifts to get my sister back and bring down the monsters who had stolen her from me. She might have found a way to bind me to her rules, but if there was any way for me to break them, then I would.

I wasn't going to leave my destiny in the hands of some deity. My fate would be my own.

MONTANA

CHAPTER TWO

I rose from the deepest slumber of my life, leaving the presence of my sister behind. I'd seen her kneeling in the dirt, her hands clasped around a blade just like Nightmare, while a warrior of a man had knelt with her. I'd seen enough to learn who he was. Magnar Elioson. The same slayer who had left the crescent scar above Erik's hip. His sworn enemy. And hell, I'd seen so much more than that too.

Somehow, Callie was still free, not here in New York, not a prisoner of General Wolfe. She was out there in the world somewhere safe, and despite the horror of our situation, I was overwhelmingly relieved about that sole truth.

I wasn't sure how my mind had connected with Callie's, but deep down, I knew it wasn't the first time. The dreams I'd been having since we'd been parted had only grown more vivid, and the moment I'd learned of Dad's death, there had been no denying the knowledge that passed between us. A suffocating, all-consuming despair had followed me into the deepest of sleeps, my mind lost between the here and there, unable to grasp onto anything more than the pain of his loss.

As the haze finally lifted, I was left with a lump of solid ice in my chest and grief weaved through my body like a hungry snake, devouring any light it found. This sorrow was made of purest darkness, twisted so deep within me that I was certain I'd never be free of it.

Although I could finally leave sleep behind if I wanted to, I kept my eyes clamped shut, sure that when I woke, I'd have to truly accept Dad was dead. Gone. This wasn't just a dream or an unbearable nightmare. It was real. And the moment I opened my eyes, I'd have to face the world without him in it.

He was the person who had been a rock for me to cling onto through the stormy sea of my life. The man I loved dearer than any other. The one who had sung me lullabies, told me countless stories, had wiped my tears away, kissed my scraped knees when I fell down. He was the hand propping me up when I stumbled, and without him, I would be cast adrift.

"Callie," I murmured, tears squeezing from my eyes.

For the first time since arriving in New York City, I truly missed our apartment in the Realm. I wanted to wake in our tiny bedroom and curl up in my sister's bed. I wanted to go back to a time when Dad was alive and a life outside the Realm was nothing more than a petty hope. Where even on the grimmest of days, I'd still had the two of them to come home to.

A hand encircled mine, their touch ice against my skin, but I didn't flinch away from it.

You have to get up. You can't let this break you.

I took a breath and forced my eyes open, facing the hollow world that I didn't want to endure without my father.

Erik sat on the edge of the bed, blocking the room from view, but I could tell I wasn't in my usual bed in the castle. To my right was a wooden nightstand with a glass of water sitting there untouched. The scent of cypress carried from the vampire who was watching me, everything about him too still, too intense.

Dread weighed down my chest as I recalled speaking his name at the choosing ceremony, offering myself to him in return for my dad's protection. But now…

My lungs felt clogged with cotton wool, my breaths impossible to take. His name had left my mouth for one reason only; to secure my father's freedom. And it was all for nothing. *Nothing.*

"You've been out cold for an entire day," Erik said, his voice softer than usual.

His brow was etched with lines and his ashen eyes flickered in a way that suggested he had many things to say on the matter but was biting his tongue. He was dressed in a simple white t-shirt and sweatpants, looking like a completely different person than the last time I'd seen him. After I'd chosen him, when my mind had connected to my twin's and a flash of memories had taken hold of me, then...I'd fallen. Just a moment of memory came back; me stumbling down the steep stairs before darkness had washed over me.

I sat up, searching myself for injuries, but I couldn't find any bruises. I was dressed in similar clothes to Erik and vaguely wondered who'd changed me, though it was difficult to focus on anything but the pain slicing into my heart.

"I fell," I murmured, my voice raspy from a lack of moisture.

"I caught you." Erik promptly handed me the glass of water and I took a long sip, the thirst driving deeper until I tipped up the glass and finished every drop.

I nodded once, dropping my eyes to the empty glass and feeling as empty as the space inside it.

"What happened?" Erik asked urgently, his hand curling tight around my arm. "I had a doctor try to wake you, but he couldn't. He said you needed time, but humans don't just go unconscious for an entire day for no reason."

I said nothing, my thoughts still realigning, and I didn't have an answer anyway. But then the weight of Dad's death descended on me again so sharply, I wasn't remotely prepared. I unravelled, dropping my face into my hands and sobbing, breaking apart and aching for the company of my twin.

Erik's arms surrounded me, and he dragged me into his lap, gathering me against his chest without a word. It was exactly what I needed, and yet I shouldn't have wanted any such thing from him. But I was too shattered by my pain to do anything but curl into his body and cry against his shoulder, heavy, wracking sobs shuddering through me.

"Tell me why you're crying," he insisted in a low voice.

I circled my arms around his neck and released my grief, letting it flow and flow until it finally died away enough for me to speak.

"I can't," I croaked.

I couldn't make myself say the words. Speaking them would make them so utterly true, I could never take them back.

"You must," he growled.

As the grip of my anguish released me a little and I found it easier to breathe, clarity came back to me. Of who I was seeking comfort from, whose arms I was so tightly wound up in. I stiffened in Erik's hold, pulling back, but he kept me there with obvious ease.

My throat was thick as I looked up at him, my sadness like two flints striking together and igniting a flame of fury in the centre of my chest. *He* was responsible for this. For Dad, for everything.

"You knew Callie was free," I accused in a gasp, shoving his shoulders to try and escape him, but he didn't release me. "Did you know about Dad too? Did you command Wolfe to do that?!" My voice tore from my chest, flying free as a scream, but what I really wanted was to hurt him in a way he would feel as deeply as I felt this torment.

"Do what?" he asked in confusion, and I didn't know if he was a damn good liar or if he really didn't know what I was talking about.

An ache was growing in my chest, expanding more and more until the words bubbled up and burst from my mouth. "My dad is dead. When I passed out, my mind connected with my sister's. And I don't care how crazy that sounds, because it's true. I saw her with Dad. His neck was torn open. He had so many bite marks and there was so much blood-" I choked, shaking my head and trying to push my way out of his arms again. He let me go at last, and I got to my feet, pacing the room, wanting to tear it all apart, but I was sure nothing would ever get rid of this desperate energy.

I gazed around the expansive bedroom we were in, taking in the wooden walls rising high either side of me, the rustic furniture dotted around the space, and a long table laden with food. Everything was cream and brown and earthy. A glass door led out onto a balcony and a glimpse of the night sky was visible beyond it, the stars glinting like little diamonds set into black velvet.

"I don't know how our thoughts connected or why. But I know what I saw is true. I know it like they were my own memories," I said.

Tears spilled over again, and I wiped them hastily away on the back of my hand, turning to glare at Erik, holding onto my rage like a weapon in my fist.

"It was Wolfe," I forced out, my hands shaking, pain weaving a web inside me, every strand spun from grief.

I held so much hatred in my heart for the general. I wanted to storm from this place and find him. End him with Nightmare. Cut out his heart and turn him to dust.

Erik moved toward me in a blur of motion, seizing my shoulders to hold me still, his eyes two pits of fury. "Wolfe killed your father?"

I nodded, unable to say it again. "He's dead because of the vampire *you* sent to free him. The monster *you* trusted to bring him here." I tried to get away from him, but he didn't let me go.

"I didn't know," Erik hissed, his tone deadly. "I will deal with him, I swear it."

"No." I bared my teeth. "*I* want to deal with him. It was *my* father he killed. Bring him here and put a dagger in my hand."

"Take a breath," he demanded, and I did, my chest rising and falling as I dragged in some air. "I know you want revenge, but we have to be careful. No one can know what you are."

I released a dry laugh. "Tell that to Miles. He already figured out I'm a slayer, and I'm sure he's telling the rest of your siblings right now."

Erik's eyes turned to stone. "He knows?!" he bellowed, and a shudder ran through me, but I didn't back down.

"Yes," I breathed. "He tried to blackmail me into picking him at the ceremony." I scrubbed at my cheeks again as more tears fell. "I'm sick of playing your family's games."

"I'm not playing games with you. Not anymore," Erik muttered, harnessing his tone. He stepped toward me and I lifted my chin, assessing what he might do. "Why didn't you tell me sooner?"

I blinked firmly to stop any more tears from coming. "Because I thought you might kill me."

His jaw flexed and he shifted closer to me, head lowering.

"You *must* trust me," he said, his tone even and demanding. "I have made it quite clear that I-"

"I trusted you to free my father and you sent a monster to kill him instead! Why would I ever trust you?"

"I didn't know he would do that, Montana. Wolfe may be a cold man, but he is supposed to be a loyal one. I didn't suspect for a moment that he would go against my orders."

Heat simmered in my veins. "But you must have known my father was being tortured. You claim ignorance to the Realms, but you know about the blood banks. You know what happens to humans inside their walls. I think you know everything that goes on and you believe I'm ignorant enough to be lied to."

"I gave you my word and I intended to keep it," he snapped, moving toward me, but I backed up.

"But you didn't! And now my father is dead because of you."

He reached for me, and I slapped his hand away.

"You used him to get what you wanted from me, just like you use every human in this world. You think we're less than you, disposable-"

"You are not disposable to me," he said fiercely, his eyes igniting with all the fire of the sun. He stepped closer and my heart tripled its pace. I held up a hand to keep him back, but he kept coming, trapping me in his wild gaze. "You have awoken something in me I thought long dead, and I will not let you go because of it. No matter how much you torment or inconvenience me. I have laid claim to you, and I will not relinquish that claim now that you have chosen me in kind."

"I chose you so that my father would be freed. That makes my choice void," I snarled.

"It is far too late for that," he said quietly. "But I will not have you think me responsible for what has happened. It is Wolfe who will answer for this crime. I will see it done myself."

His fangs glinted at me, and he was nothing more than a vicious creature as he bore down on me, stalking ever closer while I retreated.

I turned my back on him and buckled forward, a racking sob tearing from my throat. It was too much, all of this. I couldn't do it alone anymore. I wanted Callie here. I wanted to crack through the glass doors before me and escape into the obsidian sky.

Erik fell quiet, his hand pressing to my back. After an endless amount of silence, he spoke in a low voice. "I…"

"What?" I sniped, something telling me he might actually be about to apologise.

He cleared his throat, his hand falling from me. "I found the blade."

Nightmare. Fuck.

My heart screamed and I whipped around to face him, unsure what he was about to do.

"No one else saw it," he said. "I've hidden it for now, but I acted without thought when I found it." He turned his hand over and I spotted the same runes from Nightmare's hilt branded into his left palm. "It didn't break the skin, so it will heal eventually. Let us hope no one notices the mark in the meantime."

I kept my lips firmly shut, saying nothing about where I'd gotten it or why I'd been carrying it with me.

"Were you planning on using that blade on me?" he asked, his voice hard and his eyes unblinking.

Still, I said nothing, and his jaw ticked in frustration.

"Speak," he urged, but my silence was my only defence now.

He sighed, lifting a hand and making me wince as I half expected a punishment for what I'd done. His hand grazed against my cheek and slid into my hair, his fingers winding between the strands.

"I cannot fathom the depths of the pain you are experiencing," he said, his brows pulling together. "I think I may have forgotten what it is to feel things so sharply. But your suffering riles me. So I will deal with Wolfe and bring horrors untold down upon him for what he has done."

"I want him dead," I said, my tongue tainted with poison.

"I will offer him endless pain before his death," he said darkly, and despite how angry I was at him, how much I blamed him, I wasn't going to get in the way of him going after Wolfe. "He will not get off lightly."

He stepped away, heading for the door.

"I want to be there," I called, determined that he wouldn't deny me this.

Surprising me, he nodded.

"Really?" I gasped.

"You're not just a courtier anymore, rebel. You are my fiancée. And if you want to be there, you will be. I will come for you when it is time for his interrogation."

Fiancée?

A breath staggered past my lips as I absorbed that word. It made it terrifyingly real that I was meant to wed this vampire. It was the last thing on my mind among every other horror I was facing, but the word jarred me now, reminding me of the predicament I was in.

Erik stepped through the door and glanced back. "This house is yours. Go wherever you please. You are no longer a prisoner." He nodded to the spread of food laid out on the ornate table. "And eat. I swear you will never go hungry again."

He shut the door and I stared after him in shock.

A single thought filled my mind: if I was going to be there when Wolfe was interrogated, I wanted Nightmare back. But Erik wouldn't have been fool enough to leave it anywhere I could easily access it.

I forced down a few bites of fruit and bread, needing to keep my strength up for this day. When I was finished, I headed to the balcony and slid the door aside. For a second, I'd wondered if it would be locked, but Erik was true to his word. I was no longer a prisoner here. Or at least, I had less chains securing me. I doubted I'd really be able to go anywhere alone, but at least I wasn't caged within the castle anymore.

As I stepped onto the balcony, I took in the beautiful view stretching into the distance. New York City stood on the horizon under the silver light of a full moon. I guessed I was several miles outside of its borders. The house I was in sat at the peak of a grassy hill, and beyond the large front yard was a vast stretch of land which had small shrubs growing on it in perfect lines.

I drank in the fresh air and found an inch of hope to hold onto between the wind and the birdsong. Callie was out there somewhere. And even though we couldn't be together through this pain, it was better this way. She had the freedom we'd always dreamed about, and I prayed she held onto it.

I clutched the railing as grief threatened to overwhelm me again. But I had to be strong. I had to be ready to face Wolfe. Because when I did, he wouldn't see me cry. He wouldn't see the pain he'd caused. I'd only let him see the strength in me. The strength that had always lived in my family. And no one, least of all a disgusting monster like Wolfe, was going to take that from us.

CALLIE

CHAPTER THREE

I flinched as a knock sounded on the door. I'd been lost in my thoughts, trying to sift through the information I'd gained from Montana while our minds had been connected. Her pain at the loss of our father had been most present, but I'd gleaned some more from her too. The worst of which was what the vampires wanted her for.

"Callie?" Magnar's voice came from beyond the closed door. "Are you decent?"

"I'm dressed if that's what you mean," I replied irritably.

I knew he was pissed at me for forcing him into this situation, but I was pissed at him too. He knew why I'd done it. And if he'd been so against the idea of me taking the vow then he should have made the implications clearer. How was I supposed to have known what would happen if he didn't tell me? He'd dangled the carrot of my slayer gifts before me and forgotten to mention the price.

Magnar pushed the door open and walked towards me holding out a steaming bowl of food. I raised an eyebrow as I accepted it, the rich smell making my stomach growl.

"I thought you were angry with me?" I asked. His behaviour was giving me whiplash. Why was he getting me things like the bath, new clothes, and now a meal? It grated against the general pissed off vibe he was giving out and left me feeling on the back foot.

"I told you I'd never see you go hungry while you're with me." He sat on the other end of the couch, keeping a foot of space between us and not looking at me. Half of me wanted him to leave me alone again. The other half wished he'd move closer and... well no, the other half of me just wanted to kick him for lumping his anger on top of the heap of bullshit I was already trying to deal with.

I took a mouthful of the stew, and it danced over my tastebuds. I couldn't remember the last time I'd tasted something so good and had to wonder how he'd managed to make something so delicious using the tinned goods he'd found lurking in this forgotten place. Magnar really knew how to cook.

I quickly spooned more into my mouth, satisfying the dull ache in my stomach, the clink of my spoon in the bowl the only sound to meet with the crackling of the fire.

"Besides," Magnar added. "You're my responsibility now."

I bristled at the implication. "You make responsibility sound a lot like *burden.*"

Magnar grunted in a way that seemed like an agreement, his words burning through me and sinking into the pit of my gut. If he wanted rid of me so badly then that was fine.

I shoved the half-eaten bowl of food back at him and got to my feet.

"I've never been a burden on anyone in my life and I won't be starting now." I strode away from him out of the room, heading straight for the front door. I didn't have my coat or boots, but I was too full of pain and anger to care. I'd lost my dad, run from everything familiar in my life, and had no idea how to start hunting for my sister who was being held at the mercy of a monster. I was done. So fucking done with all of it, and if Magnar didn't want me with him any longer, then that was just fine by me.

A nagging voice in the back of my head told me I was being childish, petulant, and utterly stupid to be turning my back on the one man capable of helping me with all of my problems, but I stamped it out. My head was too full of everything that had happened to me, everything that had gone so horribly wrong, and I needed some space and fresh air to clear it. I didn't want to be close to Magnar if all he was going to do was make me feel worse.

The mare poked her head around the kitchen door as I passed by, but I ignored her. It wasn't like I knew how to ride anyway. Although as that thought crossed my mind, I was gripped with the sensation that I *did* know how now. My ancestors had ridden horses, and their skills were mine if I wanted them. But my anger drove those thoughts out of my head again as I stalked away from the animal.

I grabbed the door handle and wrenched it wide. Cold air washed over me, and I spotted the protection runes scratched into the ground outside. The sky was clear, and the moon hung low in the sky. Frost lined the grass and my breath rose before me in a cloud of vapour.

I took a step forward and slammed into something, nearly falling back on my ass. I caught the doorframe to right myself and swore as I tried to push past the invisible barrier again. But it was like shoving against a brick wall. I couldn't leave.

I looked over my shoulder and found Magnar watching me as he leaned against a wall.

"Get rid of your stupid wards and let me go," I demanded.

"It's not the wards," he replied tightly.

"Then what is it?"

"The vow. You can't leave me or abandon your oath. Unless you wish to die to get out of it." He folded his arms as I fought against the urge to scream, realising that I was trapped in this hell of a union whether I liked it or not. I slammed the front door instead, casting out the freezing winter air.

"So I'm stuck with you?" I growled.

"It would appear so."

I hated how calm he was. I'd have preferred him to scream at me. To tell me all the reasons why he wouldn't have chosen this situation and to at least share in my anger with the goddess over it. But his face was blank, betraying nothing of the writhing emotions which must have been eating at him just as mine were consuming me.

Part of me wanted to break down again. At least tears gave me an outlet for these feelings. Holding them in made me feel like I was going to break in two. My mind swam with memories of my father and the brief moments I'd spent connected to Montana, and the pain surged in me again.

"He's going to force her to marry him," I whispered, the true root of my outburst finding its way from my lips.

"Who?" Magnar asked with a frown.

"Erik Belvedere. That's why he took her. It's why they want me too."

Magnar's calm facade slipped slightly at the sound of that monster's name. "How can you know this?"

"After I took the vow... I don't know what it was, but it was like my soul broke free of my body. And all I wanted was to tell my sister what had happened. I found her, connected to her somehow, and I showed her what Wolfe had done. She showed me some things too. I know that's what the Belvederes want her for." I took a deep breath and pressed my palms to the door behind me.

"Dream walker," Magnar murmured. "That is the gift of your clan. My mother could do such things. She could travel into people's dreams while they slept and talk with them. Or send them nightmares. I never knew another of your kind to be so powerful, most of them could simply slip through dreams without being felt, unable to truly communicate with those they visited, but perhaps you were born with the fullness of your clan's gifts, as she was."

"I know it was real. He's going to marry her." My lip curled back in disgust. The vampires were dead. The idea of being forced to marry one of them set my skin crawling. I'd imagined all kinds of awful things happening to my sister while she was held captive by those beasts, but none so abhorrent as this.

"Why would a vampire want a human bride?" Magnar pushed off of the wall and took a step towards me.

"Because a human can bear him children," I breathed, the horror of the idea stealing my voice.

Magnar stilled, his brow furrowing as he turned over what I'd said. It was like a heavy weight had fallen upon my shoulders at the admission. Uttering the words was akin to confirming their truth. Though I hadn't doubted the information Montana had passed to me in the brief moments when our minds had connected, I hadn't wanted to believe it. She was so far away from me, trapped with no hope of escape. For all I knew, they could be forcing this marriage upon her today. She could be pregnant long before I ever made it to her, and then what? What kind of half-demon creature would she be burdened with carrying? Once he'd put it inside her, there would be no way for me to get it out again. What if we got there too late?

"I have never heard of such a thing being possible," Magnar said eventually. "Are you sure that's what she was telling you-"

"She saw them with her own eyes. The half-breed children. She showed me." The memory of their too-beautiful faces and opalescent skin drew a shudder down my spine.

Magnar's composure broke and he slammed a fist into the wall. I flinched at the sudden outburst as plaster shattered from it, cascading to the wooden floor in a heap.

The horses snorted in alarm, their hooves clattering loudly on the tiled floor of the kitchen.

He turned away from me and stormed back into the living room. The sound of something heavy falling over reached me, followed by the crash of breaking porcelain.

I edged after him, my heart fluttering nervously as the destruction continued. I peered through the door just as he launched a wooden chair across the room. It shattered against the fireplace, sending splintered wood flying in every direction.

A huge oak table big enough to seat ten people ran along the far wall, and he hurled it over too, knocking more chairs flying.

Magnar whirled around, his furious eyes landing on the tub of bath water, and I stepped into the room, cutting him off before he flooded the place. He stilled as he spotted me, his gaze burning with rage.

"Do their monstrosities know no bounds?" he growled.

I moved closer, feeling like I was approaching a wild beast. He stilled, allowing me to draw near to him, and I reached up to lay a hand on his cheek, needing him to put aside his fury and give me some hope before I fell apart entirely. He took a deep breath as he gazed down at me, a wild beast, stilled by the touch of a girl.

"We can stop this. Right?" My voice was small and filled with fear for my sister. I couldn't let this happen to her. I had to find a way to prevent it.

"They will pay for their crimes in blood. I will never let them take you, Callie. I swear it on everything that I am. That fate won't become yours. And we will do everything possible to save your sister from them too." Fire swirled in his golden eyes, and I wanted nothing more than to wrap my arms around him, to break in his hold and let his promises steal away my terror.

But the irresistible urge to release him filled me instead, and my hand fell from his face. My anger at our situation flared as the vow forced me to step away from him, my mind whirling once again with the mountain of problems that stood before me.

My eyes fell on the devastation he'd caused, and a small, helpless laugh escaped my lips. "You really need to work on controlling your temper."

"My brother Julius used to tell me the same thing," Magnar replied as he followed my gaze. "We used to spar when he could see my rage building. It was the best outlet for my less desirable qualities."

"So you've always been this angry then?" I asked.

"My life has given me a lot to be angry about. I can thank the goddess Idun for that. She never tires of testing me."

I glanced up at him and I could see that chasm of sadness pulling him under once again. My own losses weighed so heavily on my soul that I wasn't sure how to bear them. I couldn't begin to imagine how he was coping with all he'd had taken from him. I still had Montana somewhere in this world, he had no one at all.

"And now she's playing the same games with me," I muttered. "Maybe I need an outlet too?"

I'd barely begun to touch on the pool of power my new gifts had bestowed on me, but I could feel them simmering beneath the surface of my skin, begging to come out and play. The idea of learning to use them filled me with longing. It was like an itch I was desperate to scratch; the more I thought about it, the more I needed to do it.

"You want to spar with me?" Magnar cocked his head as he considered the idea.

"I might pose more of a challenge than the last time we tried," I replied hopefully.

"I'm responsible for training you now, drakaina hjarta. I won't hold back, are you sure you're ready?" His gaze roamed over me, and I straightened my spine.

"I'm ready," I replied determinedly.

I could feel the memories of so many slayers dancing on the edge of my mind. It was like a well of knowledge just waiting for me to dip into it, like I'd lived a thousand lives already and all of them led me here.

Magnar's posture shifted slightly. It was such a minute change that I was sure I wouldn't have noticed it before, but everything about my senses seemed sharper now. He'd transferred his weight onto his right leg, and I could see the attack coming.

His hand snapped out, primed to grab my arm, but I twisted away from him before he could catch me, my ancestors guiding my feet.

A faint frown crossed his face, and I couldn't resist the urge to smirk at him, the rush of that simple move igniting something deep within me.

"You're asking for it now," he growled, and a thrill raced down my spine.

Magnar lunged towards me again and I leapt back, avoiding him. I laughed as my gifts came to me as naturally as breathing. The smallest smile brushed across Magnar's lips too and he hounded after me.

I backed up once more, but I collided with the couch. Before I could fix my mistake, Magnar caught me. I expected him pin me in place and tell me what I'd done wrong, but instead, he lifted me clean off of my feet and threw me over it.

I let my gifts guide my movements as I tried to recover from the shock of what he'd just done and managed to roll across the cushions, scrambling upright and regaining my feet as I hit the floor and made it to the other side of the room.

Magnar vaulted the couch, and I backed up quickly, my heart thrashing as I found myself at war with the warrior in him, the beast freed from his cage.

"Wait," I gasped, retreating further, but he ignored me.

Fear raced through me as he drew closer; he was so much bigger than me, and I was starting to think I'd been hasty in suggesting this. I held a hand up as I tried to escape him, scrambling around a dresser and shaking my head in refusal, but Magnar only laughed.

"You said you wanted to spar," he reminded me, and the look on his face told me he had no intention of backing off.

"I do, I'm just not sure I can-"

He darted towards me, and a curse escaped my lips as I twisted away from him and tried to run. The room was cluttered with broken furniture, and I jumped over the remains of a desk before grabbing a chair and holding it between us.

"Stop," I begged. "I'm not ready-"

Magnar snatched the chair and launched it away from us. It shattered against the wall, and I gasped while he smiled like a wolf about to eat me whole. My heart was pounding with a mixture of fear and adrenaline. He was enjoying this. The son of a bitch was loving every second of my panic.

He caught me again and slammed me back against the wall, the impact knocking a picture frame from its place, making it shatter against the floor.

"Asshole," I snapped, but he didn't stop coming for me. "Shouldn't you be instructing me instead of hunting me?"

Magnar towered over me, stepping closer, a wildness in his eyes which had my heart thrashing. Nerves prickled in my gut again, and I reached out for my gifts, begging my ancestors, or the gods, or whatever strange power I now claimed, to rise for me.

They flooded my flesh as if they'd simply been awaiting my call, knowledge which had been gifted from the slayers of my ancestor guiding my body into action, and I gladly let them show me what to do.

I ducked aside, then twisted forward, my hand curling into a fist. My knuckles connected with Magnar's jaw as I threw my weight into the swing, and his head snapped back from the impact.

"Ah shit," I gasped as I uncurled my fist and held my hands up in surrender, realising I'd probably just made this whole thing worse even if it had felt really fucking good to finally strike at the asshole for real. "I didn't mean to, I just let my gifts take over and..."

Magnar started laughing. He pushed a thumb into his mouth, and it came out stained with blood. My eyes widened with surprise. I shouldn't have been strong enough to do that.

"Good. Stop trying to resist them, and stop apologising. You're going to want to hurt me by the time we're done anyway."

"What?" My eyes widened in surprise. "You're not angry that I hit you? Because I kinda thought you might be about to kick my ass and spank me like a petulant brat."

"You're going to have to hit me if you want to learn anything, and I'm going to have to strike you too. That's how this works. We can discuss the spanking later."

"Are you serious?" I hissed, ignoring the spanking comment as my mind locked on the bit about him striking me. He was over a foot taller than me, and his arms held more muscle than my legs. I was pretty sure if he hit me, I'd die.

"You're stronger than you used to be. You can take it." Magnar's eyes danced with amusement, and I could tell my momentary respite was over. But that would be a fuck no from me.

"Seriously, dude, I might be filled with memories of a load of dead people, but that does not mean I'm ready to take a punch from your meat cleavers. How about we just work on the me-hitting-you part and build up to the idea of you hitting me back in a few months or years or-"

Magnar swung at me, and I jerked aside, cursing him as he let his fist strike the wall beside my head, cracking more plaster from it to fall at our feet.

"That's a no, in case I wasn't clear enough," he taunted.

Shit.

"Okay, okay, just stop. Give me a second," I said, holding a hand up between us again and trying to ignore how little that would help me if he refused to listen.

"I'll give you five. Then you're going to do this, whether you like it or not. You took an unbreakable vow after all."

I bit my tongue on the desire to curse him out, trying to dispel my fear as I watched those seconds count down in his glimmering eyes and reached for my gifts. The memories were too much all at once, but I didn't need to hold them all within my mind, I just had to let them pass through me. It felt like opening a channel and letting the water flow, the current just strong enough to guide me without sweeping me along too fast. My posture shifted as I drew in the information I needed to continue this, hoping to hell that my ancestors knew what they were doing, because I sure as shit didn't.

Magnar still held the advantage while my back was to the wall, and I could tell he wasn't going to relinquish it, but that was okay.

"Ready?" he asked.

"No," I lied.

I ducked low and aimed a punch at his kidney. He moved aside to avoid the blow, giving me the chance to get away from the wall.

I whirled around and managed to get my arm up as he aimed a punch at my head. My forearm rang with the impact of knocking his blow wide, but I was already moving on. I aimed a fist at his face, and he batted my hand away, but I followed up with a more powerful strike from my rear arm, which he had more trouble deflecting.

It was like falling into a familiar dance from there, and I trusted my body to know the steps, drinking in the knowledge I was offered and using it to learn the moves for myself.

Our movements got quicker, matching blow for blow as neither of us managed to land a hit, excitement thrumming through me as I held my own against the greatest slayer ever known. I was doing this. I was fighting. I was fucking unstoppable.

Energy danced along my limbs as my abilities swept through me, guiding my body, and a swell of exhilaration built in my chest. I was doing it, perfecting the moves I would need to take on every vampire who stood between me and my sister. I'd embraced my slayer blood, and I *liked* it.

Sweat began to trickle down my spine as I danced out of reach once more. I could feel a smile pulling at my lips. Every move I made came to me like I'd done it a hundred times before. It was as though I'd spent my life training to fight like this, learning every move until my limbs practically worked without thought. I was so fast. I was *so* strong. I was invincible and-

Magnar's fist connected with my face so hard that it felt like the entire house had just fallen on top of me.

I was thrown to the ground and pain flared through me like I'd been hit with a sledgehammer. My breath was forced from my lungs, and the back of my head slammed into the wooden floorboards as I crumpled like a sack of shit.

Before I could so much as blink the haze of confusion from my eyes, he was on top of me, his fingers encircling my wrists as he pinned them above my head and held me there.

His weight immobilised me and his long hair fell forward as he peered down at me, his eyes glittering with amusement, my defeat undeniable.

"Do you yield?" he asked casually, not even having the decency to seem out of breath while my chest heaved and my heart thrashed frantically, sweat sticking strands of golden hair to my cheeks.

Okay, I am not goddamn invincible.

I couldn't move. I could barely breathe as he crushed me into the floorboards. My mind spun from the injury to my head, and I could taste the blood which ran from my nose into my mouth. My gifts slipped away from me again as the floodgates closed, and I was pretty sure he'd broken my fucking nose.

I tugged pointlessly at my wrists, my bare feet scrambling against the wooden floor as I tried to think of some way out of his grasp, but it was clear that I was done.

"What the fuck was that?" I snapped.

"A girl playing at being a warrior," he replied with a shrug. "It was cute."

"Fuck you." I yanked on my wrists again, but it did nothing.

"Do you yield?" he repeated.

"You broke my motherfucking nose," I hissed, tasting blood from the injury.

"I barely struck you. Your nose is fine."

"Fine? I'm choking on my fucking blood here!"

Magnar rolled his eyes, transferring both of my wrists into a single hand before taking hold of my nose between two fingers and squeezing it.

Pain flared at his rough inspection, and I thrashed beneath him, but he stopped as fast as he'd started.

"See? No break. Now stop bitching and yield. Unless you're just stalling for time so that you can remain pinned beneath me?"

"You seriously won't get off of me unless I admit you won? The fact that I'm bleeding on the floor beneath you doesn't make that clear enough already?" I hissed.

"Apparently not."

"Fuck you," I repeated.

He grinned like a demon but didn't move.

"Fine," I snapped. "You win, I yield, you're a living cunt of a sledgehammer and all that jazz."

"A living cunt of a sledgehammer?" he mused. "You're a sore loser."

"No, I'm a crushed one," I snipped, wriggling to try and get free, but that only served to make me grind against his hard body.

His smile widened, turning into something dark and feral, and I could tell he'd enjoyed the spar as much as I had - at least until the end. "Next time, I won't go so easy on you."

"That was easy?" I asked, realisation falling over me that I was not, in fact, a badass, gifted warrior bitch who didn't need any training. From the look in Magnar's eyes, we had barely begun.

"Yes, you cocky little mouse," he said, his grin widening. "This is lesson one, and it will only get harder from here. You made your vow, and there's no escaping it. You will be forged into a true slayer, Callie Ford, and your training will be the most gruelling experience of your life. Welcome to the consequences of your actions."

MONTANA

CHAPTER FOUR

E rik didn't come back during the night, and in the morning, I found my eyes stinging from the tears I'd cried but dry at last. My body felt heavy, numb, but I had several reasons worth rising for today. Callie sat at the heart of them all, but vengeance sang louder than the rest.

I finally left my room dressed in jeans and a black sweater, my feet firmly in sneakers, the notion to run never too far from my mind. But Wolfe's death would be mine first. And what I needed to secure that was Nightmare. Erik may have been planning some vague punishment for what the general had done, but I didn't trust his word on it being enough. Wolfe deserved a slow, agonising descent into hell and nothing less.

I embraced the quiet of the house as I moved to the door, turning the brass knob, and opening it. Alone time was how I coped with things best, and I was glad of it now.

I stepped into a bright corridor with dark wooden floors, sunlight streaming through high windows in the roof above. It felt like an attic space, the roof tapering into a triangle above me. The rafters were engraved with odd symbols and words written in a language I couldn't decipher.

Gammel kjærleik rustar ikkje.

I moved along, passing sun-drenched potted trees sitting beneath high windows, their leaves tilted towards the light like a thirsty creature taking a drink. I found a twisting staircase that wound down through the house like a vine curled around a tree trunk, following it deeper into the belly of Erik's home. I passed corridors leading this way and that, glimpses of light and lustre beckoning me to them, but I kept heading down until I reached the ground floor, figuring I would start my hunt at the bottom and work up. But from the size of this place, it looked like I was gonna have one helluva job finding Nightmare. I tried to listen for its voice, or perhaps sense it, but all was still.

I found myself in an expansive kitchen-lounge area where the walls were cream, and the wooden floor was a soft hazel. I walked toward a large fridge at the far end of the room, surrounded by a nest of cupboards. I tugged it open with a scowl, expecting my fury to sharpen at the sight of the blood hidden there, but my brow creased in surprise. There was no blood; it was packed solid with food. More food than had ever been stocked in my family's kitchen, an obscene amount. Enough to feed my entire apartment block.

My stomach felt leaden this morning, and I had no desire to eat anything in front of me, despite knowing the insult that would offer the people of my Realm if they knew how I'd dismissed it.

Shutting the fridge, I moved to the wide basin and poured myself a glass of water, drinking it down in a few gulps. I placed the glass on the side, focusing on the quiet that stretched out into the house, wondering if there were any guards lurking close by. There could be fifty hiding in the shadows and I'd never know, their footsteps lighter than a breeze against the floorboards.

I moved through the living area where plush sofas sat angled towards a giant TV on the wall, then stepped into another empty hallway. At the far end of it was a colossal bookshelf covering the entire wall. My mouth parted as I approached it, running my fingers over the bound spines, my heart longing for all the words inside them. So many stories, so many truths. I'd only had a handful of books to read my entire life, and I'd often imagined what it would be like to have access to more. The information they held about our world was unfathomable, knowledge I had never had a chance to claim.

I dragged my mind back to the task at hand, wondering where Nightmare might be hidden. Though a doubt flittered through my mind. Perhaps it wasn't here. Maybe it was back in the castle or even somewhere else in the city. But as I focused, a very faint feeling made my heart jolt with hope, just the touch of a vibration in the air. Excitement fluttered through me at the possibility that I could find it with my mind somehow, like I was linked to its very essence. I shut my eyes, trying to reach out to the blade so it might draw me to it, and the sensation grew a little stronger.

I moved on through the house, playing hot and cold with the blade as I tried to narrow down where it was, the hum of it increasing and then decreasing depending on where I went. My path always led me back to the bookcase, but after searching all over it, I had to accept it wasn't there.

I gave up and headed to the exit I'd found further down the hall, the wooden door arching at the top and set into a beautiful alcove where coats hung on iron hooks. A small, frosted window allowed the daylight in from outside, creating a circular pool of gold around my feet. I reached for the latch and turned it, wanting to test how far my freedom really extended. Or if Erik's word was bullshit like I suspected.

To my surprise, the door opened and a frosty breeze caressed my cheeks, the grass in the yard twinkling with morning dew.

"Good morning, Miss Ford." A guard stepped into view like a ghost materialising from the afterlife, making me jerk back in alarm. She had a large sword strapped to her back, her black uniform criss-crossed with leather straps that held other sharp daggers in place. Her face was a vision of soft angles, and her eyes were glowing with intrigue. "Prince Erik has asked me to keep an eye on you."

"Of course he has," I muttered, folding my arms. Just as I'd suspected, I was no more free now than I had been before the choosing ceremony. "He also said I'm not a prisoner anymore."

"You're not. It's entirely for your protection. After the attempt on your life the other night, the prince wishes for you to be given the highest security available."

"And that's you?" I asked, narrowing my eyes. She was slim, slightly taller than me, but she held hardly any of the intimidation some of the other vampires did. She had an easy nature about her that didn't seem all that threatening, and yet I knew I'd be a fool to dismiss her. The wickedest kind of monster might wear the friendliest face.

She laughed softly. "I assure you, I am one of the finest bodyguards in the New Empire. Prince Erik sired me himself." She inched closer, her chin rising. "I'm adept in all forms of combat, I have served the Belvederes for four hundred and eleven years, and not one vampire has crossed me and survived the interaction."

My brows lifted. "Oh."

"My name's Sabrina. Would you like me to show you around the garden, Miss Ford?"

"No, that's fine." I moved to step past her, but she barred my way, still smiling.

"I'll have to follow you. I can remain twenty paces behind if you'd prefer, but those are Prince Erik's orders."

My lips pressed together. This was my new way of being chained, I was sure of it. I'd been a mutt in a cage and now I was upgraded to a dog on a leash.

"And what if I want to leave the yard?" I asked, eyeing the large sword on her back.

She shrugged. "I'll come with you. You have a car at your disposal."

I frowned, figuring I couldn't exactly drive myself anywhere anyway. "And what if I want to leave the city?"

She laughed in surprise. "To go where?"

"I don't know...back to my Realm?" I suggested, curious to see how far I could push Sabrina.

"Well, you need a passport to travel out of the state, Miss Ford. You'd have to ask your husband-to-be to organise that for you."

I narrowed my eyes at her, feeling like she was countering me on every move with annoying grace. "And will the prince be informed of wherever I choose to go *within* the state?"

"Of course. But only if he requests the information. He isn't spying on you, Miss Ford."

"Montana," I corrected, growing annoyed with the formalities. I wasn't nobility. She was just doing as she'd been told by my captor.

"Oh... I really must insist."

"Don't call me Miss Ford," I pushed. "Montana, okay?"

"Okay," she gave in. "So, Miss Montana-"

"Cut the Miss," I said. "Just Montana."

Sabrina hesitated, obviously struggling to let this go.

"Alright...Montana." I could tell how uncomfortable she was about this. She was probably going against Erik's wishes, but if she was my bodyguard, I wasn't going to have her talking to me like I was one of the royals.

"So, Sabrina...Erik hid a gift for me in the house," I said, faking a bright smile as if I was enthralled with the game. "I've been looking all over for it, but I can't find it."

Her eyes lit up. "How romantic."

"Yes, but I think he's taken the game a little too seriously because I've searched everywhere with no luck. Do you have any ideas where he might have hidden it?"

"Hm... come with me." She strode into the hallway, heading toward the bookcase which encompassed the far wall. My heart sang as she paused in front of it, sure Nightmare was near and maybe Sabrina held the answer.

She gave me a mischievous look before taking hold of a red leather-bound book and tugging it backwards. A click sounded and a secret door swung inwards at the centre of the bookshelf, setting my pulse racing.

"It's his favourite place in the house," she whispered with a glint in her eyes.

"Sabrina, you're a genius." I hurried toward the door, stepping past her and entering a room which took my breath away.

A spiralling wooden staircase with an intricate iron railing sat at the heart of the room between shelves that reached all the way above me to a circular skylight. The stained glass cast the place in deep red and amber tones, making the floor ripple with colour, the image at the centre of the glass a tree with delicate branches and an equally intricate fan of roots below. The same symbol that was housed within the royal crest.

I moved further into the room, taking in the shelves which were stacked with beautiful objects. Hundreds of them, perhaps thousands. Giant stones that glittered, items made of gold, brass, iron, glass, wood. All in different shapes with different purposes I couldn't even begin to fathom. There were books too, looking so old that their covers were brittle, spines cracked, and pages bent from how often they'd been pored over. Some of the names were written in that same language I'd seen in the rafters, but others I could read.

"Prince Erik adds to his collection regularly. He travels often, and always returns with an old artefact or two," Sabrina said as she followed me into the room then pointed to the staircase. "There's a seating area up there. When he's not working, he can always be found here. But only me and a few other guards know about it. When the prince is here, he doesn't want to be found."

"What is all this stuff for?" I asked, moving to a pedestal where a large spherical object sat in bronze clasps.

"Well, that's a globe," she said, moving to admire it. "A map of our world."

I reached out, pushing it to make it spin, hundreds of countries winking at me as it whirled before my eyes.

Sabrina stamped her finger down on it like a cat catching a fly between its paws, pointing to a location marked New York.

"We're here," she said, and I peered closer, trying to match this map up with the torn one Dad had shown us of our country. I grazed my fingers over the ocean which was so tantalisingly close to where we were now, grief slamming into me again so fast that it was like being thrown into that ocean and sinking away into its depths. We had often dreamed of finding our way to the sea, the three of us on a sun-baked shore where the sand was golden and the water brightest blue.

I withdrew from the globe, turning to the shelves and swallowing back the emotion welling in my throat. I didn't want to break down in front of Sabrina. I just had to keep it together. Find Nightmare.

My eyes prickled as I walked to the closest stack of books, trailing my fingers over the spines. Dad would have loved the chance to read through these. He'd often spoken of the library he'd visited before the Final War. He said a book was a portal, and when life got tough, you only needed to enter one to forget your woes for a while.

"This is a telescope," Sabrina said, and I turned to find her picking up a long brass object. "One of Galileo's very first creations."

"Who?" I questioned, but she moved on, picking up a circular gold object.

"This is a compass, used by a naval officer to cross the oceans long ago."

"I see," I said, unsure how that thing could possibly help someone cross an ocean.

I noticed a brass instrument with a long horn-looking thing on one end, and my heart jolted as I moved toward it.

"I've seen a picture of one of these before. It's a cumpit," I said with a little smugness at finally recognising something.

"Oh, um," Sabrina cleared her throat. "It's called a trumpet, actually."

"Right, yeah, that's what I said," I muttered quickly, mentally cursing myself. "Look, is it okay if I have some time alone in here?"

"Of course, Mis- Montana." She bowed her head, placing the compass down and exiting the room, closing the door behind her.

A breath of relief sailed past my lips. This room was like a glimpse inside Erik's mind, a look into his many lives, and I wondered what drove him to collect pieces of the past like trophies.

I crept up the iron staircase, reaching out with my senses as I tried to locate Nightmare, sure it was close, like a fragment of my soul was calling to me.

"I know you're here. Where are you?" I whispered.

I reached the top of the stairs and found myself on a wide balcony, and between two rows of shelves was a red wingback armchair. Beside it was a table with a book resting on it, its cover black with a single symbol on its surface in white, similar to those I'd seen in the rafters. I moved toward it, the scent of Erik everywhere in this place, cypress trees and rain. I wondered if he'd care that I was trespassing on his sacred space, if he might be angry that I'd found my way to the heart of his den.

I stood by the chair, detecting a thrum of energy coming from beneath it. Bending down, I slid a wooden box out from under the seat and my pulse quickened.

I pushed the top off and found Nightmare wrapped in a thick sheath of leather, the weapon humming excitedly as we reunited. Unravelling it, I took the shining gold blade in my grip and released a sigh of relief.

Moon Child, it purred.

I had no idea why I was so attached to this thing, but it immediately swept calm through my veins, soothing the aching grief in my soul.

"My dad's gone," I breathed, unsure why I was telling a hunk of metal my darkest pain. But it had always brought me comfort before, and I needed that now more than ever.

We shall end the one who did this.

I nodded, my veins surging with energy at the thought.

Drive me into the culprit's heart.

Determination gripped me as I tucked the blade into the back of my jeans and pulled my sweater over it. I spotted a row of scrolls lining a shelf and moved toward them, taking one in my hand. Carrying it to the box, I wrapped the leather around it and pushed the box back into its hiding place. I didn't know how long it would be before Erik figured out I'd taken the blade, but I hoped it would be long enough for me to kill Wolfe with it.

I turned toward the staircase, but my eye caught on the book Erik had been reading, a niggling urge to know what lay within it taking hold of me. A page was marked with a raven feather and my fingers itched as I picked it up, carefully opening the large tome and taking the feather between my finger and thumb.

The words swam before me for a moment as I adjusted to the small, printed text. A paragraph was circled in red ink. Slowly, I deciphered the words Erik had highlighted, my heart hammering in my chest as I sensed I was crossing a line here that the prince would not be best pleased with.

Andvari: Master of gold. Mythology recounts him in many forms. From a god, to a dwarf, to a powerful mortal.

The legend speaks of a magical ring, Andvaranaut, which held great power. It was one of many pieces of treasure possessed by Andvari, and the other gods often tried to steal it from him.

"Montana!" Sabrina called to me. "Prince Erik has summoned you to the city, we must leave immediately."

I nearly dropped the book in alarm, quickly placing the feather back inside it and resting it down where I'd found it. I pushed away my annoyance at Erik for beckoning me like a pet and hoped more than anything that this was to do with Wolfe.

Jogging downstairs, I hurried out of the secret room, closing the bookcase door behind me and finding Sabrina holding a fine navy coat for me. I put it on, adrenaline racing through my blood at the thought of what was coming.

Sabrina led me out into the yard, and we followed a winding stone path around the house. The building was built from wood, huge logs stacked high, one on top of the other, right up to a slate roof.

We reached a wide stone driveway where a black car was waiting, and two more royal guards stood either side of it, looking far more imposing than my present company.

Sabrina opened the back door for me, ushering me inside, and my heart climbed into my throat. As I settled into my seat, I reached behind me and quickly slid Nightmare into a pocket inside the coat. Sabrina followed me into the back of the vehicle, placing her sword over her lap, an air of severity falling over her, giving me a glimpse at the deadly creature she really was.

"What's this about?" I asked as the two guards got in the front seats.

"I'm not sure," she replied, then called out to the guard in the driver's side. "Gus, what news do you have?"

Gus glanced over his shoulder at me, his eyes deepest chestnut brown and his face a picture of hard angles. "Prince Erik has made an arrest in the city."

Resolve found a space in my chest and blossomed like dark flowers.

I'll kill you for what you've taken from me, Wolfe. You're about to find out what happens to those who hurt my family.

MAGNAR

CHAPTER FIVE

1000 YEARS AGO

Julius still hadn't returned, and I was beginning to grow irritable. We'd been tracking a lead on the whereabouts of the Revenant, Miles, for the past three months, and now that we were finally getting close to a breakthrough, the trail had gone cold.

I huddled against the freezing rockface in my thick furs and tried not to shiver. I was unsuccessful.

My anger over losing the vampire who fancied himself a god was doubled by the fact that he had led us to the top of this goddamned mountain before he'd disappeared.

It didn't make sense. We'd been right behind him. I'd seen him with my own two eyes when he'd fled, taking this trail while his disciples slowed us down. The climb was sheer and treacherous. There was no other way to the summit and no way he could have passed us to make it back down without falling from the cliffs and dashing his brains out on the jagged rocks below.

Immortality wasn't enough to make him capable of surviving that fall uninjured. Even if he'd decided it was worth breaking his body to escape us, I was sure we would have seen signs that he'd taken that option.

I cursed him again as I waited for my brother. Night was drawing in and I was beginning to wonder if we were about to fall prey to some trap ourselves. Perhaps instead of fleeing, Miles was really lying in wait somewhere, hoping to ambush us on the way back down.

The savage in me hoped that was the case. It had been three days since I'd cut through the most recent of his immortal offspring, and Tempest hungered for more blood. I'd promised the blade a meal of Revenant souls, and my first target should have been within reach.

I shifted my gaze beyond the patch of scrub I was using for shelter and looked towards the horizon. The sea twinkled in the distance, cold as steel and twice as deadly. It called to me in a way that I couldn't quite describe. A part of me hungered to travel the seas like our Viking cousins. I wished to see new worlds, fight new foes. Perhaps once I'd rid the world of the Revenant scum, I would.

I focused on the sea, almost convincing myself that I could hear the crash of great waves against the rocks. Yes, that noise called to me, but it was more than just a promise of adventure. It was a whisper of freedom. If I crossed the seas in the name of the gods, would they release me from my bond to Valentina?

I rubbed my hand over my chest, wishing I could remove the tattoo that sealed my betrothal bond to her. It was the one mark on my skin which I wasn't proud of. Every other scar or tattoo meant something to me. But that mark just felt like a chain binding me to a fate I didn't want.

I still hadn't married her. Eighteen months was a long time to keep her waiting. But the prophet had only foreseen our betrothal, and until someone foresaw an actual wedding, I was keeping up my end of the bargain. Not that Valentina saw it that way. She tried to convince me to choose a date at every opportunity.

I didn't for the life of me understand why she was so desperate to bind her soul to a man who didn't desire her. The more she insisted she loved me, the more I bucked against the idea of tying myself to her. I knew it was pointless. In the end, the gods would expect me to fulfil the promise I'd made to her. But I'd seen true love in my parents. Every look they exchanged, every touch, even their disagreements were filled with passion. I knew what love looked like, and Valentina wasn't it.

A branch snapped a little to my left and I pulled Tempest into my grasp. I recognised the breaking branch as Julius's signal that he was approaching, but we could never be too careful. There was a Revenant on the loose, and despite it seeming as though he'd eluded us, I wasn't about to count on it. Such a powerful being stood a good chance against two slayers, even if we *were* the youngest clansmen to ever take our vows.

Julius appeared and I relaxed a little.

"What took you so long?" I asked in frustration. "My limbs are ready to drop off."

"Well, we wouldn't want your infamous backside to freeze now, would we? Perhaps we should have brought Valentina with us to rub it better for you."

I snorted a laugh. It wasn't really fair of us to mock her as we did, but my wife-to-be had become the subject of many such jokes recently. I knew she was only keen to follow the directions of the gods, but I found it hard to respect someone who was so desperate for their approval that they would forgo their own opinion. She was so eager to believe we were fated to be together that I doubted she even cared about who I truly was. Nothing I did could diminish my image in her eyes, and it had become somewhat embarrassing.

"Did you find signs of the monster?" I asked, turning the subject back to our hunt.

"No. I'm beginning to think you were right; he found a way to escape us again. Perhaps he never truly took this path. He could have doubled back or maybe he jumped from the cliffs lower down? A few broken bones wouldn't stop him for long." Julius scrubbed a hand over his short hair and sighed.

"But why?" I asked, the question itching at me like a fresh wound. "He's avoided us until now, but I had the distinct impression that he'd led us here to finish our quarrel with him. Why turn and flee at the final second? What made him blink?"

"I don't know, brother," Julius replied with a shrug.

He never questioned the vampires' motivations the way that I did. He preferred to focus on hunting them down and killing whoever we found. Wondering what made them tick wasn't high on his list of priorities. But it always infuriated me. If we could only know what they wanted or where they would strike next, then we could get ahead of them.

Instead, it always seemed that we ended up like this, following cold trails and staying one step behind them. It was infuriating. They almost seemed to know what we'd do before we knew ourselves.

"Something doesn't feel right about this," I grumbled as I began to lead the way back down off of the godsforsaken mountain. "I *know* he was going to face us. If he changed his plan, there has to be a reason for it. And the fact that we have no idea what that is makes me feel more uneasy than I can explain."

"Have the gods spoken to you to make you so concerned?" Julius asked.

He always questioned me when I had gut feelings like this, but I was rarely wrong.

"No. As always, the gods remain silent in every aspect of my life besides my marriage," I replied irritably.

Julius clapped a hand on my shoulder and led the way out of our hiding place so that we could start our descent.

The path was even harder to navigate on the way down, and loose rocks rolled beneath my feet at each step, threatening to send me tumbling to the foot of the mountain.

The daylight was fading fast, and our progress only slowed as it became more treacherous to choose where to place our feet. I was half tempted to call a halt to our journey and make camp until daylight. Not that we'd be able to get much sleep between huddling on a rock face and the howling wind tormenting us.

Ignoring my better judgment on the safety of our descent, we carried on. I wanted to put the damned mountain behind me and find somewhere warm to see out the night. There had been a tavern in the last town we passed through and, with a bit of luck, someone there might be persuaded to give us some information on where Miles could have headed. Tongues tended to loosen after a few drinks, and a bribe or threat might be all it took to track him down.

An icy wind buffeted us as though it was trying to fling us from the rocky outcrop we clung to. I frowned up at the dark sky as specks of snow began to fall.

"Curse this weather," I swore. "I should have brought a storm-weaver with us."

The members of the Clan of Storms weren't strong enough to fully change the weather unless they worked together. But a strong enough clansman would have been able to provide us with a warm wind at the very least.

"Oh? And who would you have chosen to join us? I'm sure you wouldn't have selected Valentina. Elvard creates more wind from his ass than he can conjure from the elements. And I'd sooner freeze my manhood off than spend weeks in the wilderness with Hoft," Julius joked. "I'll settle for a village girl to warm my bed tonight and accept the bastard storm while we're stuck in it."

"You have a point," I conceded.

There was more than one reason that we had chosen to travel alone to take on Miles. Two warriors were quicker, less noticeable, and more likely to be underestimated by our enemy. If I'd brought a full host after him then he would have fled far sooner than this. Aside from that, I enjoyed my brother's company above that of anyone else. If I was going to spend weeks alone with anyone, then it would always be him.

I'd hoped that Miles's ego wouldn't have let him run from the two of us. A mighty Revenant afraid to face two slayers in the wilderness? Surely that couldn't be the case. But it would seem that I'd misjudged him again.

CALLIE

CHAPTER SIX

I stood in the small washroom and inspected my nose in the mirror. Magnar had insisted it wasn't broken and I begrudgingly had to agree. It still hurt like a bitch though.

The sun shone in through the large window and gave me plenty of light to see by. Despite the fact my intention had been to look at my injuries, my gaze kept snagging on my reflection instead. We'd never had a decent mirror in the Realm, and I'd never seen such a clear image of my own face before.

The blue in my eyes was more intense than I'd realised. It sparkled like the colour of the sky on a perfect summer's day. The kind of day that sent the vampires scurrying away to skulk in the shadows.

Aside from that, I felt like something had changed in the girl who looked back at me now. Like the gifts I'd been given were shining through my skin, adding a touch of warmth to my once washed-out complexion. My hair seemed more vibrant too, almost glittering as the sunlight caught on it.

I twisted my fingers through it, beginning to braid it like I always had when standing before our mirror at home. The familiar movements sent a surge of longing through me as if any moment now Montana would start pounding on the door, insisting I hurry up while Dad called us through for breakfast. I'd never miss the Realm, but I'd always miss that.

"Don't," Magnar said softly behind me, and I turned to find him standing in the doorway.

"Don't what?" I frowned.

He reached out and stilled my busy fingers. I dropped my hands as he gently teased the braid back out of my hair. My scalp tingled while he worked my hair loose again, and his gaze slowly slid to meet mine.

Neither of us moved towards each other. We couldn't have even if we'd wanted to. But the air that flowed through the inch of space separating us felt alive with energy. The bitter words and hateful anger that had built between us washed aside as he looked at me like that, nothing but the simplicity of our situation remaining. We were bound to one another now, our fates set on the same path.

My lips parted with the desire to say something that might make our situation better, that might explain my reasoning, might somehow apologise for the way I'd forced him into this bond, but I didn't have the words.

Magnar let out a heavy breath and released my hair. "If you're done admiring yourself, the morning is wearing thin."

He turned and marched away from me, making me feel like he'd just dumped a bucket of cold water over my head, and I scowled at his back.

I glanced at myself in the mirror one last time, confirming I'd removed all the blood from my face before I hurried after him. I ran my fingers through my loose hair, wondering if he simply preferred it this way. Why else would he have cared how I wore it?

"I wasn't *admiring myself,*" I clarified as he led the way out of the farmhouse. The horses were waiting for us, and Magnar had already placed our meagre belongings onto the mare's back in preparation for our departure. "I was checking the damage you'd done to my face with your massive fist."

"If you don't care what your face looks like, then why would you bother?" He untied the rope securing the stallion to the fence without turning to look at me.

"Well, I definitely prefer my nose straight, so if you could avoid punching it again then I'd appreciate it," I snipped.

"No promises. If you don't want me to punch your perfect face, then you'll have to stop me from doing so."

My gut tightened. "You think my face is perfect?" I asked.

Magnar stilled halfway through checking the mare's lead rope and shot me a scowl. "I didn't say that."

"You did actually." I stepped closer to him, my mouth pulling into a taunting smile.

"Get on the horse."

"Not until you admit it," I pushed.

"Alright." Magnar dropped the lead rope and closed the distance between us.

I looked up at him expectantly but instead of admitting what he'd said, he lunged at me, giving me no time to reach for my gifts. He caught me around the waist, and I squealed as he threw me over his shoulder. I tried to fight my way out of his grip, but he held an arm clamped heavily over my legs and wouldn't release me.

"Put me down," I demanded, thumping his back to try and force him to comply, but he ignored me.

He tossed me over the stallion's back so that I laid across the horse face down. I scrambled to push myself upright as Magnar jumped up behind me, but he grabbed my arms and yanked them behind my back.

"Elder, what the fuck are you doing?" I bit my tongue in frustration as it forced me to speak that stupid word in place of his name again.

"Reminding you which one of us is in charge here," he growled, using his elbow to pin me down while I fought to get up.

I cursed him colourfully as he used the reins to tie my wrists at the base of my spine, immobilising me in the uncomfortable position.

"Very funny, asshole," I snapped.

Magnar's hand clapped against my ass suddenly, and I gasped in outrage as heat flooded my veins.

"Let's see how mouthy you are after spending your morning like this," he commented.

"You're not serious?" I snarled.

Magnar laughed as he kicked the stallion into motion, and we left the farmhouse behind. I started thrashing before him, cursing him out in every way I could think of, but between his forearms pressing into my spine and the bouncing gait of the horse, I mostly just smacked my face into its shoulder and achieved nothing.

"I think you need to learn a bit about respect, novice," Magnar mocked.

I struggled in vain to free myself, but he'd tied the reins too tightly.

"You have got to be fucking kidding me," I spat. "Let me go!"

"I will. In an hour. Once you've had time to consider the filthy words that keep pouring from those lips of yours, and what better way you might address the man you chose to bind yourself to."

His laughter drowned out my shrieked insults as the stallion picked up speed and we thundered away into the trees.

When my hour was up, Magnar slowed the horses and drew them to a halt.

Fury was simmering with rage in its sheath at my hip and I was glad to have at least one person on my side. Even if that person was more of an object.

I hadn't stopped swearing at him the entire ride, but that did little to fix the damage to my ego as horsehair and sweat clung to my face. Bruises bloomed on my body from where I'd been bounced against the beast's shoulders more times than I could count too.

"I think we've made enough of a commotion to draw the vampires to us," Magnar announced.

I struggled pointlessly against my bonds, no longer interested in his plan to capture a vampire and torture the train station's location out of them. All I wanted was to be cut free and try to regain what little of my dignity remained before kicking him solidly in the balls.

"Are you going to let me go now?" I demanded through gritted teeth.

Any humour I might have been able to find in the situation had long faded, and I was about ready to kill him. My hands had gone numb, and my face was sore from rubbing against the stallion's shoulder. I doubted I'd ever get the stench of horse from my skin either.

"Just as soon as you apologise," Magnar replied, running his fingers across the skin on my wrists beside the point where they were tied, toying with the reins there. I tried to jerk away from his touch, but I couldn't escape him.

"Never," I growled.

"Perhaps you'd like another hour to think on it?" He caught my hand and tugged it, sending a spike of pain flaring through my shoulders.

I bit down on my tongue, refusing to make a sound in response.

"I hate you," I hissed.

"Fair enough." He nudged the stallion into motion, and I cried out for him to stop.

"Alright, alright!" Anger flared through me, and suddenly I realised I didn't have to let him treat me this way. I had my gifts now. I was capable of fighting back. "I'm... sorry," I muttered, the word causing me physical pain.

"That's better." Magnar tugged the reins free and took my arm to help pull me upright.

But instead of allowing him to help me, I opened myself up to the memories of my ancestors and jerked my elbow back, catching him in the chin. I threw my weight into him before he could recover and knocked him off balance.

Magnar fell sideways, slipping from the stallion's back, and victory sailed through me for an all too brief moment, before my stomach lurched as he caught my ankle and yanked me down with him.

I cursed as I fell on top of him in the dirt and threw a punch into his side.

He grabbed my waist and tried to propel me beneath him, but I jammed my knee into the earth, halting his progress. Before he could try anything else, I snatched Fury from its sheath and pressed it to his neck.

"Now *you* apologise," I snarled as I glared down at him.

He relaxed his grip on my waist but didn't remove his hands.

"I don't owe you an apology," he replied calmly, but his eyes glittered with some emotion I couldn't place.

"You just hog-tied me to the back of a horse for an hour," I snapped as I pressed down on the blade. Fury hissed encouragement, bathing in the glory of us holding the upper hand. "So say you're sorry."

"I'm not sorry. Look what you just managed to do because of it."

My brow furrowed as I tried to understand what he was saying.

"You shouldn't be this good, Callie," he said. "Your gifts are far stronger than any I've ever seen. You know how to do things you've never been taught. It's more than enhanced instincts. Do you know how many warriors have ever gotten me on my back like this?"

My grip on Fury loosened and I moved it away from him a fraction. "How many?"

"Since I completed my training? Just one. My brother was the only warrior who could match me in combat. No other mortal has ever gotten me in a position like this."

My lips parted at his words, and I withdrew my blade, allowing him to push himself up onto his elbows.

"It wasn't like this for you then?" I asked. "When you took your vow, you didn't... I mean, I *remember* all of this. It's like I've lived a thousand times before. All the lessons those slayers learned are there, just waiting for me to tap into them. When I give myself to them, it's like I don't even have to try. I just know what to do."

Magnar studied me for several long seconds. "No. It wasn't like that for me. I can feel some instinct from my blades which helps to guide my hand and enhance my skills. But I trained for years to be able to do what I can. I have no memory of other lives."

"So, I'm not a slayer like you?" I asked, a sliver of doubt passing through me. If what was happening to me wasn't normal, then what did that mean?

"No. You're something else, Callie. You're magnificent."

I snorted in disbelief. "If I try to make you repeat that, will you hog-tie me to the horse again?"

"It's entirely possible." He gave me a wicked grin, and I was

70

suddenly very aware that I was still straddling him in the dirt, his hips between my thighs.

He didn't move to get up, his gaze raking over me, heat rising in my skin as I stared back at him. The warrior from a time beyond memory. He was impossible, infuriating and utterly breath-taking. I wanted…

I suddenly remembered not only the fact that I couldn't have anything at all from his body like that anymore, but also the horsehair which was still stuck to my face and no doubt made me look like a fucking yeti while I salivated over the perfection of the man beneath me.

I shoved Fury back in its sheath and stood up, stalking over to the mare and snatching one of the water bottles from the bags on her back. I poured it over my face, scrubbing the sweat and hair from my skin before taking a much-needed drink.

Magnar moved to stand in my shadow, and I avoided his gaze as I offered him the water bottle. I wasn't sure whether to be pissed at him or thrilled to have bested him, and the conflicting emotions were running circles in my skull.

He accepted it, his fingers brushing against mine, the heat in my skin flaring again. He didn't pull back right away, and I was reminded yet again of the curse that accompanied my vow. I shouldn't have wanted what I wanted from him, but it wasn't so simple to remove the memory of his mouth on my flesh, his hands bringing me to ruin, the thought of his cock in his fist and how desperately I'd wanted it.

I cleared my throat, certain he would read those sinful thoughts all over my face if he so much as glanced at me. I couldn't move any closer to him even if I'd wanted to act on the heat between us again, and I had no idea if he still wished he could move closer to me anyway.

I stepped away from him, aiming to clear my head as I looked out into the trees, but goosebumps travelled along my flesh and the strangest sense of unease filled me as I took in the view. I raised my eyes to look out into the forest to my left. Fury burned at my hip with a surge of heat, and I snatched it from its sheath.

They're coming. It seemed excited at the prospect, but I still had trouble feeling that way about facing the bloodsuckers.

Magnar moved closer, placing himself between me and the oncoming danger without a word. He removed Tempest from his back and turned his attention to the forest.

I focused on everything around us and the skin on the back of my neck prickled as I felt them drawing closer. Something foul was coming our way.

"Are you ready?" Magnar breathed.

"I hope so."

"Remember, we need to keep one alive if we want to find out where that trail station is."

"Train station," I corrected. "And how am I supposed to capture one of those things?"

"You're not. Just make sure you don't kill the last one standing and I'll deal with catching it."

"Okay," I replied.

"Tell me how many are coming," Magnar instructed.

I strained my ears, tightening my grasp on Fury to help me concentrate. My ancestors had hunted these monsters for generations. They knew all the signs. I closed my eyes as I allowed their expertise to flow through me.

"A small group..." My fingers tightened on the runes lining Fury's hilt. It could sense the dark power which allowed the vampires to exist beyond death. "Six lesser vampires and-" I swallowed thickly. "Two Elite."

"Good. Get ready."

Would I ever feel ready for this? I pulled more memories into me, filling myself with the knowledge of my ancestors as the vampires drew closer. I straightened my spine as I stepped out from behind Magnar and took my place by his side.

I glanced at him, and the corner of his mouth lifted in approval.

The vampires arrived in a swarm of motion, pouring towards us through the thick trees. The horses snorted in fear, shifting back, and I sprinted to meet the vampires at Magnar's side.

Magnar released a war cry as he fell into battle with those on my left, and I raised Fury, gritting my teeth as I raced on.

Two male vampires rushed towards me like the wind. I ducked aside as the blond swung his blade for my neck and brought Fury up in time to parry a blow from the other one.

My heart pounded with adrenaline as I spun back towards my first opponent, and Fury sliced deeply across his gut as I fell into the knowledge of my ancestors and ducked beneath his guard with more ease than should have been possible. The vampire howled in pain as I leapt away again and turned my attention to the other.

He bared his fangs at me as he swung his sword, and I barely managed to get Fury up in time to block the blow before it could cleave me in two.

"The Belvederes want her alive, you fool!" a female shouted from somewhere behind me.

I traded blows with the male vampire again and again until I finally spotted an opening and twisted beneath his blade. I drove Fury home in his heart, and the sound of falling rain filled the air as he fell to ash and was swept away on a cold breeze.

Victory flooded me, but I couldn't spare it any attention as I swung my focus back to the vampire I'd wounded. He'd collapsed to the ground, clutching at the unhealing injury I'd given him, cursing violently and hissing like a feral cat as he saw me coming. He scrambled back, grasping the wound on his stomach which continued to spurt bright red blood despite his efforts to hold it back. A slayer blade was no simple sword, its bite felt as keenly as a strike of sunlight to the monsters it was created to kill.

He tried to raise his sword in defence, but his injury made him slow. I batted his sword aside with a swipe from Fury and delivered a kick to his face, knocking him back into the mud.

Magnar was there before I could finish what I'd started, driving Tempest through the vampire's heart. I looked up at him in surprise as he swung Venom at something over my shoulder. The clash of steel rang out beside my ear, and I cringed away from it as Magnar took on the Elite who had snuck up behind me.

I frowned down at Fury, surprised the blade hadn't warned me. It was like it could hardly sense the Elite at all. I focused on trying to feel for his presence, and only the faintest response came back to me.

I backed away from the ferocity of their battle and scanned the trees for the rest of the vampires. The female Elite stood on the far side of the clearing, watching the chaos through narrowed eyes while making no attempt to join the fray. She held something in her hand, but I couldn't make out what it was from this distance.

Three sets of clothes marked the ground where Magnar had finished the lesser vampires, which meant one was still unaccounted for.

My heart pounded as I twisted back and forth, trying to locate my adversary while Fury burned in my palm. It seemed to be screaming a warning at me, but I couldn't figure out what it meant.

Higher!

I turned my head skywards a fraction too late as the vampire leapt out of the tree. She collided with me, knocking me onto my back, her fingers locking around my elbow, immobilising the arm which held Fury. The shock of the impact severed my connection to my gifts, and I was suddenly left flailing beneath her with nothing to rely on but my own determination to survive.

Her free hand caught my chin, and she forced my head back, exposing my throat.

"We have the right to bite," she snarled a moment before her teeth pierced my skin.

Indescribable pain flooded through me as her venom met with my blood. It burned like fire, clawing a path through my veins until it echoed within my skull, blinding me.

I kicked and thrashed at her, yanking on the arm which held Fury, trying to swing it at the monster who had immobilised me, but her grip was iron as she continued to feed on my blood.

Rage boiled beneath my skin. An inferno lit in my heart and my free hand swept across the forest floor until my fingers met with what I was looking for.

I grasped the heavy rock in my palm and threw every scrap of my slayer strength into my arm as I slammed it into the side of her head.

Bright blood flew, splattering across my face as the vampire was thrown off of me, but I wasn't done yet. I rolled over, punching her in

74

the gut and moving to straddle her in the dirt, pinning her beneath me and swinging the rock again. Something cracked as I smashed it down into her stunning face, and more blood spurted over my clothes.

"I. Am. Not. Food!" I screamed at her, enunciating each word with every strike of the rock.

She tried to get away from me, but then I remembered Fury in my other hand, the blade screaming for death, eager to see this done.

Teach her! it begged, and I slammed the blade down into her chest, finding her heart. I crashed forward as she turned to dust beneath me, pressing my hand into the dried leaves to right myself.

My chest heaved as I pushed myself to my feet and turned back to face the Elite across the clearing. She stared at me with wide eyes, and I realised she clutched a cell phone in her hand. She held the thing in front of her, pointing it at us as if it could see us too.

I swung my arm back with a battle cry and launched the rock at her with all my strength, but she leapt aside before it could hit her.

The other Elite screamed in pain, and I looked over to find him impaled upon Tempest. Magnar had driven the blade through his shoulder and pinned him to a huge tree. Smoke rose from the wound in a murky cloud as he tried to claw it from his flesh.

Magnar faced the female Elite too, leaving the male where he was.

"Help me, Marla!" the vampire cried, but she was already backing away.

"I'm sorry, Carlos," she replied, her dark eyes widening with fear as Magnar advanced on her.

"Tell your master I want my sister back!" I yelled at her as she turned to flee. "And I'll kill every vampire between me and her if that's what it takes to get her. Including him."

Marla glanced between me and Magnar, then sprinted away into the trees as fast as her enhanced body could carry her. I took a step towards her, intending to follow, but Magnar's hand landed on my shoulder.

"We'll struggle to catch her now," he grunted before pointing across the clearing to the Elite he'd impaled against the tree. "We've got what we need anyway."

Carlos screamed again, more smoke rising from his hands as he tried to rip Tempest from his shoulder, and the blade seared the flesh from his bones with the power imbued in it.

I huffed out a breath and nodded my agreement, turning my back on the fleeing Elite and facing the one we'd captured instead.

My neck continued to burn like an open flame was pressed to my skin where the vampire had bitten me, but I clenched my teeth against the pain as we moved towards the Elite.

"We want to know how to find the grain," Magnar snarled, his voice a deadly warning.

"Train," I interrupted, and Magnar grunted his agreement before continuing.

"You will tell us before I end you. It's up to you how long that takes."

The Elite sneered at us, his eyes darting between Magnar and I, hatred brimming in his gaze.

"My master will tear the flesh from your limbs and-"

Magnar lifted Venom and stabbed the vampire in the thigh. He screamed so loudly that birds flew from their roosts in the trees above us.

"The train," Magnar said patiently, calmly, like he had all the time in the world and would gladly spend it here seeking this answer.

The vampire started swearing loudly, threatening to murder us in all kinds of impressively imaginable ways until Magnar stabbed Venom into his gut.

The violence was different to the furious heat of battle where the need for survival was a rushed, brutal thing. This was more savage, the coldness with which Magnar executed each strike something far more terrifying than the rage he displayed in battle. But I refused to turn away from it. I'd sworn to do whatever it took to rescue Montana from these monsters, and I wouldn't back down from that vow. Besides, they were nothing more than demons wearing the faces of the mortals they'd once been. They had no mercy for the humans they corralled inside the Realms, and I had no mercy for them in my heart either.

I bit my tongue as Magnar repeated the process again and again, blood spilling, the vampire screaming in agony while refusing to answer his question.

"If this doesn't motivate you enough, then I can start severing limbs and burning them before your eyes," Magnar growled eventually. "You only need a heart and a tongue to tell me what I want to know, and I'm perfectly willing to remove everything else if that's what it takes."

The vampire glared at him, but I could see his resolve floundering. Blood poured from his wounds, and he panted heavily, his end an inevitability which only contained more or less of this torture depending on his choice to speak. He looked half dead; any mortal would have succumbed to such injuries already.

I clenched my hand into a fist, my nails biting into my skin as my gut prickled uneasily.

He's already dead. He's a monster. This is the only way to get to Montana.

I didn't doubt Magnar's threats about the steps he would take to retrieve the information we needed, and I was pretty sure the Elite could tell that too.

"What does it matter anyway?" Carlos spat. "The station is heavily guarded. The trains carry all the blood from the west coast back to the east. You won't get within five miles of it without them killing you."

"Your concern is touching but unwarranted. Just tell us where it is," Magnar replied flatly.

The Elite hesitated and Magnar raised Venom again, considering his options before placing the blade against the vampire's ankle, lining up a strike.

"Thirty miles northeast of here," Carlos said hastily. "East of Realm G. Not that it'll do you any good."

"How many of your kind guard it?" I asked quickly, my heart leaping as we got what we needed.

"What difference does it make?" he muttered.

Magnar swung Venom back, readying the blow and Carlos's eyes widened with fear. "It varies. When they're gearing up for a delivery, like they are now, more are drafted in. Around eighty lessers working shifts with ten Elite in command."

"And when you say delivery, you're talking about all of the human

77

blood you've stolen from the people of the Realms. Right?" I snarled.

"What else would hold such value?" the vampire hissed.

Magnar swept Venom through the air and ended him before we had to listen to any more about his love for our blood. Carlos's body dissolved before my eyes, and my lip curled back with disgust as the dust blew across the clearing, some of it sticking to my clothes.

"We have a destination then," Magnar said, sounding satisfied.

I nodded but the motion sent a jolt through my neck from the bite I'd received, and I cursed at the pain.

I pressed a hand to the wound as the burning continued to blaze wildly, my attention fast returning to it. I looked down at my fingers as they came away bloody with a hint of silver venom swirling through the red, my gut knotting with distaste.

Magnar noticed and a growl of anger ran through him. "Come."

He rummaged through the vampire's pockets where his jacket still hung from the tree, held up by Tempest's blade. Magnar took a smooth, black stone from one of the pockets, then removed Tempest from the trunk, releasing the impaled clothes so they fell at its base.

He jerked his chin in a command for me to follow and led me back to the horses.

"What is that?" I asked, unable to contain my curiosity any longer, my eyes on the black stone which Magnar still held in his fist.

He glanced back at me and offered me the stone. "The vampires have a god helping them too. That rune helps them hide from our blades. Luckily, very few of them were ever made, so only the Elite will carry them, and not many of them at that."

I accepted it and frowned down at the black stone which filled my palm. It was polished to a high shine, and the rune carved into it was similar to those which lined Fury and yet also entirely different. Nausea rolled through me as I held it, and I was gripped with the desire to throw the thing away.

"It's horrible," I said, shoving it back towards Magnar. "Why are you keeping it?"

"I need to destroy it. If I leave it here, then it's just a weapon waiting to be used against us. Better that I bring it with us and break it as soon as I can."

We reached the horses and Magnar placed the stone into one of the packs before removing a bottle of water from it.

He stepped towards me, and I lifted my chin so he could wash the wound. I wasn't entirely sure how much water we had left, but the pain was sharp enough that I didn't care.

Magnar leaned close as he poured the water over the bite, flushing it clean, his touch gentle, the heat of his breath on my flesh making goosebumps rise.

I swallowed thickly, setting my eyes on a tree across the clearing, ignoring the tightness in my gut as I let him work.

"Well, we know where we're going at last," I said, forcing my mind away from the similarities of this situation to when he'd first kissed me, when his mouth had taken me captive entirely and his hands had-

I bit down on my tongue, pushing those memories from my mind, reminding myself that we couldn't repeat that again anyway and trying to focus on what mattered.

"We do," he agreed, his voice rough with grit, and I wondered if he was thinking about that night too. "And we also know what they'll be carrying on that train."

"What are you thinking?" I asked, sensing there was more to his words, that cunning glint returning to his eyes.

"That it's about time we asked for a little help from Idun."

My eyes widened in surprise as he mentioned the goddess, but his jaw was set with determination, and I didn't question him. If he thought she might help us, then I wasn't going to stop him from asking.

I just had to hope that the price of her assistance wouldn't be too high.

Magnar finished flushing my wound, then raised his gaze to meet mine. The tension in that small space dividing us had my heart thundering to a heady rhythm, and as he took my cheek in his large palm, I fell entirely still.

"You could have died today," he said roughly, his thumb swiping over my cheekbone, brushing ash from my skin where the vampire's blood had splashed my face.

"I lost my connection to my ancestors," I admitted. "For a moment, I was just a helpless human at the mercy of a monster. But then I found that rock and-"

"Next time, do better. You're a slayer, not a human. Don't forget it again, novice," he snapped, his eyes flashing with the darkness of the creature who had just tortured a vampire to death. I stumbled back a step in surprise as he released me suddenly and stalked away.

I bit down on the inside of my cheek as the desire to stalk right after him and remind him that I was brand spanking new to this bullshit rose in me, but I forced the impulse aside and turned away from him instead. There was only one thing I needed to be focusing on right now and it wasn't the moody son of a bitch with a pair of flashy swords. Montana was out there waiting for me, and we'd just discovered the way to get to her.

MONTANA

CHAPTER SEVEN

We travelled into the city and the pale daylight was soon drowned out by the shadows of the colossal skyscrapers that stood sentinel either side of the roads. We moved away from the central streets where the darkness was heavier, and only a few vampires roamed the area, looking at ease in their homeland. As we arrived outside an enormous building with imposing stone pillars supporting the entranceway, trepidation seeped through me.

Sabrina got out of the car, glancing up and down the street before gesturing for me to follow.

I stepped out, gathering my coat around me as I gazed at the menacing structure, thinking of what was to come. Of Wolfe trapped in there with my father's blood on his hands. The rage that caused me was so potent that a mist of red seemed to curtain my vision, my teeth grinding in my mouth and Nightmare urging on the violence I ached to deliver.

The driver rolled down his window, looking to me. "Tell Prince Erik to call us when you're ready to go home."

I nodded, irrationally angry that Erik had declared I was free now when I clearly wasn't. Though why I had expected more of him than that, I didn't know.

I followed Sabrina up the stone steps into the fluorescent light of an entrance hall with a white marble floor and flags of the New Empire hanging from golden poles on the far wall. Several guards stood around the place, backs ramrod straight and weapons on display. An iron door between two of them was the only way forward, and Sabrina promptly guided me toward it.

"Prince Erik summoned his fiancée," Sabrina told the guards, and my gut tightened at hearing the word again.

If Erik really expected me to marry him, he was going to be sorely disappointed. But my next moves were unclear. Escape was my only option, but it was hard to think of anything beyond Wolfe right now.

The guards opened the door for us, bowing low as we passed, and I scowled at them, feeling very much like a bird in a gilded cage.

We walked down a dreary corridor, and an officer greeted us in a navy uniform. She had short hair and a sharp nose; a gun was at her hip and a sword was strapped to her back. She exuded an aura of authority that made my skin prickle.

"Just this way, Miss Ford," she said, opening another security door and guiding us through it.

The officer pressed her finger to a panel beside a door on our left and it slid open. I followed her into a dark space with a window overlooking another room. Inside it, Erik had his hands around Wolfe's throat as he held him against a concrete wall. The prince's shirt was splattered with blood and torn in places, his hair a wild mess of dark strands and his face twisted into a vicious snarl. His fangs were bared, and he was nothing but an animal with prey in its jaws, ready to deliver another ruthless blow.

My breathing stuttered as I absorbed the sight, moving as close to the window as I could get.

"Please – I wouldn't betray you, master," Wolfe begged, his voice sounding through a speaker on the wall beside me. "The girl is lying! How could she possibly know such a thing to be true?"

Erik threw him across the room with such force that he smashed into the opposite wall, crumpling on the floor like a rag doll. My breath hitched at how easily he laid into the general, a monster who had seemed so unbreakable before now.

Wolfe groaned, nursing a wound on the back of his head, his fingers shaking as they came away wet with blood. He rose cautiously to his feet, more blood staining the wall, the damage Erik had done to him abundantly clear. Fear was etched into his beautiful face, and I revelled at the sight, my breaths quickening as I drank in his pain, wishing every drop of it on him for what he had done to my father.

Nightmare emitted a sense of satisfaction against my side, purring beautifully in recognition of the vampire's pain.

Erik stalked towards Wolfe once more, his knuckles wet with Wolfe's blood and a manic darkness in his eyes that didn't frighten me for once. This was the power needed to bring Wolfe to his knees, and as much as I wanted to be the one causing that pain, perhaps Erik was the only one capable of inflicting true agony on this asshole.

"Lie one more time and I'll turn you to ash, Wolfe," Erik snarled, and I felt I was seeing the most feral side of the prince, the layers of his beauty peeled back to reveal the beast within.

I was half aware he was doing this for me, making Wolfe suffer in penance for my father's death, and there was a part of me that couldn't help but be grateful for that.

Wolfe raised his palms, trembling as he tried to keep Erik away. "Please, please, your highness. Her father tried to escape from the blood bank, I was only trying to stop him. To bring him here as you asked. I may have been too rough, I may have injured him, but he was alive when I last saw him. If he is dead, it wasn't my intention. You know how fragile humans can be."

I bared my teeth, fury tangling with my veins. "Liar!" I shouted at the glass, but if either of them heard me, they didn't show it.

I sensed Sabrina shifting closer to me, seeming uneasy.

"So you admit it?" Erik growled. "You bit him? You *drank* from a human?"

Wolfe cowered, looking left and right as if the answer would appear out of thin air. "I- I was injured. I needed blood. I wasn't thinking straight," he pleaded his case, but it wasn't convincing.

Pain welled inside me at the thought of what Dad had gone through, and I screamed my anger, wanting to break through the glass and get into that room.

Erik threw a punch to Wolfe's gut, making the general double over and cough blood. He groaned, stumbling back to get away, but Erik kept coming, throwing another punch to his head before snatching his collar and slamming him into the wall, sending a crack through the stone and shaking the very foundations of the building.

"It is illegal to drink directly from humans," Erik spat.

"Forgive me, sire!" Wolfe wailed. "It won't happen again."

"No, it won't," Erik said darkly, releasing him and stepping back. "You're finished, General."

Wolfe lunged forward and tangled his hands in Erik's shirt, his fingers grasping frantically. "No - *please*. I'll never drink from a human again, sire. It was one mistake. I shall make up for it."

"It is far too late for that," Erik hissed.

Wolfe shrank back, shaking his head, and a coldness filled his eyes that made a chill creep down my spine. "They're beneath us, why does it matter? Why should I be punished for it?"

His words sent a jolt of hatred through me that cut deep enough to tear a fissure into my heart.

"He was more than you'll ever be!" I cried, and Sabrina rested a hand on my arm as if to comfort me. But there would be no comfort from this pain, it was too profound, too raw.

Erik punched Wolfe hard in the face, splitting his lip wide and making his head snap back against the wall with a loud crack.

Wolfe snarled his fury, touching the wound as it slowly healed. "I have been loyal to you for hundreds of years - how can you be so unforgiving?!"

Erik glared at him with disdain. "Because I suspect this isn't the first time. You have a taste for it, don't you, you piece of shit?"

Wolfe slowly nodded, a glint of salvation in his eyes. "Yes, that's it, I am a slave to it, your highness. It's the curse. It has taken root in me. Please help me recover."

"We are all a slave to the curse, Wolfe. Our nature may drive us to bite, but we can be better than that if we so choose," Erik said, and my breath stalled at his admission.

Did he want to bite me just as Wolfe had bitten Dad? Was he always one poor choice away from giving in to that twisted urge? The possibility left me reeling.

Erik continued, "The curse does not guide our actions. You made your decision, and it was the wrong one." He moved toward the door, then glanced back. "We are far from done here."

Wolfe cowered against the wall, holding his head in his hands as a whimper escaped him and Erik exited the room, slamming the door behind him.

Wolfe looked broken, pathetic. And I had no pity for him. He deserved every ounce of the pain Erik had given him.

The door beside me opened and Erik stepped into the room, his ash grey eyes landing on me.

"Come," he commanded.

I strode toward him with my head high, not liking the way he summoned me, but I wasn't going to miss out on the opportunity to pay Wolfe a visit.

"Out," he barked at Sabrina and the officer, and they promptly obeyed, following us from the room.

As Erik turned away and I kept to his side, Sabrina tried to follow us, but he glared at her in warning. "Stay here. No one goes in that room, no one watches, and no one comes with us, understood?"

She nodded quickly, looking a little taken aback before she fell still, and Erik led me around a corner out of sight.

We approached a door where a final guard was standing, and I quaked with my hunger for revenge. Nightmare buzzed with a keen anticipation, and I let that feeling roll into me, taking courage from its presence.

One sharp jerk of Erik's chin sent the guard scurrying away out of sight and leaving us alone in the quiet stone corridor.

I gazed at the door, desperate to go in there and deliver Wolfe the death he was owed.

Erik took my hand and turned me to look at him with an intensity in his eyes. "His death is yours." He took a serrated knife from his hip and placed it in my palm. "Strike deep and true. No hesitation, rebel."

I startled at the icy feel of it but nodded firmly. I could do this. For myself. But most of all, for my family.

Erik reached out and brushed a lock of hair from my face. I took in his blood-speckled face and the wildness in his eyes that told me this had all been for me. That he was bending rules for me that should never be bent. Especially not for a human.

I pushed him away, needing to remain cold and not let any ounce of warmth into my chest. Because right now, I didn't hate Erik Belvedere, I revered him as the dark god he was. And I believed that he had never intended for my father to die, that he hadn't known what Wolfe would do, because why else would he have dragged him here and punished him so severely?

"Thank you for understanding the importance of this to me," I said. "And for believing me about Wolfe."

His brows drew low, his eyes shadowed. "My brothers and sister are all I have. I may have grown numb to the world, and time may have ravaged the light in my soul, but I shall never forget how to love them. If someone took my family from me, I would seek the bloodiest of vengeance in payment for their deaths. That is the least you deserve."

My throat thickened at that word on his lips. Love. It was at odds with him, this tainted creature who surely couldn't feel so deeply as to love. But I'd seen how Miles adored Warren, how Clarice had shown concern for Erik. It was no illusion. It was a truth I could no longer deny.

"There is a saying my people once had. Gammel kjærleik rustar ikkje," he said in an accent that rolled easily off his tongue.

"I saw it carved into the rafters at your house," I said in realisation, and he nodded once.

"It means 'old love does not corrode'," he said, and something about those words sent a rush of warmth through my chest. Because they were true. Truer than any words I'd ever heard. My love for my family was as long living as I was, and it would never be tarnished, never fade or alter or shatter. It just was and always would be.

I swallowed the ball of emotion rising in my throat. "I won't forget that."

Erik's mouth twitched as if he wanted to say something more, staring at me without a single blink. Instead, he opened the door, leading the way inside, and I stepped into the room where Wolfe awaited us.

"Master, I beg of you-" Wolfe started in terror, reduced to a quivering wreck on the floor. And it felt damn good to see him like that, stripped of his position of power.

"Quiet," Erik barked, stepping aside so Wolfe's piercing gaze landed on me, then dropped to the knife in my hand.

"What's going on?" he whispered to Erik, but he didn't reply, simply shutting the door and approaching Wolfe at a slow, prowling pace.

Erik took his arm, hauling him in front of me and shoving him to his knees, his hand fisting in his silver hair as he presented him to me.

"No! Prince Erik, please!" Wolfe howled, gazing up at me in fear.

"You killed my father," I hissed, and Wolfe shrank back against Erik as I shifted toward him. "Admit it," I ordered, and Wolfe stared at me in disbelief.

"How can you bring her here to kill me?" Wolfe begged Erik. "She's a slayer, master. Our sworn enemy!"

"Yes, she is. And she will be your end," Erik snarled.

Wolfe struggled but Erik held him with ease, gripping his hair tighter to keep him still. I hesitated on the strike, unsure what to do next. When I had killed the vampire at the castle, it had been in self-defence, adrenaline and fear fuelling my motions. But this was different. This was an execution, and now that I was faced with it, I wasn't sure how to go through with it.

Let me help you, Moon Child.

I dropped the steel blade to the floor, reaching into my coat and taking out Nightmare, the blade glinting wickedly.

Erik raised a brow. "I can't hide anything from you."

I kept my eyes on Wolfe, the gold glimmer of Nightmare reflecting in his eyes.

"Get away from me, wretch!" Wolfe bellowed. "You are nothing, and I will not die by the hand of a worthless hu-"

Erik slammed his face into the floor before hauling him back to his knees again, his nose dripping blood.

"I will rip your worthless tongue from your mouth if you dare speak to her that way again," he spat, and Wolfe whimpered, bowing his head in submission.

I stepped closer, raising Nightmare, a tremor rolling through my body.

I had to do this. I wanted to. And no force on earth would stay my hand in this act.

"This is for my father," I breathed as tears scorched the back of my eyes, the loss of him so sharp it felt like an open wound in my chest.

But I wouldn't let my tears fall. I would be the last thing Wolfe saw, the daughter of the man he had torn from this world. And he would know that I was not nothing. Not to him, at least. Because I was his death.

I let the blade guide my movements and aimed it directly at Wolfe's heart. Gathering my strength, I took a breath and released all of my grief into the strike, bringing it forward at speed.

"Stop!" Strong arms surrounded me and I was yanked backwards so that Nightmare met nothing but air. Fright made my heart pound, and I lost my grip on the blade, the hilt clattering as it hit the floor.

"What the fuck is this?!" Fabian roared as he locked me in his hold.

I struggled against him, but it was useless. My heart sank toward my stomach and anger flared through the core of me.

"Let me go," I demanded, fighting to break free, but he was unrelenting.

"Erik, explain yourself this second," Fabian barked.

Sabrina rushed into the room, looking unsure of how to act as she assessed the two royal brothers.

"Wolfe drank from a human. He killed the father of my fiancée," Erik snarled, shoving Wolfe to the floor, and slamming his boot to his chest.

"So you brought a human here to kill him?!" Fabian roared, his booming voice resounding through my bones. "The punishment for such a crime is banishment, not death. And certainly not death by a fucking courtier's hand."

Erik bared his fangs, looking deadly as he pressed his weight down on Wolfe. "She is no longer just a courtier, and Wolfe disobeyed a direct order from me."

"It is still not enough to have him killed. Are you insane, Erik? This could start an uprising in the city," Fabian hissed.

My heart juddered. Was that true? Had Erik really risked all that just to hand me my revenge?

"An uprising, brother? Isn't that what you want anyway?" Erik accused, a terrifying look in his eyes. "I know what you're planning. You want to take the crown for yourself alone. You want me dead."

"You are losing your fucking mind. How many times do I have to tell you I did not try to kill you?" Fabian said in anger.

I clawed at Fabian's arms, but he still wouldn't let me go, his grip almost bruising.

"Unhand her," Erik commanded. "She isn't yours to touch."

Fabian shoved me away from him and I nearly fell over, but Erik snatched my hand, dragging me to his side and clamping me there.

"So many of my men have died, Fabian," Erik growled. "Do you really expect me to believe you're not behind it? That you weren't involved in the bomb that killed two of the courtiers? A haphazard attempt on my life perhaps?"

"Listen to yourself," Fabian snapped. "Why would I set a bomb to kill you? I know it wouldn't work."

"I know you are plotting my downfall," Erik seethed. "I have intel. Hard fucking evidence."

"From who?" Fabian demanded, his face skewing in confusion.

"That is none of your business," Erik said, recomposing himself and pulling me tighter against him. "Although I am sure you are aware of those I have had watching you, because half of them have ended up dead. Faulkner did not string himself up in a tree and gut himself, did he, Fabian?"

"Faulkner?" Fabian gasped. "You think *I* had him killed? My own Elite have been dying too, Erik, I am obviously not involved."

"Those Elite are dead because I retaliated," Erik revealed, and a shudder of fear went through me. They looked ready to rip each other apart, fangs bared and muscles tensed.

Fabian shook his head, a dark comprehension filling his expression. "You fucking idiot, brother. By the gods, how could you be so stupid?"

"You strike at me, Fabian, and I'll strike back," Erik snarled, but there was a hint of doubt in his tone.

I gazed between the two of them, trying to work out if Fabian was telling the truth.

"I am not the culprit," Fabian insisted. "But I know who is."

"Who?" Erik whispered, clutching me even firmer and making me curse.

"I…" Fabian's eyes moved to me. "We should talk in private."

"You can speak freely in front of her," Erik said, and I glanced up at him in surprise.

Fabian looked down at Wolfe who was in a trembling heap on the floor.

"Not here," Fabian said, then gestured for us to leave the room.

Erik stepped off of Wolfe, pulling me down to crouch beside him.

"Apologise," Erik snapped at Wolfe, but at the same time he forced my hand toward Nightmare beside him. I grabbed it quickly, stuffing it in my coat as panic scattered through me. What if Fabian had already seen it?

"I'm s-sorry, sire," Wolfe stuttered at Erik.

"To *her*, you piece of shit," he ordered.

I stood upright, hugging my coat tight around me, and my pulse drummed in my ears as Wolfe's cold gaze moved to me.

"Sorry," he whispered so lightly I barely heard it.

Erik booted him in the ribs before snatching my arm and tugging me out of the room past Fabian.

Sabrina followed us, keeping close to my side, her eyes darting between us as she awaited orders.

A ping sounded from Erik's pocket, and he took out his phone, gazing down at the screen. His brow creased and his jaw pulsed with anger, setting me on edge even further.

"What is it?" I asked, and Erik hesitated a moment before showing me the screen.

A video played, revealing Callie within a group of trees. The brutal-looking slayer was with her, killing a vampire with a savage strike from a glimmering golden sword. My heart soared, relief and hope colliding within me as I reached for the screen just as the video ended, pausing on Callie's expression as she glared at the camera recording her. A blade was in her grasp, stained with blood. It looked just like Nightmare. And her hair was caught in a breeze, loose and more golden than I'd ever seen it. She looked…incredible. A force to be reckoned with.

"You're still trying to catch her," I said in fury, my gut clenching.

"I'll bring her to you," he said.

"No." I stopped walking, yanking my arm out of his hold. "You owe me. You-"

"Quiet," he clipped just before Fabian stepped into the corridor, and I bit my tongue.

Erik promptly stuffed the phone into his pocket, leaving me with an imprint of my sister in my mind. She was okay. Still alive. And fighting against the vampires like an angel of death.

Holy shit.

"Call the car and take Montana home," Erik rounded on Sabrina.

"No, I want to hear what Fabian has to say," I demanded.

Fabian glowered as he slammed the door behind him.

"I'll ensure he repeats everything to you," Erik said, the shade in his eyes saying he would not be swayed on us parting. "I'm going to follow in Fabian's car."

Fabian's upper lip curled back. "I'm not going anywhere with you unarmed."

Erik shrugged. "Bring a weapon then, brother. But if it comes to a fight, I will need no such thing to defeat you."

"Arrogant as always," Fabian hissed.

"You're both arrogant," I muttered, and their eyes whipped towards me. "And I think your rivalry is pathetic. Family is all you have in this world, and it can be taken from you in the blink of an eye. I'm glad I never wasted a second of my time on such pointless feuds. Maybe you've gotten complacent with your immortality, thinking no end will ever come for any of you and that your time is limitless. I thought that about vampires too once, but now I know the truth. You can die. And with so many years stretching out before you and so many enemies lurking in the shadows, the odds are that one day you will."

I strode past them down the hall, leaving them with surprised looks on their faces, and apparently no words to say in reply.

My heart warred in my chest and Nightmare hummed softly like it was trying to soothe away my agony. But this grief was here to stay, a jagged splinter lodged deep into my heart, never to be pulled free. At least I could say my time with Dad had been full of love and no wedge had ever been driven between us. We'd adored one another right until the end, but the hardest part was that I never got to say goodbye.

CALLiE

CHAPTER EIGHT

We'd ridden for hours through the woods in silence, slowly making our way northeast towards the train station. Magnar's arms were loose around me, but the heat of his body at my back was as constant as the sun in the sky.

He was searching for something, but he didn't tell me what it was, his silence back in full force. Every now and then he would call out for Idun, demanding she appear to speak with us. But so far, there was no sign of the goddess.

Finally, the sound of running water reached me, and the stallion raised his head hopefully as he turned towards it.

Magnar let him have his way and he upped his pace to a trot in anticipation of a long drink. The mare whinnied excitedly as she followed, and I couldn't help but smile at the simplicity of their problems. If only water was the single thing I needed.

The further we went, the louder the roar of the water became.

"What is that?" I asked as the sound filled the space between the trees, drowning out everything else.

"Have you never seen a waterfall?" Magnar asked.

"I've never seen much of anything," I reminded him, the bitterness in my voice clear enough. "There was no free-running water in the Realm. We had to go to the bath house to wash, and we were given rations of drinking water."

"The Belvederes have a lot to answer for," he growled. "It is one thing to have seized power, but to have robbed you all of your freedom so completely is beyond words."

"Well, I'm free now, mostly," I muttered, trying to ignore the chains of the vow I'd taken. I was certainly free of fences and blood donations anyway.

Magnar's grip tightened around my waist. "I'll show you the world, drakaina hjarta," he growled, his lips brushing my ear, my skin prickling at the touch. "Nothing will ever be kept from you again."

I wasn't sure what to say in reply to that. I was so desperate for it to be true that I couldn't think of anything other than the life I'd once dreamed of with my family and the possibility that I might claim it now. My dad never would though.

We made it through the trees and found the river which had been causing such a cacophony.

My mouth fell open as I spotted the waterfall cascading over a sheer drop on the far side of a large pool which trailed away to our right, the river continuing off into the trees. Moss-covered boulders lined the edge of the waterfall and the greenery around it rose up towards the cloudy sky. It was utterly stunning. I never could have imagined such a thing existed.

The horses waded straight into the shallow water which lapped against the pebble-lined shore and bent low to fill their bellies.

"We should take advantage of this while we can. We'll bathe and refill our water supplies while the horses have a rest," Magnar said, sliding from the stallion's back and raising his arms to catch me.

I didn't need his help dismounting or even riding the horses anymore now that I had access to my ancestors' memories, but he had insisted on me still riding with him all the same, claiming it made more sense to use the mare for our packs. My protests had been met with a threat to hog-tie me in place again, so I'd given in, but I had no intention of playing the helpless human any longer.

I ignored his offered arms, instead turning my back on him and dismounting on the other side of the horse before wading back out of the water to remove my clothes.

Magnar followed me, his eyes tracking my movements so intensely that I turned to confront him about it, but I paused as I met his gaze.

I could have sworn his eyes were dimmer today. Sometimes they sparkled with the heat of the sun and other times they burned like the simmering coals of a dying fire. He was still so sad. I knew the grief he was feeling all too well now, the two of us bound in that, but I still had hope. Montana was still out there somewhere. Magnar had no one, and I had the feeling that me taking the vow had only made things worse for him.

There were probably a thousand things we needed to say to each other, but none of them came to mind.

Magnar turned away from me and began to remove his clothes, leaving his bare back to me, exposing the ink and scars adorning his deep bronze skin.

I unzipped my coat too, stripping out of my clothes without a word and trying to ignore the bite of cold wind which nipped at me as I exposed my skin to it.

Once he was in his underwear, he strode into the water and dove beneath its surface. I watched as his shadow surged through the water, heading towards the falls and leaving me far behind on the bank.

Magnar reappeared again after several long seconds, halfway across the pool. I watched with interest as he began swimming. Dad had told us about people doing such a thing before the Realms, but the water in the bath house wasn't deep enough for me to ever have tried. The idea of diving into the pool terrified me, but it also intrigued me in a way that ached to be satisfied.

I reached for my gifts as I continued to undress and grinned as I found what I was looking for. I may have had no idea how to swim, but my ancestors sure did.

I tossed my clothes in a pile and took a deep breath to psych myself up as I ran into the water. It was *cold,* but I forced my mind away from the temperature as I continued running until it was deep enough for me to dive under the surface.

I opened my eyes to a world of green reeds and shimmering light. My arms and legs knew what to do, and I began to move beneath the surface, laughter bubbling in my chest at the ease with which I did it. *This* was freedom.

As I powered through the water, I realised the cold wasn't affecting me the way I would have expected. Though I could certainly feel the chill of the pool against my skin, it wasn't reaching down to my bones. I could ignore it in favour of continuing my swim. It was as though my body was better able to resist its attempt to subdue me. Just another way in which my slayer gifts had strengthened me.

My head breached the surface, and I was surprised to find myself halfway across the pool. The horses meandered back and forth in the shallow area by the shore, and I watched them as I managed to tread water.

I leaned back, floating on the surface and looking up at the sun as it tried to punch a hole through the clouds.

A huge wave of water washed over me, and I screamed in surprise as Magnar began to laugh. I started flailing desperately, my arms and legs moving in panicked motions as shock severed my connection to my gifts and I became a girl who knew as much about swimming as I did about flying. Fuck all.

I slipped below the surface, then somehow breached it again, coughing up water as I flailed like a lost octopus, arms and legs everywhere, my head beneath the water as often as it was above.

"I can't swim!" I shouted before I sank once more, a foot poking up in the air.

This time, no matter what I tried to do, I couldn't get close to the surface again. Every movement I made seemed to send me deeper, and my heart thundered in fear as I stared up at the promise of oxygen too far above my head.

A stream of bubbles shot from my mouth as I cursed my ancestors for abandoning me at this precise moment.

I willed my gifts to return to me, begging my ancestors to re-establish the connection but I couldn't find it. The more panicked I became, the further it seemed to recede.

A hand found mine in the darkness and relief flooded through me as I was wrenched back towards the surface.

As I made it out of the pool, I was deposited on a hard, glassy platform and I doubled over, my hair curtaining my face. I began coughing violently, my body desperate to expel the water from my lungs.

I sucked in air as the raking coughs finally subsided and pushed my hair aside, ready to yell at Magnar for nearly drowning me. But Magnar wasn't beside me.

I gasped as I looked around at the pool of water which extended away from me in every direction. Somehow, impossibly, I was kneeling on top of the water's surface.

I pressed my hands against the liquid beneath my knees and though it still felt wet, it was undoubtedly solid.

"What the fuck?" I breathed as I looked around, hunting for some answer to whatever strange magic had caused this.

Magnar stood on a similar patch of solidified liquid a few feet to my left. The water separating us lapped against the edges of our small islands, keeping us apart. I pushed myself upright, frowning at him in hopes of gaining some answer to what was happening.

"Show yourself, Idun!" Magnar bellowed. "We don't have time for your games."

The air crackled with energy, and I turned to look at the waterfall, feeling a pull towards it in the pit of my stomach.

As I watched, pink petals began to fall among the cascading water, slipping over the boulders and tumbling down to fill the pool around us. I frowned as they crept over the edge of my island and slid across my toes, and I tried to move away, but they persisted, creeping over my feet and up my legs. Their touch was gentle, like a breath fluttering against my skin, but the strange sensation set me on edge.

"What the hell is this?" I asked as I tried to smack the petals off.

"A gift." The voice that spoke was as soft as silk, its tone filled with promises, the fact of its existence scaring the living shit out of me.

I stilled, obeying the urge to trust the voice as the petals covered my body, forming a full-length gown. It hugged my figure, sweeping into a long train beyond my feet which travelled over the water behind me.

Magnar frowned as he watched the petals dancing across my skin but said nothing of them, like somehow this impossible magic wasn't even surprising to him.

A breeze filled with the warmth of summer blew around me, trailing through my long hair until it tumbled silky and dry down my back. My limbs tensed with the urge to run as far from this place as I could get, but something about this power held me still, whispering calming words inside my mind and urging me to remain where I was.

The rushing sound of the waterfall fell quiet, and I realised with a jolt of surprise that the water had stopped moving. It looked as though it had been frozen between one moment and the next, a deep and profound magic taking root in the nature around us. The centre of the waterfall parted like a thick curtain and a woman stepped out, smiling at Magnar like he was an old friend.

Words couldn't describe her beauty. It pained me to look upon the perfection of her features. She was sunlight given life. Her dress was a shimmering waterfall which flowed over her body in a never-ending cascade of silver and blue. It didn't make a sound as it continued to move across her skin, but it was alive with motion, impossible as it was.

"It's been a long time, Magnar," she sighed, her voice like the trilling of birdsong in spring.

"A thousand years has passed, and yet you still kept me waiting when I called you. So you can't have missed me too much," Magnar replied, and I wondered how he dared to speak to the goddess with such disdain.

"You know you were always my favourite," she purred as she took a step closer, her bare feet pressing to the water as if it were land.

"Then I should hate to be your enemy. For being your favourite never did me any favours," he growled.

"You wanted true love, didn't you?" Idun asked as she stopped before me. I blinked at the insinuation, instinct making me want to recoil as she looked at me like I was some great achievement of hers instead of my own person.

I could only stare at her as she reached out to brush a finger along my cheek, her touch thrumming through me like the beating of a drum.

"You have taken every chance of that from me," he replied bitterly.

"I only said you would find it. Not that you could have it." She smiled at him, and it was a cruel thing. Her gaze travelled back to me, and my heart pattered with fear as she lifted a lock of my hair, the words making my thoughts scatter in alarm. Surely she wasn't saying that I was meant to be the love he'd been seeking? We might have been attracted to each other, but we infuriated one another beyond measure. If true love looked like this, then it was a hell of a toxic bonfire. I scoffed internally at the idea, ignoring the way my heart thrummed in my chest like a hummingbird. "I thought you'd appreciate this." She pulled it close to her own hair, and my eyes widened with surprise as I realised it was the exact same colour as mine.

"That is the only similarity I see. And you kid yourself if you believe I covet your beauty so," Magnar said angrily.

Idun's eyes hardened and she released me, snapping her fingers. The petals fell from my skin and blew away on a cold breeze, so I was left standing in my underwear again.

"You're boring me, Magnar," the goddess murmured as she moved to join him, and I sagged in relief as her presence withdrew. "I hope you're not here to complain about *this* again." She reached out and pressed her finger to the tattoo lining the skin beneath his heart.

"I have no interest in discussing my obligations to the dead," he replied irritably.

"Oh yes, Valentina is long dead," Idun agreed but her gaze sparkled with amusement. I frowned, wondering who the hell Valentina was and what they were talking about. "So what is it you want from me?"

"I made a promise to you," Magnar replied.

"I am aware of your unfulfilled promises," she said, and her expression darkened with anger.

"A lot changed while I slept, and it is much harder to finish what I started now. We are the last two slayers left in existence and a sea of vampires lay between us and the Revenants."

"The last two? How romantic that notion is." Idun's gaze swept over me again, and I shivered beneath her scrutiny. She lost interest quickly and turned back to Magnar, running her hand down his chest as she leaned closer to him. "Get to the point," she breathed.

Magnar seemed frozen in place, and he ground his jaw as she continued to caress him. "I want poison. Enough to taint their entire stock of blood."

Idun laughed, releasing him and the clouds parted in the sky, letting the sun pour over us. "*That* I can do."

A vine sprang from the water, twisting itself towards her before curling around her outstretched arm. Two apples grew from it, one was deepest red and the other shimmering gold. She plucked the red one from the branch and held it out to Magnar.

I was looking at a goddess. An honest-to-shit deity in the flesh. I wasn't sure if I'd hit my head or had stumbled into an entirely new existence, but I was having a whole shit-heap of trouble accepting what I was staring at.

"Any who taste this shall die. Even those who are dead already."

Magnar accepted the apple, his gaze fixing on it in a way that suggested he was disturbed by it.

"Including the Belvederes?" I asked hopefully, my tongue finally loosening.

"No. Not them." She glared at me angrily, and I recoiled in fear. "Their gift cannot be so easily removed. But..." She smiled as if she'd just thought of something exhilarating. "I *could* help get you past your enemies too."

"The poison is more than enough," Magnar replied quickly but her gaze stayed fixed on me.

"Nonsense." Idun plucked the golden apple from the vine and took a bite. She moved towards me as she chewed on it, her motions as fluid as the water she walked upon. "A touch of immortality and they'll believe she's one of them."

"Don't!" Magnar snarled as he took a step towards us, but more vines sprung from the water, immobilising him.

Fear washed over me as the goddess approached, taking another bite from her apple and letting the juice run down her chin.

"Hush, Magnar, it won't last for long. Just long enough to get you where you need to go."

Idun reached out and grasped my chin, pulling me closer. I was a slave to her, unable to move as she leaned in and pressed a kiss to my mouth. The juice of the apple washed over my lips and the sweetest taste danced across my tongue, like honeyed fruit. She released me and I gasped as my skin tingled with her power, the strength of it simmering within me, aching to burst free.

"Hurry up now. You only have until midnight." Idun smiled and the water beneath me suddenly turned to liquid again.

I sucked in a huge breath moments before I was submerged and the icy pool swallowed me whole.

I began to panic as I started to sink, but Magnar's arm clamped tight around my waist. He dragged me back to the surface, and I gasped as my head met with the cold air once more.

He swam to shore, pulling me along with him, and only released me once the water was shallow enough for me to stand.

"What did she do to me?" I asked shakily as the echoes of her power continued to race beneath my skin.

"She made you look like one of them. Like an Elite," Magnar replied, and I noticed his eyes had moved away from me like he didn't want to see what she'd done.

I dropped my gaze to the water which lapped around my waist, and it stilled, forming a mirror in which my face was reflected back at me.

My skin glimmered with an unfamiliar coolness and my eyes were icy and hard. My features were still my own, but they weren't at the same time. Every minor imperfection had been smoothed out. Every tiny thing that made my face my own was gone. I was looking at the face of stranger. A statue given life.

"So…that was a motherfucking goddess," I pointed out, in case he hadn't noticed and I'd actually lost my mind.

"It was," Magnar agreed darkly.

"And she said…she called me, or implied that I was-"

Magnar stepped closer to me, catching my throat in his grasp, lifting my chin so I was looking right at him.

"Do you believe the gods get to decide who you love, drakaina hjarta?" he growled, a challenge in his expression which didn't fully mask the distaste he was feeling as he studied my changed appearance.

My mind whirled with the impossibility of what we'd just seen, but the pounding lump of muscle in my chest still beat hardest for the one love in my life that I had left. Montana was the only person I cared for like that. The only one I could ever see myself offering that depth of feeling to. Romantic love had never been on the cards for me, had never been something I coveted or even wanted. So why was my tongue sticking on the denial that had risen to it?

"My heart is my own," I told him.

Something in his golden eyes shuttered at my words, the lethal creature in him all that remained within their depths.

"As is mine." Magnar released me, jerking back like he'd been fighting to maintain even that small contact against Idun's rules, and I dropped my gaze to the mirror-like water once more, scowling at my vampiric appearance.

"It won't last," I said as I fought off the disgust I felt, sweeping my hand through the reflection and casting it away. "But she's right; this will help us."

"Let's go then. The sooner we get to the train, the sooner we can get *you* back." Magnar headed away and my mind trailed over the things Idun had said. There were so many questions I wished to ask him, like who the fuck was Valentina, and why did Idun seem so hung up on Magnar? But I got the strongest feeling that he didn't want to answer them.

I followed him out of the pool, wringing the water from my hair as I went and heading back to my clothes.

If Idun wanted to give me this gift, then I'd be sure to use it well. The vampires guarding that train had no idea what was about to hit them.

MONTANA

CHAPTER NINE

Erik escorted me to his car outside the prison and Fabian trailed after him with a sour expression.

He opened the door and urged me to get in, but I resisted. "I want to come with you." I glanced at Fabian, my stomach knotting at the cutting look he was giving me. But I damn well wanted to hear what he had to say.

Erik leaned closer. "We'll talk about Wolfe together when we return to the house, but there is much I must discuss with my brother before then." He took my arm, giving me no choice but to enter the car, then bending low so his face was close to mine. My heart thudded hard as he kissed me, lips rough and firm against my own, sealing his words with a silent vow. His eyes became shadowed as he stepped back, and the line of heat striking across my cheeks told me I should have withdrawn from that kiss. It may have been brief, but I'd had plenty of time to pull away, and I hadn't.

"See you soon, rebel," he said, the glint of victory in his gaze making my lips purse.

I slid across the seats and Sabrina dropped in beside me, blocking him from view. There were already two guards in the front of the car.

didn't see why it was necessary for me to have so much protection, but I didn't have much choice in the matter either. This newfound freedom sure felt a lot like remaining a captive.

A dark mood fell over me as the driver pulled away, leaving Erik and Fabian together while another car pulled up beside them. A guard opened the door for them, but they remained talking on the sidewalk, their expressions tense.

My mind was firmly on Wolfe and how close I'd been to ending that monster, but the chance had been taken from me, snatched away at the very last moment. I despised the idea of living in a world where the vicious general still existed, and Nightmare blazed with its agreement.

Sabrina didn't ask me about what had happened, and if she was curious, she didn't show it. She kept a watchful eye out of the car window, her hand stroking the hilt of her sword, and I wondered if it gave her as much comfort as Nightmare gave me.

We sailed down streets, winding through the vast city, the gleaming windows reflecting the gunmetal sky above.

The driver slammed on the brakes, and I lurched forward in my seat with a gasp. Sabrina's hand shot out, pressing to my chest, and pushing me back in my chair.

"Keep your head down," she barked.

"Is that ashes?" the guard in the front said in horror.

"Fuck," the driver growled.

I frowned, leaning forward to look through the windshield to see what they were talking about, and a lump formed in my throat as a large figure came into view at the end of the road. He was dressed in a dark cloak, standing in the centre of the street in the midst of the carnage.

Fear forged a path up my spine.

Ash lined the pavements among piles of clothes. Signs of recently killed vampires. And it was clear who was the culprit.

The beastly man took a step toward us, his hood concealing his face, but I knew from the quaking in my bones that I'd seen this monster before. This was the vampire who'd brutally killed Faulkner on the grounds of the castle.

"Turn around, get Miss Ford out of here," Sabrina commanded the driver.

My heart staggered as the figure moved like a wraith, lifting a bow and arrow in his hands and aiming it directly at our car.

"Move!" I yelled as the driver did nothing but stare.

"Get down!" Sabrina screamed, throwing herself onto me just as the man loosed an arrow and it smashed through the windshield like a bullet.

I cried out as her weight pressed me into the seat, her strength immobilising me. My heart tumbled in my chest as I tried to push free of her, needing to breathe. Ash cascaded over us, and I coughed heavily as it hit the back of my throat.

Sabrina's grip loosened as she realised she was crushing me, and I twisted sideways, frantically searching the front seats.

A large arrow was embedded in the driver's seat with runes carved into the wooden shaft, the remains of the guard now scattered everywhere.

Icy fingers clawed at my insides as I gazed out at the demonic figure in the road. He drew another arrow back, and I shuddered with terror. I glanced over my shoulder to try and spot Fabian's car, but it hadn't caught up. I didn't even know if they were on the road yet.

"Drive, you asshole! Take him down!" Sabrina barked at the other guard, and he dove into the driver's seat, slamming his foot to the accelerator.

Panic flashed through me as we sped toward our attacker. He never moved, never even flinched as he loosed his next arrow, the deadly weapon whistling our way at an impossible speed.

It sailed through the hole the first arrow had created in the glass with perfect accuracy. The guard driving tried to jerk aside, causing the car to veer violently to the left, but the arrow struck true. His body exploded in a shower of ash, and I screamed, grabbing onto the seat in front of me to stay upright.

The car mounted the curb and collided with a streetlight, forced to a sudden halt.

Sabrina was out of the vehicle before I could catch my breath, wielding her sword in a flash of speed.

"Stay in the car!" she shouted, but it was unnecessary. I had no intention of going out there where a psycho was waiting to pick me off.

I reached into my coat, taking Nightmare into my palm and willing it to prepare me for what was coming. It offered no words of encouragement, no hunger for death, just a steady silence like it couldn't even perceive the danger I was in.

I chanced a look out of the rear window, desperate for Fabian's car to appear, but there was no sign of it.

Where are you, Erik? Hurry the fuck up!

Fear trickled through me. What if this was one of the rebels who wanted to drink my blood? What if I was about to be caught and dragged away to some horror house where more rebels were waiting to hunt their freshly acquired blood bag?

I peeked out at the road, gazing after Sabrina who was facing the danger head on, proving herself as the undefeated warrior she'd claimed to be. At least so far. Arrows flew at her again and again, but she knocked each of them aside with her sword, scattering them across the concrete. The hooded man shouldered his bow and released a silver blade from his belt instead.

Sabrina ran at him with a battle cry, lifting her sword high, and her opponent advanced with a keen hunger for the fight. She was all that stood between me and death, and I feared she was about to find her match in this deadly creature.

I shot another look out of the rear window, praying Fabian's car would appear at any moment, wondering if I should try and run instead of wait. If they didn't show up soon, I'd have to.

Come on, come on.

I gripped Nightmare tighter, and it hummed with energy in my palm, but I couldn't read the new sensation it was giving off.

A cry and clash of steel told me Sabrina was now in hand-to-hand combat with our attacker. With a terrifying clarity, I realised no one was coming. Sabrina was going to fall to this vampire's wrath, and I'd be next on the list.

I may have managed to kill one of them before, but I didn't fancy my chances against that beast who had already taken down so many of his own kind.

So I made a decision I prayed I wouldn't regret and shoved the side door open, steeling myself to make a run for it.

Sabrina swung her sword, but the vampire ducked the blow with a swift agility and caught hold of her by the throat. With inhuman strength, he threw her across the street, her back colliding with the wall of a building before she crumpled to the floor. I felt his eyes fall on me from within that dark hood, and my heart flew into my throat as he started sprinting toward me.

I retreated fast and slammed the car door in a panic, hunting for a way to lock it. There was nothing. No button, no anything.

"Shit," I cursed, shuffling back across the seats and holding Nightmare up, ready to fight for my goddamn life.

He closed the distance between us and terror carved a path through my chest as he ripped the door open.

"No!" Sabrina screamed.

I lunged with Nightmare, slashing at him, but the blade felt dull and heavy in my grip, not aiding my movements at all.

He caught my wrist with a bemused laugh and twisted it sharply. Pain flared up my arm, my fingers flexed, and Nightmare hit the floor. I cried out in horror, kicking and kicking, desperate to keep his hands off of me, but he kept coming, trying to get hold of me.

"Stay still!" he bellowed just as my foot connected with his face.

His hood fell back, and shock juddered through me as I took in his rugged features and short, dark hair. Dark bronze skin and the hue of blood flared beneath his flesh, his features angular, handsome, and roguish. He wasn't a vampire. He was human.

But he was still a psycho trying to kill me, so I threw a punch straight at that disarming face with all the strength I possessed. He swatted my hand away like it was a fly, then caught my knees, shoving my legs further into the car and following me into it. His immense weight fell onto me, crushing me beneath his bulk and panic gripped me in a cold fist.

"Get away from me!" I threw another punch and this time it landed against his solid jaw, but he barely seemed to notice as he released a wild laugh, climbing over me into the front seat and pressing a button to lock the doors. A button that had eluded me until now.

"Damn feisty, you are," he said in light amusement, and I wanted to kill him for his mirth alone.

I threw myself at the door, trying to get free, but it was shut tight, and the window wouldn't open either. I kicked it with all my strength, but there was no way to escape without releasing the locks.

The engine roared, pulling away from the streetlight before speeding along the sidewalk, knocking a garbage can flying. The front passenger door was still wide open, and Sabrina sprinted toward it in a rush of motion.

"Faster!" I yelled to her.

She leapt for the car with a cry of determination, but the madman in the front seat swerved violently to the right, driving the car right into her. She slammed to the ground, and I gasped as the wheels went over her, the car bumping as the car struck the ground again.

"How's that taste, bloodsucker?" the wild man crowed, another laugh pitching from his throat.

"Sabrina!" I called in alarm, unsure why my heart squeezed for a vampire, but she had done nothing but try to protect me.

Scrambling upright, I gazed out of the rear window, searching for her. She pushed herself to her knees as her body healed, looking fierce even with the tire tracks on her chest.

"Montana!" Erik's voice reached my ears and my heart soared as I spotted him and Fabian chasing us on foot, their car abandoned in the road. They were gaining speed by the second, moving at a fierce pace that went beyond what their vehicle was likely capable of.

"You're dead," I said, turning to my kidnapper with glee.

The man angled the rear-view mirror toward them, his deep bronze eyes flashing with malice. "Fucking Belvederes."

I dropped forward, feeling under the seats as I hunted for Nightmare. Its warm hilt brushed my fingers, and I snatched it up with triumph. It sang a warning in my veins as I grabbed hold of the front seat and placed it against the man's neck.

"Stop or I'll kill you," I snarled in his ear, my heart thundering like the hooves of a galloping horse.

He barked a laugh and grabbed my wrist, pulling my hand away from his throat with a ferocious strength. "I'm saving you, fool. How about showing some gratitude to your hero?"

"What?" I breathed in disbelief. "Who are you?"

He prised Nightmare from my hand, dropping it into his lap before tugging up his right sleeve. I spotted a slayer's mark on his skin, glaring back at me and sending my thoughts into a wild spiral.

"A slayer," I gasped.

"Not just any slayer, damsel, I'm the *best* godsdamned slayer."

A force like a tonne of bricks hit the back of the car, and I was thrown forward as the vehicle skidded around a corner. Erik was holding onto the back of the car despite the manic way the slayer was driving, his fangs bared and hellish fury flaring in his eyes.

Our gazes locked through the window, and his face contorted with an animal-like possessiveness. He slammed his fist through the rear window, and I flinched, covering my head as glass rained over me.

"Not today, parasite," my kidnapper snarled, turning the wheel so sharply that the car spun one-eighty. I held on for dear life as the tyres screeched and the scent of burning rubber filled my nose. Erik was thrown into a streetlight, sending the whole thing flying across the road and crashing into a building.

"Wait!" I screamed as the slayer slammed on the brakes, then started reversing toward Erik at high speed.

I punched his cheek, but he didn't stop, his teeth gritted and hatred making his jaw pulse.

Erik moved like the wind, darting aside before the car got near him, then he lunged toward the side door, tearing it clean off its hinges with a screech of metal.

My heart flew into my throat as I stared at the vampire prince who had taken me captive, who had forced me to do as he bid, but who had also made my heart beat harder than ever before; in rage, in passion, in lust and hate. Half of me wanted to reach for him, and half of me wanted to run and never look back. I was torn in two, and it made me realise how deeply he'd gotten under my skin, how I'd started to see something in him that was almost human. An enticing scrap of decency. But that wasn't anywhere near enough for me to rush back to him, even if I had started to change how I saw his kind. Though I was terrified to admit it, even to myself.

He reached for me, and my fingers twitched with the urge to reach back, to let him steal me away and keep me as his. But I blinked out of that madness, defying the chains he wanted to place on me, knowing I deserved freedom and a life where no vampire ruled my fate. And as I made that decision, the slayer made it for me too.

"Don't you dare, Belvedere." He caught my hair, dragging me into the seat beside him as he accelerated up the road, turning the wheel so violently that Erik was hurled to the sidewalk once more. My face almost collided with the dashboard, and I pushed against it to get myself upright, a growl on my lips.

I turned and threw a hard punch at the slayer's jaw for manhandling me, and he frowned. "Stop it. Why aren't you being a good little maiden, singing my praises and stroking my ego? I like it when they do that. Go on, do that."

"No." I threw another punch and he let me continue pounding on him as he drove the car, scowling all the while and not seeming the least bit affected by my assault.

The car bounced wildly, creaking and groaning like something was seriously wrong with it, and after another few blocks, it came to a shuddering halt.

"Stay here," the man growled, jumping out of the car and snatching his bow.

Stay here? Was he insane? He may have made an attempt at freeing me from the vampires, but he was also clearly unhinged, and I was in no way inclined to stay with him.

I crawled into the driver's seat, turning to face the chaos that was ensuing in the road as a cry came from behind me.

I spotted Sabrina running up behind Erik and Fabian, her sword in hand and determination brimming in her eyes. The slayer shot an arrow at her with vicious precision, and a gasp hitched in my chest as I willed her to move. Her face twisted in fear as she tried to deflect it, but the tip hit home, and for a split-second, surprise registered on her features before she exploded into ash.

Shock rolled through me, leaving me blindsided.

He killed her. He fucking killed her. And impossibly, I actually gave a damn about it. Because she might have been a vampire, but she had also been kind to me, had tried to protect me.

Erik released a cry of anguish for his fallen guard, his eyes narrowing on the slayer with a heathenish anger that knew no bounds. But with a growl, he tore his gaze from him and fixed his sights on me instead, setting my heart hammering.

"Keep him busy!" Erik roared at Fabian before making a beeline for me, powering up the road in a blur of speed.

The slayer took something from his pocket and tossed it between him and the Belvedere brothers before Erik could get close.

A bang sounded and white smoke billowed into the sky, surrounding us in seconds. I coughed as it bit at my throat, hastily climbing out of the car, and hurrying along the road in the thick smog, usure where I was headed only that I needed to move and never stop moving.

The roar of an engine sounded nearby, and the wind was knocked out of me as someone grabbed me by the waist. I was dragged onto a motorised bike and tossed over the knees of my kidnapper, flying along the road at a furious pace.

"Let me go!" I screamed, biting and kicking, desperate to get free.

The bike was so fast, the world became a blur around me, and it was suddenly far too dangerous to keep struggling. If I fell, my head would be dashed to pieces on the road, and I did not want to end up dead because of this crazy asshole.

We moved away from the smoke and sped through the city at an impossible speed, leaving Erik and Fabian behind in the fog. I had to close my eyes to escape the flood of movement around me, the blur of it making my head spin, especially from the awkward angle I was perceiving everything from.

Shouts echoed away into the distance, but Erik's voice carried above them all.

"I'm coming for you, rebel!" he roared, his words sending a tremor through me that caused a mixture of longing and fear. "And hear me now, slayer. If you have left a single scratch on her when I hunt you down, I will ensure you know the kind of agony that only exists in the merciless depths of the afterlife. There is no path treacherous enough to keep me from her."

MAGNAR

CHAPTER TEN

1000 YEARS AGO

By the time we made it to the foot of the mountain and retrieved our horses from the woodland where we'd left them, it was well past sunset.

The night was deathly cold and despite my thick furs, goosebumps lined my skin.

We quickly found our way back to the road and set the horses at a gallop, aiming for the last village we'd passed through.

The snow grew heavier as we travelled and began to stick to the frozen ground. Soon, the road and everything surrounding it was obscured in a blanket of white, and I had no doubt that anyone else would have lost their way.

By the time we spotted the lights of the tavern through the maelstrom, the snow had gathered into deep drifts and the horses had been reduced to an awkward trot.

Baltian whinnied his protest at every available moment, but there was little I could do to ease his discomfort until we made it to the shelter of the stables.

When we finally arrived, I dismounted and led him straight inside, holding the door for Julius to follow with his horse.

The stable boy hurried out of the last stall where a small fire had been lit to keep him warm. His eyes widened as they fell on us, and he hesitated short of trying to take the reins. Baltian snapped at him playfully, and the boy raised an eyebrow.

"Point me to a fresh stall out of the wind," I said when he failed to offer any greeting.

"I'm sorry, sir, but with the storm, we've been overwhelmed with guests and there are no stalls left," the boy squeaked.

He was skinny enough that I knew he didn't get three square meals a day. That might have made him look younger than his years, but I put him at around twelve. He cowered like he expected me to strike him for his words.

"That's not a problem," I replied. "You can move some of the other horses to share a stall."

"But sir, people have paid-"

I took a step closer to him and he shrank again as I towered over him. I resisted the urge to laugh at his terror and pulled a heavy coin from the pouch at my belt.

"Now we've paid more," I said as I tossed it to him, and his eyes widened in disbelief.

The coin meant little to me; we had more money than we could count thanks to what we'd taken from the Sacred Followers. Apparently, Miles appreciated financial offerings alongside the blood of virgins, and I was always happy to relieve him of both.

I held up a second coin and the boy stared at it like he couldn't believe his eyes. "One for you to keep yourself if you hurry. Your best stalls, finest grain, and extra straw for their bedding. I'll stable him myself though, and I warn you not to approach him. Baltian will bite your fingers off without thinking anything of it."

"I'm sure I'll win him over, sir," the boy replied dismissively as he eyed my warhorse. "Just tie them there and head into the tavern."

"You'll regret that," Julius joked as he quickly tied his stallion's reins to the hitching post. He pointed an accusatory finger at Baltian.

"That horse is meaner than any man I've ever met."

"I'm sure I've met worse," the boy muttered as he turned away, clearly having no fear of animals despite his nervous disposition.

I considered insisting on helping him with Baltian, but he'd made his choice, and I was keen to get into the warmth of the tavern. No doubt he'd be coming in to find me the moment I started on my meal, but if he wanted to take his chances with my bad-tempered steed then that was up to him.

Julius headed straight for the tavern, and I followed him quickly, looking forward to shaking the cold from my bones.

Many heads turned our way as we entered the large bar area. The low doorway meant we had to stoop to enter, and with our heavy blades, towering height, and muscular builds, I knew we cast an intimidating shadow.

Ignoring the stares, we headed straight for the bar and elbowed a space into existence before it. No one dared to protest as they scrambled to get out of our way, and I eyed the other patrons while Julius ordered food and drinks for us.

"And two rooms," I added, giving my attention back to the portly man behind the bar who looked likely to be the owner.

"I'm sorry sir, I'm afraid we don't have-"

I waved off his objections and slammed four heavy coins onto the bar. "Find them. I don't care who you have to toss out."

The bartender licked his lips greedily as he eyed the coins. "I may be able to find one-"

"Two," I replied firmly, fixing him in my gaze and making it clear that this wasn't a negotiation.

He quailed under my stare and nodded as he slid the coins into his pocket. "Of course. My wife enjoys the odd night sleeping down here before the fire. I'll have the maid make up our own room and I'm sure our daughter will be happy to give up her bed for your companion."

I glanced along the bar at the red-headed beauty he indicated and noticed her attention lingering on us. Julius smiled at her wolfishly. I doubted she'd have to give up her bed; it looked like she'd be sharing it.

"Good. We'll take a table in the back to enjoy our meal, and I have extra coin for information on a man we're trying to find. He passed through here yesterday. He would have stood out as clearly as us but in very different ways. He has many names, but he is a demon with the face of an angel." I watched the man's reaction for any sign that he knew who I spoke of, but his expression remained blank. I guessed parasites didn't need to stop for food.

"I'll ask around and send anyone who saw anything your way," he assured me.

"His passage might have been marked by a strange death or two. Has anyone died unexpectedly? Perhaps with signs of an animal attack, bite marks on their skin, a great deal of blood loss?" Julius asked.

The bartender's gaze moved to a group of sombre-looking men in the far corner and nodded. "Old Mac was killed last night. There's some disagreement over what did it. Some say a wolf, but then why would it leave the body behind? Wolves kill for food. Besides, we haven't seen sign of wolves around here for years."

I pushed an extra coin across the bar and exchanged a brief smile with Julius. "If anyone knows any more about it-"

"I'll send them to you," the bartender replied eagerly, weighing the coin in his palm.

He pointed us through to the back room where a tired-looking woman was wiping down a recently vacated table. The men who had been asked to leave it cast irritated looks at us, but they didn't voice their objections as they moved back out to the bar.

While we enjoyed our meal, several men and women approached us with tales of Miles and what had happened to Old Mac. Unfortunately, none of the information we gleaned gave us any explanation for his sudden disappearance. It certainly seemed like he'd been meaning to face us here but then the trail had gone cold.

As the fire burned low and most of the patrons headed home or up to their rooms, I began to lose hope. If we couldn't find a new lead, then we might as well abandon our search and head back to re-join the clan in the south. The last time Miles had disappeared on us, it had been months before he resurfaced.

Julius tried to convince me to head to my room, but I waved him off dismissively. It wasn't like he was taking his own advice about sleep; he took his leave with a smirk and disappeared with the redhead as expected.

My mind swirled with questions about Miles. He was up to something; I just knew it.

I was so preoccupied that I hardly noticed when a slim figure slipped into the chair opposite mine.

"I hear you're looking for information about the demon," the woman said, and I looked up at her as she pushed the hood from her head. She had long, dark hair which framed her wide eyes, and she glanced about nervously as if she was worried someone might overhear us.

"I am," I replied, leaning closer to her.

The few men who remained in the bar were drunk or passed out. I doubted any of them were capable of eavesdropping on us even if they had a mind to.

"Can we talk in private?" she whispered, leaning closer to take my hand. She turned my arm over and brushed her fingers against the slayer mark on my skin. "I know what you are. My mother was born of your blood too."

I stilled, my eyes sweeping across the room. Few people knew what we really were; they saw only warriors or mercenaries for hire. Mostly they were too afraid of us to look too closely.

"Come then." I caught her hand and pulled her to her feet, leading her behind me up to the room I'd been given. Anyone watching us would presume I was going to bed her, but if she was worried about her reputation, she didn't voice it.

I pressed the door closed behind us, and she moved away to perch on the edge of the bed.

"My mother left her clan for love when she was younger than I am now," she explained as she unclasped her cloak and set it down beside her. She wore a deep green gown which was fine enough to tell me that her family had money. I wondered again why she wasn't more concerned about her reputation. "But she taught me all about the vampires and how to spot them. So when I saw them, I knew exactly what I was looking at."

"Them?" I asked curiously. We'd managed to separate Miles from his vampire companions some days ago. Julius and I had fought the three who had been travelling with him, and they'd paid for his head start with their lives. As far as I knew, there were no more vampires in the area.

"Yes. I spotted the two of them creeping through our orchard. And I know the next bit might sound insane, but when my mother died, she left me a dagger. I keep it with me always, and when I saw those monsters, it *spoke* to me." Her eyes were wide like she thought I might laugh her out of the room, but I knew the voice of the blades well.

"She gave you a slayer blade?" I asked, moving closer to her.

"Yes." She sagged with relief as she realised I believed her, and she pulled her dress up to remove the blade from a sheath strapped to her thigh.

"What's your name?" I asked as I reached for it.

"Elissa," she replied.

I took the weapon in my hand, and it hummed excitedly. *Greetings, Magnar the Great. Defender of the scattered clans.* I frowned at the strange name it had given me. The scattered clans? As far as I knew, the clans had made camp close to each other in the lands to the south. I pushed my consciousness into the blade, searching for its name and origin.

"Your mother was from the Clan of Oceans, this blade is Vortex." I handed it back to Elissa, and she bit her lip as she looked at the runes carved into its hilt.

"If I tell you what I know, will you take me with you when you leave?" she asked. I raised an eyebrow in surprise, and she hurried to explain. "I wish to be free. This blade calls to me in a way that makes me feel *alive*. But my father has given my hand to a man three times my age. I'm to marry him on Saturday, and I just don't think I can bear it."

"You want me to steal you away in the night and make an enemy of every man in this town?" I asked in amusement.

I wasn't entirely opposed to the idea, even if it did sound a little insane. I could do with something to lighten the mood of this trip now that it appeared to have been for nothing.

"You won't have to face any angry townspeople," she replied with a shy smile. "My father will kick me out and send me packing himself if... if I'm ruined before the wedding. My betrothed will never take me if I'm not a virgin."

I barked a laugh at her brazenness. "Is that so? Well, I happen to know a thing or two about unwanted betrothals myself. You know if you re-join your clan and take the vow, you may end up betrothed all over again, right?"

"I don't care," she breathed. "I'd take a warrior husband over an old man with rotten teeth any day. Please take me with you." She reached out to touch my hand, and I felt my resolve fade. It didn't matter to me if every man in this town hated me for stealing her, and if I could save her from an unwanted betrothal, then I should do so. I wished it were so simple for me to break my oath to Valentina.

"Alright. Elissa of the Clan of Oceans, I give you my word that I will return you to your people."

Her face broke into a radiant smile, and I could see her fighting the urge to cry tears of relief.

"Thank you... sorry, I didn't get your name?"

"Magnar Elioson of the Clan of War."

"You're the son of the War Clan's Earl?" she asked in astonishment, and I was impressed that her mother had educated her so well in the ways of our people.

"I am. Are you going to tell me about those vampires now?"

"Yes, of course. I saw them in our orchard, like I told you, and Vortex urged me to follow them. There were two of them; a man and a woman more beautiful than any people I'd ever seen. Their skin glimmered in the moonlight, and they moved without making a sound. They met the one you seek on the edge of my father's lands. He was angry, his fine clothes torn and filthy. He was complaining of taking a leap from a cliff and breaking his ankle, though I saw no sign of any wound-"

"Mortal wounds do not bother the vampires for long unless they are inflicted by a slayer's blade. Go on."

"The woman apologised to him for ruining his plans, and he was angry that they had. I missed some of what passed between them, but

I think he mentioned a trap being spoiled. She told him that it was unavoidable because his brother needed him to return to the west. She also said that Fabian's plan was finally coming together and that they'd have to unite their strength if they hoped to succeed. He didn't seem entirely convinced by her claims, but the three of them turned and ran west at great speed. They were gone before I even stepped out of my hiding place. Then the blade led me to you."

"I knew it," I growled.

Miles *had* been meaning to face us on that mountain. The fact that he'd abandoned his ambush could only mean that something bigger was happening. And if he planned to meet with one of his brothers, then I would do whatever it took to meet him there too.

I was half tempted to drag Julius from his bed and leave right away, but there wasn't much point. The storm still raged outside, and the horses needed their rest as badly as we did.

I began pacing the room as I tried to figure out what all of this meant. As far as I knew, the Revenants hadn't been together in years. They spread themselves far and wide to hide their hunting habits from the humans and split the attention of the slayers. If they were meeting up, then it must have been for something important. I would have to return to the clans and tell them of this.

The sound of fabric hitting the floor drew my attention back to Elissa, and I stilled as I found her standing naked in the centre of the room.

She'd clearly been serious about me ruining her for her future husband, and I hesitated for half a moment before closing the distance between us. It would have been rude to refuse, and I could do with the distraction from my swirling thoughts.

CALLIE

CHAPTER ELEVEN

Fury burned hotter than I'd ever felt it as we finally closed in on the train station. I could *feel* the vampires as we approached them, the blade warning me each time a group of guards came near. We changed our path multiple times as we travelled through the forest to avoid discovery, always one step ahead of them, thanks to our weapons.

It seemed like too much security to me. As far as I knew, no one had ever successfully escaped the Realm before. And even if they had, a human would pose no threat to the vampires. So the only reason for their patrols which made sense was that they were expecting us. I guessed after burning down the blood bank, this was the next logical place for us to come. We'd destroyed a batch of blood while we were there, and Wolfe had killed the humans they'd been using to harvest it. I could only imagine that this supply train was desperately important to the bloodsuckers now. And I couldn't wait to obliterate it.

The sun was concealed behind dark rain clouds and thick shadows filled the space between the trees, but the woodland was beginning to thin, letting more light in up ahead.

Magnar pulled the horses to a halt, and I sighed heavily as he slid from the stallion's back. This was it. We couldn't get any closer with the horses in tow. It was time to set them free.

I dismounted too, patting the stallion on the neck in thanks for all he'd done for us.

Though I hadn't spent long with the beautiful creatures, parting from them filled me with sadness. They'd become a part of our little group. The four of us had travelled for miles and spent hours in each other's company. Sending them off to face the unknown left a pit of sorrow in my gut. Where would they go? What would they do now that the whole world was open to them?

The mare moved towards me, leaning low as I stroked her nose affectionately. She nuzzled me, her deep eyes almost seeming sad too. Like she knew this was goodbye.

Magnar removed the packs from her back then took the reins off of them. They watched us calmly, waiting while we prepared to set them free.

"So this is it?" I asked, and Magnar nodded.

"There's no way to bring them, Callie. We need to do the rest of this on foot."

I knew my misery was a little over the top, but I couldn't help it. The horses had been better friends to me than most of the humans I'd known in the Realm. And once we walked away from them, I knew we'd never see them again.

"Run fast and stay free," I whispered as I stroked them both one final time, a lump of emotion building in my throat.

I stepped back and Magnar placed a hand on my shoulder, guiding me away. We headed on between the trees, and I glanced back as the sound of their hoofbeats drew my attention. The stallion took the lead as he trotted away, and the mare whinnied as she hurried after him. I watched them go with a smile tugging at the corner of my lips. I could have sworn they understood that they were free now and that they were happy about it too. It was all I'd yearned for since forever, so what was there truly to be sad about?

I brushed a single tear from my cheek as I turned back to face the trail, focusing my mind on what we needed to do now.

"You have a softness in your heart which you try to hide," Magnar murmured.

"I don't think so, Elder." I grimaced as that stupid title slipped past my lips.

Instead of growing used to that word replacing his name, I was finding it more infuriating each time it happened.

"That is because you've been forced to spend your life denying it. You built walls to keep people out so that their loss wouldn't hurt you, but the only reason it could do so is your capacity for love. If you were not capable of it, then you wouldn't have had to shield yourself from it. You are prone to love and kindness. I just hope becoming a slayer doesn't steal any more of that from you," he replied.

"Why would it?" I asked.

"We live a hard life. We're ruthless when we need to be and fierce in the pursuit of our goals. Sometimes such things grind away the goodness within you. I have lost more than I ever could have imagined in my hunt for the Belvederes. It has corrupted the good in me and left a tarnish on my soul. So much so that sometimes I doubt the path I chose," he admitted.

"I know that you've lost more than I could ever comprehend," I replied slowly. "But you *are* good, Elder. You saved me when I didn't even want to be rescued. You've protected me despite the fact that I'm practically a walking target for the vampires to aim at. Hell, you even offered a psychopathic vampire a fair fight after you disarmed her. I've never met anyone who would do a fraction of what you've done for a stranger. I'm not sure I've met many people who would go so far even for someone they loved. It's just not what people do. At least not anymore. Without you, I'd be lost now; chained to a monster who wants to marry me and force me to have demon children with him. Because of you, I know we'll save my sister from that fate too."

Magnar didn't reply but he touched a hand to my shoulder, and the darkness in his gaze lifted a little.

I kept close to him as we crept through the trees towards the train station. We still had a long way to go, but with Fury reassuring me, I wasn't worried about being discovered. At least not yet.

We crouched low in the long grass at the top of a sweeping valley. Far below us, the train was waiting at the station. It lay poised like a snake, its white paintwork glimmering faintly in the dim sunlight which made it through the clouds, glinting like wet scales.

At least thirty vampires stood guard around it, watching the area closely. Instead of the blades they often carried, they held heavy machine guns and eyed the shadows with suspicion, making sure no one approached.

Halfway along the platform, huge grey boxes were being loaded onto the train.

I tugged at the collar of my dress uncomfortably. We'd found a store leftover from before the Final War on our way here and had raided it for clothes suiting my disguise as one of the Elite. The grey dress and knee-length boots looked like the kind of thing I'd seen them wearing when they'd visited our Realm. I'd found a long, red coat to wear over it, and though it wasn't quite like the robes a lot of them wore, I was confident I would pass for one of them.

My porcelain features, courtesy of Idun, were more than enough to disguise me anyway. All I had to do was act like I knew exactly what I was doing and walk straight into the thick of them. And if for any reason it didn't work, I knew they wanted me alive. So I should have the opportunity to escape if it all went to shit.

"I think we need to figure out a way to get you into one of those boxes, Elder," I said as the vampires continued to load the train.

There was no other way onto the sleek vehicle that I could see, and we needed to get Magnar inside somehow. Hopefully once he was onboard, I could just stroll on. I'd have to figure out a way to release him from the box once the train was moving.

Magnar grunted in agreement, though he didn't sound too thrilled about the idea.

"Let's hope they're big enough," I mocked. "We wouldn't want to be discovered because of your oversized ass."

"I think you know well that it isn't my ass which is oversized," he replied roughly, and I bit my tongue on a reply to that insinuation.

"So you think you'll fit?" I pushed.

"I'm sure I'll fit somehow. The more pressing issue is going to be getting down there unnoticed."

I nodded, watching yet another patrol of vampires marching across the valley, swords and guns ready to take out anyone who approached.

"What if we caused a distraction?" I suggested. "Set a fire like we did before?"

"We don't want them to suspect anything. We need to do this without them noticing us at all," Magnar replied, shaking his head.

I bit my lip, running my thumb over Fury's hilt. The blade was beside itself with so many vampires close, urging me into action. It hungered for their deaths and was clearly disappointed with me for holding back.

"Well, I could be the distraction. I can just walk down there, turn all eyes to me and make a fuss about them not doing their jobs properly. While they're looking at me, you can find a way in," I suggested.

"Are you ready to walk into that vipers' pit?" he asked, eyeing the patrolling vampires with distaste.

"Are you worried about me, Elder?" I asked, turning to look at him, a smirk dancing on the edges of my lips.

"I'm responsible for you," he replied dismissively, not looking at me. He'd barely laid eyes on me since Idun had bestowed this gift on my features, and I could tell he hated it.

"Well, I'm a big girl. I'm sure I can manage." I gripped Fury briefly in my pocket to steal some courage from it. "I'll see you down there." I rose to my feet, and Magnar caught my hand as if he was going to stop me from leaving.

"Be careful," he warned, his golden eyes finding mine.

I gave him a faint smile. "When am I not?"

I pulled out of his grip and began walking purposefully down into the valley, steeling myself for what I was about to do. My thoughts fell to Dad for a moment, and the choking grief made me still in my tracks. The pain was achingly deep, and I knew it would be everlasting. The loss of him was still so impossible to believe.

I took a steadying breath, thinking of his parting words to me in a dream that was etched into my memory, never to be carved out. If his soul was somewhere out there, joined with Mom's, they were surely watching now, urging me on. They'd believe I could do this, even if they feared for my safety too. And that thought was all it took to keep walking.

It was only a few moments before the vampires spotted me, some of them raising their guns.

"Who's there?" a male shouted as he pointed a rifle at my face.

"Finally, one of you sees me," I replied, throwing as much disdain into my voice as I could. I just had to front this out and hopefully they wouldn't realise what I really was. "It took you long enough."

The lesser vampires glanced between each other nervously as I closed in on them.

"I'm sorry mistress, you should have been spotted sooner-"

"Yes. I should have," I growled. "I shouldn't have been able to get within five miles of this place without being discovered, and yet here I am."

I made it to the foot of the valley and paused before them. The four guards shifted nervously under my scrutiny and my lip curled back in distaste.

"I'm going to inspect the rest of this operation, and I hope for your sakes that I don't find any more failures."

"Of course, mistress. I'll send extra patrols into the forest now, and I'll show you anything you wish to inspect." The male vampire waved his companions away and they darted up the hill.

I hoped Magnar had moved on already, but I couldn't risk looking back to check. If they discovered him, then this whole plan would fall apart. My gut swirled with concern for the slayer. He might have been unstoppable in battle but there wasn't much he could do against a gun.

"Lead the way," I snapped as the vampire hesitated. He hurried to comply and set a fast pace towards the train station.

I focused on keeping my steps silent as I walked. The vampires' boots made no sound as they passed over the ground, and I couldn't afford to make any mistakes. But I didn't really need to worry myself about it; my gifts guided me on swift feet, and I swept through the grass with ease.

He mounted the platform, and I followed him up, pausing to survey the train.

"She's a beauty, isn't she?" the vampire gushed, following my gaze. "The finest bullet train ever created. She'll make it to New York in just under twenty hours." My heart leapt at the prospect. In less than a day, I'd be close enough to help my sister. Perhaps we really could make it in time to rescue her before the wedding.

"Why are you spouting facts instead of showing me the cargo?" I asked, lending some steel to my tone.

"Of course." The vampire bowed his head and hurried along the platform. We moved between the lesser vampires, and they all nodded respectfully as I passed. I kept my chin high and ignored them, my heart fluttering with nerves, but the disguise continued to fool them.

When we reached the point where they were loading the cargo onto the train, I stilled. Another Elite was watching over the work, his eyes narrowing as he noticed our approach. He was tall with hazel hair cropped close to his scalp and his face was deeply alluring. Strangely, for one of their kind, a scar cut through his eyebrow, continuing down over his cheek. I didn't even know it was possible for their skin to scar, and there was something about the break to his perfection that was hard to look away from.

"What are you doing here?" he asked without bothering to greet me.

"Isn't that obvious?" I asked in response, hoping that it was, because I had no real answer if not.

"Prince Fabian said we wouldn't be needing any further assistance." He glared at me like he was offended by my presence.

"I guess he changed his mind," I replied lightly. "If you want to question his actions, then be my guest, but I doubt he'll appreciate it."

The Elite glowered at me, then sighed. "Of course I won't disturb His Highness over something so minor. You may as well take over here; I need to check in with the patrols."

"You might want to keep a closer eye on their work," I said as he began to move away. "I made it into the valley before they spotted me. Who knows what the prince will make of that."

The Elite hissed, baring his fangs in anger before sprinting away so quickly that it set my pulse racing. I guessed some lesser vampires were about to be in a lot of trouble, and I had to fight to keep the smile from my face at the thought, hoping he gave them hell.

A group of lessers were transporting the boxes of cargo onto the train, but they kept their heads down as I turned my attention to them.

I walked further along the station, moving around the heap of crates towards the back of the pile. I tried to spot Magnar in the shadows, but there was no sign of him. Worry stirred beneath my skin, but I ignored it, trusting in his skills and knowing that the most important thing I needed to do was keep up this ruse. The guard continued to follow me, and I stopped suddenly, turning to glare at him.

"You're dismissed," I snapped.

He opened his mouth as if he might protest, and I raised an eyebrow, hoping he wouldn't push me because I wasn't entirely sure what I'd be expected to do if he did.

"Of course, mistress," he said, bowing his head. "You only need to call me if you require any further assistance."

He turned and headed away along the platform and I watched him until I was sure he wasn't coming back. Relief seeped through me as I was finally left alone, and I released a heavy breath. They didn't suspect me. Idun's magic was working.

I eyed the lessers who were loading the train, but they seemed keen to avoid my attention and were putting all of their effort into their work, keeping their backs to me as much as possible. Which just so happened to be perfect.

I wetted my lips and stepped between the crates, trying to remain casual while inspecting the boxes for a likely spot to hide a seriously big bastard. I reached out to lift the lid of one and found stacks of material within it. I frowned as I released it, moving on to check another crate. This one held coils of copper wire. I'd been expecting blood, maybe some bat cages, coffins, or little photos of lifeless bloodsuckers laying on sun loungers in the middle of the night, but these were just normal supplies, not even that vampirish at all.

As I made my way to the far edge of the platform, I found more and more items which I guessed had been gathered from the area, left over after the Final War. I supposed the vampires had uses for them, but I began to wonder where the blood was if it wasn't here. None of the crates were refrigerated, and I had to assume it would need to be kept fresh. Which meant they must have been loading it somewhere else.

"Callie?"

I paused as I heard Magnar's whisper and turned slowly, trying to spot him. A flutter of movement caught my eye, and I made my way between the crates until I discovered him.

"You made it alright?" I asked, eyeing him for any sign of injury.

"Your arrival distracted them enough to let me slip by," he confirmed.

"We need to get you into one of these crates," I said, glancing around to make sure no one was paying me any attention.

"There's some empty here," he replied. "I've already stowed our things."

I squeezed through a narrow gap, checking over my shoulder to make sure we were still alone and joined him beside the empty containers. They'd been left a little way back from those that were waiting to be loaded onto the train, but Magnar had already shifted one closer.

He pushed the lid aside before vaulting into it. The space inside was just big enough for him to lay down with his legs curled against his chest in a foetal position.

I grinned down at him as he forced himself into the uncomfortable space.

"I'll get you out as soon as I can," I promised.

"I'm sure you aren't enjoying this at all," he replied dryly.

"Absolutely not," I agreed as I shoved the lid back into place, locking him within the crate.

I removed Fury from my pocket and carved a line into the side of his box and the one which held our bags so that I'd be able to locate him again on the train.

I replaced the blade as soon as I was done and headed back towards the other side of the platform, closer to the train. The lesser vampires were working quickly, and the stack of boxes were being moved fast onto the train.

"How much longer do you expect this to take?" I asked, throwing as much irritation into my tone as possible.

"We are well on track to finish within the hour, mistress," replied a female with thick, curling hair. "Are you going to travel back to New York with the delivery?"

"Of course I am," I replied, relieved that she seemed to expect this.

"Would you like me to show you to a suite on board?" She seemed eager to please me, and I took the opportunity to use her to my advantage because I had no fucking idea what to do from here.

"Yes, thank you." Her eyes widened in surprise at the thanks, and I hurried to cover up the mistake. "Are you waiting for an invitation to proceed or just planning to stand here all day?"

"Sorry, mistress, right this way."

She headed off along the platform, leading the way to a set of doors near the front of the train. I glanced back at the crates of cargo which were still being loaded and hoped it would be easy to find my way back to them once I was onboard.

The vampire moved inside, and I followed her, making an effort to keep my features neutral as I was surrounded by more luxury than I'd ever seen in my life.

Red carpet led the way down a long corridor, and we began to pass smooth white doors with gold numbers painted on them. The vampire kept going until she reached door nine and slid it open for me.

The room inside was bigger than the one I'd shared with Montana back in the Realm. To the left of the door was a double bed with a thick comforter, and a blue curtain was pinned back beside the bed which could be used to conceal it. To the right was a table with two padded armchairs and an open door which led to a small ensuite.

I stepped in, frowning at my surroundings and working to hide the anger rising in my gut. The vampires *travelled* in better conditions than those I'd been given to live in for my entire life. This thing was just another reminder of why I was so determined to see them fall.

"I can have a chalice of Realm A delivered," the vampire offered.

"Warm, if you prefer?"

My lip began to curl back, and I forced it to stop before she noticed I didn't have any fangs.

"No," I snapped, wanting rid of her as quickly as possible. "That won't be necessary, I intend to rest a while. Just make sure I'm not disturbed."

"Of course, mistress. We should be all set to leave within the hour. Just call me if you need anything before then." She bowed her head and backed out of the room, closing the sliding door between us.

I let out a long breath as I sank down onto the bed, suppressing the laugh which threatened to bubble up from my chest. I'd just tricked a bunch of bloodsuckers into thinking I was one of them with nothing more than a taste of a magical apple and fancy new dress. My life was officially unbelievable.

So far, so good.

Now all I had to do was wait for the train to depart. Then I'd have to figure out how to release Magnar on a train full of vampires without any of them noticing. Simple.

MONTANA

CHAPTER TWELVE

The slayer eventually slowed the bike, and I could see the world more clearly, discovering we'd entered a ruined part of the city. The buildings close by were crumbling to dust, and we had to weave through debris on the road as we moved.

"Let me down," I demanded, trying to push myself upright and wondering if we'd slowed enough for me to risk jumping off. Though he'd easily catch me again and I didn't want to risk the broken leg.

We went over a bump and my face slammed into his crotch.

"Get your dick out of my face," I exclaimed, clinging to his legs as I tried to steady myself.

"Never heard that before. Most women can't wait to get my dick in their face. Besides, you're the one cuddling it."

"I am not cuddling it," I snarled, wriggling to get further down his lap, but my hand accidently slapped between his thighs, my palm riding the thick ridge of his cock beneath his pants.

"Argh," I growled, snatching my hand away.

"By the gods, stay still, will you? We can get to that later."

"If you put that thing anywhere near me, I'll rip it off," I warned.

"Whatever happened to damsels in distress?" the man asked, grinning down at me.

"I am in distress." I pushed him as he veered the bike down a dark alley, darting between fallen pieces of mortar.

"You're not a damsel though. You kept punching me throughout my valiant rescue. It was pretty distracting, actually. Like a moth dashing itself against a burning log. Totally pointless and entirely suicidal."

The bike slowed and we finally came to a halt. The slayer pulled me upright, keeping hold of my wrist as he dismounted the vehicle so I couldn't run, his grip firm enough to tell me I'd have no chance of breaking free. He was frighteningly large, with dark eyes that seemed to bore into my soul, the mischievous glint in them doing nothing to ease the frantic pounding of my pulse. And despite holding back my fear beneath a layer of fury, I was really terrified of what he was about to do next.

I spotted Nightmare tucked into his belt and lunged for it in a bid to fight, no matter the outcome.

He smacked my hand away, shaking his head. "That's mine for now, damsel."

"Give it back. And don't call me that," I ordered, and he smiled a crooked smile, raising a brow.

"You need to calm down, Montana."

I stilled at my name, shock jarring through me. "How do you know who I am?"

"I've been watching you since you arrived in the city. And if I recall rightly, you didn't seem so happy about being the vampires' little pet, so why don't you relax and take a breath of free air at last?"

I gazed around the ruins, looking up at an old bell tower beside us which stretched toward the sun glowing behind the clouds. The walls were tarred with soot from a long burnt-out fire, but the structure was well intact compared to the surrounding buildings.

"I don't feel so free." I gestured to his hand around my wrist.

"Well, you've got the look of a flighty little cat in your eyes, and I'm starting to fear they've brainwashed you. So just as a precaution, I'm going to keep hold of you. Or...I guess you can stay out here and take your chances with the hungry freaks living in the ruins."

As if on cue, a horrid shriek sounded from the depths of the shattered buildings and my heart hammered uneasily. Going towards them without Nightmare was a hell no, but staying with this asshole didn't exactly appeal either.

"Let's get inside and we can talk," he offered, his voice softening, and I eyed him suspiciously, thinking over my situation.

On the one hand, he had just helped me escape from the rule of the vampires I'd been fighting against since I got here. I had every reason to run from them now. Isn't that what I'd wanted?

But somehow, when I thought of leaving Erik behind, knowing I may never see him again, I felt something I didn't know how to express. Like leaving him had brought on a hunger in me that could only ever be sated by him. But it was foolish to think that way. I should have been weeping with joy about what this slayer had done for me. I was free. Truly free at long last – minus the muscular hand currently latched around my wrist.

"I'm going to take that as a yes," he said, steering me toward the entrance of the bell tower, and I guessed I didn't have much choice.

The slayer approached the door, pushing it open and nudging me into the dark space.

He released my wrist, giving me a hard look. "Don't. Run."

"I don't like being ordered around. I've had enough of that from *them*."

He frowned like he gave a damn about that. "Don't run, *please*. I have things to tell you. Important things."

Another shriek came from out in the ruins, and a shudder tracked down my spine.

"I'll stay for now," I said. "But manhandle me again and I really will rip your dick off."

He barked a laugh. "You'd be lucky. That's a slayer dick. Blessed by the gods. It even glows in the dark."

"That's ridiculous."

"I know, yet here we are." He turned and swept back out the door, leaving me with the image of his cock shining like the sun, trying to decide whether he was bullshitting me or not.

Dust rose in my nostrils, and I gazed around the cold place, wondering what this guy was about to tell me. I had to admit I was curious about him, why he'd come for me, what he'd meant when he said he'd been watching me.

Erik's parting words to us rattled through my head, his promise to hunt us down and reclaim me. I thought of him out there somewhere, tearing the world apart to find me, and I wasn't sure how to feel about that. Since that night at the bar, things had shifted between us more than I liked. A spark of want catching light and blazing into something wholly toxic, yet entirely irresistible. He'd crawled quietly beneath my skin, and I wasn't prepared for such an abrupt parting.

The slayer returned, rolling his motorised bike into the room and resting it against the wall before locking the door with large deadbolts. When he was finished, he turned to me in the near darkness.

"Up." He pointed toward the only other door in the room, which was a small wooden thing that was hardly any taller than me. He led the way, ducking through the little doorway, his shoulders barely squeezing through as he went. We emerged in a stone stairwell, and he guided me up it, climbing higher and higher until we arrived at the top of the tower.

Stone archways were set into the four stone walls that let cool air rush through the space. Hanging above us was a huge bronze bell which must have been far older than me, and perhaps older than most humans currently walking the earth. A pile of blankets was laid out to one side of the space under a tarp which had been strung up with some rope, and beside it was a stash of food. Tin cans and plastic-wrapped items were among the hoard, and beyond them was a pile of weapons. Steel blades, even a couple of the vampires' swords.

How long had he been living here?

The slayer released his bow from his shoulder, placing it down with his quiver of rune-carved arrows. He took Nightmare from his belt and turned it over in his palms with a soft sigh. "Hello, beautiful."

"Hey, that's my blade," I insisted, striding toward him, intending to grab it.

He turned away from me, his eyes fixed on its golden hilt. "Did you miss being with a true slayer?" he cooed, stroking Nightmare as if it was a pet. I reached for it in frustration, but he shouldered me away. "By the gods, I've longed for my old sword. You're not quite the same as Menace, but you're very, very pretty."

"Stop it." I tried to get to Nightmare, but he looped a leg around mine and knocked me to my ass on the floor with irritating ease, his eyes still on my blade.

I glared up at him, the urge to fight pouring through me. Nightmare was *mine*. It was like a piece of me he was pawing with his meaty fingers. I lunged upward and my hand brushed the hilt, but he lifted it out of my reach.

Friend of Moon Child, Nightmare whispered, and the slayer's brows rose in surprise.

"Friend?" I asked mistrustingly. Nightmare had never steered me wrong so far, but was it just being swayed by this asshole flirting with it?

"Hm." The slayer chewed the inside of his cheek as he contemplated the weapon. "Gods be damned, it appears Nightmare is loyal to you. And she's not so happy about me taking her."

I opened my mouth, shocked that he knew its name.

"Then give it back," I demanded, reaching for it again.

He eyed me with a smirk, holding the blade out to me in an offering.

I tried to take it, but he flipped it over in his hand, catching it by the hilt then pocketing it. "Nah."

I glowered at him, my dislike of this man growing quickly.

Reaching down, he snatched my outstretched hand and pulled me upright with a powerful tug. He kept my hand in his grip, shaking it firmly. "I'm Julius. It's nice to meet you at last."

My eyes narrowed as I pulled my hand away. "Who are you, what are you doing here, and what did you mean when you said you've been watching me? Because the stalker vibes aren't doing you any favours right now."

"That is a very, very long story," he said, gesturing for me to sit on his makeshift bed under the tarp. The cold wind was whipping strongly through the space and that tarp looked like it was doing a decent job at breaking it.

"Nice set-up," I commented dryly.

He glanced around at his little makeshift sleeping area like he was admiring it. "Great, isn't it? I feel like a harpy, all cosy up here in my nest."

"A what?"

"You know," he said. "A harpy. Like with the wings, and the magic, and the love of shiny sticks." He flapped his arms like wings, and I cocked a brow at him.

"You're odd," I said.

"Odd-ly charming?"

"No, just odd," I said, but dammit, his friendly tone cracked half a smile out of me.

"Come on. Sit in my nest," he encouraged.

I gave in, stepping past him and lowering myself onto the mattress, tucking my knees up to my chest.

Julius dropped down beside me with a slow smile growing on his face. "First things first, I want to know why you're scowling at me like I didn't just save your neck from a bunch of parasites."

"The vampires?" I guessed.

"Yes, bloodsuckers. Cursed nightwalkers, fanged fuckfaces, bitey cuntbags-"

"I get it," I cut him off, then sighed. "I'm grateful you freed me."

I looked beyond the nearest archway, taking in the sky, the taste of fresh air on my tongue.

"But?"

"There's no but," I said quickly.

"My mother always said that everyone in this world has a butt. Sentences are much the same."

"She sounds great," I said with a breath of amusement.

"Yes," he said, his brows pulling together. "So, what's the but?"

Everything I'd been through recently seemed so hard to voice. I'd seen the inner circle of the vampires; I'd lived and breathed their lifestyle. I'd witnessed first-hand how they had built an empire on the backs of human oppression, and yet...that wasn't all I'd seen. I'd experienced moments of humanity, warmth, passion, lust, even romantic love when it came to Miles and Warren. I'd felt something when Sabrina had died, and worst of all, I'd felt something between Erik and I that defied everything I'd ever stood for when it came to vampires. But perhaps it was all a veil of lies, perhaps Erik had lured me in like he was made to lure my kind. A deadly trap set by a design of nature or, if I believed him, by the gods. Though a stirring in my gut told me that wasn't it.

"But," I whispered, my throat thick as I feared whether I should voice this at all. "I…"

I couldn't find the right words. It felt like an insult to humankind to voice it. That I'd seen some good in the monsters. And what did it matter when you weighed it against all the bad?

"You've been through a lot," Julius said in his rumbling tone. "I have observed some of the things you've been forced to do. I've seen you in the arms of that monster, Erik…"

My head snapped up, my heart thundering at his words. "He didn't rape me, if that's what you think."

Julius's jaw pulsed. "Well, whatever hell he has put you through, understand that I will not judge you for it. I know what they are capable of. What Erik is capable of."

"What do you mean?" I asked, certain I wouldn't like the answer.

"He murdered my father in the worst way imaginable," Julius hissed, and horror crashed through me. "He is the lowest of them all. A soulless beast, a creature with a heart as black as coal."

I turned away from him, gazing around the bell tower, eyeing a glimpse of the city far beyond the archways.

"He killed your father?" I asked, my voice quavering a fraction, thinking of my own father with a tug of pain in my chest.

"Yes…a thousand years ago there was a great battle between the slayers and the vampires. My father was the only survivor, and Erik Belvedere – or Larsen as he went by back then - turned him into a vampire and sent him back to my village, hoping he would kill the rest of us. My own brother had to end his life. To rid him of the vile curse he'd been infected with."

The weight of those words settled over me like cold water crashing against my skin, chilling me to the bone.

"A thousand years ago…" I stared at him, taking in his youthful face and the impossibility of what he was saying. "But you're human."

"Close. I'm a slayer. Still, I'm mortal all the same, but my mother put my brother and I into a deep sleep, to awake when a new chance arose to defeat the vampires. A prophesised moment. But…I slept too long." His throat bobbed. "I believe I may have lost everything."

"I'm sorry," I whispered.

Julius sighed wearily, giving me a sincere look. "As am I. One day, I'll bring justice down upon all of their heads. If only my brother were here to see it…"

His eyes darkened with sorrow, and I saw the pain of grief in his eyes, recognising it all too well.

"Is he dead?" I asked gently, and he nodded.

"I believe so…I am the only slayer left. At least I was. But now there is you." His eyes brightened a little with hope. "I have been spying on the Belvederes for months. This last week I've heard whispers…some of the vampires say you have slayer blood. And now I know it is true." He reached for my arm, pushing up my sleeve to reveal the mark there, his skin burningly warm, such a contrast to Erik's frosty touch. "We're all that's left."

"We're not," I gasped. "My twin sister is like us. And she's with another slayer called Magnar Elios-"

Julius grabbed me, tugging me closer by the back of my neck.

"What did you say?" he boomed, making my heart jolt in my chest.

"Magnar Elioson," I repeated, trying to push him back, but he was like an immovable wall.

He gaped at me, pulling me so close that his face was just a few inches from mine, as if he was trying to read the truth from my eyes.

"By the gods." A smile grew on his face, wider and wider until he pulled me into his arms and crushed me to his chest in a fierce hug. "Holy shit!" He started laughing, rocking me from side to side as my face was pressed into his shirt, his muscles bunching so tightly around me I could hardly breathe.

I shoved away from him, and he let me go, his scent of sage and moss lingering in the air between us. "You know him?"

"He's my brother," he announced, rising to his feet and moving to one of the arched windows, gazing out toward New York city in the distance. He glanced back at me with a hopeful smile tugging up his lips. "Do you know where I can find him?"

I shook my head, sadness falling over me because I didn't know where to find my sibling either. "I think my sister is still on the west coast..."

He nodded, but a determined look filled his eyes. "Well, there is no doubt he will come here once he learns of the Revenants' location. My brother will want the Belvederes' heads, and we will sever them together." Pride filled his tone and my gut dipped with concern, the sudden thought of him attacking Erik unsettling me.

I felt like a traitor to my own kind as I ran my thumb over the slayer mark on my skin.

What's happened to me? Why don't I want him dead anymore?

Clarice and Miles hadn't shown me any cruelty, and though I should have wanted their lives for the sake of humankind alone, I found that when I was confronted with it, I didn't really want that anymore. I couldn't hide beneath any notions that I'd been bewitched or brainwashed, because when I really looked within, all I saw was the raw truth of my feelings. And something had changed.

"What's your plan?" I asked, shaking off the confusing thoughts. "Why did you bring me here?"

Julius rounded on me with a grim look. "I only wanted to save you, but now I wonder..." His eyes glazed with thought as he approached me, kneeling down at my feet. "Montana, we are the last slayers. And when Magnar arrives, there will be enough of us to take on the royals. You must take your vow." He snatched my arm, and I tugged away from him in alarm.

"What vow?"

"The vow to become a true slayer, to pledge yourself to the cause to end the vampires. To bring them to their knees. I can train you. I *will* train you. I'll be your mentor and the goddess will guide you-"

"No," I asserted. "I'm not staying here with you to take part in some suicide mission, I'm going to find my sister."

"You must fight. It's in your blood, Montana. It's who you are," he insisted, his gaze scraping over me. "I'll teach you how to strike them from this world for good, one undead monster at a time."

I shook my head, picturing Erik turning to ash like the last vampire I'd killed. I might have hated him, been unimaginably angry at him too, but a piece of me was fighting against all of that. I'd seen glimmers of the man he'd once been, and the thought of driving Nightmare into his heart made me sick.

"Why are you resisting your true path?" Julius growled.

"Because it's not my path," I snapped, and he eyed me darkly before releasing a low breath.

"I understand. You need more time. You can come with me on my next mission in the city. We will gather intelligence, prepare ourselves. And when the time is right, you'll take your vow."

I glared at him, my teeth grinding together at how quickly he dismissed my answer. "Stop acting as if I'm some broken creature. I told you my answer. Don't speak as if you know my mind better than I do. I said no. You're a stranger and a killer, that much I know about you, so I'm not going to blindly place my faith in you, even if you did risk your neck to free me."

"I'm hardly a killer, I just put the dead back where they belong." He raised his chin. "You'll trust me in time. We were destined to meet," he said with a touch of reverence to his voice, then he pointed at the food beside his bed. "Let's eat and discuss our next move. Erik and his vile family will no doubt meet soon. And we will be there to listen in."

My ears pricked up at that.

"Is that possible?" I asked curiously.

"Yes, Idun has helped me adjust to this new world. I now hold the knowledge which allows me to spy on them." He grinned and snatched a couple of packets of food from the floor, passing one to me.

After everything I'd been through, I wasn't remotely hungry.

"Who's Idun?" I asked, thumbing the packet.

"The goddess who created the slayers," Julius revealed, and I had to accept I was starting to believe in these gods. Erik had spoken of them too, and it was hard to deny the truth of them in the face of everything I'd seen.

I lowered my eyes to the food in my hand. "I saw you at the castle. You killed a guard in the grounds."

He released a breath of amusement. "As a message to the royals." He bit into the oat bar he was holding, swallowing it down in two bites. "I've been picking off their Elite when I can, killing anyone I can get information out of. Mostly on Erik. I've hungered for time alone with him but the bastard travels in packs. Today I had a choice...fight him or take you."

"And you chose me," I whispered, and he nodded.

"I most likely would have died standing against both he and Fabian anyway. But if Magnar is coming here, I will not run from a fight again with him at my side. You should see us in battle together, it is a thing to behold, Montana. We're unstoppable."

I didn't doubt his words, and they left a shiver in my bones that I couldn't shift.

"Tell me, did you notice any weaknesses of Erik's when you spent time with him? Or did he speak of any places he often goes alone?"

My pulse drummed in my ears and the intensity of his gaze made anxiety war in my chest.

"No," I muttered.

"There must be something," he pushed.

"There isn't."

"Come on, damsel. Give me an in that'll see the bastard dead for what he did to you."

"Perhaps I don't want to see him dead," I blurted before I could stop myself, and Julius's features twisted in disbelief.

"He was your captor," he growled, eyes flaring.

I shook my head, then nodded, unable to deny it. "Of course he was. But I still won't help you kill him."

"You're confused," he snarled, taking my shoulders and shaking me. "They brought you here. They want to violate you. Rape you and make you bear children for them. How can you vouch for a monster like Erik Belvedere?"

"He promised I would never have to do that," I said, but it sounded so foolish coming from my lips now, especially with Julius looking at me like I'd gone insane. Perhaps he was right. Perhaps I had. "Anyway, I am not *confused*. I know my own mind."

"You think his word holds any value?" he scoffed, looking furious. "His tongue is built for lies. Everything about him is a façade designed to trick you."

"I don't think that's true," I bit back, but I could see how he was looking at me. Pity was carving a path across his face, and he leaned back, his rage giving way to it. "Don't look at me like that. Like I'm just some victim of his."

"You are though," he said sadly. "But your blood will out. You'll remember what he is, given time."

"I know what he is. I'm not saying he's a damn saint, Julius. I've just seen more to some of the vampires than endless brutality. That's what I expected when I met them, but I think they make choices just like we all make choices. Good decisions, bad ones. They're living in the grey, just as we are."

"No, Montana," he said, looking me dead in the eye. "They live in shadow where nothing thrives but malice. We live in the light, and in that light, we must forge the good. They are not capable of creating something without taint. Anything more you thought you saw was a charade, I assure you. They have no souls, no morality, no tenderness."

"I think you're wrong," I said.

"Well, I know I am right, so we shall agree to disagree until you see sense."

I ground my teeth, seeing the wall in his eyes, his refusal to hear me.

"Look, your weapon will know the truth." Julius took Nightmare from his pocket, holding it out before him. "Tell me if your slayer has been brainwashed by the vampires."

I reached out, brushing my fingers over the hilt, wanting to hear the answer it provided, and the blade thrummed with a rich energy that rolled deep into my chest. When it spoke to us, Julius's eyes widened and a dawning fear encompassed his features, setting my heart thumping with trepidation.

Warrior born and monster made…Moon Child walks the path of salvation. Erik Larsen walks the very same path. A monster must be made, Julius Elioson. It is time.

CALLIE

CHAPTER THIRTEEN

I sat in the plush armchair, peering out of the window at the platform as the train rumbled to life around me. A shiver raced down my spine as a soft vibration built beneath the floor at my feet and I swallowed a lump in my throat as I tried to remain calm.

My heart fluttered with a mixture of fear and excitement. I'd never ridden in any kind of mechanical vehicle before, and I had no idea what to expect from the train once it got moving.

I pressed my hand against the material at my thigh where Fury was now strapped to my leg. The blade's constant anger at its proximity to the vampires flooded through me and I smiled. It was nothing if not consistent. But despite its bloodthirsty urgings, I wasn't stupid enough to head out into battle with the monsters who surrounded me.

I watched as lesser vampires hurried back and forth along the platform, double checking that everything was ready for our departure, calling out to one another and seeming more human than I'd ever seen their kind before. Not that they had any warmth to them, or any redeeming qualities that I'd noticed, but the vampires in the Realm had always been so stoic, almost ethereal, never hurrying, more like statues than living creatures. Not that they were living. But the vampires who were working to prepare the train for departure were hurrying, looking hassled and even irritable occasionally, their faces actually showing emotion from time to time. I wasn't really sure what I'd thought vampires spent their days doing when they weren't monitoring the Realm, but I guessed I'd expected them to be lounging about drinking our blood all day, not employed with monotonous jobs.

In the time I'd spent waiting with my heart rioting in my chest, no cry had gone out to say that Magnar had been discovered, and as the vampires closed the train doors, I felt a knot of tension release in my gut. We'd done it. Both of us were onboard the train and the vampires were none the wiser.

I expelled a long breath.

A silver clock hung on the wall beside the door of the opulent room, and I glanced at it for the hundredth time. One minute until two. Idun said her gift would wear off at midnight, so I needed to find Magnar before then. We would have to find a place to hide for the remainder of the journey once we'd poisoned their blood supplies and my gift had faded. If I was honest, I was longing for that moment, far preferring the idea of hiding from them to lurking in plain sight like this. Spending time among them felt anything but natural and I couldn't wait to separate myself from them as soon as I could.

I got to my feet, my nerves making me too jittery to sit still. I paced back and forth once, then realised I could be seen through the windows if any of the vampires on the platform looked my way, so I stopped myself. I glanced around, uncertain what to do before my gaze landed on the door in the corner of the room. I escaped into the ensuite so I could pull myself together without the risk of being observed.

The bright lights illuminated my unnaturally perfect face in the mirror as I leaned against the closed door and tried to quiet my thundering heart. I scowled at my reflection and the creature who stared back at me looked utterly terrifying.

Despite how helpful my Elite features had proven, I was more than ready to regain my own face. Nothing about the way I appeared seemed natural to me, not the exact symmetry of my features or the way my golden hair hung perfectly. I didn't even think it was appealing. It was the face of a monster. A pretty lie designed to lure prey. And the sooner I was back to myself, the better.

I released a breath, pushing away the anxiety which had been trying to take a hold of me and focusing my mind on the task at hand.

You can do this, Callie. Buck the fuck up.

I left the bathroom and reclaimed my chair beside the window, finding the platform almost abandoned. Only a few vampires remained, and they were backing away from the train as doors slammed shut and calls went out. The guards held their guns at the ready as if they still expected something to go wrong, their eyes on the trees which stood beyond the platform. Little did they know there was already a snake in their midst, their enemy within the heart of their operation.

The sound of the engine built to a whirring hum and a faint judder rumbled through the room. I gripped the arm of my chair as the train slid out of the station, fear clogging my throat and making me swallow thickly.

"It's perfectly safe," I muttered to myself. "Dad sent me here. He wouldn't have done that if it wasn't safe." Despite the words being designed to calm me, adrenaline pounded through my limbs and my stomach swooped disconcertingly as the train picked up speed. The desire to run gripped me, but there was nowhere to run to now.

The view outside my window began to blur together, the valley slipping away quickly until we shot across a wide-open field. I had to work hard to keep my breathing calm as the world raced by outside, my eyes skipping from point to point as I tried to take it all in. My brain scrambled to keep up with the rapidly changing view and I could hardly comprehend the speed at which we must have been travelling.

I gripped the arm of the chair so tightly that my bones showed white through my skin.

We were moving *so* fast. I never could have imagined such a thing was possible, and I couldn't help wondering what would happen to a person who fell from something travelling at this speed. Nothing good. That was probably why the windows didn't open. But that didn't stop me imagining the train crashing, or simply speeding right off the tracks, or just burning up from moving so fucking fast.

As I fought to accept what my brain was seeing, one clear thought found me and I clung onto it with all I had, using it to push back the panic and free myself from it.

I'm coming, Monty. All the vampires in the world can't stop me.

My heart began to slow again as the view outside became less daunting. The speed shouldn't have frightened me. It was my ally. It meant that I would be with her all the sooner.

The door behind me slid open and I jolted with surprise, a spike of fear racing through me as a vampire stepped into the room. I pushed myself to my feet and turned to face the Elite I'd met on the platform, uncertain what he could possibly be here for.

Fury seethed angrily where it was hidden against my leg and I shifted my position slightly, hoping he wouldn't notice the shape of the blade through the grey dress.

"Well, that went smoothly. As expected," he said as he leaned against the door frame, his gaze roaming over me slowly.

"Yes, everything went to plan," I agreed, wondering why on Earth he'd sought me out and what the fuck I could do to get rid of him again.

"I presume your report to your master will reflect that then?" He folded his arms, drawing attention to his biceps as they bulged through his white shirt. I got the impression it was intentional.

"Of course," I agreed.

"And just who is that?" he pushed. "Because we've never met before, and I was sure I knew all of Prince Fabian's sirelings. So who exactly sent you here to check up on us?"

My pulse pounded in my ears, and I swallowed nervously, hoping my statuesque face didn't betray an ounce of my fear.

"Who do you think?" I asked, not knowing which of the Belvederes was the most likely to be poking their nose into Fabian's business.

"*Of course.* Prince Erik is always hoping to find something he can use against my master," the Elite sneered, taking the bait and providing his own answer. "I should have known."

"Well, now you have your answer, I'd like to get some rest before we reach New York," I replied icily, hoping he'd get the hint and leave me alone.

He nodded and glanced back out into the corridor, but he didn't leave.

"I apologise if I was a little... abrupt. It's my job to see to my master's best interests. I'm sure you understand."

"I do," I agreed.

My palms were growing slick, and I clasped them together, hoping to hide the human reactions of my body. I might have looked like one of them but the longer he spent here, the more likely he was to notice the flaws in my disguise.

"But there's no reason for our sires to get between us." He turned back to look at me and his face lit with a dazzling smile as he dropped the haughty attitude. "I'm Benjamin. Ben if you prefer."

My mind raced with ideas of how I was going to rid myself of this vampire. He clearly had no intention of going anywhere, and my skin crawled as I noted the look in his eye, the way his gaze was tracing its way down my body. Hell to the fucking no. I needed to get rid of him. All the time I was trapped in his company, the more likely it was that he'd catch me in a lie. I couldn't let him discover what I really was, but I had to play along until I found the right thing to say to get him gone.

"Lauren," I replied, my mind landing on the name of a girl I'd known in our Realm. She'd been mean and selfish, so her name seemed fitting for a vampire.

His smile widened and he slid the door closed behind him, taking a step towards me. My gut plummeted as the immortal predator stalked closer. My slayer gifts weren't entirely reliable, and I seriously doubted my chances against one of the Elite regardless. Even Magnar found them challenging to defeat.

"This is going to be a long journey. I'm sure we could both do with a distraction to pass the time." His gaze slid over me, and my heart raced faster as I tried to think up a way to get out of this situation without giving him what he wanted because fucking a bloodsucking, reanimated corpse was definitely not on my to-do list.

"How did you get that scar?" I asked, eyeing the silver line which marred his face.

I hoped to stall him with conversation while I struggled to think of a way out of this which wouldn't alert his attention.

He raised the eyebrow which was broken by the scar and gave me a lopsided smile. "Do you like it? In a world so full of beauty, I've begun to think a little ugliness is quite becoming. I got it a long time ago in the final purge of the slayers. The one who gave me this faced a rather brutal end...Of course, that was before the anti-biting laws came into effect." He sighed wistfully. "Were you around when we could drink from the vein?"

"Umm, no, I wasn't," I said, hoping he didn't keep asking me questions because I really had no idea how to answer them.

"A shame. Not that I'm saying we should go back to that, of course. We all have to evolve." He stepped towards me purposefully, and I forced my mind away from the hunger in his eyes.

"Like I said, I'm tired, so-"

"Don't worry, Prince Erik will never find out, and there's nothing like the thrill of sleeping with the enemy." He prowled towards me, and I shifted so the chair was between us. I wasn't sure if I should shut him down outright or feign interest. What if vampires didn't take no for an answer? Maybe they were like animals who just took what they wanted by force. Nothing would surprise me.

"No thanks," I said coolly. "I'm really not available."

His gaze shifted to my hand where it gripped the back of the chair, and he lifted an eyebrow. "You don't wear your mate's ring. He cannot mean so much to you if you don't wish to declare your loyalty to the world."

My mind swirled as I tried to figure out what he was saying. He must have thought I'd been telling him I was married or something of the sort. I quickly pulled the necklace holding my mother's wedding ring out from beneath my dress to show him.

"I keep it close to my heart," I said, hoping the vampires clung to some sentiment like that. I doubted the monsters were capable of love, but it seemed like they held onto the idea of it if Montana's situation was any clue.

"Or you keep it out of sight so that you can pick and choose when you wish to remain loyal to him," the Elite purred as he moved around the chair.

I backed up but his lips lifted as if we were playing some game. Cat and mouse with a vicious animal probably wasn't a good idea.

"No. Really, I-"

He shot towards me in a sudden motion, that unnatural speed taking me off guard as he caught me around the waist and pushed me against the wall.

He pressed his body to mine, his grip tight around my waist and his muscles firm with tension.

My skin crawled from his touch, and I fought to keep the revulsion from my face.

"There's no need to play hard to get. I won't tell a soul..."

"I'm not playing," I growled. "I seriously don't want-"

He yanked on my dress, ignoring my words, and the material split up the side, his cold hand pushing inside it, meeting with the warm, human skin of my hip before I could even begin to curse him out.

My heart pounded with adrenaline. Fury screamed a warning. The vampire's eyes widened in shock and confusion, and I was all out of options.

"What are-"

I snatched Fury from its sheath against my thigh and slammed it into his heart before he could figure it out.

"Motherfucker," I hissed as the Elite dissolved into ash before me, his stunned expression breaking apart and scattering across the floor amidst the heap of his clothes.

I shuddered, relief sweeping through me at the ease of that strike, but it was swiftly followed by panic. I couldn't be discovered. If someone realised he was missing, then our whole plan might fall apart before we even got close to New York.

I stared down at his clothes and an idea filled me. If he'd come here looking to fuck me, then I could make it seem like that was what had happened.

I hurried to lock the door to my room, glancing out into the corridor to make sure no other vampires had been alerted by that altercation and sighed in relief as I found it empty. With the door secured, I moved back into the room and made a hasty plan.

A vase filled with yellow tulips sat on the small dining table and I quickly grabbed the flowers out of it then tossed the water into the basin in the ensuite. I shook out Benjamin's clothes and moved them out of the way before hurriedly gathering his dusty remains into the vase.

I glanced around in search of somewhere to put him, then grinned to myself as I found my answer and tossed what was left of him into the toilet. I flushed it, biting my lip against the bark of laughter that rose in my chest at what I'd just done. If I hadn't been terrified that I might be discovered and killed at any moment, then that would have been fucking hilarious. He was a piece of shit and I was flushing him away like one. The laugh found its way past my lips, and I thought of Dad and Monty, knowing what a kick they'd get out of that too.

The amusement turned to pain, and I shook my head to clear the mixture of mirth and grief-filled thoughts as I focused on my plan again. I needed to finish this before any more vampires appeared, and I had to find my way to Magnar who must have been far past the point of uncomfortable by now.

I moved my attention back to the vampire's clothes as I continued with my plan. Unbuttoning his shirt, I tossed it over the arm of the chair then threw his pants on the floor beside the bed.

I kicked his underwear into the middle of the room, refusing to touch it with my bare hand, but making it look convincingly like he'd stripped off in the throes of passion.

Next, I pulled off my dress and dropped it to the carpet too. It was ruined anyway, and it would have looked strange if none of my clothes were present.

I crawled onto the bed and yanked on the sheets until they were a crumpled mess, then I stuffed the pillows beneath the duvet and arranged it to look like two people could be concealed beneath them. Finally, I dropped the curtain to half hide the bed so that only the end of the bulging duvet could be seen from the doorway.

I stepped back and surveyed my work with satisfaction, certain that anyone looking into the room would believe we were in the bed having just fucked the life out of each other. Or the death out of each other. Or whatever gross things it was that bloodsuckers did to each other while naked. I just hoped no one would hang around to make sure.

I grabbed my long red coat and buttoned it up to hide the fact I wasn't wearing anything beneath it, then glanced at the clock. It was two-thirty. I needed to find Magnar while my gift from Idun held and I could still move about the train unnoticed.

My stomach was alive with nerves, and I took a deep breath as I placed my hand on the door, ready to head out into peril once more. Who knew how many vampires waited beyond the safety of this room? If they noticed anything amiss, then I was done for. But Magnar was relying on me. And I wouldn't let him down.

Besides, I was starting to get a taste for this kind of danger.

MONTANA

CHAPTER FOURTEEN

Julius had been deep in thought ever since Nightmare had spoken to us. He wouldn't answer any of my questions, and so far, all he'd done was spew curses whilst pacing back and forth around the top of the bell tower. I'd given up trying to speak to him and descended deep into my own thoughts.

I had no idea what Nightmare had meant by its words, but the fact it had said I was 'walking the path of salvation' had to be a good thing, right? But that didn't shed any light on what Nightmare had in mind for me. Or Erik.

What the hell was I supposed to do from here?

I was stuck in a tower with a guy who had a thousand-year-old vendetta against Erik, and nothing was going to make him forget about his father's murder. Why should he? If Erik had really killed him, how could Julius ever see past that? I knew the ache of vengeance, how keenly I needed to see Wolfe die for stealing my own father from this world. Julius had a right to secure his vengeance too. I just felt so damn conflicted about the vampire he was hunting. It should have been black and white as it had always been with the creatures who ruled my kind, but I couldn't shake the feeling that it wasn't so simple anymore.

My heart was heavy with all of it, and I kept thinking of Dad, my thoughts always ending with him. I so wished to speak to him now, because he'd know just what to say to make everything right. Then the knowledge that I would never again hear his voice left me with such a cloying sense of loss that I withdrew deeper into myself, burying my face against my knees.

After a while, a distant howl caught my ear, and both Julius and I stiffened as my head snapped up. The hairs on the back of my neck prickled to attention as another howl joined the first and soon, an entire chorus filled the air.

"Fuck. Give me your coat," Julius demanded, striding toward me with purpose.

"Why?" I balked, but he didn't stop coming, bending low and wrenching it from my shoulders. "What the fuck?"

"Fabian has a pack of familiars. Dogs. He's been trying to catch me with them for weeks. But I've laid my scent all over these ruins for miles, they can't find me. But *your* scent will lead them right here. I'm such a fool, I should have laid the trail earlier."

I drew in a breath, rising to my feet, the fear of being caught again hitting firmly home. Erik was still hunting for us, his parting promise to find me echoing in my mind. And it looked like Fabian was helping him.

"What are you going to do?" I asked as Julius tied my navy coat around his muscular waist.

"I'll lead them astray and I'll kill as many of them as I can."

The barks of the dogs drew closer, and my heart stuttered with anxiety as Julius took up his bow and tied a rope to an arrow. He stepped up into one of the arched windows and tied the rope off on a broken metal railing jutting from the wall. Lifting the bow, he aimed at the building opposite, tugging his arm back and pulling the string taut. He let it fly and the arrow sailed through the air, burying itself in a wooden awning on top of the building's roof. Satisfied, Julius promptly shouldered the bow and quiver.

"Right." He turned to me. "You're not going to do anything stupid like run off."

"Of course not," I said, though I wasn't yet decided on how long I was going to keep my word on that. There was no reason for me to stay here now, my only plan was reuniting with Callie. I just had to figure out how to find her.

"No, I *know* you're not." He grabbed my wrists, dragging me towards the wall.

"Hey, get your hands off of me," I hissed, trying to break his hold, but he was far too strong.

He used the loose end of the rope that was tied to the railing to tether me in place, binding me there while I fought to get free.

"You asshole. Let me go," I ordered, keeping my voice low as another howl pitched through the air and set my pulse racing.

Moving back to his bed, he picked up a sock among his things before returning to me.

"No screaming," he warned.

"Don't you *dare* put that thing near me," I gasped, jerking away as he grabbed my jaw, forcing my lips to part. He stuffed the thing in my mouth, then tied the ends behind my head.

I grimaced at him, praying the sock wasn't dirty as he stepped away, admiring his work.

"Lucky for you, I found a bunch of clean linen in the ruins a couple of days ago." With a grin, he took off his belt and looped it over the taut rope stretching between the buildings.

I scowled, a heated anger flowing through me at how quickly he'd made a prisoner out of me. Which made him a damn hypocrite considering how pissed he'd seemed about the vampires keeping me captive. I swear this world was full of motherfuckers who wanted to steal away my freedom, and I was so fucking sick of it.

Julius gripped the ends of the belt tightly, then launched himself out of the window.

I gasped against my gag, leaning as far forward as I could to watch as he slid down the rope at high speed, landing with silent grace on the building opposite.

He vanished down a set of stairs and I turned my attention to the street, frantically searching for any sign of the dogs.

All was quiet, but trepidation niggled at my gut. They couldn't be far...

Julius reappeared on the street below, his hood pulled up as he moved into a shadowy alley opposite the tower, rubbing my coat across the wall as he went.

My breaths came quicker as he headed away, and I tried to wriggle my hands free from the rope. It was no good. He'd tied it too well, leaving me trapped here.

Rage coiled in my gut. How could I have thought for a second that I was actually free? Now I was just someone else's damn prisoner.

Eyeing the sharp piece of railing extending from the wall, hope filled me, and I clambered up onto the stone ledge, resting the rope against it. I started rubbing it back and forth, determined to liberate myself.

If any of those dogs found me, who knew what they'd do? I didn't trust Fabian one bit, and even if he hadn't been responsible for Faulkner's death, someone had still tried to kill me just days ago. I sure as shit hadn't ruled him out, so I wasn't going to be a sitting duck if his familiars tracked me down.

The howls drew closer, and I worked harder to break my binds, rubbing them back and forth while the rope frayed. With a snap, it fell loose, and my heart swelled with triumph. Ripping the sock from my mouth, I knelt down on the ledge of the closest window and gazed out at the road below.

The pounding of paws carried this way, and I ducked low in fright as the first of the creatures arrived. A huge black dog appeared with drool foaming at its mouth, its soulless eyes seeking its prey between the shadows. The beast's powerful jaws looked capable of crushing bone, and I shrank further into my hiding place as it padded alongside the tower, not daring to breathe.

One second passed, then two, each moment dragging into the next.

The dog lifted its head, sniffing the air, and I was sure it was about to discover me. But with a bark of excitement, it darted down the alley Julius had taken, and I released the breath trapped in my chest.

My pulse hammered in my ears, adrenaline thick in my blood.

What would I do if the slayer was caught? Run from here? Or go back to the city?

I racked my brain for answers, wishing Julius hadn't taken Nightmare, wondering if it might have any more words of wisdom. Though, honestly, the riddles it spewed didn't make any sense to me. Monster made? Was that something to do with the vampires? Was it referring to Erik?

My thoughts tumbled over one another, and I wished I had more to go on. Julius had refused to share his thoughts with me on the matter, and I hated being kept in the dark. He knew something about those words that he wasn't saying, and I was desperate to learn what he was hiding.

Though I was free, I hadn't considered leaving the tower. I'd made up my mind. I'd wait for Julius to return and force answers from his lips.

Hours passed and the sun sank low behind the haze of clouds, lighting them in pink and amber tones. It wasn't long before darkness engulfed the world, but my eyes soon adjusted to the dim space around me. An icy wind was picking up, and without my coat to keep me warm, I soon buried myself in Julius's blankets.

After a while, a huff of exertion carried to my ears beyond the closest window. My heart clenched, but a moment later, Julius hauled himself over the ledge and my fear ebbed away.

"Shit. Where are you?" he growled.

"Here," I said, sitting up from the pile of blankets to reveal myself.

He sighed his relief, moving toward me and kneeling down. "I should have known I couldn't keep a woman of slayer blood bound with rope. But I'm glad you're still here. You trust me then?"

"Not in the slightest. But I have questions, and you're going to give me answers to them."

He grunted, then prodded my side. "Move over. It's been a long time since I had someone to share warmth with." I didn't miss his suggestive tone but wondered if he could see the glare I gave him in the darkness.

I shifted to give him room and he pulled the blankets across both of us, snuggling up close beside me.

"Are they gone?" I asked, shamelessly huddling against him, the heat of his body like a godsend as the cold drilled into me.

"I laid trails all over the ruins and back into the city. They'll be chasing their tails until sunrise. Most of them will be anyway. One of them got Nightmare in the eye."

I sucked in a breath as he pressed something warm into my palm.

"Calm down, it's just the blade." I could hear the grin in his voice as my fingers wrapped around Nightmare's hilt and a soothing energy rolled into me.

"Lucky for you," I reminded him.

"Ah, the dick rippage. I haven't forgotten. Give me a bit of credit though, damsel. I have more tact with women than sticking my cock in their hand and hoping for the best. I think I would have lost my dick long ago if that was my signature move."

I snorted a laugh and he chuckled, the sound vibrating through me, though I kind of wanted to kick him for continuing to call me damsel.

"So, are you ever going to share your thoughts on what Nightmare told us earlier, or are you going to continue being a cagey shithead?"

Julius scooted somehow closer, and it was hard not to melt into the heat that radiated from him as the wind picked up. "Do you know about the prophecy?"

"The what?" I asked, my brow furrowing.

"Hm," he sighed. "Alright, let's start from the beginning."

"Tell me everything," I urged, curious to hear his story.

"A god called Andvari is responsible for the vampire curse," he revealed, making my heart pound out of rhythm. "Long story short, the Belvederes' parents royally pissed him off and he cursed their children to hunger for human blood forevermore. But in order to do so, Andvari stole from a goddess called Idun. He fed the Belvederes her immortal fruit to create the curse."

"Okay..." I breathed, trying to let myself believe such things.

Julius went on, "So Idun created *us* in retaliation. The slayers. We're born to end the curse Andvari made. Which either means we have to wipe the vampires from the face of the earth, *or* we have to break the curse by figuring out the answer to Andvari's prophecy."

"Which is?" I pressed, a creeping sensation inching through me.

Nightmare vibrated in my palm at his words, encouraging me to believe every one of them.

He took a breath. "A warrior born but monster made, changes fates of souls enslaved. Twins of sun and moon will rise, when one has lived a thousand lives. A circle of gold shall join two souls, and a debt paid rights wrongs of old. In a holy mountain the earth will heal, then the dead shall live, and the curse will keel."

A shudder went through me as a ripple of power emanated around the space, and I swear the wind howled even louder. I recognised some of the words from those Nightmare had spoken to me, but I didn't understand my involvement in it all.

"What does it mean?" I asked in a hushed tone, and Julius took my hand, squeezing my cold fingers, and I couldn't deny myself the heat he offered.

I turned to him in the darkness, finding his eyes twinkling at me as the low light of the moon fell across the tower. "I don't know. But I have some questions since Nightmare spoke to us earlier. It called you Moon Child...do you know why?"

"No," I breathed. "I mean...the only connection I can think of is that my parents used to call my sister and I their sun and moon."

"And you mentioned she's your twin," Julius murmured thoughtfully, his grip on my hand growing firmer.

"Yes," I said as I realised what he meant. "Do you think we're the twins of sun and moon the prophecy talks about?"

"I don't know," he answered, his tone dark. "But maybe. It is possible you and your sister play some part in breaking the curse."

The weight of that prospect settled on me, and I turned the words of the prophecy over in my head, trying to work out what they could mean. "It says the twins will rise when one has lived a thousand lives. Could that mean...when one of us is immortal?" I shuddered at the thought, and I felt Julius shrugging his shoulders.

"Perhaps. There is only one part of the prophecy my brother and I were ever clear on. The holy mountain is a place of the dead. We called it Helgafjell in my time. I suspect this curse must be broken there in some way. A debt paid..." He shook his head, having no more answers.

Silence pooled between us, and Julius reached into his pocket, taking out a phone.

"Where'd you get that?" I asked in surprise.

"Stole it off that guard I killed." He grinned mischievously, but as I thought of Faulkner's final screams and the pain in Erik's eyes when his guard had turned to ash, I didn't find it all that amusing. "This is connected to cameras in the castle grounds." Julius pressed a button on it, showing me the screen. "Every blind spot, every weakness the royals have in that place is right here in my hand."

My mouth parted in shock as I leaned forward, eyeing the live videos playing in tiny boxes on the phone. Julius tapped on one and it expanded, showing the steps leading up to the castle. A couple of guards were standing by the road beyond them, looking around and sharing the odd muttered word with one another.

"Now what?" I asked.

"Now, we wait for the Belvederes to show up," he said, and my heart thrashed at the prospect.

The minutes ticked by, the silence broken only by the roaring wind and the odd howl pitching away into the night. The minutes turned to an hour, and in all that time, nothing of note happened but a change of guards.

My mind began to wander, fantasy lands calling to me, promising me escape from my own thoughts. But for some reason, I didn't want to shy away from the world anymore. I didn't want to forget the pain caged in my heart over Dad, or how I longed for my twin. Because those things might have been raw and crushing, but they were vital pieces of me that tied me to my family. I realised since I'd been stolen away into the clutches of the vampires, I might not have been free, but I had been wide awake, aware of life in all its beautiful brutality. And I didn't want to shut myself off from it anymore.

"Looks like we've got some movement," Julius said, and I perked up, focusing all of my attention on the screen to keep the grief at bay.

Headlights spilled over the guards at the base of the steps and two cars arrived. I held my breath as the guards hurried forward to open the doors, but Erik stepped out before they got there, still wearing the casual clothes I'd last seen him in. Fabian, Miles, and Clarice all appeared after him dressed in their royal attire, exchanging worried glances.

Erik led the way as they marched up the steps, his expression taut with rage, and my stomach tightened. He looked fit to destroy the world, his ashen eyes ablaze and his jaw flexing with every step he took.

Julius shrank the image, clicking the next one which enlarged an office with a circular glass table at the heart of it.

"I had to hack into the camera in this room." Julius tapped his temple. "Security access is only given to a few Elite. When I first awoke from my sleep, this world had changed so much, and I had no idea how to use vehicles or computers. I knew I needed to understand these things if I was to stand any chance against the Belvederes, so I begged Idun for help. Luckily, she was feeling generous, and she gifted me all the knowledge I needed and more. She's got a soft spot for me, I reckon. And who wouldn't? I am a hero after all." He beamed and I shook my head at him.

"You think a lot of yourself, don't you?"

"Delusional confidence is the key to life," he said brightly. "If you call a duck an eagle often enough, people tend to start agreeing."

"So, you're really just a duck posing as an eagle," I taunted.

"No, no, you're missing the point. You become the eagle too, see? If you delude yourself hard enough, one day it just comes true. Great, isn't it?"

"What if I think you're a duck?"

"I'm an eagle." He gave me a sharp look. "Fucking ca-caw. Now look." He tapped the screen. "They're almost at the office."

"Can you watch everything from here?"

"Only where there are cameras. I couldn't see into your bedroom, in case you were wondering."

I sucked in a breath, realising something. "Then surely someone saw the vampire who attacked me a few days ago. Why haven't the guards identified the culprit if they can see all this?"

"Attacked you? When?" Julius demanded, seeming agitated.

"Four days ago," I said, my brows pinching together. "They must have seen them on here."

Julius frowned. "The system went down around then. Nothing for hours into the night. I thought it was a glitch on my end. The next morning the streams were live again."

"Damn, who else has access to these? Who could have done that?"

Julius thought on it. "It would have to be someone with a lot of power, or the royals themselves."

I pursed my lips, thinking it over, but Julius nudged me, pointing at the screen as the royals marched into the office, taking seats around the table.

My heart skittered at the sight of Erik's fierce expression. He looked ready to murder someone, and I had the feeling that someone was Julius.

"My familiars have traced them to the Bronx ruins," Fabian spoke, and I was startled as the sound was fed back to us, clear as day. "Their scent is all over that place, but the hounds haven't yet narrowed down their location. I'll send a couple of birds too. Their keen eyes will spot them if they make a move toward the city again."

"Thank you, Fabian," Erik said tersely, fisting his hands on the table.

"Fuck," Julius growled, and my heart stammered.

"Should we be concerned?" Clarice asked, running her fingers over a golden plait down one side of her neck. "If there is a slayer of old in New York, there could be more. And how is it possible that he still lives after a thousand years?"

"I don't know the answer to that. But there is only him. I believe it is Julius Elioson. I'm sure you all remember him," Fabian said, his rust brown eyes flicking left and right.

"I've still got the scars to prove it," Miles growled, turning over his arm to reveal a silvery line on his skin.

Julius chuckled in my ear. "I almost took his hand off that day."

Fabian nodded, looking grave. "I became aware of his presence several weeks ago. I've been trying to track him down covertly."

"Why didn't you tell us?" Miles hissed, baring his fangs.

"I didn't want to start a panic," Fabian muttered. "Just days ago, he set a bomb that killed those two courtiers. And I know how attached some of you get to them. I didn't see the need in worrying you."

I looked to Julius with my heart thundering. "Did you do that?" I demanded, pulling away from him.

He shook his head fiercely. "Of course not. I'd never kill an innocent."

"But it was intended for Erik," I hissed, panic rising in me. Was I sitting beside the man responsible for killing Joshua and Brianna?

"I didn't do it," Julius swore. "A bomb wouldn't kill a Belvedere anyway. I am not a fool. Slayer blades are one of the few things capable of vanquishing the vampires."

I eyed him with concern but could see the truth in his gaze. Was Fabian lying to cover his tracks? But if Julius knew the bomb wouldn't kill Erik, then why would Fabian set it? Unless the bomb really had never been intended for Erik.

My eyes whipped back to the screen as the royals' voices rose with anger.

"You had no right, Fabian!" Clarice snapped. "We should have dealt with it together. What were you thinking?"

"Enough," Erik growled before Fabian could defend himself. "Fabian has been a fool, yes. But we have more important matters to discuss now."

"Like?" Miles asked, sitting back in his chair and sweeping a hand through his sleek blond hair.

"Like finding Montana, for one," Erik snarled. "And apprehending the slayer who took her."

"You mean executing him, surely?" Fabian interjected.

Erik's mouth twitched with anger. "Eventually, of course. But we must learn what he knows. If there are more slayers-"

"There are no more slayers," Fabian spat, slamming his hand down on the glass surface. "The remainder of them died off a thousand years ago."

"Unfortunately, brother, that is not true. I too have been harbouring some secrets, but it is time they were brought to light." Erik took out his phone, placing it at the centre of the table and playing a video. I couldn't see what it showed, but Erik explained anyway. "General Wolfe encountered a slayer in the blood bank south of Realm G. He said his name was Magnar Elioson, Julius's brother. Marla sent me this video which clearly shows it is true."

A hushed silence fell over them all, and Clarice took up the phone, gazing at the screen in fear. "Magnar is still alive? Who's the woman he's with?"

"Montana's sister, Callie Ford," Erik revealed, and my heart rioted in my chest.

Miles stood abruptly, glaring at Erik. "You know, don't you? She told you."

"Who told me what?" Erik replied calmly, but his eyes shone with a dangerous glint.

"Montana's blood is stronger than the others we've found. She has the potential to be a full slayer," Miles announced, and Clarice's mouth parted.

Fabian gazed at the blond prince, his eyes narrowing.

"I saw her mark," Miles went on. "She hasn't taken her vow, of course, but what difference does it make? If she's with another slayer now, what's to say she won't take it and they'll band together against us?"

Julius tossed me a pointed look and I firmly ignored it.

"When did we all start keeping secrets from each other?" Clarice scolded. "We're family. We have always worked as a unit." She sighed and the others looked a little guilty in the face of her accusation. She turned to Erik with desperate eyes. "Is it true what Miles says?"

Slowly, Erik nodded, and my heart crumbled to dust. They knew. All of them knew. And surely that made me a threat worth eradicating.

"Montana has slayer blood stronger than any of the courtiers brought here in the past," Erik said carefully. "She is also a twin." He took his phone back from Clarice, tapping the screen. "Look at her. Her colouring is as light as Montana's is dark. Night and day. Twins of sun and moon."

Miles and Clarice shared a look of fear, and that same fear twisted through my chest.

"The prophecy, Erik? Are you really spurting that at us now?" Fabian drawled.

"It is our salvation," Erik barked at him. "We have been wrong, all these years. Forcing humans with slayer blood to have children with us to try and bear twins. But like I always said, it was just another of Andvari's lies. Warrior born but monster made does not mean we are supposed to have children with those of slayer blood."

My thoughts muddled together as I processed what he was saying. They were trying to solve the prophecy. They thought bearing twins with a slayer was the answer. But it wasn't. It was us. Me and Callie. At least, that was what all this seemed to be pointing to.

Julius pressed a hand to my spine, lending me comfort, but there was no comforting me from this.

I focused my thoughts on their conversation, not wanting to miss anything else.

"We'll double our efforts in finding Montana's sister," Miles said keenly. "She must marry one of us. A circle of gold will join two souls."

Erik glared at him. "You are entirely dismissing what I just said."

"But perhaps we need to bear children with a true slayer," Miles suggested. "It's not like I want to, we just have to consider the possibility. We could test your theory too. How can we retrieve both twins swiftly?"

"I've already sent several Elite to find Montana's sister," Erik snarled. "But this." He bashed his fist against his phone. "Shows how deeply the rebels have gotten into our ranks. One of my own sirelings bit her. I cannot send a team after her if they will not follow basic orders. My own general is a fucking biter. And he murdered their father after I explicitly ordered for him to be released from the blood bank. It is *unacceptable*."

Clarice took a slow breath. "Look…we can handle this. We'll send only our most loyal followers to retrieve her."

"These *were* my most loyal followers, Clarice!" Erik yelled, his anger spilling over and setting the hairs raising on the back of my neck. "I cannot trust anyone. Not even the people in this room!" He turned his gaze to Fabian, who snarled in response.

"You are in dangerous territory, brother," Fabian snarled. "You have already wrongly accused me of killing your sirelings. You know the slayer, Julius, was the culprit, so why is it you still look at me with distrust?"

"Because there are things you don't know I'm aware of," Erik stated. "Montana was attacked by a vampire just days ago. In her bedroom on the castle grounds. Who else could gain access to the royal quarters unless they walked among us freely? Someone allowed an assassin into our home. There are only a few people who could manage such a thing."

"You think *I* tried to kill the girl? Why would I want her dead?" Fabian scoffed. "What is it you see in me, Erik? A traitor? Because the only traitor I see here, is you."

"Me?" Erik snarled. "In what way am *I* a traitor?"

"You had my men killed in retaliation because you believed I was targeting you. If only you would put your faith in me and stop-"

"Enough," Clarice stepped in, glaring between the two of them and taking ownership of the room. "If Erik has acted against you, Fabian, you will be compensated. But he made a mistake, and you must let that pass now. We have to unite. If the slayers are rising again-"

"They are not rising!" Fabian bellowed.

"How do you know that?" Miles growled. "We know of four in existence. What if there are more than that? And if Magnar and Julius Elioson are among them, they are Blessed Crusaders. Gifted by Idun herself. How do we know these others are not the same? How do we know we are strong enough to face them? We had to run from them before."

"Because we have an entire country of vampires at our backs," Fabian said coolly. "We have nothing to fear from four slayers. They are no more than a thorn in our side. And we will pluck it out and crush it in our palm before any more of our people are killed."

"Maybe we should consider the positives to this," Miles said thoughtfully. "If Montana and her sister are of slayer blood, they could bear the twins the prophecy speaks of."

"It is *them* it speaks of, you fool," Erik said in exasperation.

"But how do you know that?" Miles questioned in frustration. "Andvari told us that we could bear children with mortals. That must be important."

"It's just another of his tricks," Erik insisted.

Clarice gazed anxiously between them. "I hate to think we have been wrong all these years. That we've made those poor women have children when it wasn't necessary. So many of them died in the process..."

My heart stuttered at her words. Wives had *died* bearing their children? It was unthinkable. That ritual of theirs was barbaric enough, and now this?

"It's a bit late to grow a conscience, Clarice," Fabian said hollowly.

She scowled. "I'm not the one who bears them. Maybe *you* should be the one growing a conscience."

Fabian rolled his eyes. "The humans have never complained about my treatment. My wives adore me. Wouldn't you say the same of yours, Miles?"

Miles nodded firmly. "I've always given them everything they ever wanted. Montana and her sister would be no different."

"Montana is *my* fucking fiancée, Miles," Erik snarled, his eyes flaring with emotion, and my throat thickened. "No one will be touching her. None of you. Not even me," he added, seething as he stared his family down.

"Well, it's irrelevant at the moment anyway, considering she is off gallivanting with a slayer," Fabian remarked. "Perhaps she is fucking him as we speak, preparing to bring more of our enemies into the world."

Erik was out of his chair in a heartbeat and grabbed Fabian by the collar, hauling him to his feet. "Speak of her that way again and I will ensure you regret it for the rest of your immortal days."

Fabian shoved him off, brushing the creases from his shirt. "By the gods, Erik, don't tell me you actually have feelings for a human."

"Erik," Clarice whispered, her blue eyes widening. "Do you?"

Erik glared at Fabian for several long seconds before returning to his chair, not responding to Clarice. My heart twisted and writhed in my chest as I stared at him. Whatever he felt for me was dressed in sin and corrupted by greed, but it was also as undeniable as the rising sun.

I felt Julius's eyes on me, but I couldn't turn my head to face him, unsure how to express my own feelings under his watchful gaze. I wasn't sure I wanted to feel anything at all, but Erik's fervour brought on a quake in my body that I couldn't deny.

"We should focus on her sister then," Miles said. "One of us will marry her when she is caught and-"

"*No*," Erik barked, his gaze like molten lava. "You are not listening to me. The answer is not children. *They* are the answer. We must figure out what the rest of the prophecy means. We are so close to an answer."

"Fuck the prophecy," Fabian muttered.

"What?" Clarice gasped. "How can you say that? It's what this is all for. We only want to break the curse, Fabian."

"Well maybe I'm done hearing your complaints about our so-called curse. The prophecy is a lie told to drive us all mad anyway, why not enjoy the immortality we've been given?" Fabian offered.

"Why take wives then, Fabian?" Erik growled.

Fabian's eyes whipped to him. "Because I want to, Erik. Get off your high horse and join us all in the real world, will you? We're royal. The kings and queen of a whole country. We don't have to answer to anyone. If I want a human bride, I will have one. And if it solves the prophecy, great. If not, at least I had fun trying."

Erik's eyes narrowed sharply. "You have to answer to me, brother. I will always make sure of that."

"Is that why you went behind my back to have the Realms rebuilt?" Fabian mused, folding his arms.

My lips parted at his words. Erik had done that?

Clarice and Miles shared a look of alarm as Fabian continued, "Yes, I know all about your backstabbing, Erik. The Realms are *my* responsibility, stick to your own business if you know what's good for you."

"I am *making* them my business because you have done such a terrible fucking job with them," Erik said in a fierce tone. "The Realms will be brought up to the standard of Realm A within the next month, or I will expose your lie to the New Empire and we'll see what the people think of your treatment of the humans."

"They don't care," Fabian laughed. "I thought they did once, too, that's why I created Realm A. I thought it was necessary, but it isn't. Half of the city is vying for the right to bite."

"You're wrong," Clarice stepped in. "It's only a small group of rebels."

"They're the ones you see on the streets," Fabian answered. "But I know that idea lurks in plenty of their minds. Erik, your own Elite are biting on duty. General Wolfe is a prime example."

Erik's face contorted with fury. "A man you have insisted be banished for his crimes instead of killed. I'm beginning to suspect you have a higher motive."

"It is the law," Fabian answered easily.

"We make the law!" Erik countered. "Why do this, Fabian? Why not provide the humans the resources they need?"

"Because the crops do not flourish, you ignorant halfwit. The land is wasted from the toxic bombs the humans dropped on each other. They brought about this plague on their own kind, not I."

"There is more fertile land to the north. Efforts must be made to provide more food, more clothes, more comfort," Erik insisted.

"And will you feel better about draining them then, brother?" Fabian tsked. "They are food, nothing more. So long as they provide the blood we need, it does not matter how well they live."

"It matters to me!" Erik shouted, and my eyes raked over him, my chest brimming with emotion. He meant those words, every one of them.

"Stop this bickering," Miles cut in before Fabian could come back. "I vote we locate the sisters and figure it out from there."

"Yes, and we must speak with Andvari," Erik said, nodding firmly. "He will know what to do."

"He hasn't been very enlightening before now," Clarice said tentatively. "Do you think he will guide us?"

"If we are on the right track, he has to guide us," Erik said, though doubt simmered in his gaze.

They all stood, and Clarice and Miles trailed from the room, but before Erik could exit, Fabian caught his arm. "I'm sending my own men after Magnar and the girl. If I get to her first, I will decide her fate."

Erik bared his fangs at him. "Then you'd better be prepared, Fabian. Because if you touch a hair on her head, my fight will not be with the slayers. It will be with you."

They exited the room and I stared at the empty space with my heart crashing against my ribcage.

"It seems Erik Belvedere is playing games again," Julius murmured in my ear. "Though I cannot yet see the purpose behind his actions in convincing the other Revenants that he cares for you."

"You think that's what he's doing?" I asked, my cheeks heating.

Was it all an act? His efforts to fix the Realms, his plight to find me, the way he spoke with passion about me. Was I completely insane to think any of this came from the goodness of his heart and wasn't some tactic I couldn't yet see the meaning of?

"Of course it's what he's doing. That's what they all do. Any attachment he holds to you is rooted in power and avarice. It is the way of them. I've seen it many times before. Miles acting like some false god, building an army of pious followers out of weak-minded humans, Fabian playing trickster with his familiars, luring hunters to him with a prize stag only to make a meal out of them himself, and Clarice with her harems of men, baiting them for her pleasure, yet no matter how many she claimed, it seemed not even an army of men could satisfy her." He sneered. "And then there's Erik, a master manipulator, the most bloodthirsty of them all. To see him disguise himself now beneath a farse of dignity, of civilisation, it sickens me. You should have seen him bloody and draped in death, Montana. Then you would not be so willing to attempt to find the good in him."

I shuddered, the potency of Julius's words cutting me to the quick.

"Then you're not going to like what I have to say next," I said carefully.

"And what is that?" he growled.

"I need to go to him tomorrow," I said, my gut knotting at the thought, but this was bigger than me now. "If he's going to talk to Andvari, I have to be there. I need to know if the prophecy really does refer to me and Callie."

"If you go back to him, he'll never release you," Julius snarled.

"And I will not be responsible for that. I cannot let you leave."

I shifted away from him, anger pulsing through me. "It isn't up to you what I do. And staying here won't do us any good. I have to know the truth. If Callie and I can help break the curse somehow, then we have to do it."

"I didn't risk my neck just to send you back into the arms of those monsters," Julius bit at me.

I dropped my head, threading my fingers together as I considered my options. I sure as hell didn't want to be a prisoner again, but maybe there was a way to prevent that...

"So we get some leverage first," I said thoughtfully, refusing to walk back into Erik's chains without an escape route. "A bargaining chip. Something that means Erik has to do as I say."

Julius's brows arched with intrigue. "Like a hostage?"

"I didn't say that-"

"No, but I did." He smiled wickedly. "I'll take someone Erik cares about, someone he has to give you anything for." His voice rose as his excitement at the idea increased.

"Erik doesn't care about many people," I said uncertainly. "Apart from his family and..." My heart stalled as a name flitted into my head. Someone more valuable to the city than anyone else. The vampire who could control the weather and keep the sun from weakening the entire population of New York.

"Valentina," I breathed, turning to him with a rush of my own excitement.

He wrinkled his nose. "By the gods, Erik Belvedere cares about *Valentina*?"

"You know her?" I gasped.

"Of course I do," he snarled. "She was a slayer who joined my clan a thousand years ago. She was betrothed to my brother," he revealed. "When I woke from my enchanted sleep, I found her waiting for me beyond my hiding place. I saw what she had done to herself in an instant. Her face was captivating and deathly pale. She'd become one of *them*. Our sworn enemies. It disgusts me beyond belief."

His eyes darkened. "My sword hungered for her end, so I drove it through her without hesitation. But I missed her heart. I was weaker after the sleep and needed time to recover. She begged me to spare her, and I didn't know what the right course of action was. The only other slayer I'd seen as a vampire had asked for death. So I fled."

"Did you find out why she became a vampire?" I asked, my voice hushed.

"No…although I have considered confronting her here in the city. I followed her to New York after our encounter. Since then, I have been lost as to why she has accepted their ways. But perhaps this life was forced upon her…"

"She offered to help me once," I said, rubbing the mark on my arm. "I didn't know if I could trust her."

"I am not sure either. But if she is still on our side, she may be a good ally to have. Especially if she is valuable to the royals."

"She is," I insisted. "She controls the weather here. She keeps the clouds covering the sun. I've seen it myself."

Julius stared at me in horror. "Then she has retained her slayer gifts…" A slow smile grew on his face as a plan formed behind his eyes. "She is our target. Do you know where to find her?"

I nodded, a thrill rolling through me at the mad plot we were designing. "I've been to her apartment. I think I could find it again." My enthusiasm quickly scattered into a hundred doubts as I realised how impossible it was going to be to move through the city undetected. "But how are we going to get to her?"

Julius gave me a roguish look. "Don't worry, damsel. I have ways."

I tried to get more out of him, but he evidently enjoyed keeping me in the dark as he sank into his own thoughts.

I figured I had to place my faith in him, and if we pulled it off, tomorrow I would be facing Erik with a threat up my sleeve. The idea alone set my veins burning with adrenaline. How the hell was he going to react to me blackmailing him?

I pushed away my fears, my heart growing strong walls and sparking courage in my chest.

He blackmailed me first. It's about time Prince Erik had a taste of his own medicine.

CALLIE

CHAPTER FIFTEEN

I slid the door to my suite open and stepped out into the corridor. Thankfully, no one was there to see me leave and I pressed my back to the door as I released a long breath.

You're meant to be here, Callie. No one will question you if you stop questioning yourself.

I pushed off of the door and set a quick pace as I headed towards the rear of the train where they'd been loading the cargo.

I set my feet down softly, not wanting to draw the attention of any more of the Elite who may have been behind the doors I was passing. I hardly dared breathe until I made it to the end of the carriage.

Once I'd passed the suites, I crossed over into the next carriage where the lesser vampires sat around small tables on comfortable chairs. Some of them looked up curiously as I passed, but I kept my chin high and ignored them.

My heart pounded as I moved down the aisle and tension knotted in my gut. What if they could hear it? What if they realised what I truly was? I was surrounded by these beautiful monsters who hungered for my blood. I felt like a sheep creeping past a pack of sleeping wolves. They hadn't noticed me yet, but if they did, I was done for. Gifts or not,

I knew I was no match for this many enemies at once.

I kept going, fixing my gaze on the door at the end of the carriage. None of them seemed to want to question me. If they wondered what I was doing, they didn't voice it. It seemed their fear of the Elites overruled any curiosity they may have felt, and I made it past them almost too easily.

My hand trembled as I reached for the door handle at the end of the carriage and I stepped through quickly, pressing it shut again with a sigh of relief.

The next carriage was cooler than the others and no lights illuminated it. I squinted into the space as my eyes adjusted and I spotted long rows of the wooden cargo boxes.

I began moving between them, trying to spot the scratch I'd carved into the box where Magnar was hiding. As I walked, Fury tingled against my thigh and I reached beneath my coat to grab it, the warm hilt humming in excitement.

Old friends this way.

The blade urged me on, and I upped my pace as I let it guide me towards Tempest and Venom.

I moved into yet another carriage, passing more crates than I could count and feeling immensely grateful to Fury for saving me the effort of having to check them all.

As I neared the end of the long room, the blade sighed a greeting through my mind, and I stopped. A deep scratch was carved into the box on my right, and I knocked on it lightly.

"It's me," I called as I grabbed the edge of the crate and tried to haul it out of its position in the line. I grunted with effort, the huge box slipping forward reluctantly as I struggled with its weight despite the newly gained strength in my muscles.

I finally got the box clear of the shelf above it and forced the lid open with a grunt of effort.

"Took you long enough," Magnar grumbled as he sat up, rotating his shoulders.

"I would have been faster if you weren't so damn heavy," I replied lightly.

"Did everything go to plan?" he asked, ignoring my comment as he clambered out of the crate.

"Pretty much," I hedged, not really wanting to explain about the Elite who had wanted to fuck me.

"Tell me."

His command fell over me like a punch to the gut and my mouth opened, spilling the whole story to him whether I liked it or not.

"There was an incident with an Elite," my voice was flat and emotionless, but anger flared in my chest as he used his power over me once more. Since the incident with the bath, I'd been trying to convince myself that he hadn't really been able to force my body to bow to his control like this, but those hopes were dashed entirely as I was coerced into a truthful response. "He followed me into my room under the pretence of checking up on who had sent me here. Once he had me alone, he made it clear he had other intentions and he propositioned me. He persisted despite my refusal and tore my dress in his attempt to convince me. When he touched me, he could feel the heat of my skin and-"

"What?" Magnar bellowed, and my heart flipped over as I looked back towards the other carriages, praying that none of the vampires had heard him.

He grabbed me, shaking me slightly as his eyes raked over me, and I felt a touch of fear at the fire burning in his gaze.

"What did he do to you?" he demanded.

"Nothing," I snapped, pushing him back, though it didn't really do anything to help. "I killed him, alright? Stabbed him in the heart and covered it up so no one will notice. It's done."

The tension fell out of Magnar's grip, and he scowled at the narrow corridor which led between the crates as if searching for the source of his rage there.

"Good," he grunted, though it didn't seem like he was all that pleased about it.

"What's your problem?" I demanded, and he turned to me, looking like he might bite back, but then he grabbed me, yanking me against his chest and holding me tightly against him.

"You're mine to protect," he growled, his mouth brushing against my temple. "I won't let those monsters have you."

Anger, grief, pain, and torment tangled in me while I stood there in his arms, breathing in the leather and oak scent of him, unable to return his embrace. My arms felt like they were weighted with lead as Idun's laws refused to allow it, holding us apart even in something as simple as this.

He was all I had in this place, and I was all he had too. The bonds between us muddied that, complicating it and leaving it darkened with bitterness and resentment on both sides, but at the truth of us now, we were all we had.

Magnar growled a curse then released me abruptly, stepping away. With a frown, I realised that he'd just fought off Idun's control so he could hold me close for that single moment. I had no idea how he'd managed to do it. I couldn't move an inch beyond the boundaries she'd set, and yet he'd just punched right through them as if they didn't even exist for him.

"You won't be alone with them again," he said firmly, his voice dark.

"It's fine, I dealt with it. I just hope no one realises the bastard is missing before we've done what we came to do." I stepped away from him and pulled open the crate he'd used to hide our supplies.

The silence grew between us, and I knew he was holding back on something he wanted to say, but I wasn't going to force his lips to loosen.

I grabbed my pack from the crate and located some clean clothes within it. I didn't have anything else that looked right for an Elite, but I had a pair of black leggings and a black long-sleeved shirt which clung to my figure and hopefully wouldn't draw much attention anyway.

I shrugged out of my coat and hung it over the crate, turning my back on Magnar so I could at least imagine I had some privacy.

"Where is your dress?" Magnar asked, his voice dangerously low.

I glanced over my shoulder at him as I pulled the clothes on.

"I told you it was torn," I replied dismissively.

I didn't want to keep thinking about how close I'd come to being discovered. Or of the look in the Elite's eyes when he'd refused to take no for an answer.

"Just tell-"

"Are you going to force it out of me again?" I snapped before he could finish the sentence, squaring up to him despite being more than a foot shorter and currently wearing nothing but my bra and panties. "Don't you trust me enough to allow me to choose what I say now? Have I lost the freedom to speak my mind as well as the freedom over my actions?"

Magnar glared at me, and I glared right back. Tension crackled between us, and I couldn't tell which one of us would break it first. I could see the war going on behind his golden eyes as he tried to decide how badly he needed to hear every detail of what had happened to me. And whether it was worth the damage he'd do to my trust in him if he made me speak it.

He finally let out a huff of irritation and turned away from me dismissively. He was clearly unhappy about it, but he didn't force my tongue, and my chest swelled with the small victory.

"I'm fine," I muttered as I turned back to my clothes and continued with the task of dressing. "And the motherfucker is dead. The rest doesn't matter."

Magnar made a noise which could have indicated he understood, then turned his attention to the crate containing our things.

I put the coat back on and tugged my hair out from under the collar. Magnar took Tempest from the crate but left the rest of our supplies where they were, then he slid the two crates back into position, concealing the evidence of him stowing away.

"We need to hurry up and find the blood. I don't have unlimited time with this disguise, and we might need it to get past the vampires," I said.

"Come then." Magnar started to lead the way, but I caught his arm and slipped past him.

"I should go first," I reminded him. "I won't raise any suspicions. *You,* on the other hand, stand out like a bear at a tea party."

"What?" He frowned at me in confusion, and I rolled my eyes.

"Never mind. Let's just get on with what we came here for."

The next carriage held more crates of supplies, and we passed through it quickly. When we reached the following door, I eased it open and cold air washed over me.

My breath rose before me as I stepped inside, and Fury sang with victory at my hip like it already knew we were in the right place.

"This is it," I whispered.

Magnar pressed the door closed behind me and I frowned at the dark space ahead. I found a switch beside the door and flipped it on. The carriage was illuminated with pale blue light, and I gasped as I spotted four huge, glass vats filled with dark red liquid.

Curling letters were etched into the glass on each of the vats, and I ran my fingers over them as I passed through the carriage. I, H, F...G. I stopped beside the vat labelled with my old Realm's letter. Was my blood in there?

Rage and disgust flowed through me in equal measures.

I reached out and pressed my hand to the cool glass. How much blood was inside it? How many vampires would it feed? How long would this sustain them for?

I turned back towards Magnar and found him leaning over vat H as he unbolted a hatch on the top of it. Once he'd opened it, he pulled the apple Idun had given him from his pocket and cut a slice from it with his blade before dropping it inside.

As the fruit sank into the blood, it began to dissolve. Tiny bubbles spread throughout the liquid, rushing towards the glass and bursting against it. My pulse hammered as I watched the poison slipping through the blood and spiking it as simply as that.

Once the bubbles had all fizzled away, the blood fell deathly still. There was no sign of the apple or its effects.

"Holy shit, do you really think this will work?" I breathed, biting my lip as I stared into the deadly concoction.

"Idun's power is boundless," Magnar murmured. "Every vampire who drinks from this will perish."

A dark smile captured my lips as I watched him silently repeating the process with the other vats and my heart swelled with hope. We were finally striking at them in a way which would really hurt. This could kill hundreds if not thousands of the bloodsuckers. It felt like striking the first blow in a war they didn't even know they were fighting yet. But it was time that humanity fought back. And I was proud to be spearheading the assault.

Hide! Fury hissed urgently, and I flinched in surprise at the blade's voice inside my mind.

The faint sound of voices reached us, and my pulse leapt in panic.

I ran to switch the light back off and Magnar's hand landed on my elbow as he wrenched me further into the room.

I stumbled as he tugged me along and shoved me into a small gap between two of the vats. He had to turn sideways and force his muscular body through the space to follow me, and he barely made it into the darkened spot before the door opened and the lights flickered on again.

I was crushed against him in the tiny space behind the vats and I hardly dared to breathe as the vampires stepped into the carriage.

"Well, what do we have here then?" a male voice cooed.

Adrenaline crashed through my limbs, and I widened my eyes at Magnar as panic gripped me. How had they known we were here? It didn't make sense. I'd been sure none of them had followed me-

"Isn't it beautiful?" another, deeper voice replied. "I wish we could sneak a taste, but the volume has been logged. They'll know if we touch even a drop of it. This blood is destined for the royal wedding; they don't want it sampled until after the celebrations."

"So you just brought me here to tempt me?" the first voice asked.

The second vampire laughed. "I remember what it was like working my first blood delivery. It drives you mad knowing it's so close but not seeing it. So now you have."

"Thanks. Though now I'll be driven mad having seen it and not having taken a taste. I guess I'll have something to dream about the next time I sleep."

"Imagine swimming in one of those vats. I think I'd just die all over again from the pure ecstasy it induced."

The vampires laughed before switching the lights back off and heading out of the carriage again.

I released a shaky breath and Magnar eased back out of our concealed spot. I followed him and we waited in tense silence for several long minutes. When Fury's hilt cooled in my palm, we headed back through the door and kept moving until we reached the cargo crates where our things were hidden.

Magnar pulled the crate out of the line and removed our packs from it before pointing me into the space behind it.

There was just enough room behind the rows of shelves for me to crawl in and lean against the wall out of sight. He followed me before pulling the crate back into place behind us.

Magnar shifted into the corner, getting as comfortable as possible in the confined space. I sat beside him, curling my legs in front of me with a smile tugging at my lips. We'd just poisoned the vampires' blood supply and now this train was a weapon heading straight for the heart of their nest.

Dad would be so fucking proud of this.

My smile slipped, then fell away, grief taking bites out of me once more, and I curled my hands into tight fists, trying to focus on the feeling of my fingernails digging into my palms, forcing out that pain with all I could.

"Don't do that," Magnar murmured softly.

I glanced at him, releasing a breath as I forced back the tears that were burning the backs of my eyes.

"Do what?"

"Your father sacrificed himself to save you. He died so that you might live. And he did die, drakaina hjarta. It hurts. It burrows so deep inside of you that you won't ever be the person you were before knowing the pain of his passage, and that's how it should be. His love for you and yours for him should leave a mark so deep that you never truly part from him. Denying your pain over his loss won't lessen it. You shouldn't fight it."

"If I let myself feel it, I'll drown in it," I breathed.

Though there were no vampires in this part of the train, I didn't want to risk alerting any of them to our presence. We'd come this far, all we had to do now was make it off the train without being seen. I wasn't sure how we'd manage such a thing but that was a problem for tomorrow.

"You won't. You're stronger than you give yourself credit for. More importantly than that, you need to feel the pain of his loss so that you might be able to enjoy the memories of his life again. If you forever let that agony overwhelm you, you'll lose the chance to remember him with the love and joy he gave you."

I swallowed thickly, pressing my lips into a thin line as I tried to do as he'd said, tried to allow some of that pain to trickle past my defences, tried to let it claim me.

"My father tied my right arm to my side and made me use only my left for an entire year," Magnar said softly, his voice barely carrying over the low rumble of the train.

"Even when you slept?" I asked, giving him the side eye.

Magnar snorted, shaking his head. "Your mind is so literal sometimes. No, Callie Ford, he did not tie me up for an entire year; only while I was learning to wield a sword so that I might train my left arm to be as efficient as my right."

"Why? Surely using your dominant arm makes more sense," I muttered, a tear slipping down my cheek which I allowed to fall without interference.

"Because he never wanted me to be on the back foot. Never wanted me to rely too much on any one thing. If my body was to be a weapon, then every piece of me would be expected to perform with the brutal efficiency required to keep me alive. Once my left arm was strong enough, I began training with my right in kind."

I pursed my lips, trying to imagine what it had been like to grow up as he had, to have been trained for this for my entire life instead of stumbling into it through grief and a desperate need for vengeance.

"Dad used to take me out into the ruins at the edge of the Realm," I said softly, fighting through the pain of those memories and letting him have a taste of them in return for his own. "He knew I craved freedom more than anything, that I hated being little more than a bird trapped in a cage. He couldn't offer me an escape from the Realm, but he offered me an escape from the bars it built around my mind. He taught me to climb the ruined buildings, to leap between broken rooftops and how to roll when I fell so I didn't break bones. Just me and him. A taste of freedom laced in adrenaline, which loosened the crushing feeling on my chest."

The tears ran freely now, but I forced myself to let them, to feel the gaping place in my heart which should have held him close for so much longer, the aching, endless grief. He would have chosen this path for me if he'd been able to, would have wanted me free and able to fight back against the monsters who sought to cage me again.

The aching emptiness in my chest was overwhelming, the chasm of space in the inch which divided me from Magnar seeming as endless as the miles which divided me from Montana. This loneliness was hungry, devouring, taking bites out of me piece by piece and leaving nothing but my raw bones exposed in its wake. The loss of my father was too much to bear, the reality before me too enormous to conquer, and the laws of this vow that bound me felt all too much like a cage of their own.

I needed something to steal away the ache in my chest, a distraction to pull me from the darkness of my own reality.

I shifted against the wall of the train, pushing my spine against the cold metal, digging my heels into the floor to anchor myself as I looked to my right through the tears blurring my eyes.

Magnar looked back at me, a pit of pain swirling within his golden gaze too. He knew this emptiness, knew this torment.

The breath of space dividing us felt like a ravine that couldn't be breached, but I shifted my hand closer to his all the same. The urge to move away again battered against me as the laws of the vow tightened around me, but I fought it, ignoring the ache in my muscles as my hand slowly slid closer.

My fingertips brushed against his for the briefest moment, and he looked at me in surprise, his own fingers curling around mine, the heat between us pulsing through that small point of contact.

"What now, drakaina hjarta?" Magnar growled, a challenge in his words, that anger returning too.

"You mean if I wasn't bound by the magic of some goddess I only just found out exists?" I asked. "Then I'd likely use your body to make me forget my pain for a little while."

His fingers flexed around mine, my core heating at the tightness of his grip even as the power of the goddess grew, my hand trembling with the effort it took to resist her demand to release him.

I gritted my teeth, resentment building in me as I fought against her will, hating the control she had over me with every piece of my being. Even my freedom wasn't my own anymore. The bars which trapped me only ever shifting, never truly shattering.

Idun's power hit me with more force, and I snatched my hand back, sagging against the wall with a curse while Magnar grunted in irritation.

"Let's assume you'll be fucking your own hand for release instead then," he muttered, his gaze moving from me, the bite in his voice slicing at my flesh.

"I didn't ask for this you know," I snapped.

"You did, actually."

"I wanted to become a weapon fit for killing bloodsuckers, not a slave to the power of a deity set on using me for her own gain."

"And yet you sit there resting instead of honing your knife skills with this time you've been offered."

"You want me to train with you here? In this tiny space while we hide from a hundred vampires in the dark?" I scoffed.

"What's wrong, drakaina hjarta? Is that too difficult for you? Fury is small enough to wield in close quarters, and you should be able to get yourself out of a tight spot like this if you found yourself trapped in one. Vampires will always want to come at you. The closer the better. All the easier to get their teeth into you after all."

I hesitated for a beat, the unnatural swaying of the train and low hum of its engines all that surrounded us. It would be madness to do what he was suggesting. But I wasn't the type to back down from a challenge.

I shook my head as if denying him, my fingers wrapping around Fury's hilt where he couldn't see them in the dim light.

Magnar clucked his tongue at me, and I struck like a cobra, snatching my blade from its sheath and swinging it toward his throat.

Of course I didn't catch him off guard though. His hand clamped around my wrist, tugging me closer and taking control of my momentum until I was straddling him, my blade twisted to press against my own throat while still in my grip.

"You're smaller than me, so you need to be faster," he snarled, my pulse skipping at the sudden turn of my strike.

Magnar released me and I drew back, eyeing him for a moment and calling on the memories of my ancestors.

I swung Fury for his chest this time, following it with a left hook aimed straight at his jaw.

He blocked both, his forearm crashing against mine with enough force to make my wrist go numb, and I cursed him as I tried again, aiming to headbutt him while stabbing for his thigh.

Magnar laughed as he was forced to jerk aside, one hand batting Fury away, the other gripping my knee and drawing me further onto his lap.

I gasped as something hard pressed against my core, my gaze falling to the dagger he had somehow drawn and now had pressed between my legs, the blade flush with my inner thigh.

"Femoral artery," he said with a taunting smile. "One good slice and you're dead."

My lips parted on some kind of reply, but he shifted his hand, his knuckles raking over my core and stealing my breath as need rolled through every piece of me.

I moaned, biting down on my lower lip as I shifted my hips against his hand, my eyes on his as they darkened.

Magnar's grip on my wrist loosened, and I twisted it sharply, lunging for him and pressing Fury to his throat before he could stop me.

"Jugular," I breathed in his ear. "Now you're dead too."

"I can think of worse ways to go. Besides, you've made a mistake."

"How so?"

"I'm meant to be a vampire, so you should have gone for the heart. Cutting my throat won't do the job – and now you've gone and left yourself exposed."

"Exposed to what?" I said in disbelief. I was straddling him in the darkness, my blade to his throat, and he still wanted to claim the win from me. "I call bullshit."

Magnar's hand was suddenly in my hair, fisting tight and yanking hard.

I gasped as my head was drawn back, my grip on Fury slackening and Magnar rearing up beneath me, knocking it from my hold altogether.

His teeth sank into the flesh of my neck before I could I do a single thing, a noise escaping me far too loudly as I found myself at his mercy once more.

"Fuck," I gasped as he growled against my skin, the noise a sin which resounded through my flesh.

"Dead," he repeated, his other hand still between my thighs, his grip on the knife there shifting so that his knuckles rode over my clit. That was no fucking accident, and the sound which spilled from my lips let him know exactly what I thought of it too.

"Now what?" I gasped, his grip on me tightening, his arm banding around me. He pulled my hair harder, locking me at his mercy and making my spine arch against his hold.

"Now let's see if you can get free, novice," he taunted, his mouth still against my neck, the rake of his stubble punctuating his words, setting my skin on fire.

"I can't," I hissed.

"Try struggling," he suggested.

My heart thundered at the suggestion, his grip on me utterly unyielding, the chances of me breaking loose little to none. My hands were free, but I was crushed against his chest, his mouth at my neck; his blade between my legs and his fist in my hair kept my spine arched in a way that prevented almost all movement.

I gripped his forearm, digging my nails into the inked skin as I tried to push against him, his body as immovable as stone.

I lifted my hips, and his knuckles rode straight over my clit again, dragging against the seam of my pants, making my nipples harden and ache.

"That's it, drakaina hjarta," Magnar growled. "Try a little harder next time though, or you'll never break free."

I cursed him, realising his game, seeing how he'd turned this to his advantage and yet finding I didn't care about that at all. He had me at his mercy, and the only freedom he would allow me was this.

But if he thought he was winning by taunting my body with what it couldn't have, then he was so fucking mistaken.

"You're awfully chatty for a vampire set on sucking me dry," I hissed, my nails digging into his skin even harder as I pushed at him.

Magnar chuckled against my neck, laughing like he thought he'd won something here. "Do you yield, or do you think you might stand a chance at winning still?"

"I can still win," I snarled, wanting to prove a fucking point here if nothing else.

"If you say so." Magnar bit me again before I could reply, and I cursed.

My nails bit into his arms hard enough to draw blood, and I struggled against his grip on me, my hips flexing, grinding my core against his knuckles, the hilt of his knife. The friction set my entire body alight, and I bit down on a moan.

Idun's power hummed in the air surrounding us, the need in my flesh building to the point of excruciating, release dancing just out of reach.

Magnar's hold on me tightened and my chest pressed to his, my aching nipples finding the barest hint of relief between the layers of fabric that parted us. I needed this. I needed more. I was so fucking close, my pulse rioting out of rhythm, and if I could just-

My back hit the cold wall of the train and I blinked like a bucket of ice water had just been tossed over the two of us, a power beyond measure pressing me back from him.

"Fuck," Magnar muttered, his fingers raking across the stubble on his jaw while he looked at me like I was something he was just aching to devour.

I cursed beneath my breath and tore my gaze from the torture of his, shaking my head like that might clear it.

Considering she was supposed to be helping us, that goddess really was a meddling bitch.

"You should sleep," Magnar grunted, and I appreciated the fact he hadn't commanded me to do so even though he clearly could.

It had been a long day and my body was crying out for rest. When we made it to New York we'd have so much to do that we couldn't guarantee the next time we'd get to sleep. This might be the best chance we had, and it was clear Idun wasn't going to allow us to pass the time with anything more interesting either.

"So should you," I pointed out.

"I'll keep watch."

"Mmmhmm." There was no point in trying to argue with him.

If he didn't want to sleep, then that was his business, but *I*, on the other hand, was going to take as much rest as I could get while working to banish the thundering need from my body. Magnar Elioson might have been a son of a bitch, but I couldn't deny how goddamn hot he was too. Not that I was going to be making use of that fact again apparently.

My eyes fell shut and sleep came for me like a tide, the hours I'd missed rushing up on me and offering me this small escape. I gratefully fell into its embrace and let my problems fester in the back of my mind while seeking silence in the dark.

ERIK

CHAPTER SIXTEEN

1000 YEARS AGO

Daylight.

A storm of noise.

Hands on my shoulders.

"We need you! Brother, stand up, get to your feet!" The voice was Fabian's, and for a moment, I wondered if I was imagining his arms around me. After all my years in solitude in this cave, his touch was as alien to me as the heat of the sun.

He clutched my face, forcing me to look at him, and I took in the handsome, familiar face of the man I had claimed as a brother long ago.

"Speak to me," he begged, and I met his wild eyes and took in his bedraggled hair.

I opened my mouth, but no words came out, the hunger had stolen the last of them.

He lifted me, dropping me over his shoulder and carrying me through a hole in the wall. But it couldn't be possible. This had to be a hallucination because the gods had sealed that path long ago.

I gazed back into the darkness and Andvari's voice drifted into my ears. *"Time to go."*

I shook my head as a little more clarity found me among the pounding in my head. No…I couldn't leave. My debt was not yet paid.

I reached out and tried to hold onto the edge of the rocks, but Fabian dragged me away, not giving me a chance to gain purchase. I growled, but he paid me no heed, keeping me tight to his body and stealing me away from my place of penance.

He ran with me, and I squinted against the blinding light of the world despite the dark clouds hanging above. A thousand forgotten smells clutched my senses; lichen, moss, and pine.

The forest was a blur of dark green, and the rush of the river faded away, that sound had been my constant companion for so many days and nights, that my ears rang with the sudden quiet.

I tried to make my mouth form a word, but nothing came. I was a starving husk, a creature whose soul had been carved out, leaving me barren.

When Fabian eventually placed me on my feet, the roar of a battle found me, warriors clashing, steel blades colliding. The ring of metal, the cries of death, it all came to me at once, too many sensations making my mind spark and flash.

My eyes sharpened and I took in a sprawling field of wildflowers, cut down under the feet of nearly a thousand slayers.

Clarice swept through them like a tornado, killing tens of men with claws and sharp teeth, ripping bodies apart like they were made of nothing but parchment. Miles stood beyond her, wielding a shining blade and spilling guts as easily as slicing open the flesh of fruit. Other vampires joined our ranks, fighting tooth and nail, turning to dust before my eyes when slayers' blades found their hearts. But the last of them were falling fast, their numbers dwindling by the second. It was carnage in its purest form, vampires versus the slayers, an age-old fight which had culminated in this furious war.

Fabian raised his hands and a dark cloud swept closer over the hill, a swarm of ravens descending on the slayers, pecking at their eyes and bare skin. The screams made my thoughts jar, but I absorbed it all in less than two seconds, and I cared about none of it. The only thing present to me in that battle was blood. The sweetest thing I'd ever smelled after two hundred years without it. In an instant, I lost all control and gave in to the rampant thirst that was my sole desire, flooded by the desperate longing to sate this need.

I sprinted toward the nearest slayer, ripped his head sideways and sank my fangs into his flesh, drinking deep. It was ecstasy, the blood hitting my tongue and sending my mind into a frenzy. Casting him aside, I dragged the next one close, tearing out her throat with teeth alone. It was savage, the curse bared in its most ruthless form, the thirst a beast of its own that desired nothing more than to feed.

Blood. Kill. Blood. Kill.

I saw red. It stained my whole world. It rained down on me as I moved between the ranks of slayers, becoming stronger than I'd ever imagined was possible.

Andvari was close, cackling in my ear, and I felt his strength reaching into my body and lending me the power I needed to devour a whole army. He wanted this, he urged me on, branding that singular need into the essence of my soul until I became the hunger, and it became me.

The horrified cries of men and women drummed in my ears, but I never stopped. I barely saw them fall as I found more necks, more skin, more blood.

Rip. Slash. Drink.

Over and over. I made a path through the battle like a hurricane devouring the land. Not one blow found me. Not one blade touched my skin. I was too fast, too strong. The curse thumped through my veins and created a monster so fierce that the slayers didn't stand a chance.

One hundred, two hundred. I couldn't count how many fell at my feet. Soon I was climbing over mounds of bodies, desperate for the next throat, driven to madness by Andvari's power.

Three hundred, four hundred.

I barely drank now, the thirst desiring death and nothing more, turning me into a reaper for the gods, harvesting souls like summer wheat.

The rest of my kind pressed their advantage, but I could have done it single-handed. The battlefield ran red with the blood of the slayers, and I waded through it towards the final man still living, rivers of red washing down my body.

His unruly hair hung around his shoulders. He was dripping in the blood of his comrades, his eyes haunted, but still determined. He was on his knees, clutching a gaping hole in his stomach.

The only vampires who remained alive were my family, every sireling who had come to fight at our sides turned to dust by the slayers' wrath. Clarice, Miles, and Fabian closed in until we had circled the final slayer. My family's wide eyes turned to me as I approached, a mixture of fear and awe lighting their gazes.

Blood dripped steadily from my body and the tang of it surrounded me, the scent overwhelming my senses.

As the final slayer looked to me, he lifted his sword, ready to die for his cause and secure his passage to Valhalla.

Andvari's strength withdrew from me, and I gasped, shuddering as I bent forward, the release of his power like a window opening in my mind, showing me the reality of what I had done.

The hunger was gone. I was whole once again and yet more broken than I'd ever been, the horrifying knowledge of what I'd done cutting so deeply into my chest that I released a shuddering cry, stumbling forward and nearly crashing to my knees. But Fabian slammed a hand to my shoulder, steadying me before I could fall.

I lifted my head, gazing across the massacre I'd caused with a suffocating wave of guilt.

"Brother, you can finish the last. You have saved us all," Fabian said in reverence.

"No, I..." I shook my head, pain flaring through my un-beating heart, disgust rising in my throat. I had done this. I was responsible.

I had risen the debt on my head by a thousand lives. I was more than a monster; I was an abomination.

I stepped back from the final slayer who was glancing between us as if trying to decide who to lunge for. Even in his injured state, he hadn't given up.

I drew closer, lowering to my knees before him.

"*Erik*," Fabian barked at me.

The slayer slashed his sword toward me, and I caught his wrist, crushing it in my grip. He was weak, and it took little more than a squeeze to make him drop the blade, the hilt making a thunk as it hit the ground and Clarice hurried forward to kick it out of his reach.

I gazed into the golden eyes of the warrior and reached out, pressing a hand to his warm cheek. Though he was growing colder and the light in his eyes was fading, life still thrummed in his veins like a fragile hummingbird. He crashed backwards onto the ground, groaning in defeat. I leaned over him, frowning as I drank in the last of the life in his eyes, a terrible weight of guilt holding me hostage.

"Freya," he whispered, his eyes distant, looking beyond me toward the afterlife. "I love you, dear wife. I wish I could come to you now."

"You won't make it off of the battlefield," I rasped. "You have lost too much blood, slayer."

He reached up with a shaking hand and gripped the back of my neck, but he didn't seem to see me. "My sons, my boys. Magnar...Julius, take care of your mother."

"Finish it, Erik," Miles muttered. "It is not right to leave him this way."

Andvari drew near, and I shuddered as his presence slipped over me. *"Warrior born and monster made."*

Shock flooded me as I found new meaning in the words, an answer offered in my moment of devastation. Was the god encouraging me to turn a slayer into one of us? Was that what the prophecy meant?

I'd never sired a human before, but I'd seen the others do it. And if this was the path to breaking the curse, I had to do it. Lifting my wrist to my mouth, I dug my fangs in deep to cut into my skin then held the wound to the warrior's lips.

He choked and spluttered but was too weak to fight me off. When I was certain he'd swallowed my blood, I lifted his wrist and slid my teeth into it, releasing my venom into his veins.

He gasped in horror, turning pale beneath me, trying to pull his arm free of my grip. His eyes glazed as the venom took root in his body and I extracted my fangs from his skin.

"Is this it?" I asked Andvari, but he only chuckled in response.

My kin were moving closer, muttering as they watched.

If I was right, the curse would be broken. This slayer would be a vampire and perhaps that meant he would be given back his life too, the moment my brothers and sister were remade as human.

"This has to be it," I said in desperation. "Forgive me."

I took hold of the man's head and his eyes widened as he realised what I was about to do. A sharp crack cut through the silent air as I snapped his neck. He fell still and I looked to my family, finding concern in their eyes.

"A slayer, Erik? Is that a good idea?" Miles asked, moving closer. His blond locks were drenched with blood and his usually soft features looked hard for once, battle-worn and tainted with sins of his own.

I reached out to Andvari for an answer, but he gave me no confirmation.

The slayer beneath me jerked with life and I stood above him, watching as the wound on his stomach knitted over. He reared upwards, his eyes wide as he clutched his throat, the first moments of bloodlust finding him.

I knew how hungry he'd be in these first moments, so quickly pulled a body closer for him to feast on. The man fell on it like an animal, drinking the blood of his comrade before regaining his senses and lurching backwards. His beard was thick with blood and his eyes wide with horror.

"You can go home now," I said as he rose to his feet.

He gazed at me with a burning intensity, then lunged toward his sword on the ground and I was surprised to find he could still touch it. The four of us tensed, but he didn't fight us. Instead, he fled, running across the battlefield at high speed, and I turned my face to the grey sky, praying Andvari would show himself.

"Is this enough?!" I roared, but no answer came. Only the low whispers of my family reached my ears.

"Good idea," Fabian announced. "He will kill his entire clan."

My throat tightened as I turned to my brother, fear stroking my heart at that possibility. And as Andvari's taunting laughter reached me once more, I realised I'd been tricked by the god once again. My action would equal more death, and I would never be rid of the blood on my hands.

No...what have I done?

MONTANA

CHAPTER SEVENTEEN

I gazed out of the bell tower with trepidation in my heart. Although it was almost morning, the moon was still out, and the stars were still twinkling. But we had to leave this early, wanting to catch the dawn - which Julius said was the time of day when most vampires retreated into their homes. The night was when they thrived, their strength at its peak.

It had been hard getting sleep crammed under the blankets next to Julius's huge form, but even harder with my thoughts caught in a tailspin.

I needed to go back to Erik on my own terms. Walking into his household wasn't something I was going to take lightly, and I refused to be a captive again. The plan Julius and I had come up with was not only reckless but downright dangerous. But if we pulled it off, Erik would have to abide by the rules I laid out for him.

Julius was busy packing his belongings into a bag. When everything from his steel blades to the smoke bombs and food was tucked inside it, he lifted it onto his back, then strung his bow over his shoulder.

"We won't be able to come back here after today," he said.

"Why not?"

"It's only a matter of time until the familiars locate this place." He held out his cloak. "Here, you'll get cold. I don't tend to feel it as much. You'll find that too if you take your vow. It'll unlock all of your gifts."

"I'm good with the cloak thanks," I said and took the black material, wrapping it around my shoulders. "But what do you mean by gifts?"

He grinned in that carefree way of his. "Slayer gifts. Agility, speed, strength, and so much more. If you're curious enough, we can go ahead and do the vow right now."

"I'm good," I said firmly. "Shit like that sounds like it has a catch anyway."

"Yeah," he muttered. "There is a couple of those. Here, you'll be needing this." He took Nightmare from his belt, his eyes glittering playfully.

"When did you take it back?" I patted my pocket where I'd tucked it before going to sleep.

"Had to give you a reason not to run off in the night, didn't I?"

"Light-fingered asshole," I muttered.

"No, Montana, I will not lightly finger your asshole." He shook his head at me sternly.

"I didn't say that," I balked.

"Uh huh," he drawled like he didn't believe me.

"Has anyone ever told you you're incredibly annoying?" I asked.

"No one. Ever." He shrugged. "Why?"

"I think you know why."

"No, I'm entirely in the dark here." He smirked, then offered Nightmare to me. "So, are you taking it or not? It is more loyal to you than me after all. Besides, I have my bow. And maybe I'll get my old sword back today if Valentina decided to keep it."

"After she pulled it out of her stomach?" I teased, taking my blade and relaxing at its warming touch.

"Yes. By the gods, I doubt she will forgive me for that."

"Do you think you can handle her if she decides to fight?" I asked with a tug of concern in my chest.

"Without a doubt." He said no more as he headed across the space toward the stairwell, shouldering his quiver and bow as he went.

I followed, tucking Nightmare inside a pocket in the cloak he'd leant me. "How are we going to get back to the city without the familiars spotting us?"

"We're not," Julius said simply, and my heart rate quickened.

"But if Fabian sees us, he'll send an army to catch us," I pressed as we headed down the winding dark stairway.

"Trust me, damsel," he urged.

"I will if you stop calling me that," I said airily as we arrived on the ground floor.

"Deal." He unlocked the door, then strode toward his bike and rolled it out onto the street. "On you get," he said, patting the leather seat as I stepped outside.

"What? I don't have to ride draped over your lap today?" I asked dryly.

His eyes gleamed with mirth. "You can if you prefer it."

I pressed my lips together, fighting a smile at his tone before I swung my leg over the seat.

"Place both feet on the ground to keep yourself upright," he instructed, and I did as he said.

"Twist the throttle back when I tell you." He pointed to one of the handles and I gazed at the wall opposite with unease, guessing that was how he had been making this thing move yesterday. "You won't go anywhere, it's not in gear."

"Okay…" I said nervously, unsure what he was planning.

He kicked his foot down on a pedal on the bike and the engine rumbled to life, the vibrations echoing through me.

Julius swung his bow from his shoulder, placing an arrow into it in a fluid motion. "Now!" he shouted, and I twisted the right handle hard.

The engine roared and smoke billowed from a pipe at the back of it, causing one helluva cacophony. I gazed at Julius in alarm, thinking of the familiars, but he gestured for me to continue, aiming his bow toward the sky. A shadow swooped overhead and Julius loosed his arrow. It plunged into the chest of a raven and the animal exploded into dust which rained down on us.

"Keep going!" Julius cried just as the sound of howls picked up in the distance.

My pulse drummed in my ears as I continued to make the engine thunder with noise, drawing Fabian's familiars right to us.

Another shadow sailed overhead, and Julius shot two arrows at it in quick succession. The small finch avoided the first, but the second hit home and it burst into grey ash.

A bark caught my ear and I turned sharply to face the noise, spotting a huge brown dog at the end of the street.

"Julius!" I shouted and he turned toward it, releasing another arrow.

The dog dodged it as it sprinted toward us, gaining speed by the second, soulless eyes set on us with intent.

Julius was calm in his movements, and he pressed another arrow to his string, but my heart beat out of control.

I gasped as the dog came within a foot of him, launching itself into the air, its sharp teeth bared. The arrow slammed into its chest, and it crumbled to dust, showering over Julius as he turned to me.

"Enough." He knocked my hand from the bike handle and the engine softened to a purr. "The birds would be here if there were any more of them."

My heart stumbled as three more dogs rounded onto the street, charging toward us at a ferocious pace.

Julius threw his leg over the seat in front of me, forcing me to scoot back. I grabbed his waist as he pulled the throttle and turned us violently in the opposite direction to the hounds.

Their barks fell behind us as we took streets left and right, tearing down roads littered with bricks and chunks of concrete. Julius dodged them with incredible agility, swerving between the debris and making my stomach swoop with every sharp movement.

I gripped his waist tighter, holding on for dear life as the wind pulled my hair out behind me.

"What about the dogs?" I yelled in his ear.

"Forget them. They won't keep up!" Julius shouted.

"But Fabian will know where we are," I called.

"Not for long," he laughed, taking a ninety-degree turn at a terrifying speed.

The bike tilted hard to one side, and I clung fiercely to Julius as my right knee nearly brushed the concrete.

The bike swung upright as he sped down a shadowy alleyway, and I started to relax my body so I fell in sync with his movements, adrenaline flowing through my veins.

A thrill went through me, and a laugh escaped my lips. "Holy shit."

"Idun showed me the way of these things," Julius called to me. "Fucking exhilarating, isn't it?"

"It's incredible," I cried.

We closed in on the ruins of a building which had a huge hole blasted into the front of it, the sign of a bomb dropped years ago. Julius didn't slow as we approached, and I flinched as the bike sped up a slab of concrete jutting from the ground. I gripped Julius with my thighs, holding on even tighter as the bike zoomed over the edge of the concrete and we jumped a mound of rubble before landing with a thump in the dark building, leaving my pulse thrashing wildly.

The sound of the engine echoed off the walls and my stomach flew upwards as we descended down a steep ramp into a pitch-black space.

We slowed to a halt and Julius cut the engine, then kicked a stand down before dismounting the bike, lifting me off of it and planting me beside him. I didn't have a moment to ask questions as he took my hand and started leading me deeper into the darkness.

"Keep quiet in case there's hungry freaks down here," he murmured.

"We called them rotters," I whispered.

He grunted in amusement. "I like that. I'll use it."

After a beat, a light illuminated the space, and I spotted a flashlight shining on Julius's phone. The bright blue glow lit up what seemed to be an underground parking garage.

Ancient vehicles sat around the space, left to rot after the Final War. The ghosts of the past seemed to linger around us now, watching from a time left behind. It was cold in here, damp too, and the old vehicles were kind of eerie, looming out of the dark in silent rows like forgotten gravestones.

"This way," Julius urged, his hand still gripping mine as he guided me through the rusted carcasses of cars and trucks, leading me to the back of the lot.

It should have felt awkward, but I found his presence weirdly reassuring, and I wondered if it had something to do with our slayer blood. Like something in me recognised our shared ancestry.

We arrived at a crumbling wall with a hole at the base of it and Julius crouched down, crawling into the gap and squeezing his broad frame through it.

I bent low, gazing after him with a flicker of anxiety.

"Come on," he called from beyond the wall, and I steeled myself, dropping to the floor and belly-crawling through it.

Julius helped me up on the other side and I took in the dank tunnel ahead, illuminated only by the light on his phone. Without it, the dark would have been impenetrable, and I didn't like the idea of relying on that tiny device to keep the way lit.

"What is this place?" I asked, my face scrunching as a smell of decay carried to me.

"The old sewage system," Julius said, lifting his shirt up to cover his nose.

I mimicked him and was immediately relieved of the vile scent by at least eighty percent.

"This will lead us under the entire city. Vampires don't pay any attention to the old tunnels running beneath their streets. A river of shit isn't something they want to deal with," Julius explained with a low laugh. "It's how I've been getting around undetected."

My heart jolted at his words. "That's genius. And totally disgusting."

"I know. Only a filthy animal would roam these tunnels."

"They sound perfect for you then," I said lightly, and he sniggered.

"I'm only filthy in the good ways."

I could hear the smile in his voice as he walked away, and I headed after him, trying to ignore the slap of my footsteps as I moved across the damp floor. The guy was arrogant as hell, but he was funny too, and I was quietly starting to like him. Not that I'd be telling him that anytime soon.

Julius walked silently, and I wondered how he managed it considering his bulk. A vampire would hear me coming far easier than they would hear him, and I wondered if that was one of the slayer gifts he'd mentioned. I was a little curious about all that, to be fair, but his insistence for me to take some vow was not remotely appealing to me. It sounded like the elusive gods were involved, and from everything I'd learned about them so far, they didn't sound like creatures I wanted anything to do with.

I gazed up at the green algae coating the curved ceiling and walls, hoping this would be the worst we had to deal with on our journey. The river of shit he'd mentioned was surely a joke…

I followed him quietly through the winding passages as he seemed to know exactly where we were going. We didn't stop for what felt like an hour, and I was starting to wonder how close to the city we were.

"Right." Julius lifted his phone, bringing up a map which showed the whole of New York City.

I sucked in a breath, moving closer as I took it in, every street and building labelled right before my eyes.

"The palace grounds are here." He pointed, zooming in on a rectangular expanse of green on the map. "That's about a mile from where we are. Do you think you could figure out where Valentina lives on here?"

I took the phone, studying the streets and figuring out the route I'd taken from the castle grounds with Erik, finding the New Empire State Building and following the path from there with my eyes.

"We took a right here…" I trailed my finger along it, searching for the block of apartments where Valentina resided.

I frowned, zooming in closer and orientating the map.

"I think it's near this street." I said, tapping the screen. "But I'm not entirely sure." I bit my lip, not wanting to let us down this deep into our plan.

"We'll head there and check it out. Maybe you'll recognise something once we're above ground."

I nodded as he took off at a fast pace and I jogged to keep up.

My gut coiled as we closed in on our destination. How were we going to pull this off? What if we couldn't find her apartment? And even if we did, what if she wasn't there alone?

Eventually, we arrived beneath a manhole in the ceiling with a ladder running up to it. We'd passed several of them since we'd entered the city's borders, but this was the first time Julius stopped.

He gazed at the phone, checking our position before pocketing it. "We're a few streets away, but this manhole comes up in an alley, so we should be safe to exit here."

I nodded, my heart fluttering as I moved closer to the ladder. I was painfully reminded of the drain I'd used to escape the Realm. The last day I'd spent with Dad...

Emotion built a lump in my throat, and I blinked back tears as I drew closer, needing to keep it together right now.

"Are you alright?" Julius asked with a frown, and I nodded stiffly, forcing the pain away and burying it deep inside me. This wasn't the time to dwell on that, but I wondered how long I could keep bottling up my grief until it spilled over again.

Julius placed his hands on the ladder, pulling his shirt down from his mouth and nose. "I'll go first. Wait for my signal."

I nodded again, watching as he scaled it and pushed the metal plate above his head. The faint light of early morning fell over us, and I held my breath while Julius climbed out.

I bit hard into my lip, almost drawing blood as I waited for him to return.

Finally, he ducked his head through the hole. "All clear."

I took hold of the cold rungs and started climbing. As my head raised above the manhole, I lifted my chin to release the shirt from my nose and sucked in a breath of fresh, clean air.

I got to my feet and gazed left and right down the dark alley we were in, between two tall tower blocks. Julius quietly slid the cover back onto the drain and stood upright, his eyes wheeling to the road at one end of the alley. A couple of cars sped by, but it was mostly quiet.

I wondered how we were supposed to go anywhere without being seen, but Julius answered by heading to a fire escape on the nearest wall. "We'll climb up and get a look at our surroundings. We can make our way across the roofs to remain undetected."

I frowned. "How are we supposed to do that?"

"Run and jump." He shrugged, and I gazed up at the sprawling gap between the two buildings above us with trepidation.

"Are you crazy?" I hissed.

He grinned widely. "No. I'm a Blessed Crusader. That jump is nothing to me."

"Well lucky you," I said. "Unfortunately, I'm not a Blessed *whatever,* and I am not throwing myself off the edge of a building to work out how far I can jump."

"That's why you'll be on my back," Julius said smoothly, moving beneath the fire escape.

He leapt upwards, catching hold of a rusted ladder, and dragging it down to the ground.

I groaned, gazing at him as I realised I had no choice in this.

You can do this. Just climb to the roof and he'll do the rest. Don't focus on what 'the rest' is.

Julius gestured for me to go first, glancing over his shoulder toward the road. "Better get moving."

I nodded, taking a breath before stepping onto the ladder and making my way up. He was hot on my heels, and I tried my best to keep my footfalls quiet as I climbed, though I was nowhere near as silent as him.

When we reached the roof, I dropped over a low wall onto a wide square space filled with grey gravel. The city stretched out for miles around us, and I took a moment to admire it as I caught my breath. Lights twinkled in some of the windows as the morning barely seeped into existence, the pale pink glow on the horizon the first sign of the rising sun.

Julius took my arm, guiding me toward the far edge of the roof and pointing down at the streets. We were on the highest apartment block in the vicinity, and even though it was still fairly dark, I was overly aware of the windows pointed our way across the road.

Julius seemed to consider it too, taking my arm and pulling me low to the ground as we peered over the wall.

"Recognise anything?" he asked as I looked out across the area.

I scanned the streets, trying to locate something familiar. To our right was a series of tower blocks, and I was fairly sure I'd seen one of those red-brick buildings from Valentina's window.

"Over there…I think."

Julius nodded, stroking the fresh stubble on his chin. "Ask Nightmare if it can sense my sword. If Valentina has it, it'll know."

I reached for the blade and rubbed my fingers over the hilt. "Can you sense Julius's sword?"

"Menace," he prompted, reaching for Nightmare too.

Menace is close, it whispered, and I gave Julius a hopeful look.

"Good enough. We can ask again when we're closer." Julius stood, gesturing for me to do the same. "On my back." He turned away from me and I looped my arms around his neck with a flicker of anxiety.

Hopping up, I wrapped my legs around his waist and held on tight, my face pressing to his quiver of arrows.

"Are you sure you can do this?" I asked, my stomach knotting.

He just laughed like a madman, running toward the right of the building at a tremendous pace. My lungs stopped taking in air as he sprang onto the low wall at the edge of roof, using his momentum to propel himself forward and leaping from the edge.

My heart lurched upwards as we flew across the space and landed heavily on the roof below us. He didn't even stumble as he kept running, launching us onto a balcony on the next building before grabbing onto a drainpipe and starting to scale it.

"How can you do this?" I breathed in shock.

"I'm goddess-gifted, damsel."

He picked up his pace, climbing so fast that I forgot to curse him out for that nickname, instead glancing down at the dizzying drop below and focusing on not losing my grip.

We made it to the top and Julius crossed the roof, turning toward the tower blocks and taking a running leap to the nearest one before I felt entirely ready, but maybe I'd never be prepared for this.

We crashed into a fire escape and Julius swore as he lost his footing, nearly sending us tumbling backwards off of it. He snatched hold of a metal platform above us and I gripped onto him tighter, sure we were going to fall, my heart pounding like mad.

"Don't worry," he said through gritted teeth. "I've never fallen yet."

He hauled us onto the platform, and I took a steadying breath, trembling as I clung to him. "Please keep up your streak."

"Planning on it. Now ask Nightmare again," Julius commanded, and I released him with one shaking hand, feeling for the blade inside my robe.

It didn't answer with words this time, but it sent a trickle of electricity into my palm. I could sense the sword was near and as I shut my eyes, I felt the connection to it humming in my own veins.

"It's close. A few hundred feet or so," I said, and Julius let me down, turning to face me.

"We can cut through the back alleys from here," he said, lowering himself onto the ladder and descending to the platform below. I followed, willing my heartbeat to slow, and I was glad as hell when we made it to the ground.

We were in a narrow alley beneath the fire escape, and Julius looked to me for directions, not seeming remotely shaken by the death-defying bullshit he'd just pulled off.

"I think it's that way." I pointed toward a narrow path leading behind the buildings and jogged toward it, sensing Nightmare's connection to Menace growing even stronger.

Julius kept at my heels, and as we passed a few more apartment blocks, I stumbled to a halt, gazing up the black tower to my left.

"This one," I gasped, certain it was Valentina's home.

Julius beamed at me, gazing up at the sheer wall before us. Circling around into the alley, we found another fire escape that led up several floors.

"One more climb," Julius said with a grin, jumping up and pulling down the ladder before gently resting it on the ground. "What floor is it?"

I recalled chasing Erik up the stairwell when we'd come here together, panting my goddamn lungs out as he made me scale the entire building.

"The top one," I said bitterly, putting Nightmare away.

"I'll go first, stay close." He sprang onto the ladder, climbing it at speed like nothing he had done so far had caused him to need a breather. I hurried after him, muttering curses. He moved like the damn wind and was as silent as a pigeon fart.

My arms ached, but adrenaline kept me going and I followed as quickly as I could.

When we'd made it to the top, I sagged forward, resting my hands on my knees as I caught my breath, this building firmly my nemesis now. If I had to climb it once more in my lifetime, I'd burn the damn thing to the ground.

"If you take your vow, you'll find this all a lot easier," Julius whispered with a grin.

"I don't even know what the vow is," I panted, standing upright as he approached the window, my side aching like a bitch.

"It's a promise to end all vampires. But thinking about it...if you take it, we won't be able to hook up. So let's keep that option wiiiiide open."

I scowled at him. "That's never gonna happen."

"Never is a long time, and I'm pretty irresistible." He winked and I moved closer, choosing to ignore that comment as I gazed into the dark hallway.

Julius ran his hands along the bottom of the window, trying to pull it up, but it was clearly locked.

He turned to me with an intense look, all jokes fast abandoned in the face of our mission. "I'll have to break it, then we'll have seconds to get into Valentina's apartment. We move fast, attack quickly, and subdue her before she can alert anyone."

I nodded, the reality of what we were about to do sinking in hard. I unsheathed Nightmare, trying to mentally prepare myself for this.

What if she's too strong? What if we can't pull it off?

I took a breath. We'd come this far. We had to try.

Julius flexed his fingers before grabbing hold of the base of the window again and wrenching as hard as he could. Wood splintered and the pane flew upwards.

He leapt through the gap, and I scrambled after him. He was at the door across the hall in seconds, slamming his boot to the centre of it. It crashed open and he stormed into the apartment.

My heart was in my throat as I sped after him and silence reached my ears from the apartment.

Julius started knocking doors open, searching for Valentina with wild abandon. We reached the living room, and a chill ran down my spine as I found it empty.

Where is she?

Turn! Nightmare screamed and I whipped around just before someone collided with me.

Strong hands forced me down, smashing me into the coffee table and trapping Nightmare beneath me.

Another weight fell onto me, and I could hardly breathe as the two bodies slammed into one another.

"*Yield,*" Julius snarled.

Valentina cursed and she stilled on top of me. I managed to roll beneath her and wriggled my arm out, my hand tight around Nightmare as I prepared to defend myself.

"Julius?" Valentina gasped.

He dragged her off of me and I got to my feet, unsure what to do as I rubbed my bruised limbs. Would I really be able to fight like Julius if I took my vow? It was pretty tempting when he suggested things like that.

Julius stared at Valentina, his knife pointed at her heart, ready to strike the moment she made one wrong move, and the look in her eyes said she knew she was in trouble. She was dressed in a slinky black night gown that barely concealed her curvaceous body, yet it hadn't slowed her down in the slightest. She'd leapt at me like a damn lioness from the long grass.

"What are you doing here?" Valentina said in disbelief, backing up and bumping into me. She evidently had no worries about me being a threat and the fact sparked irritation in me.

Her dark eyes slid to me, and a frown filled her stunning face. "Montana? What's going on?" Her gaze fell to Nightmare and a flicker

225

of recognition slipped into her expression. "By the gods, I knew you were one of us."

"I'm not sure *you* count as one of us anymore," Julius snarled, his gaze promising death if she made one wrong move.

I walked around to join him, shifting Nightmare in my grip and raising it defensively in case she attacked.

But she was all too calm. Too compliant. Why wasn't she fighting?

"I knew you were in the city," Valentina spoke to Julius. "I hoped you'd come to me after what happened between us. When you'd had time to think on it. Surely you know you can trust me?"

Julius lowered his blade, glancing at the window as rain pattered against the pane. "I don't know any such thing. You're one of *them* now. How could you do this to yourself?"

Valentina hung her head and her dark locks fell forward around her face. "I had no choice, Julius. They attacked me, turned me into one of them. You and your brother were locked in a hundred-year-long sleep and there was nothing I could do. So I decided to remain alive, to wait until you came back. To warn you." The light in her eyes dimmed.

Julius's upper lip curled. "And yet my brother and I *didn't* wake. We slept *nine* hundred years, not one."

"I know...I called on Idun for answers. She told me your mother bound you in a longer sleep. To save you. She feared you would die in the final battle," she breathed.

"My mother would never do such a thing. She would not have deprived us of the chance to end the Revenants," Julius growled, his face taut with emotion.

"Then who else? She was the only Dream Walker who was powerful enough to do it," Valentina whispered, but his expression said he refused to believe it. "All these years, I've waited for you both to wake. For my allies to return." She glanced at me with a soft smile. "I tried to help you, Montana. Really. But we're outnumbered here. And I knew you didn't trust me."

"I still don't trust you," I admitted, but I couldn't deny that she did seem relieved to see us.

Julius stepped towards her threateningly. "You didn't have to work for them. You could have run. Or parted the clouds and weakened them all with the sun."

"Even if they'd been weakened, I couldn't take on a thousand vampires single-handedly, Julius," Valentina pleaded. "They would have killed me."

"Then you should have died trying," Julius spat. "That is why we take our vow. To do what we must to end them."

"I couldn't have killed them alone, but I haven't wasted this time among them. I've learned their secrets, earned their trust," Valentina said, her brow wrinkled with distress. "I longed for the day you and Magnar would wake. You know how much I love him. We're destined to be together, he's my betrothed. And now you've come to me, we can find your brother together and-"

"No," Julius snapped. "That's not why we're here."

"Then why are you here?" Valentina looked between us, a flicker of fear in her eyes. "You attacked me before, Julius, have you come to finish the job?"

"You'd be dead already if that was the case," Julius said. "I assume we don't need to gag you as you haven't screamed yet?"

"Of course not. None of this is necessary. If you need my help, I will gladly give it," Valentina said, and she did seem pretty genuine.

"Sit down." Julius pointed at the couch and Valentina backed up, dropping onto it with wide eyes.

I kept beside Julius, my grip firming on Nightmare in case this was a trick. Valentina was strong as hell, and she might just be biding her time to attack us.

"You're going to do exactly as we say," Julius growled, and Valentina nodded, pressing her lips together.

"Stop the rain," I commanded, and her eyes whipped to me. "And get rid of every single cloud in the sky."

"It's going to be a beautiful fucking day in New York, and I am ready to see the sun rise," Julius added.

Valentina inhaled sharply, turning to face the window. My heart skittered with excitement. The whole of the city would be affected, but I didn't know how weak the vampires would be in the sun's rays.

"Now," Julius ordered, and Valentina shut her eyes, concentrating.

Slowly, the rain ebbed away, and the rising light of dawn grew brighter and brighter behind the clouds. I faced the window, enraptured by the sight of the sky clearing, the clouds fizzling away and revealing a powder blue sky.

Between the skyscrapers, the sun was just cresting the horizon, and as the final clouds dissolved, its beautiful rays flooded the room.

I turned to Valentina, expecting her to wince or burst into flames or...something. But she just blinked, looking at ease.

"It's not working," I muttered to Julius.

"It will," Valentina replied. "But it doesn't affect me. I'm a vampire but I'm a slayer too, and our people were made to walk in the light. The sun doesn't hurt me, and I can still wield our blades. I don't even have a scar after you stabbed me Julius...I'm still waiting for an apology for that."

"You're going to be waiting a very long time." Julius smiled but there was no light in it, and Valentina tutted her annoyance.

A scream caught my ear and I hurried to the window, spotting cars coming to a halt in the road. Vampires ran from them into the closest buildings, cursing and wailing as they went.

Triumph pounded a fierce tune in my chest, and I turned to Julius, who threw me a victorious grin.

"The city is ours," he announced, and a laugh escaped my lips.

"That was far too easy," I said, gazing down at the streets as they emptied entirely, vampires racing for cover from the sunlight, clearly hurt in some way by its touch.

We did it. The streets belong to us. We finally have the advantage.

"What are you going to do now?" Valentina asked uncertainly.

I wondered how badly Erik was going to react to this. He was likely losing his shit right now, but I didn't care. Frankly, I was looking forward to seeing the look on his face when he found out I had a hand in this.

"So..." Julius glanced around the room, then plucked Valentina's phone from the coffee table. "We're going to record a little message for the royals."

"They'll already be sending a team here to find me," Valentina said frantically. "You haven't got long."

"They will be panicking about the sun for a while yet," Julius said thoughtfully. "But don't worry, when they do turn up, you won't be here."

"Where will I be?" she breathed.

"You'll find out soon." Julius beamed, angling the camera at her. "Now if you really do want to help us, I suggest you start begging Erik Belvedere for help like a good little vampire sireling."

Valentina gaped at him, her eyes flashing to me then back to the phone. "I-I-"

"Do you need some encouragement?" Julius snarled, lifting his steel blade as a threat.

"No!" she gasped. "Please, Julius, don't hurt me."

He nodded his approval of that, and she kept going, begging Erik for help, putting on a damn good show of being terrified.

When Julius was satisfied, he pocketed the phone and folded his arms. "So, Valentina…Nightmare tells me you still have Menace. Where is my baby?"

Valentina's face grew cold. "It's mine now. You drove it into me. How could you do such a thing? I only came to be with you when you rose from your sleep. But you attacked me."

Julius stalked toward her with a scowl. "Look at yourself. You're one of *them*. A cold, lifeless thing. Menace saw what you were before I did. And my vow will always guide my hand. I did what I had to."

"I would never have hurt you," Valentina said, on the verge of tears. "I came to be with you. We're family."

A pang of pity ran through me at her pained tone, and I shot Julius a look, wondering if he should cut her some slack.

"No, we're not. You never married Magnar. I have no allegiance to you. So where the fuck is she?" Julius growled. "Tell me or I'll rip this place apart and find her myself."

Valentina sighed and a tear slipped from her eye. "In my bedroom. It's in a box beneath the bed."

Julius looked to me, jerking his chin in an order. I didn't like being

229

bossed about but figured I'd rather he stayed there watching Valentina instead of me.

I strode from the room, locating her bedroom and heading into it. The place was decorated in dark blue tones with pictures on the walls of mountains and lakes. I headed to the bed, dropping to my knees and feeling for the box, a fierce energy rolling into me as my fingertips grazed the wood. I pulled it out and opened the long oak container. Inside was an incredible weapon. The golden sword glittered as if beams of pure sunlight lived in the metal. I took the hilt, raising it up, finding it almost too heavy to carry.

I reached for its energy and a savage presence pressed into me, resisting my touch. Slowly, it opened up to me, revealing its name. *Menace.*

Nightmare sighed in my pocket, seeming happy to be united with the sword, like greeting an old friend who had finally come home.

I carried Menace back to the living room and Julius let out a groan as he spotted it. Darting toward me, he snatched the rune-decorated hilt and raised it above his head with a gleam in his eyes.

"Oh my love, how I've missed you. Did you miss me too?" He swung the sword through the air with amazing agility, sweeping it in arcs as if he and the blade were involved in some strange dance.

Valentina pouted as she watched him. "I miss my old blade too, Julius. The vampires keep it locked in an armoury deep beneath the castle with the rest of the slayers' blades. Vicious is so close, and yet I can't get to her."

"Well if you prove yourself, Valentina, perhaps one day I shall help you retrieve her."

"Thank you," she murmured.

I turned to Julius with my heart beating wildly in my chest. "What now?"

"Now, it's time for you to go. Step into the streets. Walk to the castle if you like. Walk and walk until someone comes out of the shadows to take you to the royals." A wicked glint shone in his eyes and strength seeped into every bone in my body.

"Damn, I should have brought my walking shoes instead of my ass kicking ones," I said, and he barked a laugh, while Valentina attempted a vague noise of amusement.

"I'll be waiting where we agreed," Julius promised. "If Erik wants Valentina freed, he will have to let you go. I'll give you until sundown. When night comes again, they will rise against us. So do what you have to and do it fast." He took Valentina's phone and tapped something on it before handing it to me. "Show Erik the video. Threaten the hell out of him. And if you need me, press this button, and call me." I eyed the screen as he demonstrated how to find his number.

I nodded, taking in a deep breath before I pocketed the phone and headed toward the exit. I marched straight across the hallway to the window and climbed out onto the fire escape. Sunlight danced through the air and lit the alley in warm tones. I smiled as I descended to the ground and walked out onto the street where cars were abandoned everywhere.

All was quiet. And as the sun shone down on my back like a shield of protection sent from the gods themselves, I started walking toward the castle with power coursing through my veins.

We're on equal ground now, Erik Belvedere. And oh, how quickly your world crumbles in the light.

CALLIE

CHAPTER EIGHTEEN

The sun shone through the clouds in lazy shafts, punching holes in the blanket of grey overhead. I turned my head towards the sky and smiled as sunlight spilled over me, filling me with its warmth.

I was standing on the top of a hill, looking out over a reddish-brown desert interspersed with cactuses and enormous rock formations which were too incredible for words. A shadow circled overhead, and I spotted a bald eagle soaring across the cloud-filled sky. It watched me, wheeling through the air in lazy circles before turning and flying away.

I tracked the path of its flight, and in the distance, I noticed a line of greenery which marked the start of a forest. But right here, nothing substantial grew. It was a playground for the wind and the creatures who thrived in its mischief.

I looked down and found myself wearing the strangest clothes. A thin cotton shirt lay beneath fighting leathers similar to Magnar's. The outfit was sculpted to my curves, cinching in at my waist while revealing much more of my chest than I was used to revealing.

Fury was in my hand, its presence warm and reassuring, but somehow it wasn't the same as usual. Like its personality was missing, *a dullness where its wit and bloodlust usually lay.*

A warm breeze picked up and my long hair was tossed around me, the sun glinting off of it as if it were actually made of spun gold.

The sound of clashing steel reached me, and I turned to look down the hill at my back, blinking in surprise at what I found there.

A fearsome battle was taking place between four figures who were bathed in the sunlight spilling through a hole in the clouds overhead, and a tide of vampires clung to the shadows surrounding them.

I stepped closer, recognising Magnar even from this distance as he swung Tempest in a mighty arc, destroying more vampires than I could count, ash billowing away on the wind.

More monsters swarmed forward to take their place and he lunged at them too, his powerful body moving to the rhythm of the battle like he'd been born for it.

The man to his right roared a challenge as he cut through foe after foe of his own. His skin was paler than the others, but his hair was as long as Magnar's and braided with golden beads, as was the long beard which coated his jaw. He raised his sword above his head, and I recognised Venom just before it carved a vampire from nose to navel, finding his heart along the way and scattering him to dust.

My mouth fell open as I realised who the man was. I was looking at Magnar's father. The man Erik Belvedere had murdered and turned into a vampire.

This wasn't my dream. Magnar must have fallen asleep beside me on the train, and I'd found my way into his.

Holy shit.

I glanced around, wondering if I should try to get out of here, to step out of this place and leave him to the privacy of his own mind. I felt like I was spying on something personal by intruding in his dreams and yet at the same time I ached to know more, and with no way of knowing how to remove myself, I simply kept watching as the battle played out.

My gaze drifted to the other man who was fighting alongside Magnar and his father, and I gave in to my curiosity as I watched them. He was around Magnar's age, his dark hair cropped short but his muscular build so like the others that I knew it must have been his brother, Julius.

Magnar laughed as he decapitated a vampire and Julius moved with him, plunging a blade through its heart to finish it off. They fought seamlessly side by side, like two parts of the same body. Their laughter echoed up to me again and again as they killed without end, brutally and mercilessly. Destroying the undead like they were born to do.

The final warrior was a woman with rich brown skin and dark hair pinned into braids along one side of her scalp. She was beautiful in all the ways the vampires weren't, her face flushed with the radiance of her warm blood, her body a weapon carved with nothing but effort and dedication. Everything about her screamed life and joy.

A vampire lunged towards Magnar's back, and she threw herself between them, swinging an axe as she screamed in defiance. A mother bear protecting her cub – even if that cub was twice her size.

The battle raged on, and Magnar fought beside his family with a smile on his face, the likes of which I'd never seen in the real world. He was happy here, surrounded by those he loved, and that only made the pain in him more apparent than ever.

I couldn't help but stare, captured by this legendary family. Everything he'd lost in his crusade against the vampires. It made my heart ache to see it. And yet I couldn't turn away.

The final vampire finally fell to dust at their feet and the four of them embraced each other amidst the heap of ash and clothes left behind.

Magnar released his family and suddenly turned towards me, the hillside I'd been standing on somehow sinking, flattening out and placing me much closer to them now.

"There she is!" he called, and his smile made my heart stumble. It was so wild and carefree, the feral beast still there but somehow tempered by the love around him.

"You missed all the fun, Callie," Julius teased as he spotted me too. His tone was filled with warmth, his grin this familiar thing that made me feel like we were friends despite the fact that I'd never met him. My gaze roamed over his powerful frame and the features which were at once similar to his brother's and yet unfamiliar too. His eyes were lighter, and he had a dimple in his left cheek as he gave me that roguish grin, everything about him spelling trouble.

I opened my mouth to reply but I wasn't sure what to say. When I'd found myself in my father's dream, he'd known I wasn't supposed to be there. He'd recognised the fact that I was real while everything else wasn't. Montana and my mother hadn't directly interacted with me like this, as if we were the same, both figments of the dreamscape we found ourselves in.

I could see the difference between Magnar and his family in this place. He was solid; a more defined object in the centre of everything else. The others only existed in his memory and imagination. But he didn't seem to have realised that I was different yet.

"You didn't look like you needed my help," I said as I walked down what remained of the hill to join them.

Fury fizzled out of existence now that the vampires were gone and my hand was left empty.

Magnar's mother smiled at me, reaching out to tuck my hair behind my ear in a gesture that felt maternal and utterly bewildering. I couldn't remember my own mother doing such things, so accepting that kind of attention from a stranger was more than odd.

I looked up at Magnar and found his eyes shining with joy. This was everything he'd lost. Everything he wished to have back and would never be able to claim. His father had been stolen from him during his lifetime and his mother and brother were lost to the reality of the time that had passed while he slept at the mercy of the gods.

He took a step towards me, and a chill raised goosebumps across my flesh as the wind caressed my skin. I glanced down and found the cotton shift missing from beneath my fighting leathers, the fabric gripping every curve of my body. I was pretty sure my tits were about to bust out of the damn thing at any moment.

What the fuck? I frowned in confusion, wondering if he'd done that intentionally or not. Either way I was going to kick his ass for it.

As I looked up at Magnar again, I found him closer to me, my heart leaping in surprise at the sudden change.

His family were sitting behind him, gathered around a fire which hadn't been there before and the light was shifting, the sun dipping towards the horizon beyond the clouds.

"Look at you, drakaina hjarta," he said roughly, his eyes tracing every inch of my face, his fingertips brushing against my arm.

"Magnar-" I began, meaning to tell him that I was real before demanding answers about this bullshit outfit.

I was more than ready to call him out on his shit, but I didn't think he should say anything else to me without knowing that I was truly in his dream. He might not want me to be here. I was intruding on his thoughts, seeing things which belonged to him, and he shouldn't have to share unwillingly. Even if he was an ass.

"Say that again," he said, his voice low.

"I haven't said anything yet."

"The part where you said my name." His eyes flashed with a wicked realisation and my lips parted as I understood what I'd done.

He was standing so close to me that I could feel the heat from his body, but Idun's rules still had to be keeping him from closing the distance. Except that they hadn't stopped me from speaking his name...

"Magnar," I repeated, and a thrill raced down my spine as his eyes burned like liquid gold.

He lifted a hand and ran his fingers along my jaw before sliding it into my hair and cupping the back of my neck firmly.

My heart pounded as I stood, captured in his gaze while he drank me in, a thousand sins growing in the depths of his eyes, luring me in.

"Why am I dressed like a porno Viking?" I growled, remembering my anger with him over that as he stepped into me, his body pressing flush to mine.

"What's a porno?" he asked, the corner of his mouth twitching with amusement as he looked down at my outfit, taking in the way my tits were close to bursting free of it.

"They're magazines people used to jerk off over before the world fell apart – one of the most valuable trade items I ever found out in the ruins, and they have lots of photographs of women dressed up as ridiculously as this in them."

"What's a photograph?"

I opened my mouth to try and explain that particular technological advancement, but apparently Magnar didn't really care to hear it.

His fingers knotted in my hair, tugging my head back sharply as he leaned in, his stare locked on my mouth. Despite all the reasons I had to kick him in the balls instead of giving in to this, I tilted my chin up as he closed the distance between us. The moment before his lips met mine felt like an eternity which stretched away without end. My whole body ached for him, the heat between us only burning hotter now that we'd been forced apart.

He was a bad idea, the worst fucking idea, and yet I couldn't stop circling the thoughts of his mouth on my body, aching for the press of his skin against mine. A longing grew in the depths of my core, begging him to take me captive despite my better judgement, and he seemed in no way inclined to refuse.

His mouth claimed mine and every inch of my skin came alive beneath his touch as his tongue pressed between my lips and he kissed me like he wanted to devour me. I gripped his forearms, pulling him closer as our kiss deepened, losing myself in the feeling of him even if he was a beast and an asshole and had dreamed me up a ridiculous outfit.

His free hand fell to my ass, and he lifted me into his arms with no effort at all. I wrapped my legs around him, my fingers fisting in his hair as I sank my teeth into his bottom lip, moaning at the feeling of his solid cock driving against my core.

Magnar released my lips, his mouth grazing down my neck, the grip he still held in my hair forcing me to arch my back, exposing my neck as he took command of my body. Clearly Idun's rules didn't extend to our dreams, and he had no problem at all with breaking them here.

"I think I'll play with your body until you're begging for release, then deny it to you in payment for this bond you forced upon me," he growled, yanking my leathers down and forcing my breast free of it. His teeth clamped down on my nipple as I opened my mouth to call him out on that shit, and I cursed his name instead.

Magnar leaned forward suddenly, laying me down on a thick bed of furs which appeared beneath me, his body rearing over mine, his thick length grinding over my clit through the barrier of our clothes.

A tent rose up around us, sealing us away from the world, and I *blinked up at it in surprise, taking in the thick fabric, the scent of smoke in the air, the wholly alien world which appeared so simply around him. This was the world he'd known. The life he'd lived. I wanted to marvel at the magic of the dream, but his presence stole my attention from everything that surrounded us.*

His mouth continued to move across my skin, trailing lower as I moaned in pleasure.

I caught his shirt in my hand and pulled him back, kissing him again as he pressed me down into the furs. Why did it seem so much simpler to do so inside the confines of this dreamscape? Not only because Idun's magic prevented this in reality but also because I felt no inhibitions here, no fear for what might become of us, no anger over what we'd already become. I wanted him and he wanted me. In this place, that was all that seemed to matter.

My grip tightened on his shirt and I wished it wasn't there so I could feel the warmth of his skin against mine. As soon as the thought crossed my mind, it disappeared.

Magnar reared back, glancing down at himself in surprise, and a deep laugh fell from his throat, making my toes curl as his body rocked against mine. I smirked up at him as my fingers slid over his chest, following the curves of his muscles, the savage cuts of his scars and the twisted lines of Norse tattoos.

As I traced a line beneath his heart, I realised the tattoo which should have been there was missing. I frowned at the spot and Magnar followed my gaze. He took my hand in his, lifting it from his chest and raising it to his mouth.

"I never wanted her," he said as if that explained it, his teeth grazing the pads of my fingers. "I wanted the freedom to do this."

"This?" I asked, cocking my head as I watched his expression, noting the darkness which had slipped into his gaze at this topic. "You don't strike me as the chaste type, Magnar. I get the feeling you did this as often as you pleased with as many partners as you desired."

"I'm not talking about fucking, drakaina hjarta," he replied roughly, a tempest building in his golden eyes as he pressed a kiss to my forearm where my slayer's mark stood out against my skin before raising my

hand above my head and pinning it in place. My heart thundered with anticipation as he lowered himself over me.

When he kissed me again, it was filled with more urgency, and his other hand trailed the length of my body before landing on my belt.

He tugged on it, releasing the buckle, and tossing it aside. His hand moved beneath my battle leathers, pushing them up, finding my flesh beneath as he gripped my waist and drew me against him.

I wanted to stay precisely there, to indulge in every one of the promises that each touch of his skin against mine offered, but a nagging voice in the back of my head kept reminding me this wasn't real. And it wasn't honest either. He didn't know that this was truly me.

I gave myself another moment with his weight pressing me into the furs, his mouth on mine, then pulled away from him with a curse.

"Stop," I breathed.

Magnar pulled back and looked down at me, savage amusement dancing across his features. "Are you sure?"

"Not really. You're a lot of things, Magnar, but a bad lay doesn't seem like one of them." I bit my bottom lip as I looked at him, my gaze trailing down his body again before I forced myself to admit what I was. "But I'm not like everything else here."

I wasn't really sure how to tell him that I'd invaded his dream, but it seemed like a pretty important fact given the way we were tangled together.

He tilted his head as if he didn't understand what I was saying, and I released a breath as embarrassment clawed at me.

I waved a hand, demonstrating what I meant by making the tent dissolve around us. We were still laying on the furs, but a clear sky filled with twinkling stars hung above us, a coyote calling to the moon somewhere in the distance.

"Oh, that."

"Yeah, that. Isn't this freaking you out at all? I'm inside your head right now."

"I know," he replied, shrugging one huge shoulder. "My mother was the first of your kind to dream walk. Did you really think I couldn't tell what you were as soon as I saw you?"

My mouth fell open in surprise as I tried to understand why he'd gone along with it for so long if that was the case. Wasn't he pissed at me beyond all reason over the whole vow thing?

"But I thought... don't you care about Idun's rules?" I asked.

"If Idun gave a fuck about us, she wouldn't continually bind us to promises we didn't want to make. She knew what you were to me when you took your vow. Forcing us apart amused her. There was no reason why she couldn't have removed that restriction on us," he growled, and his eyes flashed dangerously.

"But why would she do that?" I didn't understand what the goddess would gain from toying with those who were trying to fulfil her wishes.

"Because she can. She's a jealous, fickle thing and no doubt despised the idea of me lusting after anyone but her. Not that she desires me for herself. My life is simply a game to her." Magnar rolled off of me and cupped the back of his head in his hand as he lay beside me, staring up at the stars, causing them to roll and riot in the sky above while we watched. "She enjoys testing my loyalty." He scratched at the skin above his heart where his tattoo should have been.

"Why don't you have that tattoo here?" I asked.

I could tell he didn't like talking about it, but it was obviously something that mattered to him, and I was sick of secrets and half-truths. My life had been filled with them growing up in the Realm and I just wanted honesty from the world I found myself in now. Even when that truth tended to hold a whole heap of shit within it.

Magnar sighed and I knew he didn't want to answer, but to my surprise, he did. "Before I slept, I was betrothed to a woman I didn't choose for myself."

The sky lightened abruptly, and I sat up as I found myself beside a huge fire and surrounded by more canvas tents than I could count, an entire Viking campsite unfurling around us at nothing more than a thought from Magnar. A wooden log formed beneath my ass, and we sat on it as Magnar's people moved about us, laughing and eating, an entire world coming to life before my eyes. One which had died a thousand years ago for me but couldn't have seemed like more than a few months ago to him.

A woman stepped between a pair of tents on the far side of the fire and walked towards us. Her dark hair was delicately coiled into braids along one side of her head and her blue dress hugged her figure, everything about her seeming so carefully constructed, at a contrast to the brutal war camp she passed through. She had deep eyes and full lips which pulled up into a smile as she approached Magnar, but he gave her no such look in reply.

"There you are, husband. I came looking for you in your tent last night, but I must have missed you. Were you walking in the rain again?" Her tone was playful, and she dropped down into the space between us, forcing me to shift along or risk her ass landing on my knee. I frowned between them, that title making my gut knot, suspicion writhing through me.

She placed her hand on Magnar's thigh, leaning close to him suggestively, and my posture tightened uncomfortably as the memory played out. She was beautiful in a very precise way, every movement she made seeming practiced, flawless, designed to attract attention. Her pale skin was unblemished, not even a freckle to be seen, and her voice was low and seductive.

"I told you not to call me that. I'm not your husband yet," Magnar replied, and though he appeared relaxed, I was sure I could detect irritation lacing his tone.

"Well, if you keep me waiting much longer, I may just have to set the date myself. It's been three years, Magnar. You can't keep hiding behind the desire for revenge." Her hand shifted further up his thigh, and I wondered how she managed to press on with her point while his face turned stony, the warrior in him rising to the surface of his skin. I half expected him to stab her at any moment, and I had to admit she was tenacious as she refused to back down despite the warning signs he was giving off. "Your father would want you to be happy, he wouldn't have expected you to wait so long to live your own life-"

"Don't presume to know what my father would have wanted," Magnar snapped, pushing her hand off his leg. "And you forget that I am the Earl now. I decide when marriages should take place, and there have been no signs to suggest I should prioritise ours. The gods demand *justice for our people, they have no interest in our union."*

"You swore an oath to me," she hissed and the hairs on the back of my neck stood up at the sudden shift in her tone. I got the distinct feeling that she wasn't the type to back down to anyone and that this argument wasn't the first they'd had on this subject.

"And I have the scar to prove it," he spat. "I have not broken my word. We are betrothed just as the prophet said we would be. But until I rid the world of the Revenants, I have no intention of taking the arrangement any further."

Magnar stood and strode away. The woman stared after him with her chin held high. Instead of the tears I expected, an icy steel formed in her gaze as though she was figuring out her next move, plotting instead of retreating. I got the impression she wasn't going to accept that answer without a fight.

She fizzled out of existence, and I flinched as I found Magnar sitting on my other side. He was no longer lost to the memory but sat looking at me expectantly, like he wondered what I made of the woman he had been betrothed to.

"Why didn't you want to marry her?" I asked.

"Many reasons. But the main one was that I didn't love her. Marriage seems like one hell of a cage to lock yourself into with the wrong person. The gods demanded my betrothal, that was enough chains." He shrugged and looked away from me, frowning into the fire, his jaw ticking with irritation.

"So when you tried to warn me that taking my vow might mean I had to accept a husband I hadn't chosen, it was because you knew how that felt?"

"Your heart should be your own to give or refuse. No matter what path you choose to follow in this life."

The wind picked up and he caught my hair as it blew across my face. He swept it aside, cupping my cheek in his calloused palm. The fire disappeared and the tent sprang up around us once more, leaving us alone again.

"If I was allowed to choose, I'd pick my own path. One that forced nothing on me and demanded only the blood of my enemies."

I looked into his golden eyes, my body aching with the desire to taste his mouth again. I bit down on my lip to try and hold back the urge to follow that impulse.

"Why is it so easy to forget all of the shit between us here? I know that I'm pissed at you for that control bullshit, I know that I should want to punch you at least as much as I want to bite your lip instead of my own, and yet, right now, option B is far outweighing the others."

"That's because dreams tend to be either good or bad. Perhaps if you'd come calling on me in a nightmare, this might have played out differently, but unless you twist it to become such a thing, I think you'll be begging me to taste your sweet cunt again in a matter of seconds-"

I punched him squarely in the chest just for being a cocky asshole, then climbed into his lap and bit his lip hard enough to draw blood.

Magnar laughed into my mouth, his hands gripping my ass as he tugged me down against him, rolling his hips beneath me so that I could feel every rock solid inch of him grinding against my clit.

Every fibre of my body came alive beneath the touch of his lips against mine, the taste of his blood staining my tongue. And I ached for more of him, consumed by the desire to give myself to this feeling. I was standing on the edge of a precipice, and it took everything I had not to fling myself off.

I ran my fingertips across his jaw, smiling as his stubble grazed my skin. He was the perfect sin, just waiting for me to fall to ruin at his feet.

His hands pushed beneath my leathers, skimming the skin at the base of my spine, and I arched my back, moulding my body to his.

I pulled away and cursed as I looked into his eyes.

"None of this is real though, is it? I can't really say your name or do this..." I trailed my hand down his chest, holding his gaze as I skimmed his waistband and his grip on me tightened.

"It feels pretty real," he countered.

I rested my fingertips on his belt buckle. "But it's not."

His gaze slid over me and he grunted in acceptance. "No. It's not. But you're unlike any slayer ever born, drakaina hjarta. If you can master your connection to your gifts, you won't need me to teach you for long. And once you aren't my novice, you can come climb into my lap and beg me to do whatever it is that's dancing through that dirty mind of yours."

"I keep telling you, you'll be the one begging, asshole." I rolled my eyes, but my mind reeled with the implications of what he was saying. If it was true, then maybe I would be able to break free of his control over me sooner than I'd hoped.

His thumbs brushed across the curve of my hips and his gaze travelled over me in a way that made me feel like he was about to test my resolve in halting this. A knot of longing tightened my muscles and the temptation to change my mind pulled at me, but I shook my head.

I forced myself to reject the temptation and a thick coat formed over my body. Magnar's battle leathers returned too, and he released a breath of disappointment.

"This dream is turning into a nightmare," he growled.

"I'm worth the wait," I countered.

He leaned closer and kissed me one last time, his hands pushing through my hair and igniting a flame in the pit of my stomach.

"You will be," he promised, and my body trembled with the insinuation as the dream slipped away and I was drawn back to our confined hiding place on the train where the laws of the vow flared into place and ensured we couldn't cross that line in reality. Not until Idun decided to have mercy, but I had the feeling she was not a merciful being and I was far from done witnessing the depths of her scorn.

MONTANA

CHAPTER NINETEEN

I walked along the quiet streets, sensing eyes on me from the surrounding windows. The wind picked up, tugging my hair out behind me, and Julius's cloak fluttered around my legs.

My pulse thumped to a wild rhythm as I took this stand against the vampires, the whole city shut down because of the plan I'd concocted with the slayer who had been causing chaos for the royals.

If the gods truly existed, I reckoned they would be watching now, turning their gaze towards the lone human striding into the heart of the beasts' lair, the deadly creatures subdued by the sun that blazed at my back.

As I closed in on the castle grounds, a dark car sailed towards me with blacked-out windows, and I raised my chin to face it head on.

A feeling in my soul told me Erik was inside, and as the vehicle rolled to a halt before me, he stepped out of the driver's seat. He'd come alone. Perhaps tipped off by one of the many onlooking vampires.

Everything about him appeared more feral than before, his shirt creased, untucked, his hair a mess of dark strands, but it was his grey eyes that held the wildest chaos.

My heart pounded fiercely at the sight of him, my feet coming to a halt as I gazed upon my captor with his entire empire clamped in my fist.

He winced against the beating sun and dark veins spread out around his eyes, proving he wasn't immune to its effects.

With a flash of movement, he was gone, and my heart jolted violently as he appeared behind me, capturing my throat and yanking me flush against him.

"Rebel," he growled in my ear, and a shiver chased its way all the way down my spine.

I held my nerve, my hands balling tightly at my sides.

"I hear you've been looking for me," I said lightly, and he released a low growl.

"I've been hunting for you from dusk 'til dawn. Have you returned to me as you promised upon choosing me?"

"I don't recall making any promises," I lied.

"And yet here you are."

He released my throat and twisted me around in his arms, his hand moving to grip my chin instead.

"Did he hurt you?" he asked roughly, inspecting me for injuries, turning my head to one side as if he expected to find bruises.

"No," I said, batting his hand away. "And I haven't come running back to you like an obedient little human if that's what you think."

He snarled, but I realised it wasn't at me, his eyes flicking to the sky and the dark veins around his eyes deepening. The sun was taking its toll on him, and though I'd expected to feel satisfied watching him hurt, a knot formed in my chest instead.

"You have to get out of the sun," I said quietly.

Nodding stiffly, he caught my hand as if he expected me to run away, guiding me to the passenger's seat and steering me inside the car.

He dropped into the driver's side a second later, slamming the door with a groan of relief.

"What the fuck is Valentina playing at?" He gazed out at the sky with concern, then turned to me with a fierce look. "How are you here? How did you escape?"

"We should go somewhere private. To talk." I tore my eyes away from him, gazing firmly out of the window. I had to stick to my plan. I couldn't let him rattle me.

"What does that mean?" he growled.

"It means we need to talk," I said simply.

"I need to go to Valentina's apartment," he said decisively, and I shook my head.

"She's not there. And you won't find out where she is until after we've spoken."

"I cannot very well leave the sun shining and disabling my entire city," he snapped.

"How many more times do I have to say it? Do as I tell you, or you'll never get your precious clouds back." I shot him a hard glare and he stared back at me in shock, his muscles tightening.

We remained in that intense stand-off until he muttered something under his breath and turned the car around.

"Put your seatbelt on," he commanded, and the warning in his voice had me doing as he said.

The moment I had it in place, he slammed his foot to the accelerator and we sped up the road, the momentum pressing me back into my seat.

He didn't drive to the castle as I expected but headed onto a highway, driving at a terrifying pace, avoiding old, rusted cars which had been abandoned sometime in the past, weaving between them so suddenly that it made my breath halt in my lungs. When I realised we were leaving the city, uncertainty ran through me.

"Where are we going?"

"To our place in Westchester," he said, his jaw ticking with frustration. "You want privacy? You're about to get it."

He reached into the pocket of the door, taking out a pair of sunglasses and sliding them on.

My throat thickened as we tore along the road toward a patch of green in the distance, mentally preparing what I was going to say to him. It had to be delivered perfectly, every word tempered with confidence. I wasn't going to let him get me on the back foot ever again. It was my turn to play games, and he'd better dance to my tune or I'd never return Valentina to him.

We finally rolled up to the iron gates of Erik's property in the suburbs, tall brick walls stretching away into the distance either side of it. A guard stood outside with a black umbrella above his head, his body tucked in tight beneath it and a look of worry about him. His skin looked kind of shiny, and I noticed a bottle of sunscreen poking out of his pocket, though surely that wouldn't make any difference to his predicament.

Erik rolled his window down a crack as the vampire stumbled over, wincing as he moved.

"By the gods, what are you still doing out here?" Erik demanded.

"It's my duty, sir," the vampire replied in a desperately dry voice, sounding like he was parched beyond belief.

"What's your name?" Erik asked.

"Egbert, sir." He bowed low, then yelped as the sun fell over his ass as it escaped the shade of his umbrella.

"Report to me after your shift. You deserve a fucking promotion."

Egbert's eyes widened with awe. "Absolutely, your highness. Thank you, thank you." He stood upright, scurrying over to the gate and punching in a code on a keypad, letting out tiny yelps every time he did so, and I noticed a few blisters on his fingertips. I almost felt bad for the guy.

The gates parted and Erik drove us up the gravel drive toward his large log home which had arching windows at either end of it. I hadn't had much of a chance to admire it from the outside before, and this place was something from a fairy tale. A woodland sat off to one side of the property and huge oak trees cast shade over the far side of the slate roof. A winding path led away into the woodland, and birdsong carried through the air like the softest kind of music.

The sun shone down on the garden, bringing the green grass out in a vivid colour, the morning dew glittering in the light. I'd nearly forgotten what it was like to see the sun in full force. It was dazzling. Freeing. And it gave me a strength I never wanted to be rid of.

Erik parked as close to the house as possible and yanked up the parking brake, tossing his sunglasses onto the dashboard with a clatter. He gazed out at the sunlight with a flicker of unease in his eyes. Shoving the door open, he moved around the car in a blur, yanking my door wide before I had a moment to do it myself. He lifted me into his arms and my stomach lurched as he took off at the same impossible pace.

In seconds, we were inside, and my head spun as he planted me on my feet.

"What's going on?" he demanded, giving me a hard look that told me to behave. But that was the last thing I planned on doing.

I wet my lips, gazing around the quiet hallway, the dark wood floors and scent of cedar and rain everywhere, like this house was an extension of him.

"I'd like to sit down," I said, figuring I was going to make the most out of having this power over him. He sure as shit had done the same when he'd been in control of me, and I wasn't going to make this easy on him. "And I want a glass of water. And a sandwich."

"A sandwich," he deadpanned.

"Yes, a nice one." I folded my arms.

"Anything else?" he clipped.

"That'll do. For now."

"Come," he growled, capturing my hand and dragging me further into the house.

We arrived in the open plan lounge and kitchen area, and he nudged me down onto the couch but remained on his feet, staring down at me. I ground my teeth, irritated by his attempt to intimidate me.

"Well?" I prompted and I could tell it was taking every ounce of restraint he possessed not to lose his shit.

He shot into the kitchen in a blur, filling a glass with water, grabbing two slices of bread and slapping two pieces of cheese into the middle of it.

"With mayonnaise," I said lightly, and he growled in anger before snatching a jar from the fridge, fetching a knife and making one holy hell of a mess as he spread it onto the bread with wild abandon. I'd tried the sauce at one of my evening meals at the castle, and the taste had made me groan. There was far better food in the world than I'd ever been aware of, and I was still discovering new ones every day.

"Have you never made a sandwich before?" I frowned at his poor attempt.

"No, actually," he muttered.

"Oh, right," I said in realisation. "Forgot you were a thousand-year-old undead monster for a second there."

He tossed the hastily made sandwich onto a plate, then strode over to me with it in one hand and the glass of water in the other. "Here."

He placed them down on a side table and I took a sip of the water, biding my time as he just stood there with his jaw ticking. Damn, he was hot when he was angry. Which was pretty much all the time, unless he was bored.

I took a bite of my sandwich – which was seriously good compared to the dry shit I'd been given to eat in the Realm - and Erik released a low growl as I took my time over it.

"Your presentation leaves a lot to be desired, but fuck me, that tastes good." I took another bite and his gaze narrowed.

"You are testing my patience," he warned.

I sighed and placed my sandwich down, preparing to deliver the blow of what I'd done. "Julius and I have taken Valentina hostage."

I took out Valentina's phone, holding it up and playing the video.

Several painful seconds of silence rang out as he stared at it. His eyes narrowed, his nostrils flared. Then his fury unleashed full force. "You did what?!"

I fought a flinch at his ferocious tone, leaping to my feet so I didn't feel so vulnerable beneath him. "I will not be your prisoner again, Erik. I needed some leverage on you. And now I have it. The sun."

His mouth parted and he gazed at me in utter disbelief. He grabbed me by the shoulders, staring right at me with his penetrating eyes, pulling me close and making my heart beat erratically.

"How many more times are you going to surprise me? Fuck calling you 'rebel'. You're a hurricane. A goddamn mercenary. You've taken on the whole city single-handedly."

A grin pulled at my mouth and pride swelled inside me. "Not quite single-handedly."

His eyes darkened to pitch. "Julius Elioson." He plucked at the cloak around my shoulders, then tore it from my back, throwing it to the floor. "You're going to tell me where he is this instant."

"No, I'm not actually." I folded my arms and his jaw flexed in agitation. "You don't hold the reins anymore, Erik. *I* do."

I could see I had him right where I wanted him, and it felt damn good after everything he'd put me through. Never in all my life had I held power over a creature such as him, but to claim it over one of the vampires who had declared himself a prince of my land was satisfying beyond words.

"By the gods, what am I going to do with you?" He carved his fingers through his hair, and I took in the toll I'd taken on him. The frustration in his eyes, the stress etched into his perfect features. He was a monarch on his knees, and I was the one who'd put him there.

"Firstly, you're going to tell me about the prophecy." I jutted up my chin and his brows arched in surprise.

"You know?"

"I know," I replied. "And Julius and I have some theories that I need to discuss with you. And Andvari, too."

He rubbed his temples with one hand as if this was giving him a headache, though whether his kind could feel things like that, I didn't know. "Can you stop mentioning that slayer as if he's your fucking partner?"

"Well, in a way, he is," I said, unable to resist the chance to jab at him some more.

His lips pressed into a hard line. "You've clearly had a lot to say to each other."

"Yeah, I learned a lot. Remembered some stuff too. Like where I belong."

"Which is where exactly?" he asked sharply.

"Far away from here. Somewhere with people who treat me like an equal."

A V formed between his brows. "Well, rebel, this really is quite the stand you're making." His tone dropped to a dangerous level and heat burned deep in my bones, spreading out into every corner of my body. "I suppose you have more demands you'd like to air?"

"Yes." My mouth was dry as I readied to spell this out for him. I had to say this right. To stand my ground and make Erik bow to my wishes. "I'm giving you until sundown to take me to Andvari. To tell me everything you know about the prophecy and…" I took a breath, preparing to reveal the final blow. "Then you're going to let me return to Julius, no questions asked."

Erik looked like he was about to spontaneously combust, anger flowing freely through his eyes. "You expect me to let you go back to a fucking *slayer*? An enemy of the empire? A man who has killed my people, murdered them in cold blood. Sabrina was my best guard for over four hundred years and now she lies in an urn. Do you understand the magnitude of what you are doing right now? I am not someone to be blackmailed."

"But you had no problem blackmailing *me*. Hanging my family over my head. My dad-" I choked on the word and turned sharply away from him, determined not to let him see me come undone. "My dad is dead because you sent a bloodthirsty monster to retrieve him."

"I know," Erik breathed, and I sensed he was inches behind me, moving ever-silently. "And I…I'm so sorry, Montana. So deeply sorry I cannot even begin to express it."

Those words were my undoing, the cage trapping my grief splitting open and baring my soul for all to see. Tears made it free of my eyes and a heavy sob racked through my chest. I didn't want to break, but I'd been choking down these emotions for too long, and with his apology, something shattered in me. Because all I wanted was to hate him, but part of me knew that Wolfe was truly to blame and that Erik's words were sincere. He had never meant for this to happen. And I didn't think it was just to keep me under his thumb; he understood the importance of family. It was all he had, just as it was all I had. The only people he cared about in this wretched world.

I may have wanted to dismiss the vampires as soulless beings with no capability of such things, but I just couldn't do it anymore. And it changed everything. So deeply that I didn't think I would ever be the same woman I was before I left the Realm.

Erik tentatively slid an arm around me, and I fought the urge to lean into his embrace, needing someone, anyone in that moment. But it shouldn't have been him I turned to. If Callie could see me now, she'd be sick to her stomach.

I pulled away, taking a deep breath before turning back to him, harnessing my pain. "The sun stays out until you've given me what I asked for."

His brows lowered and unease crept over his features. "I will. But you never needed to force me, rebel. I would have given you anything you wanted regardless."

"Even letting me return to Julius?" I scoffed.

His eyes clouded, jaw tight. "No…not that."

"Then here we are," I announced, pushing my shoulders back. "So, are you going to tell me about the prophecy?"

"I need to tell you something else first." His adam's apple bobbed and he reached for my hand, his cool fingers winding around mine, and a foolish, twisted piece of me had missed that feeling. "I have been a man adrift in a sea of chaos for an unknowable amount of years. It took losing you to find myself. To remember some of what I once was. My desire to keep you is purely selfish, I know that. But every day you are with me, I think I regain a little more of myself. It's like catching drops of moonlight. There was a moment in the midst of the night that I thought I may never see you again, and I cannot tell you the depths of fear that caused me. I've known you for so little time, and really, I know you hardly at all. But I want to. Because in a thousand years of torment, you are the first thing to break the monotony of my immortality. You have awoken me to the world again."

"Erik," I breathed, his words powerful enough to rock the foundations of my soul.

"You're still my fiancée," he added.

I ground my teeth, tugging my hand away, the sweet moment shattering just like that. "I'm not a willing fiancée. And I don't intend on going through with the wedding."

He released a feral growl which sent electricity right down to my toes. "You *chose* me."

"To protect my father," I said coolly. "I never wanted to choose anyone. And now my choice is void because you didn't protect him, did you?"

"I tried."

"You failed," I spat. "You may have apologised, you may even be capable of really regretting it, but you can't change it. So, what difference does it make? You're full of pretty words, Erik, but where are your actions to match it?"

I tried to turn from him again, but he pulled me to him, bringing my fingers to his lips and grazing his mouth across my knuckles.

"Then don't forgive me," he said darkly. "You want actions? Then strike at me. You carry your slayer blade still, so draw it and wield it against your enemy."

He dropped my hand and pulled his shirt off, dropping it to the floor and turning his palms out towards me to show he wouldn't fight.

"Stop it," I rasped, taking in his muscular body, the tension lining his broad shoulders, his skin like moonlight given life.

"Do what you must," he insisted. "Take your price from my flesh. Scar me or kill me. The choice is yours."

"This is a test, isn't it?" I said, shaking my head at him in disbelief. "Or another trick."

"There is only one way to find out," he said, grey eyes fixed on mine.

He was so much bigger than me, imposing in every way and so beautiful it hurt to gaze upon his face. He had been my affliction far too long, a nightmare constructed to haunt me. And the anger of it all welled over, the injustice of what he'd done, not just to me but to humankind, spilling through me in a torrent. He was offering me an end to all that, a chance at vengeance. And how could I refuse it?

I took Nightmare into my hand and the blade buzzed frantically, though it felt more like a warning than a plea for blood. I was too focused on the task to pay it much heed, a frantic energy racing through me as I raised the slayer blade and held the tip just shy of Erik's chest, aimed right at his hollow heart.

"I hate you," I growled, the hurt over my father's loss tearing through the centre of me.

"Then prove it, rebel," he pushed, and I pressed the blade to his skin, making him bare his teeth as the metal singed him.

"You'll have to try harder than that," he goaded me, and I pressed harder still until a bright red drop of blood spilled, sailing down his skin.

My eyes flicked up to meet his and I saw the cracks of humanity in his eyes, the man he had once been standing in the wake of a god's wrathful curse. And it hurt me to see the suffering in his eyes, wishing I could free the man trapped in this beast instead of casting him to ash alongside it.

Before I even realised I'd made the decision, Nightmare slipped from my grasp, hitting the floor with a dull thunk, and I wasn't sure which of us moved first, only that we were colliding, mouths coming together with a tangible want that went beyond anything I had ever felt before.

His hands snared me as I looped my own around his neck, arching into him and tasting the desire on his tongue.

"Hate is superior to love," he spoke against my hungry lips. "Its fire burns hotter than any hellfire, but you've made me believe there is a greater desire that lives between the two, neither one nor the other, forged from the most destructive elements of both."

"I can believe that," I said breathlessly, my nails biting into his neck as I tiptoed up, our lips meeting again and moving together. Heat burned deep in my core and lust drove me to the brink of madness as he crushed me against him, my breaths coming heavier.

"I don't want you almost as much as I do want you," I admitted. "And I despise the part of me that needs this."

"I'll never be good for you," he said gruffly, his warning lost to my lips as our kiss deepened once more, my hands trailing down his muscular arms, his cool skin like frost against my fingertips. "And I do not hold enough morality to stop this, but I must know the answer to this if I am to prepare myself for it…are you going to leave forever when you return to Julius?"

"You'll really let me go?" I asked, leaning back, though his hands were still firm on my spine, keeping our bodies pressed together.

"You have given me little choice," he muttered, and venom flowed between us once more, the stark truth that he wouldn't free me if he could get away with it. I'd still be his prisoner now if it wasn't for

Julius. And that truth made me bitter all over again.

I hadn't thought far beyond what would happen once I left Erik. I had to hear what Andvari said first, but if the prophecy didn't actually involve me, what then?

The answer was obvious. I'd run. Leave the city and go in search of my sister.

"That would be best," I admitted. "This thing between us doesn't lead anywhere good."

"I cannot promise I won't look for you,' he said.

"Even if I don't want to be found?" I questioned thickly.

"Tell me then, that you never wish to see me again."

The intensity of his stare seared right to my soul, and I found myself unable to lie. Because that was what it would have been if I declared outright that I could walk away without ever thinking of him, without a small part of me hoping we would share another moment together.

"I deserve more than a prison for a life," I said instead. "If you cared about me, you'd let me walk away."

"But I could give you everything," he said, sincerity lacing his voice.

"Everything except freedom," I said. "Your cages are far prettier than the one I'm used to, but they're still cages."

"You can have anything from me if you choose to stay."

"I will never choose to keep shackles on my wrists," I said passionately.

He gazed at me, unmoving, becoming as still as a predator in the grass, but for once, he wasn't hunting. He was contemplating the world laid at his feet, and I wondered when the last time was that he had been refused his desires.

"Let's talk about the prophecy," he muttered, dropping onto an armchair, his mood sullied.

"Okay," I agreed, not wanting to dwell on the twisted craving inside me.

I was so goddamn confused, torn apart by logic and emotion. My family would have been horrified to learn of my confliction, and that knowledge forced me to bury this distress deep and refuse to acknowledge it.

"What did Julius tell you?" Erik asked, and I noted his ire at speaking the slayer's name.

"You really hate him," I stated, and he nodded stiffly.

"Julius and his family terrorised me and my siblings for years, hunting us like animals with the sole desire of ending our lives. So forgive me if I am not more delighted by his reappearance."

"Well maybe he had reason to, considering you turned his father into a vampire and sent him back to his clan to kill his people."

Erik's eyes turned to stone. "That is not how it happened. And I am not going to waste time discussing an event that occurred a thousand years ago. Tell me what the slayer said to you about the prophecy."

I sighed, relaying what Julius and I had discussed. Erik listened patiently, his hands stacked on his lap. If he was concerned, he didn't show it. But when I revealed our suspicions that the prophecy involved me and Callie, he leapt from his seat.

"I have wondered that myself," he said, a hopeful light entering his eyes.

I wanted to tell him that I already knew his thoughts on the subject, call him out on everything he had said in that room with the other royals while Julius and I had been listening in, but I wasn't going to give away the slayer's access to their cameras.

"I need to speak with Andvari. You have a way, don't you?" I pushed, thinking of his bedroom at the castle and the eerie voice I'd heard in there.

"Yes," Erik said. "I can speak with him through mirrors."

"Then what are we waiting for?" I took a step toward the exit, but Erik shot into my way in a surge of movement.

"I will do it alone."

"No," I said immediately. "It's my fate too. I want to hear it for myself."

He ran a hand down the back of his neck. "Rebel…"

"Erik." I folded my arms, his stubbornness only reflected back at him.

A glimmer flickered in his eyes, amusement making his lips twist up at the corner. "Fine, but you must promise me something first."

I nodded slowly, my eyes narrowing.

"That today will not be the last day I ever spend with you."

It seemed like such an easy promise to make, but it would be a cardinal sin cast against my name too. Because if I agreed, I knew it wouldn't be purely out of the need for him to take me to Andvari, it would be to feed the dark creature in me who yearned for Erik Belvedere.

But if I gave this vampire an inch, he would take a mile. The city was suffocating, and all of their rules and tricks were too much to bear. I didn't want to stay.

"I can't promise that," I exhaled.

"Then at least tell me this…" He stepped closer, his eyes a sea of ink. "If your darkest desires could speak for you, what would they choose?"

A burning sensation grew in my throat, and my heart fought against my ribcage like it was trying to escape my chest.

"You know the answer to that," I murmured, trying to step past him, but he caught my arm.

"Yes, but I believe it will do you good to admit it. You should never feel shame for the pieces of you that lie in the shade."

"There's damn good reason for that shame. It's trying to keep me safe."

"I would never hurt you."

"Wanting you is hurting me. You stand for everything I hate. And if I give in to it, then it insults the life I've led, it insults the people I love."

"Humans have such a short time here in this world. I've seen them come and go like flashes of fire in a scalding pan. All you have is the chance to burn as brightly as you can while you're here, and if you live your life in the pursuit of ideals, you will never truly live."

"So, I should forgo my morals for the sake of petty lust?" I scoffed.

"No," he growled. "That was not the intention of my words."

"Then what was the intention?" I demanded.

"Follow the path your heart yearns for deepest," he said. "If that path leads you away from me, then so be it. But you'd best be honest with yourself and leave no room for error, rebel, because today's choices are tomorrow's regrets. Humans do not get the luxury of a do-over."

"I know my own mind. I'll make the right choice."

"Just do it for you, not for your sister, or society," he insisted.

"There's merit in sacrifice, in following the path that's right and in protecting myself from my own detrimental wants," I said.

"Is it me you're convincing, or yourself?"

I glared at him, done with this conversation.

"Take me to Andvari," I commanded, my blood feeling all too hot in my veins. "I think you've forgotten who's in charge here, and you're wasting my time."

"As you wish, rebel," he said, features grave. "But I hope you're prepared to meet the wicked creature who made me. Because if the vampires frighten you, you will not know peace in the face of the gods."

CALLIE

CHAPTER TWENTY

I kept my eyes closed despite the fact I'd woken as soon as I'd left Magnar's dream behind. The place between our minds felt separate to who we were. Had I just been kissing him or not? Did the fact that we'd just shared a dream change anything about how we acted going forward?

"You're you again," Magnar said, his voice low so that it wouldn't carry.

I opened my eyes and looked up at him from beneath my lashes. "What do you mean?"

"Your face is no longer that of a vampire. Idun stuck to her word for once. Thank fuck for that."

I raised a hand to my face, my thumb brushing over my bottom lip as I tried to figure out if I felt any different. I wasn't sure if Idun had actually done anything to me physically or if it had just been a mirage. Either way, I was pleased to be myself again. Resembling a vampire was enough to make my stomach turn.

"You didn't think it was an improvement then?" I asked, lifting an eyebrow in amusement.

"Their type of beauty isn't appealing to me in any way. A stone may be filled with colour, but it will never hold warmth or life. I would sooner have your face precisely as it is, not carved from porcelain and hiding poison."

"You'd just prefer it if I dressed myself in revealing battle leathers?" I asked, raising an eyebrow.

Magnar snorted in amusement. "They lacked practicality, but they held a certain appeal. If it had truly been a dream version of you, I imagine you'd have remained silent for far more of it though."

"Sorry I lack the preferred control over my smart mouth," I scoffed.

Magnar laughed. "I'm sure I could find a way to silence it given less interference from the gods."

"Well, in the meantime, you'll just have to make do with admiring my perfect face," I taunted, reminding him of what he'd said about me before.

Magnar let out a deep breath. "Vanity doesn't suit you."

"Oh, I disagree. In fact, now that I have your indisputable testimony to my perfection, my ego has increased beyond limit. If we ever find any other mortals out here in the wilds, I'll be sure to fuck as many hot men as I can get my hands on without ever having to question their attraction to me or waste time on flirting."

"You won't fuck any man while you're under my protection," Magnar growled darkly, his voice thick with that raw power, his words wrapping me up in knots and binding me to them.

"Oh, fuck you," I snarled, punching him in the bicep hard enough to make my fist ache.

"If that dream is anything to go by, that's precisely what you're hoping I'll do," he taunted, catching my wrist when I swung for him again and dragging me close enough to taste his breath on my lips.

"It was *your* dream, not mine." I scowled at him, and he gave me a taunting grin before releasing me as fast as he'd caught me.

"Keep telling yourself that. Maybe I should start demanding a more respectful attitude from my novice though. I'll have to think up ways to punish you every time you're disrespectful or indecent."

"Me, indecent? That's rich compared to you, barbarian." I rolled my eyes.

"You have no idea just how indecent I can be."

I fixed my attention on my boots, ignoring the way his voice made my skin prickle.

"Just so long as you don't hog-tie me to a horse any time soon, we'll be good,"

"Don't tempt me. Besides, I could command you to be as respectful as I desire," he reminded me, and I pursed my lips at the thought of it.

"You *could*. But I think you secretly enjoy me taunting you," I pointed out.

"Just as you secretly like being told what to do."

I scowled at him in response to that. "I'm sure you wish that was true. It would make me so much better suited to your company."

"I think you're well enough suited to me as you are." Magnar looked at me with enough intensity to make me squirm, the proximity of his body to mine making my blood pump far faster than it needed to.

Now that we were back under the restrictions Idun had placed upon us, all I could think about was the way his body had felt pressed to mine in that dream. And the fact that I was unable to lay so much as a finger on him only made the lust I felt for him sharpen.

I shifted slightly, trying to release the tension in my shoulders from spending hours sitting up, jammed against the wall. My neck was stiff too and I longed to climb out of our uncomfortable hiding place and stretch my limbs. Heaven only knew how bad Magnar was feeling; he was twice my size and had spent over an hour packed into a crate before joining me here.

The train coasted to a stop, and I held my breath as silence fell over everything.

I leaned to my left, looking through the small gap between the crates as I waited to see what would happen now. Ideally, we wanted to make it off the train unnoticed, but hopefully it wouldn't be the end of the world if we were seen. I was doubtful that the vampires would have any suspicions about the blood being tainted; no poison should have been capable of killing a vampire, so they'd have no reason to fear it. But if we wanted the element of surprise on our side when we staged our rescue attempt on Montana, then it would be better if they didn't know we'd crossed the country.

I wanted to ask Magnar what to do but I was afraid to disturb the unnatural silence, certain the bloodsuckers had to be close. I strained my ears, trying to hear some sound of the vampires disembarking. The train was stacked with valuable cargo. So why wasn't anyone coming to unload it?

A heavy hiss sounded and a door slid open on the opposite side of the train.

Magnar leaned closer to me so that he could peer through the gap too, the rough bite of his stubble grazing against my jaw.

Blazing sunlight poured inside, and longing stirred within my gut. It was like my soul ached for the sun's warmth on my skin.

Still no sound came. No vampires appeared to unload the cargo. Nothing.

"Do you think they've figured out we're onboard?" I breathed as the seconds dragged. "Maybe they're waiting for us to come out of hiding?"

"Perhaps," Magnar replied slowly. "Either way we can't stay here all day."

He shifted forward and began to shove the crate out of our way. My heart seized as it scraped across the floor, the noise sounding a hundred times louder in the deathly silence.

Magnar crawled out and stood in the centre of the carriage, looking around carefully before beckoning me to follow him.

He gave me his hand and pulled me to my feet. My muscles tingled in a way that was close to painful as the blood flow returned to them after hours cramped in the tiny space, but I ignored the discomfort and focused on our surroundings.

Magnar rolled his shoulders, stretching his limbs and releasing the tension from his muscles.

I placed a hand on Fury, but the blade was surprisingly calm... almost happy. It was like it knew something I didn't.

"What's going on?" I whispered.

Magnar removed the lid from the crate that hid our supplies and handed me my dark blue coat. I pulled off the red one I'd been using to disguise myself as an Elite and threw it into the crate in its place. He wrapped his fur cloak over his shoulders and replaced Venom and Tempest in the sheaths across his back.

Finally, he lifted the pack filled with our waning supplies onto his shoulders, then he shoved the lid back onto the crate before sliding it into line again.

I eyed the open door at the end of the carriage with mistrust. Where were the vampires? Why would they leave the cargo sitting here like this? It felt like a trap, but then why hadn't they sprung it yet?

Magnar stepped in front of me, drawing Venom as he headed for the door on silent feet. I stayed close behind him holding Fury ready too, reaching for my gifts and letting the lessons of my ancestors spill through my body.

As Magnar made it to the door, he paused, and then a soft laugh fell from his lips.

"The gods are smiling on us," he said, stepping aside so I could see past him.

Blazing sunlight brighter than I'd ever seen poured down from the heavens, filling every shadow. It heated the air so it was impossibly warm for the time of year and my coat quickly began to feel like a prison for my skin.

"What does this mean for the vampires?" I asked as I peered up at the periwinkle blue sky.

The colour woke something primal in my blood, and I could feel it flowing through my limbs, energising me and filling me with the desire to act. I wanted to run, stretch my legs, and push my body to its limits. A smile tugged at my lips as I realised what I yearned for: I wanted to hunt the vampires.

"They cannot function in the sunlight. It weakens them immeasurably. The lesser vampires will be reduced to little more than breathing husks if they are caught in it. The Elite and the Belvederes can resist it a little, but they will be slowed to the point of causing us no challenge at all. They will not be released from its power until the sun sets or the clouds reclaim the sky."

"So that's why no one has come to unload the train?" I asked. "They can't face the sunlight?"

The idea of it forced a laugh from my chest. We were surrounded by vampires and yet they couldn't make a move towards us, couldn't even bear to peer out of a window where they might be able to see us. They all cowered inside, hiding from the thing which gave everything life. It was as though the sun highlighted what they were; there was no place for the dead beneath its rays.

"Come, we should get away from here while the gods are feeling generous." Magnar stepped into the sunshine, and I followed him.

I tilted my chin up, taking a moment to bathe in the heat washing over my skin. My coat was stifling, so I pulled it off, wanting to be free of it to feel more of the sun's touch.

The platform stretched out on either side of us, and I turned, trying to figure out which way we should go.

To our left, sparkling skyscrapers reached up towards the sun, bigger than any I'd ever seen in the Realm or the ruins surrounding it. They glinted in the dazzling light, promising wealth, and luxury beyond their walls. I had no doubt that that was where the vampires lived. We would only need to locate the most ostentatious building of all to find the Belvederes and my sister.

I took a step in that direction, but Magnar caught my arm, halting me. A deep frown had formed between his brows and his grip on Venom was so tight that his knuckles were turning white.

"It can't be..." he breathed.

"What is it?" I asked, glancing around nervously at the abandoned platform.

Magnar didn't reply. He turned away from the glimmering city abruptly, tugging me along for a few steps before releasing me. He moved quickly, his stride lengthening until he fell into a run. I began running too, adrenaline surging through my veins as I tried to figure out what the hell he was doing.

Magnar leapt from the platform, landing on a patch of moss-covered concrete beyond the tracks and started sprinting.

I looked around uneasily, trying to understand why we were running, needing to know if we were being chased or on the hunt. Fury gave me no clues, nothing to go by at all, so I had no choice but to scramble after the slayer and demand my answers from him.

"Elder!" I called as the distance between us increased. "What are you doing?"

I jumped from the platform and hurried after him as he ran towards a tall, wire fence.

He glanced over his shoulder for the briefest moment, taking in the wide space which had opened up between us.

"Keep up!" He turned away from me and yanked the fence high so he could slip beneath it. His command fell over me and my legs started to move faster through no desire of my own.

Motherfucker!

I gritted my teeth in anger as I reached the fence at an impossible pace and yanked it up to follow him. As I ducked beneath it, my coat got caught and was tugged from my arms. I tried to turn back for it but Magnar's power over me wouldn't allow it. He had moved further away, ducking into the ruins that lined the city.

Disappointment surged through me as I left the coat behind. I'd spent my whole life without the warmth of such a garment and the piece of clothing had become immeasurably important to me. It was a symbol of my freedom from the vampires, and I knew I'd miss it once this sunshine relented and winter reclaimed the sky. Thanks to that asshole, I'd be shivering again come nightfall.

I sprinted after Magnar, cursing him between each breath as my legs moved faster and faster. The crumbled remains of old buildings rose up around me and I weaved between them as if the wind carried me.

A small part of my brain marvelled at the speed I was moving at. I'd always liked running in the Realm, but I knew I'd never have been able to move this fast before. My gifted muscles urged me on, and despite the distance we were covering, I still wasn't growing tired.

Magnar scaled a sheer wall ahead of me before dropping over it to the other side and disappearing from view. I gasped as my legs carried me straight towards the wall too and I leapt into the air with a shriek of alarm, the brickwork careening towards my fucking face.

I slammed into the wall at a point which had been way above my head and somehow my fingers found gaps in the brickwork to cling to. I scrambled higher, climbing the wall like a damn spider before finding myself at the top of it.

The drop on the other side must have been two floors high but Magnar was already tearing across the fractured street beyond it.

The urge to jump filled me and I fought against it as terror licked along my spine. That fall would fucking kill me.

I locked my muscles in place, gritting my teeth as a bead of sweat ran down my back, the urge to keep moving building beyond compare within me. I wouldn't do it. There was no way in hell that I was going to-

I screamed like a banshee caught in a hurricane as I leapt from the fucking ledge. The wind whipped my hair out behind me as I plummeted towards the tarmac and certain death.

I'm dead, I'm dead, I'm dead. This is going to hurt like a motherfucking bitch-

My feet hit the ground and I tumbled into a roll, springing upright again easily.

My scream stalled in my lungs, my heart thundering in utter panic, and I twisted to look back up at the wall I'd just dived from and somehow survived.

No fucking way.

Before I could process the insanity of what I'd just managed with the slayer gifts I'd been given, my feet began to move once more.

A deep howl sounded somewhere further within the ruins, and Fury grew startlingly hot in my hand, making me curse in alarm.

Hide, Sun Child, it hissed urgently, but I couldn't hide. I couldn't do anything but bow to Magnar's command to keep up with him, and he was still well ahead of me.

More baying howls met with the first and a fresh fear swept into me. Something bad was coming my way.

I swung around a corner, chasing Magnar as he ducked out of view. He ran like the wind, dragging me behind him on an invisible chain.

When I caught up with him, I was going to fucking kill him. He was a piece of shit, and I was going to remember that the next time

I got distracted by his hotness. I'd be sure to focus on how much his personality made me want to throw rocks at his damn head instead. St*upid, hot motherfucker.*

My soul bucked against the control he had over me. I'd yearned to be free for as long as I could remember, and I was going to break myself out of his servitude if it was the last thing I did. Apparently that day wasn't today though.

A dark shadow fell over me and I glanced up, spotting a huge owl circling overhead, its eyes trained on me, and my gut plummeted as I recognised it for what it was.

Kill it, Fury begged, but the Familiar was too far above me, even if I could have stopped running for long enough to try.

"Elder!" I yelled angrily, wondering why he was ignoring the bird or if he hadn't even noticed it. Whoever controlled it had certainly seen us now. It wouldn't be long before they found a way to get to us. The blazing sun was likely the only reason they weren't here already.

Magnar ran on, ignoring me as he circled a building which was mostly intact and moved out of sight again.

Watch out! Fury hissed as I raced after the warrior bastard, but I couldn't do anything other than run.

A huge shape pounced from the shadows and collided with me in a tangle of fur and claws.

I screamed as I was thrown to the ground, my back hitting the concrete hard, knocking the air from my lungs as I reached for my gifts.

The huge black dog tumbled off me as we hit the ground, but it quickly regained its feet, leaping at me again with drool-coated fangs bared at my throat.

I swung Fury with a snarl of rage, but I missed its heart, the blade only slicing into its shoulder as Magnar's command forced half of my attention onto regaining my feet and chasing after him once more.

I cursed as the wild dog leapt at me again and I kicked out, catching it in the side of its jaw and sending it flying away from me.

I took a step towards it with Fury raised to finish the undead beast, but Magnar's command jerked me to a halt, my own body betraying me.

Fear flooded my veins as I turned my back on the snarling dog, and I began running again.

The dog howled as it raced after me and the voices of its companions joined it from the surrounding streets as they drew closer too.

Shit.

"Elder!" I bellowed as I sprinted after him and the dog snarled dangerously close to my back, its breath washing over my skin. "Release me!"

The howls of the other beasts closed in, and I threw a glance over my shoulder, finding six huge dogs right on my heels. My gifted muscles meant that I was fast, but those dogs were gaining on me with every adrenaline-fuelled step, and I was helpless to stop the impending fate from playing out.

Fury begged me to turn and face the beasts, but I was powerless to stop the pounding of my feet as they closed in. I might have been moving like the wind, but those dogs were faster.

I leapt over a low wall and moved to run on, but heavy paws collided with my back, knocking me from my feet once more as the first of the dogs caught me.

I managed to twist beneath it, raising Fury as the dog's weight slammed me onto the ground. The beast spiralled into ash as my blade found its heart but the fall was more than enough to let the others catch up.

I scrambled backwards, the urge to chase Magnar colliding with my desperate desire to survive.

The pack of dogs leapt for me, and my heart thundered as I tried to break free of Magnar's command and focus on fighting them.

A snarling brown beast made it to me first and I kicked it, forcing it back before its teeth could find my flesh, swiping at it with my blade and whirling towards the creature closing in on my left.

The urge to catch up to Magnar disappeared as he threw himself between me and the rest of the pack, swinging his blades as he fought to keep them off of me, finally having realised that we were under attack.

The massive brown dog pounced again, its weight slamming me back onto the concrete, jaws snapping in my face and rancid breath filling my nostrils.

I screamed in defiance, shoving it back and stabbing Fury into its side as its teeth lunged for my throat. I stabbed it again and again, my hand growing slick with too bright blood as I missed its heart. I forced its neck back with my other hand as it snarled and bared its teeth, my muscles trembling with the power of its attack.

But suddenly, the monstrous dog stilled, its bulk pinning me down as it stared into my eyes with a clarity that hadn't been there before. I sucked in a breath, certain I was seeing the vampire who controlled it gazing down at me. Dread filled my gut as the vampire continued to watch me through the beast's eyes, its gaze calculating, assessing. Fear spilled through me like a spear of ice piercing my heart as I took in the darkness in that creature's eyes. The watcher knew me now. And he would come for me.

The dog burst into ash, my heart leaping in shock as its weight suddenly fell away, and I scrunched my eyes shut against the remains tumbling over me. A wooden clatter reached my ears, and I rolled upright, noticing an arrow carved with runes lying on the ground beside me.

Magnar still fought with one of the huge dogs, but he drove Tempest through its chest as I pushed myself upright, and the ruins fell eerily silent around us once more.

He looked up at me as I closed in on him, but I didn't give him a chance to say a single word before my fist connected with his jaw.

He stepped back, surprise flashing through his eyes a moment before I swung at him again.

"Callie," he began angrily as he managed to block my punch.

I released a growl of pure rage as I ducked beneath his arm and aimed for his face once more.

"You nearly got me killed!" I snarled. "Your stupid fucking command could have ended my life, asshole."

He deflected another strike, and I twisted away from him before sending my foot crashing into his chest. Magnar stumbled back, raising his hands between us as if I might be convinced to stop, but I was too pissed at him to even consider it.

"You know I didn't mean for you to-"

"I don't care what you meant to do, you son of a bitch. You had no fucking right to do that to me! I could have died because you decided to go on some power trip instead of just explaining why the hell you ran off like that."

I swung at him again, but he caught my fist in his hand, stalling my attack with his iron grip. He grunted with effort as I pushed against his hold with the full force of my gifted muscles, and he barely managed to knock my knee aside before it could collide with his balls.

With a surge of strength, Magnar spun me around and pinned me against a crumbling wall, the brickwork digging into my spine as he caught my other wrist the moment I tried to swing Fury at him.

"This is what you signed up for, Callie," Magnar snarled angrily, his face inches from mine as he immobilised me against the wall. "I didn't want you to take the vow. I never wanted to have this power over you, so you should remember that every time you let your anger get the best of you like this. *I'm* not the one who did this to you."

He glared at me, and my chest rose and fell heavily between us.

"Fuck you," I spat.

Magnar looked like he might just murder me, and I was pretty sure I was throwing the same look right back at him.

"Nice to see your efforts with the fairer sex haven't improved in the last thousand years, brother," a voice called from beside us, and I flinched in surprise, my head snapping around to look at the beast of a man who was standing between two buildings to our right.

An icy calm washed over Magnar, his expression blanking out as he turned his head to look at the stranger who approached us with an easy smile on his face.

My mouth fell open as I recognised him from the dream I'd stolen my way into and Magnar's hands fell from me, our argument utterly forgotten as Julius held his arms wide in greeting.

"I thought I sensed your blade here, but I didn't think it was possible that I'd find *you* too," Magnar breathed in astonishment, then a laugh fell from his lips which was so free and pure and full of love that I couldn't help but feel the power of their reunion in the core of my being.

They clung to each other fiercely, and I felt like a splinter had been pulled from my heart as I watched them reunite. Two brothers from the past, finding each other in another lifetime.

MONTANA

CHAPTER TWENTY ONE

Erik led me through the house and my thoughts clashed together. How could I have let him know I wanted him? A vampire. My dad would be turning in his grave if he knew I held such feelings in my heart. It went against everything I believed. And yet, I couldn't shake the feeling no matter how hard I tried. I yearned for Erik in a way that defied all I stood for, this ruinous connection between us reeling me closer with every second I spent in his company.

I followed him to the bookcase in the hall with anxiety rippling through me. I didn't feel remotely ready to face a god, but if I was going to get answers, this was the key to getting them.

Erik pulled the red book that opened the secret door, and it swung inwards.

"After you." He placed his hand on my back, encouraging me into his private space, and the air seemed thicker somehow as he closed the door behind us.

He moved up behind me, his fingers tracing the length of my spine, then his mouth fell to my neck, and I arched into him in surprise.

I clutched the back of his head, my nails digging in as his mouth moved to my ear, leaving a trail of fire in its wake.

"Don't," I whispered, though I didn't want him to stop.

"I think we're long beyond pretending we don't want each other," he said roughly, though he stopped touching me all the same.

"No, I'm good with pretending," I said airily, stepping away from him, and he released a breath of amusement.

"I'm not." He stepped forward, but I twisted around and folded my arms.

"You're procrastinating," I teased.

"I am," he admitted. "And I would like to do so a little longer."

"That would be a bad idea," I said firmly.

"Do tell me why." He hounded after me as I headed to the spiral staircase and started walking up it.

"I assume the mirror is up here with your other secret things?" I asked, ignoring his question.

"Why are you running from me?" He ignored mine.

I picked up my pace, jogging up the stairs, but a shadow surged past me, and Erik appeared at the top of the steps, barring my way forward.

"Password." He quirked a grin at me.

His sudden playfulness was so disarming, it was impossible not to steal a moment of light with him. Hell only knew I'd had enough of the dark.

My mouth curved into a taunting smile. "I don't know. Erik's an arrogant royal ass-twat?"

"That was my second choice, but I decided to set a more physical password." He tapped his lips, grey eyes full of the game.

I scoffed and tried to duck under his arm.

He caught me fast, pressing me back. "If you want me to play by your rules, rebel, do play by mine."

I laid my hands on his chest, stepping closer as I gave in. "Am I warm?"

"Very." His eyes flickered with lust.

I slid my hands up to his neck, tiptoeing toward his lips. "Warmer?"

"Volcanic."

I slid my hand between us, offering him my middle finger right in front of his eyes, and he released a rumbling laugh. "Why do I have to work so hard for you?"

"Because sometimes the great Prince Erik doesn't get to snap his fingers and have anything he wants," I said, dropping my hand.

He captured my chin between his finger and thumb. "At least give me a taste. Drive me to madness with the memory of you, it's the least I deserve."

Damn, those words were hard to resist. I leaned into his kiss and my heart melted like hot wax, pouring through me in a waterfall of pleasure. The heat between us ignited once again and want took hold of me, binding me to this beast who could so easily break me.

He drew me close, my hands riding the swell of his biceps, sliding over his firm shoulders, and gripping tightly. He tasted like the devil, temptation in its rawest form.

His hands slid down the length of my spine, cupping my ass and driving me against him, reminding me of how he'd taken possession of my body before. The way his fingers had moved inside me, his savage claiming of me that had crossed my mind far more times than I wanted to admit.

A strange energy washed over me, followed by an icy breath of air on the back of my neck, making me stiffen in Erik's arms.

"Well, well, I do hope this display isn't for me, Erik Larsen." A cold, powerful voice filled the room, and I nearly slid off of the step in alarm.

Erik caught me, pulling me onto the balcony, his arm locked protectively around my waist.

"Andvari," he growled. "We were just about to call upon you."

"I know, and yet how distracted you became. I fear if I hadn't come to you now, I would have interrupted something far more interesting. But I am ever the gentleman."

I gazed around the room as the shadows danced and swirled beneath the bookshelves, my heart pattering in my chest.

Erik released me, moving to one of the shelves and taking a beautiful hand mirror from between two of the books. I recognised it from his room, and my blood ran cold as I approached him, eyeing the ethereal object.

He gazed down at the polished glass and his reflection stared back at him with a strange smile. It wasn't him; I could tell that from the prickling sensation in my gut.

"Erik Larsen," the reflection spoke. "You come to me for answers… as always."

"I may have the right one this time," Erik said hopefully, angling the mirror toward me.

The reflection didn't change, despite the fact that it was facing me now. Andvari started laughing, then reached toward the glass. When his fingers touched the mirror, they slipped through the glass as easily as if it were liquid.

I gasped as a gnarled hand extended from the frame and icy fingers grazed my cheek, the touch like death itself.

In an instant, the reflection vanished, and the mirror started to expand as if the glass was made of water, spreading out before me. Erik released the handle, but the mirror remained in the air, stretching out wider and wider until Andvari was able to step through it.

Erik caught my arm, dragging me away and placing himself between us as the deity materialised. As he did so, his appearance changed to what must have been his true form. The god had long hair and a brown cloak fell around his slim body. His feet were bare and gnarled where they hit the floorboards, his eyes were opaque and his face was a hollow, beautiful thing, ancient and youthful at once.

The mirror clattered to the floor, returning to its previous size, and the noise rang out around us, sending a tremor through me.

Erik's fingers curled around my hand in a fierce grip, a growl in his throat, and I had no intention to pull away.

Andvari observed us, his eyes skimming across our faces, then down to our clasped hands.

"You surprise me as usual," he spoke to Erik in a deadly purr. "I have always seen something in you. Your heart is as strong as the day I cursed you. And unlike most of your kin, you follow the beat of it. Despite the world you have allowed your family to create, you still think of yourself as honourable, don't you, Erik? Because you resisted what they could not. Until now, it seems." His eyes skimmed over me again, and I glanced up at Erik, my heart crashing against my chest.

Erik lowered his chin, his eyes dark. "I would hardly use the word honourable."

"No, but you wish so much to hold onto your values," Andvari said. "In the deepest hours of the night, your thoughts turn to your immortal soul. You still hope for it to be saved, even now, after all you have done." The god stepped closer, leaving wet footprints as he walked.

My courage failed as he approached, the power of him a living thing, moving around us like a silent breeze.

Erik didn't answer, but his posture grew rigid, a predator poised to pounce.

"Do you think *she* is the answer?" Andvari asked, his eyes flashing to me.

I gasped as freezing hands seemed to squeeze my lungs from inside my body, forcing the air from them with untold magic. The god stole all my breath away, sapping the oxygen right from my veins. My vision darkened and my knees hit the floor as I buckled, succumbing to his unearthly power. I felt Erik's arms around me, but he couldn't do anything to stop it. I couldn't draw breath, I could hardly see, a roaring in my ears telling me the magic was only burrowing deeper.

"Release her!" Erik bellowed, and my lungs decompressed all at once, allowing air to rush back into them.

I spluttered, gripping Erik's arm for support as I tried to right myself. My cheeks flushed hot with anger as I pushed to my feet, determined to get the answer I'd come for.

I glared at Andvari with every ounce of strength I had. "Is it true? Am I a part of your prophecy?" I demanded, though my legs were still shaking from what he'd done to me.

Andvari chuckled lightly, his eyes hooded as he took me in. Erik straightened his spine as the god addressed me. "Mortal girl, how brave you must think you are to speak to me with such insolence."

"I want answers," I hissed, refusing to back down. "And you have them, don't you?"

"Yes," Andvari whispered, the air gusting around me like his breath could wield it. "Oh, how fine a moment this is." He turned to Erik. "You do not even realise it yet, do you?"

"Realise what?" Erik snarled.

"After all the years you have fought to protect your soul, a mere mortal has claimed it instead." Andvari threw his head back with a cruel laugh, and my thoughts scattered.

I stole a glance at Erik, but his face was stony and unreadable.

"Say it." Andvari abruptly stopped laughing, pointing at him. "I want to hear it."

"I am tired of your games, Andvari," Erik growled, and fear rolled through me at the tension building between them.

"One more game and I shall answer the question you seek," Andvari promised, pressing a finger to his own chest and striking an X across his heart. A glimmer of gold glowed through his cloak, then faded away to nothing, apparently securing the vow.

Erik wouldn't look at me as I tried to catch his eye, and I grew terrified of what he was about to say.

"I cannot love someone in this form," Erik said in a low voice.

I turned to Andvari as Erik's words resounded in my skull, the truth of them stinging in a way I could never have predicted. Perhaps because they confirmed this want between us was nothing but lust. I just hadn't expected to crave more than that.

"Liar," Andvari spat, and his shadow grew behind him, casting us in darkness.

His face turned to a wicked thing; his features contorted with a fury I didn't want to face. But my feet remained rooted to the floor. I wouldn't run. I wouldn't leave until I had my answer.

"Defy me again and I will have your tongue," Andvari hissed, and power stretched over me like his breath was seeping across every inch of my skin. He raised a hand, and his taloned nails pinched together in the air.

Erik coughed, jerking forward as blood poured from his mouth, dripping to the floor.

"Answer me!" Andvari roared, and the walls shuddered around us.

Fear scorched a path through my chest, and I grabbed hold of Erik, trying to help him, but there was nothing I could do.

Andvari twisted his hand in the air and Erik slammed into me, throwing me into the bookshelf, pain ricocheting through my shoulders from the impact. His weight crushed me in place, but I knew it wasn't really him. His eyes met mine with a bitter apology inside them as more blood oozed from his mouth.

His jaw trembled as his lips parted and the blood trickled down his chin. His voice was throaty when he spoke, and I could tell the pain this was causing him.

"I love you," he rasped, but I knew it was a lie devised by Andvari, the god wielding his tongue for the purpose of his sick games.

Andvari's high laughter rang in my ears as he moved his hands in a weaving motion behind us. Power flooded my body, and I lost control of my own limbs as I reached between us and squeezed my breasts.

I cried out, battling back with all my strength, and Erik's hands slammed into the bookcase either side of my head, sending tomes crashing to the floor around us.

"Enough!" Erik roared, his body trembling from the exertion it took to resist Andvari's power.

My chin lifted and Andvari forced my mouth to meet Erik's, the metallic taste of blood sliding onto my tongue.

Erik broke chunks out of the wooden shelves as he fought to keep his hands off me, but Andvari's will broke through and he grabbed my hips, his tongue sinking deep into my mouth.

Erik's hand slid beneath my shirt, fingers biting into my waist with violence as he tugged me closer, and I could do nothing but follow the orders of Andvari's power, shedding my shirt so it fluttered to the floor.

"Stop," I begged, trying to make my limbs do anything else but follow the god's orders, but I was a slave to him.

The wave of power released me, and I fell against Erik, taking in a shaky breath of relief, but my fear of what Andvari might make us do next had me trembling. Erik's hands encircled me, his back to Andvari as he shielded me from him, though I doubted anything could stop him.

"You won't have answers from me unless I am appeased," Andvari said lightly. "You have displeased me, Erik."

Erik was forced away from me and my legs moved of their own accord, walking me towards Andvari. I winced as I moved into his arms and the god's hand slithered down my spine, pulling me close. He smelled like bark and wet earth, as if he was made of nature, bound in the false body of a man.

"Perhaps I'll taste how sweet her kisses are for myself." Andvari angled his horridly angelic face toward me, and I leaned back as far as his power would allow, disgust weaving through my gut.

"Get away from her," Erik growled in a deadly tone. "Touch her and I'll end you."

"An idle threat as always," Andvari sneered, wafting his hand so Erik was knocked to the floor, forced to remain there. Andvari's eyes wheeled to me with a flicker of amusement glittering in the depths of them.

"Kiss me as if you were kissing him. I wish to know what it is that sparks his desire so keenly," he ordered, and I felt the power of the command run through me like frosty water.

For the second time, my lips were taken hostage by a monster, but I realised which of them held the true power now. The one who had weaved the vampire curse into existence, who had Erik and every one of the vampires under his omnipotent control.

I shuddered as Andvari's tongue slicked across my lips, his mouth tasting like ash; as dry as dirt and as bitter as alcohol.

"Stop it," I growled as his arms seized me, so strong I was immobilised even if I hadn't been under the power of his magic.

"Get your hands off of her!" Erik shouted, fighting to get up, but a thump of magic sent him slamming to the floor again. He cursed the god with all his might, demanding him to release me, but the prince held no power in this room. There was only one creature capable of wielding our fates now.

Andvari released me and licked his lips with his black tongue before shoving me to the floor. I scrambled away from him, backing up to Erik's side and wiping my mouth with the back of my hand, horrified at what he'd made me do. At the impossible power he held over us. He could have made us slit our own throats if he wanted.

Erik dragged me closer, and I drew comfort from his fierce hold, his fury aimed at Andvari, and a thousand-year-old vendetta blazed in his eyes. He hadn't lied to me about the creator of his curse, that was clearer than ever. He was Andvari's monster, built from bloodshed and corruption, and there was no escaping this wrathful god.

"She is sweet indeed," Andvari whispered, still wetting his lips as if savouring my taste, and I grimaced at him in disgust. "As agreed, I will answer one question. Make sure it is a good one."

Erik snarled at the god as he posed his question. "Is she the answer to the prophecy?"

"She is half the answer." Andvari smiled a wicked smile, then disappeared into a swirling shadow, leaving the mirror rattling on the floor.

"Wait!" I cried, shoving to my feet, and grabbing the mirror. "What do I have to do? How can I break the curse?"

The reflection was my own, and Andvari didn't answer, nor did he take hold of my image in the mirror. He was gone, leaving us with nothing but a confirmation and no path to follow.

"Fuck," I exhaled, throwing the mirror to the floor again.

Erik shot over to join me, the blood on his mouth now gone. Perhaps it had only been an illusion, one of Andvari's dark tricks.

"Let's go," I said, a shiver tracking through me. "I want to get out of here."

Without a word, Erik scooped me into his arms and sped down the staircase in a rush of motion. He moved through the house at speed until we were upstairs in the bedroom I'd woken in just days ago.

Erik placed me in a chair, kneeling before me and staring at me with horrors in his eyes. "I cannot undo what he did."

I pushed my fingers into his hair, seeing him in a new light after what I'd witnessed, the depths of torment Andvari had put him through. "You don't need to."

"I should never have taken you to him." He clutched the sides of my thighs, his fingers gripping my jeans and digging in hard as he hung his head.

I reached down to cup his face, pulling him up to look at me. His eyes gleamed with regret, and I ran my thumbs over the anxious creases beside them. "I can handle it."

He nodded stiffly, but he looked broken and so hollow that it tugged at my heart.

"Erik, you heard what he said, right? I'm part of the prophecy."

"I don't care," he spat, rising to his feet with incredible speed and setting my heart pounding. He glared around the room, looking ready to rip the world apart. "I will not make you a part of this. Who knows what he'll ask of you? I will not let him take power over you again."

"If this is the answer to the curse, we have to face it," I insisted, getting up and taking hold of his arm, forcing him to look at me.

He sighed heavily, shadows swirling thickly in his eyes. "You are so strong. Stronger than me. I am floored by you and your resilience. What I've put you through, what all of my kind have done to yours...it isn't right that you must shoulder this burden."

"If I can end the curse, I have to, Erik. For my family, for all the humans. For...you." My throat thickened on that final word and the truth that simmered between us.

His gaze burned into mine. He seemed transfixed and I felt my heart weakening under his scrutiny.

"I will not ask this of you," he said.

"I'm not asking for your permission," I replied. "Whatever it is I have to do to end this, I will."

"The answer to Andvari's curse will be some terrible thing, I am certain of it. And I will not lose you," he said tightly. "The first look you gave me struck a fire in my heart I'd long forgotten was there. The second stoked the flames. And every look since has turned that fire into a deadly force that sees me growing madder with every passing day. But in light of what I know now, I do not want you to want me back. I want you to despise me. To do what you do best, rebel, and goddamn *rebel*. Ignore everything I have asked of you. Ignore my demands, ignore all promises I forced you to make. Don't be mine. Don't *ever* be mine. Because if you let me have you, Andvari will have you too. He will design new games to torture me, and he knows my weakness now. You will be his latest weapon against me, and I will not let him hurt you."

"Erik," I gasped, shaking my head in shock at his declaration to protect me.

"Promise me you will turn from me now, because if I have the chance to keep you, I will not be able to resist it," he said, his brows pulling tightly together.

"It's too late for that," I said, stepping forward and leaning up to brush my lips against his. "I'm part of this. Your curse is my curse too. Let's end this together."

MAGNAR

CHAPTER TWENTY TWO

1000 YEARS AGO

"Magnar!" Julius hammered on the door to wake me, and I groaned in displeasure as I clawed my way back towards consciousness.

I tossed the blankets aside and headed for the door, only remembering that I was naked as I pulled it open.

"For the love of the gods, Magnar, I've seen your cock far more often than I ever wanted to and more in this lifetime," Julius cursed as he pushed his way into the room and bolted the door behind him.

I let out a laugh as I retrieved my clothes from the floor and pulled them back on. "What's got you so worked up?" I asked as he paced away from the door, pushing a hand through his short, dark hair.

"We may have outstayed our welcome. The barkeeper came looking for his daughter and wasn't best pleased to find me on top of her."

"Are you telling me you couldn't handle one old man without having to come crying to me?" I teased.

"One old man wouldn't be an issue, but he stormed off to raise the rest of the townsfolk against us and see us on our way. I suggest we get out of here before-" He stopped mid-sentence as he spotted Elissa in my bed. Her cheeks flamed red as she clutched the blankets over herself. "Please tell me this one is a whore and not another village girl."

"She's Ocean Clan," I replied lightly as I tossed the girl her dress.

"Thank the gods for that!"

"Oh, and she's also betrothed to someone here. Or *was* I suppose. I might have ruined her."

"*Ruined?* Who was she supposed to marry?" Julius asked incredulously.

"An old man, you can imagine why she preferred to take me to her bed." I tightened Tempest's sheath across my chest as I replaced the heavy blade on my back.

"Well let's hope they don't know about her yet. We should leave."

"He's old *and* near toothless," Elissa added as she pulled her dress on. "*And* the mayor."

I exchanged a look with Julius and we both burst into laughter.

"Well if we're going to piss off a whole town, we might as well do it thoroughly," he said.

"And my father's the magistrate," she said. "Just so we're totally clear on everyone who's involved."

I couldn't help but laugh harder as I yanked my boots on.

A clamour of noise began to grow outside, and I tugged the curtain aside, spotting a horde of angry townsfolk marching our way. They held various weapons, none of which would do much good against two fully trained slayers, but our vows forbade us from willingly engaging them.

"Time to go," I announced as I dropped the curtain and Julius yanked the door open. "She's coming with us," I added.

"Of course she is," he replied sarcastically. "Why the hell wouldn't she?"

"I gave my word, brother." We thundered down the stairs, Julius shaking his head.

"I don't think you made that decision while thinking with your head," he commented.

I glanced back at Elissa whose cheeks were still flaming red and grabbed her hand to hurry her along.

"You still want me to take you to your clan?" I asked as we made it to the door.

"Yes," she breathed, and despite the fear she clearly felt, I could tell she was desperate to be free of this place so she could return to her mother's people.

"Then let's run."

Julius yanked the door open, and we fled in the direction of the stables. I could hear the angry crowd drawing closer and my blood sang in my veins as we raced to elude them.

We rounded the final corner and skidded to a halt as we found the stable boy waiting for us. Our horses were saddled, each carrying bags filled with grain. The boy sat on a stunning grey mare and his face was set determinedly.

"I'm coming with you," he called, and I noted the fresh black eye he was sporting. "I wish only to serve you."

"Any man who can saddle Baltian is welcome to join us," I replied, and I leapt onto the stallion's back, holding out a hand for Elissa. "What's your name, boy?"

"Aelfric," he replied with a grin. "And I won't let you down."

"Yes, let's bring the stable boy on a stolen thoroughbred," Julius said with a grin as he jumped onto his own steed. "Why the fuck not?"

"Well, Aelfric," I said as the townsfolk rounded the corner and spotted us, crying out in anger while waving pitchforks and other improvised weapons. "You'd better be able to keep up."

I gave Baltian his head and he charged at the crowd, forcing a path through them as they screamed a torrent of abuse at us. The other horses followed close behind and we raced away through the snow, carving a trail for home.

It took us twelve moons to find our way back to the clans' camp. They'd moved several times in the months we'd been gone, and I had to rely on Tempest to track them down. The blade seemed to be slower to direct me than usual, and I struggled to figure out why. Usually, the closer we drew to camp and the other blades, the stronger the pull towards home felt.

But today it was more like trying to lock on to a much smaller group. I wondered if the clans had split up for a while. Sometimes bad weather or difficulties with supplies made that unavoidable. We couldn't always travel in one group.

Julius noticed the difference too, and we let out a joint sigh of relief when a collection of scattered tents finally appeared on the horizon.

Elissa was riding with Aelfric today, and I was glad to be alone as I gathered my thoughts for my reunion with my kin. It wasn't often that I had to return bearing news of failure, and I just hoped that our father would still be proud of what we'd managed. Next time, Miles wouldn't be so lucky.

I kicked Baltian into a reluctant gallop and we charged towards home. Though I would have been thrilled to return with tidings of Miles's death, it had been so long that I was just pleased to be back at all. I may have been a grown man, but I missed the comfort offered by my mother's company and the wisdom of my father. I wasn't ashamed to admit such feelings and I would relish a moment in their arms as we were reunited after so long.

The first face I saw as I reached the tents wasn't my mother or my father though; it was Valentina. She was dressed immaculately as always, her dark hair braided carefully. But there was something off in her gaze.

"Valentina, how unexpected to find you waiting for me out here," I said dryly as I pulled Baltian up beside her. The coy smile I expected didn't come, and I frowned as she resisted the urge to play our usual games of courtship. Or I supposed her games were aimed at courtship while mine were designed to tease her for her persistent devotion.

Her face was still with restrained emotion, and she twisted her hands together uncomfortably as if she couldn't decide how to deliver whatever it was she was trying to say.

"Magnar..." she began, but Julius interrupted her with his arrival.

"Valentina! What a surprise to see you waiting out here for my dear brother. I do hope you haven't been at this every day for the past few months?" He tossed me a taunting smile and slid from the saddle. "Where is everyone else?"

I followed his gaze to the empty space between the tents, a pit of unease growing in my gut. Something was wrong. Besides the camp being much smaller than usual, everything else was missing too. In place of the usual chaotic chorus of swordplay, wood cutting, children playing, and horses snorting was an eerie silence.

A sliver of ice crept down my spine. I dismounted too, tossing Baltian's reins to Aelfric as he pulled his horse up beside me.

"Where are our mother and father?" I demanded, having no space in my heart to wonder about anyone else yet.

"Your mother is in her tent," Valentina began, her hand snaking out to grasp my wrist as I began to move past her. "But Magnar-"

I pushed her aside as I began to run for my parents' tent in the centre of the camp with Julius right beside me. Whatever had happened, I didn't want to hear it from Valentina, I wanted it from my mother's mouth.

The guards looked up in alarm as we raced towards them, but they recognised us and stepped aside. I shoved the tent flap out of my way and quickly crossed the wide space inside. The pile of thick furs which served as my parents' bed lay at the back of the room and I spotted her curled among them with a jolt of surprise.

"We have returned, Mother," Julius announced as we made it to her bedside. "Tell us what has happened here."

"My sons! Oh the gods have returned you to me when I needed you most!" She scrambled out of the bed and threw her arms around both of us, crushing us tightly against her as she sobbed.

I'd never seen her cry before.

My heart constricted in my chest as pain sped towards me on swift wings.

"Father?" I asked, knowing in my heart that nothing else would have reduced her to this state. I felt Julius's posture stiffen beside me as he waited for the blow that was about to fall.

"I'm so sorry, my loves." She gripped us harder, her fist knotting in my hair as if she were afraid to release us.

"Tell me," I growled, staving off the rush of pain and grief that came for me as my need for answers persevered. I had to know who had done this. I had to know who had managed to fell the great warrior Earl Mallion Elioson. The idea of such a thing happening was beyond my comprehension and my mind rebelled at the suggestion of it.

"There was a tremendous battle. The prophets foresaw three of the Revenants reunited in one place, and the clans joined forces to march against them and finish our feud once and for all. Almost every warrior we had marched out and none have returned. I only remained because your father begged me to stay and lead the clan in his absence. Now I have to live with the knowledge that he died without me by his side."

"When did this happen?" I demanded, refusing to bow to the weight of the emotions that were piling in on me. Julius had fallen unnaturally still, and I wasn't sure if he was even breathing.

"Three nights ago." She ran her hands up and down our backs, soothing us the way she had when we were small boys. I wasn't sure if she did it for us or for herself; to reassure her that her children still lived.

"How can we be certain they're all dead?" I asked a little more aggressively than I'd intended. "Perhaps the battle rages on, maybe we should be heading out to-"

"I dreamed it," she breathed. "I managed to dream-walk with souls on the edge of death and saw what had happened. Our people were winning, cutting through their forces, and heading for victory. But the lost Revenant, Erik, returned from whatever pit of hell he's been hiding in for the last two hundred years. His hunger was insatiable. His rage unparalleled." She descended into sobbing, and I pulled her against me fiercely.

"This can't be happening," Julius breathed, and I found myself at a loss for words.

"How many of us are left?" I asked eventually, my voice cracking with the question.

"What you see here is it," Mother replied. "This is all that remains of the seven clans. Our people destroyed all of the vampires who fought beneath the Revenants, but it cost them everything."

"All seven?" I asked in astonishment. "You mean to say that this smattering of tents is it? There are no more of us left?"

If it was true, then we really were done for. It would take a hundred years for our clans to even begin to rebuild our numbers, and that would rely on the vampires leaving us alone to do so. And if I knew anything about them, then I knew that wouldn't be the case. They'd come for us now, hunt us down like feral beasts on the scent of fresh blood and try to wipe us out. If our bloodlines were lost, then humanity would no doubt fall to them too. We were all that stood in their way.

I tried to wrap my head around the idea that such a thing could have happened. Our people had been decimated. Even if all of the sired vampires had been destroyed too, we were still at a major disadvantage. They could create more vampires as quickly as they needed them. In the span of two moons, they could sire hundreds of monsters in their image. There would be no way to stop them.

As my thoughts started to spiral into despair, I heard the one sound in the world that I wished for most, shock piercing my heart as I spun towards the flaps that hung closed over the entrance to the tent. I held my breath as I failed to believe it was true, but then I heard it again.

"Freya?" my father called more urgently from outside the tent.

The three of us looked to each other in astonishment for a moment before turning and running for the exit. We burst out into the dim sunlight and found him standing on the far side of the fire pit.

"Mallion!" my mother cried in relief as she began to run for him, but he backed up sharply, lifting a hand to warn her away.

"Please, Freya, my love, don't come any closer. I couldn't bear to hurt you."

My relief slowly gave way to something far darker as I looked at my father more closely and blinked the grief from my eyes. Though he had always been a handsome man, his features looked too perfect now, his face too alluring. Something in the way he held himself had changed, like he had gone from a prowling wolf to a stalking wild cat.

I caught my mother's wrist as she tried to approach him despite his warning, the foul truth slipping through my soul.

"No," I breathed in horror as the reality of what they'd done to him weighed down on me.

"I only came back to say goodbye, my love, my sons. Please forgive me for taking such a risk, but I couldn't bear to leave you without seeing you one last time."

My mother started screaming as she realised what he was, the noise pitching through me, scarring my soul. Julius joined me in restraining her, and my father fell to his knees beyond the fire, tears streaming down his face, grief cutting him in two.

"Tell me who did this to you, Father, and I swear to you that I will end their immortal life if it's the last thing I do," I cried, my voice cracking with the pain of those words.

A heavy pressure began to build around us and the sky rumbled with an approaching storm. I had the strongest feeling that we weren't alone, the gods turning their eyes to us in this moment of truest defeat.

"It was the Revenant Erik," he replied. "Once all of our kin lay dead at his feet, he decided to force his eternal curse upon me. It pains me beyond measure, but I need to ask a favour of you, dear boy."

I let out a howl of pure rage and hatred as I released our mother into Julius's care and pulled Tempest from my back. I knew what he was going to ask me, and the thought of it alone made me want to drive the blade through my own chest. How could I live with myself if I had to kill my own father?

"I'm already dead," he breathed, his voice carrying to me despite the distance between us. "But I need you to release me from this torment. You don't know how the blood calls to me. I'm fighting it with all I have but I can't do so for much longer."

The presence around us grew thicker and I felt sure the gods were near, come to see the outcome of the trick their demon had played on my family, toying with us all over again.

The pain I felt seemed enough to cleave me in two and I used that energy to drive my blade into the hard earth by my feet. I dropped to my knees and pulled my fighting leathers off, tossing them onto the dirt so that my bare chest was exposed.

"Gods, if you are here, I beg you to release my father from this curse!" I moved to grip Tempest by the hilt, hoping to hear them speaking to me through the blade.

It's too late, Idun's voice whispered sadly beside me, and I hung my head as I bucked against the idea of accepting it. My father stood before us, his flesh and soul trapped by the curse of the Revenants.

"Please," I begged, and I didn't care that they saw me brought so low. "Please, I'll give you anything. I'll give you *everything*. Just let him live."

Only ending the curse can release him.

"If I knew how to do such a thing, I'd have done so already. There must be another way!"

The goddess seemed amused by my determination, but she didn't budge in her decision.

Prove your strength, Magnar, and I will grant you gifts enough to chase your foes to the ends of the earth. Prove your strength, and I will make it so that your very name incites fear in their bones.

I shook my head to clear it of the voice who goaded me into action. No deity nor any other being would guide my actions. My life was my own and my decisions would sit squarely on my shoulders. I needed no gods to tell me how to live.

"Please, my boy, the thirst grows stronger." My father turned his worried gaze on my mother and brother, and I squeezed my eyes shut as I made my choice.

If the gods refused to release him, then I would have to do it myself.

I closed the distance between us in eight long strides. He looked up at me with his too perfect face; the face of a stranger in place of my father. But I could see his soul still shining in his eyes. He deserved a warrior's death. He deserved to be rid of this torment.

"My sword is yours." He dragged the heavy blade from his back and held it out to me.

I accepted Venom with a feeling of dread building in every fibre of my being and weighed the legendary weapon in my hand. It was heavier than Tempest, though the length was the same.

My hand shook as I gripped it in my fist, my heart racing with the inevitability of what lay before me, agony burrowing its way into my soul. I would never recover from this act. I would never again be the man I was now. The gods had refused my pleas and the Revenants had delivered a torture beyond all comprehension to my door.

"Know that I will carry it with the promise to right this wrong that has been done to you. The Revenants will fall, and I won't rest until I see an end to their vile kind," I swore as I forced myself to raise the blade and held it ready above his heart.

"I am so proud of you, my son, never forget it," Father breathed, the tears on his cheeks summoning my own. How could I do this? How could I find a way to live with it if I did? "You will lead our people to victory against them, never doubt it."

Father looked up at me, eyes filled with regret, and I knew he wished he hadn't had to ask this of me. But I would never have allowed another to take on this burden. My love for him made this task impossible, but it also made it mine alone.

"I love you," I told him, my mother's sobs punctuated by Julius's cry of pain behind me.

"I love you too, son." He gave a final nod, the plea in his eyes undeniable, and I fought the shaking in my limbs so that I might offer him release from his pain at last.

I took a heavy breath and my muscles tensed as they fought against the need to drive the blade home.

The goddess grew anxious as she waited to see what would happen, the storm building quickly above us as lightning flashed, her impatience buzzing through the air itself.

"I love you all," Father breathed, and I forced my arm down with a cry of agony tearing from my throat, and Mother and Julius called their final love-filled words to him.

"I release you from this curse," I choked out.

Venom pierced his heart in one heavy blow and he fell apart into ash which swirled around me before catching on a breeze and tumbling away. The greatest man I had ever known, the most powerful warrior to have walked our lands, turned to nothing by the curse of the monsters he'd given his life to see destroyed.

My mother screamed behind me, and I sank to my knees once more as my own tears fell in burning lines down my cheeks.

Thunder boomed angrily above our heads, and I turned my eyes to the heavens as rain began to hammer down upon my bare skin.

A true warrior turns from no fight, Idun purred, and I felt the ghost of a hand stroking the side of my face as if she were proud of me for my part in the sick fate she'd just watched play out. *You have proven yourself worthy, Magnar Elioson. I grant you the power to destroy your enemies and lead your people to greatness.*

As each raindrop hit me, I felt a surge of power flooding into my veins. I choked on my own grief as my tears mixed with the rain and washed my body clean. A scratching pain began on my chest, and I groaned aloud as tattoos started to appear across my flesh depicting ancient runes, the likes of which I'd never seen.

I could feel the goddess pouring her power into me like I was nothing more than a vessel to be filled. All throughout the campsite, slayers cried out as the goddess imbued them with gifts too, our power growing while our pain burrowed deep and scarred us from the inside out.

But my grief hit me harder than any gift she bestowed on me, and I raised my head to the sky and roared my rage into the heavens. I wouldn't forget that she had forced my hand in this, that she had refused to help me when I had begged her to do so with all I was. But I would take her gifts all the same. Because nothing mattered to me now except the promise I had just made to the man I loved beyond measure.

I would rid the earth of the Revenants once and for all, and I refused to die until it was done.

CALLIE

CHAPTER TWENTY THREE

We followed Julius through the ruins as he led us along a route he clearly knew well. I kept a few steps behind the brothers as they walked together, talking in low voices about people I didn't know and places that no longer existed.

I didn't begrudge them their time together, but it sent a pang of longing through my heart. Their bond was so strong and their love for each other so fierce that it was no wonder I missed my sister more than ever while I trailed along in their company. I was something separate to the two of them. They'd found each other but I was still desperately seeking Montana.

"We were hiding underground but I couldn't resist the pull of the sun, so we came up here," Julius said, glancing over his shoulder to remind me that he hadn't forgotten I was there.

I appreciated the gesture, but I knew my presence paled in significance beside that of his brother.

"We?" Magnar asked with a frown.

"Ah yes... Well, she was nothing if not consistent. Always waiting on your return like a good little puppy. And I know what you're going to say, but she insists she's on our side, and we need her to keep controlling the weather like this." He pointed up at the sky and I frowned in confusion. Was he saying someone had *made* the sun shine today?

Magnar pulled Julius to a halt. "You can't mean-"

"Magnar?" a light, feminine voice spoke from the shadows and my heart leapt in alarm as I spun towards it.

A vampire stood at the edge of the wide courtyard we'd just stepped into. Her hair was dark and spilled over her shoulders in tumbling waves. She wore a tiny black nightdress which showed a whole lot of her toned body, and her full lips were parted in astonishment.

My grip tightened on Fury, but the vampire made no move to attack us, nor did the sun seem to be bothering her. I frowned in confusion as Magnar's muscles tensed and his fist closed angrily.

It took me a moment to recognise her. When Magnar had shown her to me in his memories, I'd seen a slayer woman. The figure who stood before us now was clearly a vampire. More than that; she was an Elite.

The air filled with a deep kind of pressure, and I sucked in a breath as I sensed the goddess watching us. Idun's presence brushed against me, and I felt like she could see into the depths of my soul. Whether she liked what she found there or not was hard to say.

"Valentina?" Magnar asked in surprise, his gaze sliding over her new form with unveiled disgust. "What have you done to yourself?"

"We are betrothed, Magnar," she said, her voice silky as she stepped closer. "And yet you chose to sleep for a hundred years. How else could I have been there when you woke? You made a promise to wed me."

Tinkling laughter filled my ears and I sensed Idun was still close, amused by their interaction. The sound set my teeth on edge and the hairs raised along the back of my neck. I wasn't sure if the others could hear her or not. None of them reacted to the laughter if they could.

"I presumed that you would live out your years while I slept," Magnar growled. "I hoped you'd find love with someone else."

"Someone else? But I made a promise to *you,* Magnar. It's etched into my skin." She brushed her fingertips across a tattoo that curled above her heart and I realised it was a twin to the one Magnar hated on his own flesh.

"You cannot think I would still marry you?" Magnar asked in disbelief.

Julius released a wolfish laugh. "You say *still* as if you might have gone through with it once. I don't think that was ever the case."

Valentina's eyes flashed dangerously, and Julius schooled his expression, though amusement still danced in his eyes.

"You swore an oath to me. Or have you forgotten that now you've found a new toy to play with?" Valentina's gaze landed on me, and a cool breeze gusted around us as if the wind itself agreed with her less than appreciative opinion of me.

"I'm not anybody's toy," I growled.

I didn't trust this bloodsucker no matter who she'd once been, and I didn't like the way she was looking at Magnar as if he belonged to her.

"I hope you don't feel special." she sneered, and her gaze dripped over me, full of disdain. "You won't be the first whore I've had to chase from his bed."

My gaze slipped to Magnar briefly, but I simply scoffed. "I'm not *his* anyth-"

"You won't speak to her like that," Magnar growled, cutting me off.

He drew Tempest from his back and stepped towards Valentina, clearly intending to end her now, whatever past they held meaning nothing to him in the face of what she had become.

"We need her, brother," Julius said softly, laying a hand on Magnar's arm to stop his advance.

"You think we should trust one of *them?* She's a parasite now; there's only one thing they desire and only one thing to be done with them."

Fear flickered in Valentina's gaze, but she fought hard to cover it, raising her chin defiantly.

"Wait," she breathed, raising a hand as Magnar advanced on her. "Do you really intend to break your word to the goddess?"

"I swore to marry a *woman*, not a bloodsucking leech. I also swore to destroy every vampire in existence," he replied, his voice dangerously low. "I ended my own father's suffering in much the same way. What makes you think I'd stay my hand for *you?*"

"After everything we've been through together?" she asked, backing away from him. "This is how little you respect your word to Idun?"

"It is you who has disrespected their oath. You swore to remove vampires from this earth, not add to their numbers."

Magnar lifted his sword, but he froze suddenly. It was as though his muscles had seized up and he'd lost control of his body. Julius attempted to move towards him, but he froze too, a look of panic gripping his features. My heart leapt as I tried to step towards them but found myself rooted to the spot.

A feeling like icy water ran along my limbs and I couldn't lift my blade or raise a fist. I couldn't so much as turn my head. All I could do was stare in horror at Valentina as she padded towards Magnar on bare feet.

Idun's grip on my soul tightened like a fist was squeezing my heart.

"*I told you, Magnar, you must fulfil your promise to me before I will break your betrothal.*" Idun's voice echoed around us, and a shiver raced down my spine.

Valentina's mouth lifted into a radiant smile as the goddess protected her from Magnar's wrath. She closed the distance between them, pushing up onto her tiptoes as she ran a hand along the side of Magnar's face. Anger prickled through me as I was forced to watch her paw at him like he was her property, all of us unable to do anything to stop her.

"I loved you so much," Valentina breathed, gazing into his eyes like a lovesick puppy while he simply glowered back. "We could have had it all. I gave you my heart, Magnar Elioson, but you broke it time and again. This was your last chance."

"I never wanted you when you were mortal, Valentina," he growled. "And if you truly thought for a second that I'd want you like *this,* then you are utterly deluded."

She hissed at him, baring her fangs and revealing the monster behind the mask. "Did you think I would just let you leave me alone, shamed and abandoned while you ran off to chase glory in the future?"

"I didn't much care what you did. So long as it wasn't with me," Magnar replied, and I couldn't help the surge of pleasure I felt as the sting of his words hit her.

"Well, as you have taken so much from me, perhaps it's time I returned the favour," she whispered, placing her hand on his chest. "Goodbye for now, husband."

She pressed closer to him, leaning in until her lips met his. I could see the rage dancing in his eyes as she wrapped her arms around his neck, moulding her body to his.

A feral kind of anger built in me, and I longed to rip her off of him and smash her beautiful face against the sole of my boot.

A breath sighed across the back of my neck, releasing my muscles from Idun's control.

Power flowed through my body as rage flooded me, and I ran at Valentina with Fury raised to strike her un-beating heart.

She heard me coming at the last second and turned just enough for my blow to catch her shoulder instead of ending her. I buried Fury deep into her flesh, and she spun away from me with a cry of outrage.

I caught her long hair in my hand, yanking her back before she could escape but I lost my grip on Fury as it remained lodged in her back, so I threw my fist into her face instead.

Magnar and Julius remained frozen in Idun's grasp, forced to watch as our battle played out, and I could sense the goddess's delight as I fought to destroy the vampire who had once been a slayer.

Valentina howled like a banshee and threw her arms around my waist, tackling me and sending us both crashing to the ground. I yanked on her hair and ripped a chunk of it out at the roots before punching her hard enough to break her damn nose.

Valentina cursed, managing to get on top of me and squeezing with her thighs to keep me beneath her.

Her fist slammed into my face, and I tasted blood as my cheek collided with my teeth.

I punched her solidly in the stomach, forcing her to double over so

I could get my hands around her neck.

I was going to kill this psychotic bitch.

I squeezed so hard that something popped, and she threw her weight back, breaking out of my grasp and leaping to her feet as she coughed.

I scrambled upright too, spitting the blood from my mouth as I prowled after her, the knowledge of my ancestors tumbling through me.

Valentia ripped Fury from her back with a hiss and threw it at me. I twisted aside, managing to catch the loyal blade as it passed my ear, a savage grin tugging at my lips.

Kill her, it urged, longing to pierce her heart.

"How did you learn to fight like that?" she demanded, but I ignored her question, tightening my grip on the blade and lunging at her again, aiming for the heart.

Valentina's eyes widened with fear, and she turned to flee.

I raced after her, my feet swift over the crumbing debris that lined the ruins as she sped away between the wreckage.

Magnar called out to me as I left him behind, frozen alongside his brother. But I couldn't let her get away. She needed to pay the price for what she'd become. She would die for abandoning her vow and joining the bloodsuckers. I couldn't stop, couldn't think of anything other than ending her. It was like a drum had started up inside my skull and I was powerless to do anything other than move to its beat. Some small part of me knew this was insanity, understood that I needed to stop, but whether it was the power of the gods or simply the instincts my vow had placed within me, I couldn't listen to reason. I just needed to end her.

As Valentina tore away from me, she weaved from side to side, grey clouds began to fill the sky and thunder boomed loudly overhead. I glanced up, missing the feeling of the sun on my skin as the unnatural storm built in intensity, the wind whipping around me, specks of rain dashing against my cheeks.

It made no sense, the change in the weather stirring from nothing, but I couldn't think on it, my entire focus fixed on ending the immortal life of the monster I was chasing.

I rounded a final corner and skidded to a halt as I found Valentina standing in the centre of a wide open space between the decaying buildings. A male vampire stood beside her, his mouth parted in a deadly smile which revealed his sharp fangs. If it was possible, he was even more stunning than the Elite, his beauty beyond breath taking. His brown hair was pulled back into a neat tail at the base of his neck and his black suit was immaculate, at a sharp contrast to the crumbling destruction surrounding us.

My gut told me what he was, fear coiling through me like a viper waiting to strike.

I was standing face to face with one of the Belvederes.

My breath caught in my throat as my eyes stayed fixed on his ethereal beauty. Something like him shouldn't exist. He was unnatural, enticing and terrifying all at once. I wanted to turn and run screaming from him, but he held me utterly captive in his gaze. And I was struck with the sense that it would be far more dangerous to run from him than it would be to stand my ground.

"How nice of you to save me the trouble of hunting you down, Callie," the man purred with a voice as slick as silk. "Valentina's Familiar told me where to find you, but I didn't expect you to come running to me like this," he purred, and his voice was smooth and alluring.

A little bat fluttered around his head and came to rest on Valentina's outstretched hand for a moment as she smirked at me.

A trap. This was a trap which had been laid out before my feet and I'd stumbled into it like the foolish novice I was.

"I'm pretty sure I'm the one hunting *you*," I replied, my voice low and filled with a confidence I wasn't sure I felt.

"So it's true? You've taken your vow?" His eyes were alight with curiosity as he took a step closer to me.

Adrenaline spiked through my veins but I held my ground.

"Maybe you'd like to see how my training is coming along?" I offered as Fury practically vibrated with the desire to kill this vampire who called himself royal. I widened the channel that connected me to my gifts, letting them flow into me like never before as I prepared to take him on, wondering if the combined memories of my ancestors would be enough to match this monster.

"Maybe you can show me once we're wed?" His eyes glittered as they slid over me in a way that made me feel naked. I wanted to hide from his gaze and hope that he would forget he'd ever seen me at all.

"I'd sooner die," I growled.

Lightning flashed overhead, illuminating the crumbling buildings. More vampires than I could count lay waiting within each window and doorway, and I sucked in a sharp breath. Fear flickered through me, and I wondered if I might stand a better chance if I ran after all.

"You are quite the specimen," the Belvedere said as he began to prowl towards me. His movements were fluid and feline, his powerful body a machine honed to kill. I planted my feet in anticipation of a fight I wasn't at all prepared for. I wouldn't let him take me. No matter what happened, this monster wouldn't get his hands on me. "I don't think I've ever seen such a beautiful human. Wouldn't you agree, Valentina?"

Thunder crashed violently overhead.

"She's nothing special, Fabian," she sneered dismissively but I didn't miss the irritation flashing in her eyes at the comment.

"Come now, jealousy doesn't suit you. Look at the colour of her hair. At those stunning eyes which just want to drink in the whole world. And her mouth... I could take a lot of pleasure from that mouth alone."

Thunder boomed again and the wind picked up furiously. I shivered in my thin shirt, cursing the loss of my coat as rain flooded down from the heavens.

"I get it. You want to fuck her. You don't have to pretend she's something unique in the process." Valentina glared at me as if I was responsible for the things he'd said, and I swallowed back the fear that grew in me. I was a slayer. I didn't need to fear the likes of her.

"Cat got your tongue, Callie?" Fabian asked.

He ignored the pounding rain as it drenched him, sliding his jacket from his shoulders and tossing it aside. The water quickly turned his white shirt transparent, and it clung to his muscular frame indecently. I got the feeling that was meant to be for my benefit and my lip curled back in disgust.

"I have nothing to say to you, *bloodsucker,*" I growled.

His eyes burned with excitement, and he smiled at me in a way that seemed like it was meant to be flirtatious. It only made me want to stab him more.

"Hurry, Fabian," Valentina interrupted anxiously. "Who knows how long the goddess will hold the brothers? My bargain with Idun won't buy us much more time."

"It would be my pleasure," he replied hungrily.

Fabian shot towards me in a blur of motion that defied all logic and I barely had time to react before he was upon me. He seized my arms, but I'd already prepared for it and I slammed my shoulder into his chest, throwing him off balance.

I gave my body over to the memories of my ancestors as he tried to grab me again and I twisted away from him, slashing Fury at his throat to force him back a step.

Fabian advanced once more, but I ducked low and stabbed Fury at his thigh. He slammed a hand into the side of my wrist, and I cried out as the force of it resounded through my bones, barely managing to keep hold of the blade.

"Callie!" Magnar bellowed from somewhere close in the ruins, and my heart soared as I realised he'd been released from Idun's grasp.

"Here!" I yelled as I twisted away from Fabian.

He hounded after me with a deadly desire in his eyes, but I managed to evade his grasp again and again, using all of my gifts to simply stay out of his grasp, unable to give a single moment to trying to attack.

He was so fucking fast.

In the corner of my eye, I noticed the other vampires flooding out of hiding as they moved to intercept Magnar and Julius, my small ray of hope dwindling as I backed up faster, my heart thrashing with panic.

Fabian drove me back, forcing me further from the other slayers. I screamed my defiance into his face, ducking beneath his arm and throwing myself at him in a desperate bid to land Fury in his chest but he moved so fast that I struck nothing but air.

The rain slammed down on us, running over my face and pooling beneath my feet. I slashed my blade towards his stomach as he came for me again, but he batted my hand aside with a breath of laughter, his hand gripping the front of my shirt and yanking me towards him.

"Come on, you know you can't beat me, love. You may as well stop this," Fabian growled, leaning close to kiss me, his words washing over my lips.

I swung Fury towards his throat, the closeness making it easier, and he snarled as he caught my arm at the last second, dragging me against him.

I tried to fight my way out of his grip, but his fingers locked on my elbow like iron, his hold impossibly strong.

"Let me go," I breathed, and a cruel smile graced his lips as I begged.

"Not likely, love. Stop fighting now and I promise I'll be gentle with you."

I stared into his rich brown eyes, looking right at the monster who had caused so much of the ruin which had befallen my kind, and I found no mercy there, no humanity lingering at all. This was a game to him. One he only expected to win.

He tugged me closer, and I forced the resistance to sink out of my body as he reeled me in, letting him think he'd won, allowing him to believe he had me beat.

"That's better," Fabian said, his gaze roaming over my face, lingering on my mouth, then trailing to my throat.

The moment his focus locked on the pounding pulse there, I released my grip on Fury from the hand he held immobilised and caught it in the other, driving it towards his heart in a movement so fast that victory sailed through my soul a breath before the blow could land.

Fabian lurched away from me at the last second, throwing off my aim, but the blade still drove deep into his stomach.

Bright red blood gushed over my hand as he shoved me out of his arms. I staggered back but managed to stay on my feet.

"Shit," Fabian hissed as Fury burned his skin and the stench of smoking flesh filled the air between the rain drops.

I didn't wait to see him remove the blade, I simply turned and fled.

My boots pounded through deep puddles, splashing filthy water over my legs as I ran as fast as I could, locking my sights on Magnar and Julius where they fought the horde of vampires dividing us. I just had to get to them. They were the only thing that mattered.

I sped towards them, mourning the loss of Fury as I raced across the concrete, flinching as thunder boomed violently overhead, lightning joining it with a feral blast across the sky.

Tempest swung in a high arc above the crowded bodies as Magnar bellowed a challenge and my heart lifted with hope. He was so close. I only had to reach the two of them and I knew we would be able to fight our way out of this, no matter how unlikely the odds seemed.

Out of nowhere, my face collided with something impossibly solid, and I cried out as strong arms gripped me, holding me on my feet.

I fought to free myself, looking up at my attacker and finding another Belvedere staring down at me, curiosity sparking in his bright blue eyes. His blond hair was pushed back in a boyish coif and his lips lifted in an amused smile as he resisted my attempts to break away from him.

"Got ya." He grinned.

He yanked me against his chest, clamping me in place with one arm while pulling something from his pocket.

I cried out as I spotted the needle and started thrashing against his hold with more vigour, yelling curses at him as I kicked and punched and tried to crack my skull against his nose. When that failed, I bit down on his arm where he held me, tasting something sickly sweet as I broke the skin. I spat to remove his blood from my mouth, and he shoved the needle into my neck in the space between two heartbeats.

"Sorry about this," he muttered as my limbs relaxed against my will, and my heart thrummed like a hummingbird in my chest. "We'll break the curse together. You'll see."

"No," I breathed as darkness curtained my vision and he pulled me into his arms. "No..."

MONTANA

CHAPTER TWENTY FOUR

I sat next to Erik on the cream sofa in the bedroom I'd been given in his house, the air thick between us. I'd put on a new shirt, and he had too, though I swear I could still feel Andvari's hands on my skin.

I had a deep fear in my heart that I was betraying my father by being here with Erik. Spitting on his grave after he'd died at the hands of a vampire, but I couldn't let my thoughts go down that rabbit hole. It would only end in despair, and I needed to focus.

"I think it's time you told me where Valentina is," Erik said.

"I think it's time you stopped being a bossy asshole."

He cursed in frustration. I was clearly getting under his skin, and I had no intention to stop.

"I kept up my end of the deal," he pointed out.

"Not all of it. I still have to go back to Julius."

Erik's brows pulled sharply together. "You said we would break the curse together."

"And we will. But that doesn't mean I'm staying *here*."

He growled, baring his fangs as he grappled with that, and I had no inclination to try and placate him. He had to learn he wasn't in charge anymore, and maybe he could deal with his possessive issues while he was at it.

Thunder boomed and lightning flashed beyond the window, stealing our attention. My heart thrashed and I rose to my feet, running to the balcony as a sheet of rain swept over the house.

"No," I gasped in horror, wrenching the door open and stepping outside.

A cold wind battered my cheeks as I gazed toward the city and raindrops drove against me, each one like the cold kiss of iron against my skin. The clouds were thickest over the ruins and seemed to swirl in a dangerous storm, promising my destruction.

Erik joined me and his hand landed on my arm, his fingers curling around my wrist. I jolted, suddenly feeling trapped as I yanked away from him. If Valentina had been caught, did that mean Julius had been too? Or what if he was lying in the rubble somewhere, his body lifeless and cold?

Panic seized me and I backed away from Erik as he turned to me with the storm reflecting in his eyes. I no longer had any leverage on him, and my world was spinning wildly out of control.

His phone rang in his pocket, and he took it out, lifting it to his ear, his eyes remaining on me.

"Fabian?" he answered curtly.

After a beat, he pressed his thumb to the screen and his brother's voice emitted from the phone.

"-since you disappeared off the face of the Earth this morning, the rest of us have dealt with saving the entire city."

"You found Valentina?" Erik guessed, and I took another anxious step away from him, the hairs on the back of my neck creeping to attention. But I didn't run, because I had to know if Julius was alright. That he wasn't dead because of the plan we'd made together.

"Yes, she got away from the slayers." He emphasised the S on the end of the word, and my throat thickened.

"Slayers?" Erik growled, tension lining his jaw.

"It seems Julius has reunited with his brother, Magnar. They are still at large, but no doubt my sirelings will bring us their heads soon enough."

A breath got trapped in my lungs. If Magnar had reached the city, did that mean Callie had too? Had she stayed with him? Found her way here?

Fabian went on, "I hope you're prepared for the wedding ceremony tomorrow. I've been informed that Montana has returned to you."

"The wedding is off until the slayers are apprehended," Erik snarled.

"Oh, you really aren't calling the shots anymore, brother. The wedding is on whether you attend it or not."

"Miles is forcing the issue, is he?" Erik asked.

"Yes, and I am too. I've decided to take a bride after all," Fabian mused, and something crawled up my spine, telling me to beware.

Nightmare hummed angrily in my pocket, like it sensed the danger drawing close.

"What are you talking about?" Erik snapped. "There are no more courtiers-"

"There is now. I captured Callie Ford. And she is quite the beauty, Erik. You know how I feel about blondes."

My world tipped and cascaded into utter chaos. My pulse rose out of control and panic seized me like the hand of destiny wrapping around my soul.

I lunged at Erik, snatching the phone from his hand. "Where's my sister, you piece of shit?"

Fabian's laughter rang out of the device. "Hello, Montana. You really should have picked me, then we wouldn't be in this situation now, would we? Never mind. Your sister is just as beautiful. And by the gods, is she fiery."

"I want to see her," I demanded.

"There is not a chance in hell of that happening," Fabian said. "She's under lock and key until she walks down the aisle tomorrow."

I clutched the phone tighter, my rage growing out of control. Erik prised it from my grip as more curses fell from my lips, raising it up to speak to Fabian himself.

"Are you telling me this to try and piss me off?" Erik asked coolly. "Because I'm rather pleased actually. I spoke with Andvari, and he finally confirmed that we *are* supposed to have children with those of slayer blood after all."

My brows raised in shock as I stared at him, unsure what the fuck he was playing at by lying.

A beat of silence passed before Fabian answered. "So, you'll be attending the wedding then?"

"Of course I will," Erik said easily. "Then we'll see who breaks the curse first."

He hung up and I stared at him in confusion, but mostly fear. Because I had just become his prisoner again, an unwilling bride about to be wed to a vampire prince, and nothing could save me.

"Rebel…" He turned to me, and I took a step back. "Don't run," he warned, but those words were my undoing.

I turned and fled, racing back into the house as fast as I could possibly move.

I made it to the hallway before he collided with me, but I was ready, reaching for Nightmare and wheeling around as he pinned me to the wall. Nightmare guided my movements, and the blade kissed his throat, my teeth bared as Erik's fingers latched around my wrist to keep me from striking him. Though I wasn't sure if I really would have done it.

"Listen to me, we're going to rescue your sister," he said fiercely.

"Bullshit," I snapped.

"Why do you think I lied to Fabian? I have an idea."

"I am not getting twisted up in your games anymore, Erik. Fabian has my sister, and I will do *anything* to protect her."

"Then you will trust me, because I am the key to rescuing her from Fabian," he said fiercely, and my heart began to soften with hope. "We just might have to get married first."

"What?!" I yelled, any hope I'd had dashed to pieces in an instant.

"My best people will be at the wedding ceremony tomorrow. I'll work out the details with them on how we'll smuggle her away. We won't get near her before then. This is your best chance."

I fell quiet, my heart thrashing so hard I had no doubt he could hear it. Callie was trapped between four unbreakable walls, but Erik was offering her a door to walk through if only I could lay my faith in him. And really, what other choice did I have now that Valentina had been caught? If there was even the slightest hope of rescuing Callie, I had to take it. I'd do anything to see her free. The fact was, Fabian had my sister and he was going to make her marry him. After that…I cringed, unable to bear the thought of his slimy hands all over her.

I set my jaw, staring evenly at Erik as I made my decision, praying I wouldn't regret it.

"Proposal accepted," I said grimly.

He lifted a brow and a glint of satisfaction passed through his eyes that I wanted to punch him for.

"Good," he said formally, stepping back, and I lowered Nightmare to my side.

He turned, walking back into my room, and I stalked after him.

"It's only to help my sister," I reiterated.

"Of course." He moved to a wooden cabinet, taking out a bottle of red wine and two glasses.

I narrowed my eyes. "What are you doing?"

"It's called pouring a drink." He topped up the glasses with the red liquid, holding one out to me while I gave him a dry look.

I didn't take it, gazing at the drink as the sharp scent sailed under my nose, the look of it all too similar to blood for my liking.

"I find the best plans are often made over a drink." He dropped down onto a chair and placed my glass on the table, but I had too much wild energy in my veins to sit too.

"You're really going to help me save her?" I asked suspiciously, eyeing him closely to see if I could detect a lie in his eyes.

"Yes," he said, sipping his wine. Why was he so damn calm? Did he go around proposing to women and planning rescue attempts often?

"So?" I demanded, thinking of Callie. Of her stuck with Fabian. Would he leave her alone until tomorrow?

I squeezed my eyes shut, trying to bury the horrible images springing to mind.

"Take a breath," Erik commanded.

"I can't," I groaned. "What if he's got his hands all over her?" I spat the words, heat thumping through my veins.

Nightmare whispered promises of his death in my ear, and I had the urge to follow through on them as swiftly as I could manage.

I'm coming, Callie. Hang in there.

"He's not with her. He's with Miles and Clarice. I heard them talking when I answered the phone."

"So? He could go to her now," I pressed.

Erik pursed his lips, then took out his phone and tapped a message so fast that it was sent in less than a second. "Miles will keep her away from him until tomorrow."

"Are you sure?"

"Yes. He has always made certain that the women are untouched until after the wedding. I trust Miles with this – despite the fact that he won't listen to me about the prophecy. This whole marriage and children thing is ludicrous, but he insists that it is the key to undoing the curse. The poor asshole has no other leads, and I know he hates every second of it, but he's desperate." He frowned wearily. "It doesn't mean he'll allow Fabian to hurt her though. He'll make sure the rules are adhered to."

I nodded, having a few more choice words for what I thought of their ritual. Barbaric. Monstrous. Inhumane.

"So, what are we going to do?" I asked, a knot tying in my stomach.

Erik ran a thumb across his mouth, deep in thought. "There should be a window of opportunity after the vows are taken and your sister is moved to Fabian's quarters. My sirelings could take her by force."

Doubts spilled through me. If he did that, what would happen to Callie then? Even if Erik could save her from the marriage, she would still be a captive in the city.

"And release her?" I pushed.

He hesitated. "She is the key to the prophecy, as you are."

"She can't stay in the city. She'll help if we ask her, but not by force."

"Montana..."

"Erik," I snarled.

"Let's just get hold of her. Take her somewhere secure, and we can figure it out from there."

I nodded slowly, pretending I was good with that, but my mind wheeled to Julius and Magnar. Surely they'd help if I asked them to? Deep down, I knew I couldn't risk them hurting Erik...but if they could get Callie out of the hands of the vampires, I had to gain their assistance.

"Okay," I said, my tongue heavy as I accepted what I was going to do. What I *had* to do to help Callie.

"Can you trust me to handle this?" Erik asked. "I have some of the strongest sirelings in the city. They *will* be able to take her."

I nodded. For some reason, I really did trust him to try and save her from Fabian. But it wasn't enough. I had to get Callie away from the vampires entirely.

"What time is the ceremony?" I asked, thinking of Valentina's phone in my pocket and what I was going to do the second I got a moment alone.

"Midday," he said. "At St Patrick's Cathedral." He gave me a dark look and my heart pounded hard against my ribs. "Are you sure you're ready for this? It will be risky, but I'll protect you with my life, rebel. You know that don't you?"

"I know," I whispered. And in my mind, I added, *and I'll do anything to protect my sister.*

Erik had left me to shower while he made arrangements with his people for tomorrow. Steam billowed around me as I wrapped myself in a towel and took the phone from the pocket of my folded jeans. Erik was downstairs, and I kept the shower running to conceal my voice as I called Julius.

"Shit, Montana, are you alright?" he answered, and a bubble of relief grew in me, knowing he really was okay.

"I'm fine. I heard about Callie though..."

A crash sounded in the background and Julius sighed. "Yes, Magnar is losing his mind - he keeps breaking things."

It struck me how much Magnar must have cared about Callie. "Do you think he can keep it together for a rescue attempt?"

"Yes, but we're in the dark here, Montana. We have no idea where

Callie is or what Fabian is planning."

I took a breath, my heart hammering as I revealed what was going on. "Fabian is going to marry her tomorrow. I'll be there too…with Erik."

"By the gods," Julius sighed, and I heard another gruff voice demanding to hear what I'd said. "Just wait a minute, brother," he muttered then addressed me again. "Do you know where?"

"Yes, but Julius, you have to promise me something first."

"What?" he asked.

"You can't hurt Erik. Either of you. If you come to the ceremony, you have to save Callie. Do whatever you have to, to get my sister out of there. But you can't touch him."

Julius murmured something under his breath. "That's a big request."

"I know," I sighed, my throat constricting at what I was inadvertently admitting to here. "But you have to promise me."

I could almost hear the cogs whirring in Julius's head before he answered. "Fine. But this is a one-time deal. If Magnar or I cross that fucker again, we won't hold back."

"Got it," I breathed. "But tomorrow, no matter what, Erik is safe."

"You know you're crazy, right?"

"Batshit," I agreed. "You can curse me out for it when I see you again."

"Deal," he growled, and I sensed he was a man of his word. I could trust him with my life. With Erik's too. If only this once. "There's a ceremony at midday at St Patrick's Cathedral. I don't know where it is exactly but-"

"I'll find it on the map," he cut me off. "Do you know anything else?"

"No," I replied honestly. "But I'm sure there'll be a lot of vampires there. You have to be careful."

"Same to you, Montana. Stay safe. And when we show up, I've got a ticket out of there for you too."

"Thank you, Julius."

"See you tomorrow, damsel," he said but with nothing of the playful tone he usually used.

"See you then," I whispered, hanging up and taking a steadying breath.

The mirror on the wall was fogged up and I was glad, fearing Andvari could be lurking behind it, watching me.

I shuddered, gathering up my clothes and the phone. If Erik thought to question me about whether I'd used it to call the slayers, I'd have to lie, and lie damn well.

Heading into the bedroom, I placed the clothes in a laundry basket and hid the phone under the bed.

I found some soft sweatpants and a t-shirt and pulled them on, thinking of Julius's offer to free me too. Of what I had to do tomorrow.

The world was dark beyond the window and hail stones plinked against the glass with malice. Wherever Valentina was, I sensed she was furious about something. Had she been captured by Fabian too?

I considered going to search for Erik and moved toward the door, but before I got close, a knock sounded against it. I was pretty sure it was the first time he'd ever knocked, and it brought a small smile to my lips.

I opened the door, finding him there with his black hair mussed up as if he'd been dragging his hand through it.

"It's all organised for tomorrow," he revealed, and my shoulders dropped with relief.

One way or another, I was going to get Callie away from Fabian. With two plans in place, there was no way I could fail.

"You should get some rest," Erik said, backing up, but I caught his hand.

This was it. The end. One final night with him, and tomorrow, I would run with Callie the moment I got the chance. There was no other fate for me but that. My twin and I had dreamed of a free life for as long as I could remember, and it was time we fulfilled it. But even with that decision as clear as a beacon in my heart, it still hurt to know I may never see Erik again beyond tomorrow. Perhaps, sometimes, the right decisions cut deepest.

"Stay." The word fell from my lips and goosebumps rose across my skin.

"All night?" he asked, and I knew he was asking so much more than that.

The blood rose in my veins, and I nodded, releasing his arm and backing up. He lingered in the doorway, eyeing the threshold like he knew the weight of crossing it as starkly as I did. But I'd laid out the invitation. He only needed to accept it.

After tonight, I could never put a voice to this want. It would be my darkest secret, a cross to bear alone. But it would always be mine, a memory to revisit, darkness dipped in honey.

He walked forward and shut the door behind him with a sharp click. Tension stretched through the room, expanding into every tiny space inside me too.

I opened my mouth, trying to figure out what to say. Maybe telling him I was a virgin would have been a killer idea right now, but no words came out, and Erik stepped closer, brushing a lock of hair from my neck. I didn't covet my virginity in some fairy tale way, but if I wanted to draw some lines, now was the time. Say what I wanted, how far this could go. But I wasn't even sure of the answers to those questions myself. I was caught between two powerful emotions. One telling me to give all of myself to him, the other telling me to remain as far away as possible.

"Why are you looking at me like that, rebel?" he mused, and his low tone electrified every fibre in my body.

A blush crawled into my cheeks, but I held his gaze, refusing to cower from these needs in me. It was like I was waiting for permission to do what I wanted instead of doing what I should do. Because the shoulds were clear, written in burning letters across my mind. I should tell him to leave. I should keep away. I should bury these desires and never, ever let them surface again. But the wants…they were where the devil lay. Temptation in all its beautiful, destructive glory.

And it was just one night, that was all I was asking for…

Tiptoeing, I laced my fingers behind his neck, and a rush of heat slid down my spine like liquid fire.

He took my waist, brushing his thumbs over my bare skin as my shirt rode up. I drew in a breath as desire pooled within me and charged energy scattered through every inch of my being.

"You need to tell me what you want, because I'm not going to make the decision for you," he said, his voice rumbling through me.

"I think...I want you," I whispered as if the gods themselves might be leaning close to steal away my secret and tell it to the world.

"You *think* you want me?" he echoed back at me with a smirk.

"Don't be a dick." I scowled and he released a light laugh that was filled with a joy I rarely saw in him.

"Keep going, rebel. Your dirty talk is sublime."

I smacked his arm, but he just waited for me to continue.

"I do want you," I said more firmly, my fingernails digging into his arms.

His expression was nothing but villainy as he reached down, grabbing my thighs, and hoisting me up so I had to tangle my legs around his waist to hold on. He turned around with a burst of speed and pinned me against the door, making my breath hitch at the impact.

"I think you're bluffing," he growled with a dark smile that tied my stomach in knots.

Before I could reply, he dropped his mouth to my jaw, trailing fiery kisses to the corner of my lips. I fisted my hands in his hair, but he refused to kiss me properly, skating over my lips and working up the other side of my jaw in a sweet kind of torture. When his fangs grazed my skin, a mixture of fear and excitement set my heart pounding, and my core clenched with need.

"I'm not bluffing." I tried to turn toward his lips, but he leaned away with a hungry look in his eyes.

He dropped me without warning and my feet hit the floorboards with a thump. "Are you sure? Because I've been one hell of a bastard."

"And are your bastard days over? Is the great Erik Belvedere reformed?" I teased.

"Reformed?" he scoffed. "There's no reformation for me now. But...I also gave up trying to be better many years ago, and I think it's time I tried again."

"I like it when you try." I grazed my knuckles against his cheek, the cool touch of his skin setting my pulse racing. His eyes were a sea of ash, holding a weight of memory in them that I would never know the burden of.

"When you first saw me, were you afraid?" he asked.

"Terrified," I whispered, dropping my hand.

"And now?"

"I fear what you've done, what you might yet do. But I don't fear you."

"Why is that, do you think?"

"Because…" My throat clamped around my answer, not letting it free.

"Come on, rebel. You've never bitten your tongue before now." Mirth glittered in his eyes, and I pursed my lips.

"Because you wouldn't hurt me," I said with certainty.

He nodded. "I would protect you in this life and the next. You have given me countless reasons to adore you, but I'm yet to understand the reasons you look at me the way you do."

"I've never met anyone who can argue with me the way you can," I said, emotion burning a line across my chest. "Or someone who is so infuriatingly dispassionate about everything."

He frowned as if that might be all I had to say about him, but I went on, unravelling the reasons I wanted him for my benefit as much as his. Letting it out of my head was a release I hadn't known I'd needed.

"Because despite what you might say, I've seen you fighting to be more than a monster. I've had moments of light with you that show me who you were before the curse took root in you. And even though you're stubborn and rude and you make me want to scream sometimes, you're also the first person to wake me up from my daydreams. I don't want to escape into my head when you're in the room. I am so starkly here, wide awake and living. When I'm with you, I can feel…everything."

He kissed me, his hand pushing into my hair and pulling me closer, and our tongues met in a fervent kiss.

I reached for the top button of his shirt, breaking our kiss so our eyes met. His throat bobbed as he watched me easing the buttons free. As I pulled the last one open, my hand met with his cool skin and my eyes tracked the hard plain of his muscular chest, the cut shape of his abs and the dark trail of hair that disappeared beneath his waistband.

He shrugged out of his shirt, letting it fall to the floor, and I took in his achingly perfect body, power emanating from every hard angle of his muscles to the silvery scars that spoke of the violence he'd once faced from his enemies. My fingertips trailed to the crescent-shaped scar on his midriff and his muscles firmed as I traced the shape of it with my thumb. An ache grew in my chest at the thought of someone slicing a blade across his skin, but that thought was so wildly opposite to my upbringing that a knot of guilt tightened in my chest. My family and I had been a slave to his kind, and now I was handing myself to one of them, my heart beating for him in a way it never should have.

I scraped my gaze up to meet his, and my doubts sped away as fast as a receding storm. There was a calmness in his eyes that I felt deep in my soul too, like being this close to him was right in some way that defied all reason. My heart thumped harder for him, willing me closer, and I knew there was a part of me that had fallen for him, and that part was going to shatter and crumble the moment I ran away.

But I was still here with him now, and I didn't want to waste another moment resisting the call of my heart.

Besides, it was only tonight, the hours already falling to dust, soon to be forgotten by all but us. What was one night in the entirety of my life?

He hooked a finger into my waistband, towing me after him as he headed to the bed, the look of a heathen in his eyes.

I reached up to kiss him again, but he pushed me away, knocking me onto the bed.

"Asshole," I cursed.

His eyes lit with a game only he knew the rules to. "I know every way I want you, and in what order."

"And am I meant to comply like a good girl?" I scoffed, shoving to my feet so I was standing on the bed looking down at him.

"That would be unlike the rebel I know, I suppose," he mused.

I pulled my shirt off, unclipping my bra and shrugging out of it, tossing them both away. Erik's throat bobbed as he watched, and I shimmied out of my trousers and panties, kicking them away too. It felt like a power move, but with his eyes raking across every inch of my bare skin, it took a lot to hold my nerve.

He reached for me with a hungry groan, but I slapped his hand away, making him growl instead.

"I'll have you begging by the end of this," he warned. "You won't be in charge when you're beneath me."

"I think you need a lesson in subservience," I said with a playful smirk.

"Oh, do I now?" he said dryly, taking a step forward that said I was only a few seconds from losing the upper hand. His gaze continued to move over my flesh, his appetite for me clear. "Fuck, you're beautiful. And you've put on weight."

I glanced down at my body, caught off guard by the comment. He was right; I looked far less scrawny than I had when I'd been brought to New York. Three full meals a day, along with whatever snacks I desired, was doing me the world of good, but that only reminded me of what I'd once lacked.

My thoughts jarred and Erik took my moment of silence as an invitation, stepping smoothly onto the bed, capturing my waist and squeezing the skin there.

"No more hungry humans. I promise you," he swore. "It started with you, but it doesn't end there."

"It doesn't change what's done," I breathed.

"No, we can only start from where we are. The past is written, but we get to write what comes next."

"What's gotten into you?" I shook my head at him in maddened confusion.

He just grinned and then pushed me so I fell onto the bed beneath him, taking control once more. He dropped over me, kissing my stomach and making me gasp as he pressed his hands into the sheets, his shoulder muscles tensing beautifully as he dragged his mouth down towards my core.

"Less talking. I want you screaming," he murmured against my skin.

"If you think I'm going to just-" My words turned to a wild moan as he slicked his tongue over my clit in a long stroke that sent a shiver of pleasure daggering through me.

"Oh God," I gasped, and he did it again, his cool tongue like a weapon against my flesh, disarming me with every stroke and forcing me to submit.

He was lazy in his torture of me, like he was enjoying each twitch of my body and the way I writhed every time he dragged his tongue over that sensitive place.

"Better," he commented, and I opened my mouth to rebuke him, but he was ready for that, rolling his tongue over me in a quick motion that made me cry out. He kept it up and my body began to shudder and tense, my thighs wrapping around his head as I urged him on with every buck of my hips. Nothing had ever felt this good, his mouth on me so fucking perfect that I never wanted it to stop.

My back arched as I came with a scream, his name wrapped around my tongue, my body too hot all over, waves of electricity rolling out from that perfect spot as he continued to lap at me like I was his favourite meal.

"Fuck, that was…" I slung an arm over my eyes, catching my breath and trying to recover.

"That was your warmup," he said, grabbing my hips and forcing us to roll so he was beneath me.

I gasped, my hands flying out to catch myself as I found myself on top of him, my thighs spread over his face. His hands gripped my ass, forcing me to ride his tongue, and I grasped the pillows for support, my clit so sensitive from his first assault on me.

"Erik," I gasped, trying to lift my hips, but his fingers squeezed hard, holding me down and rocking me forward a little so he could slide his tongue into me. "*Fuck.*"

He drove his tongue in and out, and I couldn't help but fall into the rhythm of it, every part of my core throbbing, hot and so wet. His fingers slid between my ass cheeks, and I wasn't remotely ready for when he slicked his tongue back up to my clit and drove two fingers into my pussy instead. My body took over, my hips rocking back and forth as I fucked his hand and that aching heat built between my thighs again, seeking release.

His tongue didn't slow, driving against me firm and fast, and the sensitivity gave way to pure ecstasy.

My fingers tore into the pillows, my knees digging into the sheets on either side of his head, and I became nothing but an animal as I followed the needs of my body, grinding against his mouth. He slid two more fingers into me with his other hand. My pussy tightened around him, clenching every time he drove them inside me, stretching me and making me work to get used to taking so much at once.

I was coming again, but this time the strength ebbed right out of my body, my pussy clenching around his fingers and making him growl with desire, the sound vibrating through my clit. My vision darkened for a moment as I rocked my hips a few more times, lost to the pleasure he fed me, before I went slack.

He pulled his fingers free of me, grabbing my hips and moving me down to straddle his thighs. I found myself sitting over the hard ridge of his thick cock through his pants, my core soaked and my body trembling from what he'd just done to me. My nipples were peaked and swollen, begging for attention, and my black hair was a mess of waves. He stared up at me, sucking his lips clean and wiping his chin on the back of his hand.

"On a scale of one to ten, how in charge of me do you feel right now?" he asked with a smirk.

"Ten," I panted, and he barked a laugh.

"Such a liar."

I shifted my hips, and he released a low groan as his cock ground between my thighs. He was so big, I couldn't imagine how he would feel inside me. His fingers had felt more than enough.

"How many men have made you come?" he asked casually.

"What – why?" I blurted, my cheeks blazing.

I wasn't embarrassed about my life choices but telling him about my inexperience suddenly felt way too exposing.

"Relax, I don't give a damn if you've fucked a whole army. I just care about outdoing anyone who's had you," he said cockily.

"I don't want to talk about that," I said.

"What else are we supposed to do while you're catching your breath?"

I ground my teeth in realisation. "You're going easy on me."

"Well, this breather is hardly for me."

"Are you holding back on me?" I asked, irrationally angered by the thought.

"I could literally snap your spine in half, rebel. So yes, I'm holding back. You couldn't handle what I'm capable of."

"Don't tell me what I can and can't handle," I growled, but what I was really focusing on was the huge bulge between my thighs and how I was actually going to deal with it. I didn't know what I was doing, and it was going to be seriously obvious if we went that far.

"Why are you so flustered?"

"I'm not flustered," I snapped.

"Montana," he said in that voice that always undid me so easily. "Talk to me."

He leaned up, shifting his hips forward so he was sitting, and I wound my legs around him. We were nose to nose, eyes fixed on each other's while my chest continued to rise and fall, yet his remained entirely still.

"Nothing, I want this. Keep going," I insisted.

His cool chest pressed against mine and my heart began to slow, the closeness of him building another fire in me.

Traitor.

The voice cut through my head, and though it was my own, it sounded like Callie's too. I forced it away as Erik kissed my neck, his touches like brands on my skin, marking me as his. I wanted this so much and yet...

You're giving yourself to one of the creatures who hunger for your blood.

I clamped my eyes shut, battling the thought away.

Erik lifted my hips up, reaching for his waistband and I sucked in a breath, panic seizing me.

Dad would be disgusted with you.

I scrambled away from Erik, off the bed, snatching his shirt and pulling it on to cover myself.

"That's enough," I said, hurriedly doing up the buttons and refusing to look at him.

He shot in front of me, giving me no choice as he caught my chin, lifting my head to meet his gaze.

"What's wrong?" he asked. "I'm right here, speak to me."

"I don't want you here. And I don't want to speak to you," I snapped, pushing away from him, my heart hammering frantically.

Dad would be so ashamed. Callie would be horrified if she knew.

I carved a hand over my face, turning my back on him.

"Forget this. We can go watch a movie or-" he began.

"I don't want that. I don't want any of this. Or you. I want you to get away from me," I demanded, the grief I'd been bottling up for days flooding out and drowning me. I was twisted up in the shame of it, for wanting Erik at all. He was responsible for so much. My parents were both dead because of the vampires, and this was how I repaid them after all they'd done for me?

"What did I do?" Erik asked, hurt lining his voice.

"What did you *do?*" I echoed as I rounded on him, my upper lip peeling back. "You caged humanity. You made us your food. You think because you want to fuck one of us that redeems everything you've done up until now?"

Erik's jaw flexed, his eyes unblinking, and I saw the darkness in him spilling back out, the truth of who he really was.

"No," he said quietly, fury and pain shading his eyes. "It doesn't."

You're an insult to humanity.

The tears kept coming and I silently apologised to my family, pressing the heels of my palms against my eyes.

"My dad would be so ashamed of me if he knew that I gave myself to-" I swallowed the last word.

"Say it," Erik snarled. "Say what I am. The creature you despise, the one worthy of your disgust."

"You're a monster," I breathed.

"Yes, and nothing I say can change who I am, Montana. I wish it could, truly. But the fact is, I *am* the monster you've hated your entire life. I *am* the beast your father warned you of. And you're right to heed his warning."

He strode to the door, and I took a step after him, regret suddenly burning a hole in my chest at the callous way I'd turned on him.

"Wait," I called, and he hesitated in the doorway, not looking back but I had his attention.

"You're right about me, Montana. And it's time you stopped falling for my pretty lies. I'm made to lure you in, right? Looks like you've finally remembered that. Congratulations."

He strode out the door, leaving it wide open, and I knew this thing between us was finally fractured beyond repair.

I gazed out into the corridor, a bitter acceptance filling me to the brim. In the face of doing the right thing, I felt little satisfaction in my heart. Just a cold splinter digging deeper and deeper, telling me I'd just lost Erik Belvedere for good.

CALLIE

CHAPTER TWENTY FIVE

My head pounded violently, and I had the strangest sensation that I was swaying. I was lying on something impossibly soft which sculpted to my body, cushioning me on it. A thick duvet lay over me, banishing the cold from my skin.

My gut roiled and I lurched upright, heaving over the side of the bed. I didn't bring anything up though; my stomach was pathetically empty.

I blinked down at the knots and whorls in the wooden floor for several long seconds as I forced my vision to stop spinning. When I was fairly sure I wasn't going to heave again, I pushed myself upright and looked around.

I was sitting on a huge four poster bed in what was probably the biggest room I'd ever been in. Dark wooden furniture took up space around the other walls; a dressing table, heavy chest and imposing wardrobe all looking back at me from the walls of my prison, but there was plenty of empty space between it all. There was a single window on the far wall too, but heavy shutters were closed over it.

I had no idea what time it was. It could have been the middle of the night, or the sun might have been blazing outside.

I shoved the duvet off of me and scowled at the opulent fixtures adorning the space. It was so lavish that it was garish. The wood was all decorated with little hand carvings, the walls hung with gothic styled wallpaper. Even the air was thick with the scent of polished wood and supremacy.

Cool air brushed against my legs, and I looked down, finding the clothes I'd been wearing gone and a thin white robe in their place, the silk shifting against my skin.

"Motherfuckers," I hissed, my hand automatically moving to my throat, inspecting the skin for puncture wounds which were surprisingly absent.

My heart slammed against my ribcage at a frantic pace, my throat dry as I fought to stay calm and figure out what I needed to do.

I fisted the sheets and closed my eyes against the pounding in my skull, focusing on my senses, knowing that freaking out wasn't going to help me now.

The room was eerily silent. I couldn't hear a thing from beyond it, not footsteps in the corridor or the wind beyond the window. Nothing.

I cursed and stood up hastily, almost falling straight back down again as my legs buckled beneath me and I barely managed to catch the post at the foot of the bed to steady myself.

I swallowed thickly, fighting the urge to heave again and focusing on the feeling of the sculpted wood beneath my palm as I flexed my toes against the cool floorboards.

Once I was confident I had control of my body, I released the post and untied the robe, anger and embarrassment clawing at me as I found myself naked beneath it. Who the fuck had undressed me while I was unconscious? My skin was so clean it prickled from the sensation, and I could feel some kind of lotion on my flesh. Every single hair had been removed from my body too, my skin as smooth as a goddamn snake.

A shudder ran down my spine as I imagined some bloodsucker washing and changing me while I was out of it. I felt utterly violated. I had no idea what else they could have done to me while I was unconscious and had no way of knowing.

I have to get out of here.

I gritted my teeth as I pushed myself away from the bed, my legs trembling beneath me as the last of the drugs they'd filled me with clung to my body. I reached for my gifts and found them harder to channel than usual; like the fuzziness in my brain was blocking them off, leaving me weak and terrifyingly human in the pit of monsters.

There were two doors in the room, so I stumbled towards the closest one, tying my robe closed again as I went. It barely covered my ass, and I ground my teeth in anger at the ridiculous garment while concentrating on making my steps firmer and fighting off the last of whatever was flooding my system.

To my surprise, the door pulled open easily, and I peered inside the new room it revealed, finding a large blue and white bathroom. I scanned the toilet, sink, and finally let my attention still on the huge walk-in shower by the far wall, as the need to defend myself sharpened. I moved towards it quickly, each step steadier than the last, adrenaline pushing the terror aside. This was a fight or flight situation, and I'd be damned if I wouldn't go down swinging.

I grabbed the shower head and yanked on it as hard as I could with my enhanced muscles, the hose pulling tight as I threw my weight against it. I strained my arms, bracing a foot against the wall and gritting my teeth before finally ripping the metal hose out of the wall with a surge of victory. A few tiles shattered and I stumbled back so suddenly that I had to catch myself on the glass door to stay upright. Water spurted out of the hole my prize had left behind and a lump of brickwork thumped to the floor by the drain.

My head spun violently from the outburst of energy and I clung to the glass door, breathing through my nose. I ignored the large puddle of water that began to grow around my bare feet as the burst pipe continued to spurt water everywhere.

As soon as I could trust my legs to hold me again, I backed up, stepping out of the puddle into the centre of the room. I snapped the shower head off of the other end of the hose with a sharp yank, then looped the hose around my fist, creating a makeshift weapon. It was nothing compared to Fury, but it was better than going without.

I headed back into the bedroom, taking deep breaths and demanding cooperation from my malfunctioning body until I was striding across the room instead of stumbling.

I tried the other door.

Locked.

No surprise there.

I took a deep breath, focusing on the gifted muscles in my legs and hoping to hell that I was ready for whatever happened next. Either way, I wasn't going to just stay locked up in this pretty prison.

I opened my eyes and kicked the centre of the door as hard as I could, the reverberation rattling through my teeth as the full strength of my slayer gifts were thrown into the strike. The heavy wood rattled, and plaster dust was knocked loose around the doorframe, but it didn't give.

"Fuck you," I hissed at the door.

I kicked it again. And again. The door shuddered and groaned as it took the battering, but it still didn't break. I wasn't giving up yet.

I took several steps back, then ran at the door, bracing my shoulder for impact before slamming into it as hard as I could.

The resounding crash that followed made the floorboards shudder, but the bastard door still didn't give way. I snarled at it as I backed up, then rammed it again.

After the fourth attempt failed, I let out a scream of frustration and hurled the shower hose to the floor in disgust.

I turned back to the pristine room and ran towards an ornate dresser, grabbing it and hurling it over. The legs smashed as it hit the ground but that wasn't good enough. I stamped on the back of it with the flat of my foot and the wood caved in.

I ripped the back off of it and hurled it across the room into a full-length gilded mirror which smashed into a thousand pieces.

A thrill of petty satisfaction rolled through me, and I turned to the wardrobe with a savage determination. I wrenched a door open, tearing it from its hinges and sending that clattering to the floor behind me too.

I hesitated as I spotted what was inside it; beautiful dresses hung in an assortment of colours, the fabrics richer than anything I'd ever seen in the Realm. I brushed my fingers over the soft material and pulled a stunning silver dress from the hanger.

I held it up before me, appreciating its beauty for a moment, my fury at the opulence of these monsters digging into my soul like claws shredding at the last of my restraint before I tore it straight down the middle. If they thought I was going to be dressing up like some walking, talking doll then they'd be sorely disappointed.

I worked my way through every item in the wardrobe until I stood knee-high in a flood of shredded material, then spat on it for good measure.

Once I was finished, I threw my weight against the side of the huge wardrobe and sent it crashing to the ground too. It broke into several large pieces, and I grabbed a big shard of wood from the centre of the pile.

I leapt onto the bed, using the makeshift knife to shred the stupid curtains which hung around it. Next, I turned my attention to the duvet, stabbing it repeatedly as I imagined it was one of my captors. White fluff tumbled out of it, and I shook it loose, filling the room with stuffing.

The whole room was destroyed, but it wasn't enough. I needed to be free. I stormed towards the window and grabbed the edge of the heavy shutters. They were nailed down, but I gritted my teeth, throwing every ounce of my enhanced strength into ripping them off the fucking wall.

The wood groaned as the fixings resisted, but they finally gave out with a splintering crash. I fell to the floor as they came loose but quickly scrambled to my feet again to peer out through the glass.

The pale light of dawn spilled in through the window and my heart sank as I realised I'd lost an entire evening and night. Magnar would be losing his shit, probably pissed as all hell too. I bit my lip as I imagined him charging in to rescue me, and fear clawed at my heart. What if they'd killed him when they captured me? He'd been fighting a horde of vampires the last time I'd seen him, and even two legendary slayers couldn't stand against an endless tide.

I forced the fear from my mind. I didn't know anything about what had happened to Magnar. He might be coming to help me, or he might not – and I couldn't let myself linger in the fear of what that meant if he wasn't. Either way, I'd be damned if I'd just wait here like a damsel in a tower needing some prince to rescue me. Real princesses picked out their own crowns and balanced them on their heads like the badasses they were. No prince required. I was more than capable of saving myself, and that was what I intended to do.

I moved closer to the window and cursed as I spotted the heavy metal bars on the other side of the glass, stopping me from using it to escape.

I was high up in some ostentatious stone building. It looked like the kind of place that should only have existed in fairy tales. A castle built in a kingdom of blood. Green woodland spread out behind carefully maintained gardens at the foot of a stone behemoth and glimmering skyscrapers stood in the distance beyond it. At least I knew I was still in New York City.

Could they be holding Montana close by too? I tried to reach out to her with my mind like I had after I'd taken my vow, my fingernails biting into my palms as I concentrated on her, but nothing happened. Not even a flicker of power blossomed at my call. I wasn't sure how I'd done it before, and if I still held the power to do so, I couldn't access it now. Perhaps Idun was playing games with us again.

I ground my teeth in irritation; if my sister was here, I needed to get her out too. But how the hell was I going to find her? I hadn't even managed to escape this one room.

The distant sound of voices came from somewhere beyond the locked door, causing the hairs on the back of my neck to stand on end as apprehension built in my gut.

"-don't know what on Earth she's doing in there, sire. And you forbade us from opening the door, so we didn't know what else to do. We had no choice but to come for you-"

"It's quite alright," Fabian replied, and goosebumps rose along my skin at the sound of his voice. "I'm sure my fiancée will appreciate some quality time with me now that she's awake."

"Of course," the other voice replied, though he didn't seem convinced.

Fiancée? Fuck that.

I slipped across the room, keeping my footsteps silent, and grabbed a sharp sliver of glass from the shattered mirror, hiding it in the pocket of my ass-skimming robe. I snatched the shower hose from the floor as his footsteps paused beyond the door, my heart thundering with the need to fight.

I scrambled up onto a chest of drawers positioned beside the door – the only escapee from my furniture massacre - and I pressed my back to the wall as I waited for Fabian to enter.

"Well, I can't hear anything going on in there now," he muttered.

"I assure you, sire, it sounded like she was tearing the walls apart. We were worried she might hurt herself or-"

I kicked a vase off of the chest of drawers and it shattered loudly. It wasn't like they didn't know I was in here so if they wanted to hear more sounds of destruction then who was I to disappoint them?

The sound of several bolts sliding open rattled through the door, and I fell into the embrace of my gifts as I prepared to fight my way out of this elaborate prison. Power flooded into me, the effects of the drugs finally seeming to have worn off, leaving me free to claim every piece of my power.

"I'm coming in," Fabian called as a heavy lock turned in the door. "And I'd prefer it if you didn't stab me again. The last wound still hasn't healed."

My lips twitched with gratitude as he gave me that information. I knew exactly where his weak spot was now.

The door opened slowly, and Fabian stepped into the room. "By the gods, you really have destroyed-"

I leapt at him from the chest of drawers with a furious snarl and flung the shower hose around his neck as I landed on his back.

Fabian cried out in surprise a moment before I yanked the hose too tight for him to draw breath. I gritted my teeth, putting all my strength into choking him as he spun around, trying to throw me off.

My ankles locked tight around his waist, my weight hanging from the hose and tightening it further.

Fabian tried to grab hold of me and rip me free, but the angle I held him at made it impossible to grasp anything besides my legs which weren't budging a single inch.

He shot backwards, slamming me into the wall at speed. The impact sent pain flaring through my body and drove the oxygen from my lungs, but I refused to let go. He did it again and again, the fourth strike forcing me loose at last, and I lost my grip on the hose with a curse.

Fabian whirled away from me and I fell to the floor amidst the broken glass from the mirror.

I inhaled sharply as slivers of glass cut into my legs and Fabian was on me before I could so much as regain my feet. He caught me around the neck and lifted me into the air, slamming me back against the wall and baring his fangs in a feral snarl.

I clawed at his hands, my nails gouging into his skin and drawing scarlet blood as I thrashed against his hold on me. He snarled, lunging towards me like he might sink those fangs right into my throat, and I kicked him as hard as I could, right in the spot where I'd stabbed him with Fury.

"Shit!" Fabian roared, launching me away from him, and I was hurled against the wall behind the four-poster bed before crashing down onto the mattress.

I scrambled to get upright again, but he shot towards me in a blur of motion, leaping on top of me and pinning me to the bed.

I screamed curses at him as I tried to fight my way out from under him, his hips pinning me in place, his fingers digging into my wrists as he held them above my head and bared his teeth at me.

"Stop," he commanded. "You can't beat me."

I stopped thrashing just long enough to spit in his face.

Fabian glared at me for a moment, my death flashing through his deep brown eyes, my heart stalling in my chest as if it knew its time was up. But instead of the brutal ripping of teeth into flesh, the vampire prince barked a feral laugh.

I'd knocked his hair loose from its tie in our brawl and it fell around his hauntingly beautiful face as he looked down at me.

"You really want to kill me, don't you, little slayer?" he asked.

"I took a vow to kill all of your kind. You're at the top of my list," I hissed in reply.

"Well next time, I would advise you don't waste time choking me; I don't need to breathe." He grinned at me like we were playing some game, and I gave him a death stare back.

"Give me my blade and I'll stab you again instead." I glanced down at his stomach where blood was seeping through his shirt, and a small level of satisfaction found me.

He noticed my attention and his grip on my wrists tightened painfully. "That will scar, you know," he growled irritably. "And it hurts like a bitch... that said, it's been a long time since I felt real pain. So perhaps I'll let it slide, in light of our new relationship."

"We don't have any kind of relationship," I growled. "I'm never going to do anything you tell me to do, and I'm never going to stop trying to kill you."

"You know, I haven't had a woman speak to me like this before, and I'm starting to think I like it. Do you know how boring life can become when you've lived for over a thousand years? This really is quite refreshing."

"What do you want with me?" I asked, though I already knew the answer. I'd heard him refer to me as his fiancée. I just needed to hear him say it.

"You find yourself in a very fortuitous position, Callie Ford. You are to be my bride." His gaze dropped to my mouth, and he pressed his weight down on me a little harder, as if he thought I might be tempted by his proposal.

"I won't," I snarled. "I'll never marry you and I certainly won't be having any of your demon children. I'd sooner cut my own throat."

Fabian sighed dramatically. "Who told you about the children? That was supposed to be a surprise. Was it Valentina? She often loses her head when she gets jealous-"

"Can you get the fuck off of me?" I snapped, not wanting to hear another word about that bitch.

"Look who's jealous now. She told me she thought you were sharing her betrothed's bed. Magnar Elioson was a legend once, so I suppose I can understand why you might have been drawn to him. But if it's power you covet, I hold so much more than him," he purred.

"He's still alive?" I asked, grasping onto the fact that he'd spoken about Magnar in the present tense.

Fabian pursed his lips like he was deciding whether or not to answer me. "For now. The Eliosons prove harder to catch than you, love. But we'll catch up with them soon enough."

"Magnar will come for me," I growled. "And he will tear this place apart before carving your black heart from your body."

"No doubt he will try. You are rather tempting bait for him after all, and I shall be ready when he arrives."

A cold fear fell over me at his words. He was right; Magnar would come looking for me and all they had to do was dangle me before him to lead him into a trap. And as I highly doubted Fabian was looking to marry a seven-foot warrior with a thing for killing Belvederes, it would equal his death. I had to escape from this monster at all costs. I wouldn't allow Magnar to come to harm because of me. I owed him a life debt and I wouldn't see it go unpaid.

Fabian's gaze dropped to the thin robe which had fallen open in our fight, my breasts fully on display, my nipples peaked and chest rising and falling rapidly. A different kind of fear came for me then. I was pinned beneath him, his hips driven between my thighs, his strength far outmatching my own even with my gifts. I was at his mercy, and I doubted a creature as monstrous as him had any of that left in him at all.

Fabian transferred both of my hands into one of his, keeping them pinned above my head as he reached for the material which had fallen open across my chest. A stillness came over me, one which defied breath and held me captive in utter terror.

"Please don't," I breathed.

I was completely under his control, and I wasn't above begging if it would spare me from the desire I could see lighting in his eyes.

Fabian's cool fingers brushed against my skin as he caught one side of the robe between his thumb and forefinger. My heart thundered as I expected him to pull it wider, to reveal more of my body to him, and I stared up at this beautiful monster in horror. But he slowly shifted it closed instead, pulling one side, then the other, tightening the knot at my waist and making sure it was secure.

His mouth lifted on one side as he looked back up at my face, seeming to find amusement in my surprise. "I'm not a complete animal."

My lips parted, but I had no words to offer him. I only stared at the impossible beauty of his face and wondered if I'd imagined the moment of decency because it made no sense at all to me.

"If I let you go, do you promise not to try and choke me with a shower hose?" Fabian went on.

"No shower hose," I agreed icily.

I just wanted his damn hands off of me and his hips out from between my thighs.

"Too easy," he said, shaking his head in disappointment, like he'd actually wanted me to keep fighting him. "What if I let you buy your freedom with a kiss?"

"I'd sooner cut my lips from my face," I growled.

He leaned closer to me, his breath brushing across my skin, and I recoiled into the mattress, trying to buy back the space he was devouring.

"Come on, slayer," Fabian breathed. "I promise you'll enjoy it."

My mind was spinning, my heart thundering, the need to escape blaring through my thoughts and making it difficult to form any real plan, but as one came to mind, I clung to it and didn't let go.

"One kiss?" I asked, my gaze falling to his mouth, to those fucking fangs. Could I really kiss a mouth which had tasted so much human blood? Could I really afford to be choosy with escape plans when this was the only one that had come to me?

"Just one. Unless you decide you want more – I'm sure I could be persuaded if you do."

My throat bobbed. This was a terrible idea. The worst. The idea of kissing a creature born of death and ruin turned my stomach, but if I could just distract him long enough…

I nodded, unable to say the words, just needing to act.

Fabian looked so fucking smug that I could only believe he thought himself irresistible, but that was fine by me. Let him think I was fickle enough to have forgotten all I stood for and all I had survived beneath the rule of his kind the moment he turned his too-perfect features on me. Let him think I was nothing but a lust-struck bitch who was utterly enthralled by the vampire prince just because he'd deigned to look my way.

His vanity would be his downfall if I had anything to do with it.

I held myself in place and let Fabian press his cold lips to mine, his kiss light at first as I froze beneath him, a mixture of shock and several moments of me questioning every decision I'd ever made in my life momentarily fixing me in place. He seemed to take my horrified stillness as encouragement though and he pressed his mouth to mine more firmly, reminding me of my plan and encouraging me to kiss him back.

I let my mouth move against his, shuddering at the brush of his fangs against my lips despite my efforts not to. Fabian seemed to think it was from pleasure though, and he released his grip on my wrists so he could push his fingers through my hair and tug me closer.

My heart pounded with excitement as I arched my spine beneath him, moving my hand between us and running my fingers down the hard plane of his chest. He groaned in pleasure, flexing his muscular body against me, his cock growing hard between my thighs.

Shit.

I needed to move faster. I released a moan, pushing my hips up against his, letting his tongue press into my mouth as I covered the movement of my hand which fell to the pocket of my robe.

With a spike of adrenaline, I took out the sliver of glass before he could realise what I was really doing then slammed it into his side with as much force as I could muster.

"Fuck!" Fabian swore loudly as I yanked the glass out again. He reared backwards to escape me, but I slashed it across his face, cutting deep into his eye.

The back of his hand connected with my cheek and my vision swam from the impact as I was knocked onto the mattress. I ignored the pain, twisting out from beneath him and holding the glass ready between us once more. My own blood coated the edges of the jagged piece of mirror, the sharp shard cutting me too, but I couldn't feel it, my need for his death far outweighing any pain.

Fabian snarled at me, his fangs bared like he might just bite me, but I didn't back down. I couldn't give in to this monster's demands. I refused to do what he wanted, and if that meant I might die, then so be it. I'd rather die a mortal death than face the fate he wanted for me.

"You're a cunning little bitch, aren't you, slayer?" he growled.

"And you're a vain piece of shit. What kind of idiot would think I wanted to kiss him right after trying to kill him? You might be pretty by vampire standards but everything about you disgusts me. If you're dumb enough to think I really might have wanted to fuck you, then the least you deserve to lose is an eye. Next time I'll aim lower." I gave his cock a pointed look and he snarled at me.

The door banged open, and a surprised laugh filled the air as I scrambled backwards and put more space between both Fabian and the newcomer.

"It seems your charms aren't working on this one, brother," the blond vampire said as he stepped into the room with a wide smile on his face. I glowered at the Belvedere who'd captured me, wondering if I should try to get my makeshift glass dagger into his heart while I had the opportunity.

"What are you doing here, Miles?" Fabian asked irritably.

"I thought I'd come and make sure you weren't trying to sample the goods before your wedding night." His gaze slid over me and the destroyed room as if he wasn't sure what he'd just interrupted.

I eyed the open door behind him like it held the answer to all my dreams. Freedom whispered sweet promises to me on the breeze from the corridor, beckoning me to take it.

"She likes it rough," Fabian said with a shrug as he moved to stand upright, and I watched in stunned fascination as his eye slowly mended itself and the skin surrounding it stitched itself back together too.

"Is that so?" Miles raised an eyebrow at me, taking in the robe which barely covered my nudity and the blood-spattered shard of glass in my hand. Something which looked disconcertingly like concern burned in his gaze and my suspicions sharpened. They didn't care about me. This was about their fucked-up ritual. "You know you're supposed to wait until after the wedding for all this? And if she doesn't want you, then there are other ways. The rules are in place for a reason, Fabian." He gave his brother a stern look and Fabian sighed dramatically.

"I don't need your help," I snapped. The day I accepted help from a

Belvedere would be a cold day in hell.

"You see? She's enjoying it," Fabian said, giving me a cocky grin.

I whipped my arm back and launched the shard of glass at him. He moved at the last moment, and it pierced his bicep instead of his heart, but it had been damn close and the beat of silence that followed my strike only punctuated that fact.

"Nearly," Fabian mocked as he pulled the glass out and tossed it aside, but I caught the look which passed between him and Miles. "You see, brother, it's just a little roleplay. The slayer who secretly lusts for the vampire. You've got to admit it's pretty hot."

Miles pursed his lips as if he didn't believe his brother for a moment but wasn't sure what else he could say.

"I just thought I'd come and give Callie the choice all of the courtiers get," he said, his blue eyes meeting mine as he spoke. "Even though there isn't time for you to get to know us properly now, you should know that you can choose which prince to wed. You can pick me if you aren't so keen on Fabian's bedroom manner for example."

Fabian bristled. "You're already going to wed that other girl."

"What other girl?" I demanded, but they ignored me, Fabian carrying on as if I hadn't spoken at all.

"As the rules dictate, *I* will be the one to wed this one," he said.

"The rules say that if a courtier refuses to choose, then she will have to marry the prince who was not selected by the others, but Callie still has the right to choose." Miles smiled at me encouragingly and I glared at him in response.

"If you are so keen to follow the rules, then why didn't you bring Erik along?" Fabian asked.

My gut prickled at the name of the worst Belvedere. The vampire who'd stolen my sister from me. The reason the slayers had been wiped out. The only way I'd ever want that creature close to me would be if I was plunging Fury through his heart.

"I think it would be a little inappropriate for Callie to share a husband with her sister," Miles said dismissively. "Aside from any other reasons. So, what's it to be then, Callie? Would you rather marry Fabian or me today?" He gave me a bright smile complete with fucking dimples. Rage built in my chest.

It wasn't a choice at all. I didn't want to marry either of them, and I wouldn't be forced to make some irrelevant decision just so they could feel better about the fact that they were planning to force me into this. Marrying either monster was exactly the same. It was a fate worse than death and I refused to play along with it. I had no intention of going through with it and I wouldn't even pretend otherwise.

"I'm not going to marry either of you," I snarled. "So you can take your fucking offer and your fake charm and shove it up your asses."

Miles's smile dropped and he glanced at Fabian as if he wanted to say more, but his brother grinned in satisfaction.

"You really won't make a choice?" Miles urged one last time.

"If you want to know what I would choose, it's this; I would choose for you to return my blade to me so that I might kill each and every one of you," I hissed.

"There you have it," Fabian said triumphantly. "She's mine."

Miles sighed and turned to leave, drawing Fabian after him.

"I just hope we're right about using a slayer for this," he muttered.

"I'm sure we are, brother," Fabian replied, his gaze falling on me one last time as he allowed Miles to lead him from the room. "And I may as well enjoy finding out either way."

"Where is my sister?!" I yelled, hounding them towards the door, but they snapped it shut before I could reach it, neither of them offering me an answer.

They locked the door behind them, and I released a frustrated scream as I was trapped yet again.

MONTANA

CHAPTER TWENTY SIX

My heart was hollow. I only had one real desire left in my desolate heart. Save Callie.

I felt awful over how things had ended with Erik last night, and that regret in itself was eating me alive.

How could you care about a monster?

Because he's not a monster…

A tidal wave of pain was on the verge of overwhelming me, my grief over Dad excruciatingly sharp once more. I'd hardly slept, tossing and turning while grappling with the confliction I faced. But this morning brought a new kind of clarity. Today would be my last day with Erik, and I couldn't leave things like this.

I headed to the door, a purpose filling my stride. I needed to find him, to explain myself better so at least he could understand that I didn't think of him as a monster. That he'd altered my beliefs and grown new ones in their place. That I was struggling with an inner turmoil and I didn't know how to express it.

I opened the door and came face to face with Nancy. Her dark curls hung close to her cheeks, and she had the sort of expression that said she'd recently been berated.

"Oh, Miss Ford, good morning." Her eyes darted down the corridor, then back to me. "I have strict instruction from His Highness, it's best we get started."

I glanced longingly over her shoulder as she nudged her way into the room, pulling a large suitcase behind her.

A voice caught my ear downstairs, and I lingered in the doorway a moment longer as I listened.

"Good morning, Prince Erik. You told me to, er, find you? About the promotion..?" I recognised the voice of the guard, Egbert, who'd remained out in the sun yesterday.

"Get out," Erik bit at him.

"Oh, it's just…you asked me to come to you after I finished my shift and-"

"Get out!" Erik roared, and the whole house trembled. I cursed as I backed up into my room and closed the door, hesitating on what to do.

Go to him.

Don't go to him.

"Prince Erik is quite anxious this morning," Nancy commented with a quaver to her voice, and I turned to her, taking in her concerned expression.

"I think that's my fault," I muttered.

"Don't be so hard on yourself," she said, shaking her head. "A man's mood is within his own control. Besides, I see no reason why he's down there pouting. It's his wedding day, and he has such a lovely bride." She gazed over the baggy pyjamas I'd slept in. "Well, he will have when I'm finished with you." Her mouth hooked up in a teasing smile and I relaxed, glad to have a familiar face on a day like this. *Dammit, Nancy, when did I come to like you?*

I moved toward her and glanced down at the suitcase. "What's in there?"

"Everything we need to turn you into a princess."

"Great," I grumbled.

It wasn't like I'd wanted this ceremony to ever happen, but at least yesterday Erik and I had been on the same team. Now we were miles apart on the most important day of my life. And not because I was getting married, because it was my only chance to save Callie. There wasn't a force on earth which would get between us now. My father had already been taken from me, and I'd walk to hell and back before anyone hurt my sister too.

"I thought maybe…you and Erik had grown closer," Nancy said as she unzipped the case. "It's a shame to find neither of you smiling today."

My heart split open and in a moment of madness, I lurched toward Nancy, pulling her into a hug. *Dammit, Nancy, why are you so likable today?*

She gasped, hugging me back as I clung onto her. "By the gods, are you alright?"

No. Not a bit. Not remotely.

I nodded, pulling away from her, vaguely patting out the creases I'd put in her dress. "I'm fine. Let's just get this over with."

She hesitated like she wanted to push me for more details, but I was shutting down like a cram. Or a clam? Something like that for sure.

"As you wish." Nancy guided me to a dresser across the room.

We set into our old routine where she made me look beautiful whilst I watched the woman in the reflection be transformed into a lie. She went overboard today, perfecting my face before adding a shimmer to my collarbone and a dash of glitter to the very ends of my eyelashes. When she was done, I looked like a strange, ethereal creature. Like something out of Dad's stories. I vaguely recalled the term 'fairy' and was sure it was fitting.

Nancy weaved my hair into an ornate plait, winding a white ribbon through it before placing tiny jewels around it.

When she was finished, she took out the biggest item in the suitcase: a white bag which clearly contained a dress.

I stood from my seat, suddenly curious as she unzipped the bag and slid out the most elaborate piece of clothing I'd ever seen. A white gown with a large, shimmering silk skirt and a lace bodice. Interwoven with the lace were gems similar to those in my hair, looking like tiny fragments of starlight.

Nancy handed me some white underwear, and I turned around before pulling on the slinky items. My breasts were pushed up, so I actually looked like I had cleavage, and the stockings clipped to my thighs made me feel kind of powerful. Maybe because one of those would be perfect for sliding Nightmare into.

Nancy helped me into the huge gown and took several minutes to do up the many tiny buttons. I glanced over my shoulder at the mirror on the dresser, taking in the beautiful lace, which was entirely transparent down my back, unsure how to feel about all this glamour. It had no purpose. Just a thing to be beautiful and nothing more. I didn't see the point in it.

When she was done, she took out two white shoes with a small heel on them.

"I know you don't like the high ones," she said with a smile, and I was glad she'd remembered. I'd rather have gone barefoot than worn something I couldn't run in. Especially today, when I knew I'd have to.

She helped me into them and adjusted the puffy dress around my legs. I felt like a doll, wrapped up in so much finery; it was like a disguise for the woman I really was.

The door flew open, and Nancy dove in front of me with outstretched arms as if she was taking a bullet. If Erik's expression could have fired one, she definitely would have been dead.

"Rebel," he snarled, stepping into the space, and dominating every inch of it.

"You cannot see her!" Nancy waved her arms, trying to hide me from view and I gazed at the back of her head in astonishment. "It's tradition!" she begged.

Erik's gaze slammed into mine, and my heart stumbled as I tried to read what he was thinking.

Ever-so-slowly his eyes drifted to Nancy. "Do you know how many shits I give about tradition this morning?"

"I-er-I-" Nancy stammered.

"None. Not one. Not even half of a squirrel shit. Now get the fuck out."

Nancy stumbled as she fled the room and Erik slammed the door behind her, his expression as sharp as a blade.

"Erik-"

"Silence," he commanded, and his cold tone sent an earthquake through my bones. The heels on my feet suddenly felt way too high to even try and outpace him in his furious rage. "If you haven't caught on already, we're going back to the old way of doing things. I tell you to jump, you say 'how high'."

I folded my arms, seething as he tried to make me bow to him again. "I don't recall ever doing that."

"Then you're going to start now. I'll help your sister today, then you can both help my family end the curse. After that, you're free. You can go live in the desert or up a fucking tree. Frankly, I don't care."

I ground my teeth, feeling so hurt that he'd do this, bringing us full circle back to where we started. But if this was how he wanted things to be, then fine. I wasn't going to waste my breath trying to convince him otherwise, and I wasn't going to let him see how much I was breaking inside. He may have been declaring to relinquish his control on me and set me free once the curse was broken, but it wasn't out of the goodness of his heart. He wanted rid of me.

"Suits me." *Except the part where I hang around here doing whatever the hell you say. I'll work to break the curse on my own terms.*

I expected him to leave, but he didn't. His eyes travelled down me, and I felt somehow more naked in the huge dress than I had last night.

"Passable," he muttered, and I bit down on my tongue, refusing to let him see how furious I was over him reverting to his nasty little habits.

I took in his attire for the first time; his hair was swept back with a sleek iron crown sitting on his head. He was dressed in a fine, black suit with a white flower attached to his chest.

"You look just like the day I met you," I said coolly. "Evil in a nice suit."

"And you look the exact opposite to the day I met you. All dressed up and obediently waiting to marry me. Guess I tamed you after all."

I huffed out a furious breath, wanting to strike at him for that comment. This could be our last moment alone together, and this was how we were wasting it?

I swallowed my pride, calling him out for what I knew to be true. "You know what? You don't have to be an asshole just because you feel something, Erik. I feel like shit too."

His jaw pulsed with anger, but his eyes told a different story. One of loss and hurt.

I stepped closer, breathing in the cypress scent of him, forcing myself to stop being petty. Because I wouldn't be getting this chance again.

"I'm sorry," I whispered, my throat barely releasing the word.

He took my chin between his finger and thumb, gazing directly into my eyes like he was about to kiss me. But instead, he crushed my heart in his fist with his answer.

"I'm not."

He strode from the room, leaving me with the wind knocked out my lungs and rejection burning the back of my throat. It looked like we were back to square one, and with the seconds ticking down to our marriage, I feared he was about to renege on all his promises.

CALLIE

CHAPTER TWENTY SEVEN

I sat on the destroyed bed and watched as the water from the burst pipe flowed out of the bathroom and began mixing with the white fluff from the shredded duvet. I felt like it mirrored the mess of emotions which were stirring inside me. I was brimming with unspent energy, but I was stuck here, waiting for a fate I'd never accept.

Some of the cuts on my legs and palms were still bleeding, and I welcomed the pain. It gave me something real to match the ache in my chest. How could I have been so stupid? Valentina had led me right into a trap and I'd fallen for it like the naive girl from Realm G that I was. Why had I let myself believe I was something special? Just because I could access my ancestors' power now, I'd begun to think I knew what I was doing with those gifts. But I was still the same caged girl I'd always been. And when it came down to it, the vampires were driving my fate yet again.

A knock came at the door, and I stilled as I looked up. The shard of wood I'd used to shred the duvet sat beside me and I reached for it instinctively, tucking it beneath the torn sheet and keeping my fingers tight around it. I wanted to be armed against whoever came through the door next. Even if it hadn't done me much good so far.

"Callie?" a woman called from the other side of the door.

I didn't reply. Why should I? These monsters didn't care about what I wanted despite any use of manners or consideration toward my feelings. She could pretend to ask my permission before she came in, but we both knew she'd be entering no matter what I said.

After several seconds, the bolts slid aside, and the door was unlocked.

"Fabian mentioned you attacked him when he came to see you," the woman said gently, and my anger stirred again at the false display of concern. "I'd prefer it if you didn't try that with me...okay?"

"How about you just open the door and let me go. Then I'll promise not to harm you," I offered.

"You know I can't do that." She sighed and pushed the door open. There was a sharp inhale as she spied the devastation that surrounded me, and I allowed myself a small smile. It was a petty victory, but I was happy to take whatever wins I could claim.

After another few moments of hesitation, the woman stepped inside, lifting her pale blue gown high to keep it out of the water which now covered most of the floor. My lip pulled back as my gaze fell on her unreal beauty, and there was no questioning who had come to visit me now. Clarice Belvedere was almost as stunning as the goddess Idun.

"When Miles told me you'd trashed the place, I thought I'd be discovering a few displaced cushions. Maybe a smashed vase...this is... Well, you've certainly surpassed my expectations."

"Maybe you shouldn't underestimate me," I replied. Although I was beginning to believe that I'd definitely *over*estimated myself. I'd gotten caught up in the idea that the gifts I'd been bestowed had instantly given me what Magnar had spent years working to achieve. But that was foolish; I may have been given access to my ancestors' memories but none of those achievements were my own. I was going to have to learn my own lessons about what it took to survive in this world ruled by my enemies, and it looked like my first challenge was already upon me. I had no idea what I was doing but I knew I had to do *something*. Perhaps if I could figure it out, then I might be able to make up for the terrible mess I'd made for myself.

"Apparently not." Clarice dragged her gaze away from the destroyed bedroom and fixed her eyes on me instead.

"What do you want?" I asked. She'd left the door open behind her and I was tempted to run for it. I knew I wasn't faster than her but if I could do something to slow her down, maybe I could get enough of a head start. Perhaps I'd be able to find somewhere to hide and slip away before they discovered me.

"You need to get ready for the wedding," she said with an encouraging smile. "I had thought we'd do it here but perhaps we should take everything to my room instead."

"I'm not getting married," I replied in a low voice, my grip tightening on the wooden stake. Dad had told us old vampire stories where a stake was always the best weapon to use against them. Maybe it was worth a shot.

"I know this must all seem very sudden and confusing. You haven't had a chance to get to know my brother and now we're marching you straight down the aisle. But I assure you, he's a good man beneath all the theatrics. He'll treat you well-"

"He's not a man," I corrected. "He's a cold, dead, monster, and I will die before I'll marry him."

She winced a little, but her moment of hurt was quickly locked away again behind her bright blue eyes. "I'm sure it's difficult to adjust to the idea of this. Normally, you'd have a few days to get to know the princes and it would be easier to-"

"I don't need to get to know him or hear any fucking songs about how wonderful he is, so you can take your platitudes and piss off."

Clarice's gaze turned icy. "Look, I really don't want to have to do this the hard way. But if that's what it takes, then I'm willing to do it."

"Don't try to pretend you're anything other than a self-righteous bitch. The reality is that you're making me do this against my will either way. So if you're gonna be the kind of person who kidnaps people and then forces them into a marriage, just own it."

For a moment, it seemed like Clarice might argue her point, that she might try and deny it, but the truth was sitting there between us like a steaming turd in the room wearing a top hat.

"Fine." Clarice snapped her fingers and six male vampires moved into the bedroom. "Bring her to my chambers," she commanded. "We'll have to do this there."

They advanced on me, and I tightened my grip on my concealed weapon as I opened the floodgates on my gifts. I knew my chances of fighting them off were fairly slim, but they'd made the mistake of making it clear just how much they wanted me for this marriage. They weren't going to kill me. But I had no such rules about them.

As the first vampire reached out to grab me, I snatched his hand, yanked him forward, and raised the stake. It slammed into his heart, and Clarice screamed in shock and horror as he fell to dust.

"Damian!" she called as if there might be a chance of him coming back from death for a second time.

I threw myself backwards as the other vampires leapt at me. I tumbled over, coming up in a crouch on the far side of the bed with the stake held ready.

I gritted my teeth as power flooded through my muscles and the vampires raced towards me as one.

The first to get close caught a kick to the chest and was thrown across the bed to crash down on the floor. I swung my stake at the second, slicing it across his abdomen so that scarlet blood flew, splattering over my white robe as he fell back.

I ducked beneath a set of grasping arms and tried to roll across the bed to gain more space, but a hand clamped down on my ankle, violently yanking me backwards.

I flipped over and kicked the vampire who'd caught me squarely in the face. My heel smashed against his teeth, and I let out a scream as his fangs pierced the skin and venom poured into the wound. Burning pain flared through my foot and my concentration wavered as I swung the stake again.

One of the vampires struck my arm and the stake went clattering to the floor.

I tried to punch and kick my way free, but they leapt on me, pinning my limbs in place and finally tying my wrists behind my back.

One of them picked me up and swung me over his shoulder before I could do more than call him a bloodsucking dickhead.

He raced out of the room at inhuman speed, turning left and right down lavish corridors before finally arriving at an ornate wooden door with a huge golden knocker hanging from it. I tried to fight against his hold on me but there was nothing I could do to free myself. I'd failed again and the knowledge left a weight hanging in my chest.

Clarice appeared beside us in a blur of motion and opened the door, indicating for the male vampire to bring me inside.

I was flipped right way up again and deposited on a soft cream sofa in the middle of a room which was so large it could have housed forty people.

White furniture stood around the edges of the space, each piece decorated with paintings of golden flowers. Everything else was very pink. The walls were a dusty rose colour, and every flat surface was filled with cushions and blankets in colours ranging from fuchsia to baby pink. The four-poster bed was absolutely enormous, and I was sure it could have slept ten comfortably.

"No wonder they call you the Golden Whore," I said. "How many of the men you've seduced with your ungodly face do you lure to that bed at a time?"

The male who'd carried me here slapped me so hard that my head snapped to the side and my ear started ringing. The mixture of pain and humiliation made my eyes burn, but I couldn't let these monsters see me fall apart. I'd never let them know how close I felt to my breaking point.

Clarice surveyed me through tear-filled eyes as she stood over me. "Damian was a part of my harem for two hundred and seventy years," she exclaimed, and I almost could have bought into her crocodile tears if I didn't know she was a heartless bloodsucker responsible for the death of countless humans in the millennia she'd spent stalking the earth.

"Who?" I asked with a frown as I fought to keep my composure.

"The vampire you just killed!" she exclaimed, choking on the words.

"Well, it sounds like he got two hundred years longer than he should have," I replied coldly.

Clarice bit her bottom lip, and I eyed her fangs warily as her hands curled into fists, her composure cracking.

"You really think we're all nothing but monsters?" she asked in a voice so low it was nearly a whisper. "You feel no remorse at all for killing him?"

I almost laughed at the question. Why the fuck would she expect me to care about killing a bloodsucker? But the look in her eyes told me she really couldn't understand it. I scowled at her, infuriated by the idea that she couldn't see what she was, what they all were.

"Imagine you'd been born into a prison where there was never enough food and you had to watch your family suffer every day. In the winter, you had to worry about freezing to death despite the fact that there were warm clothes and blankets laying unused on the other side of the electric fence you're not allowed to cross. And you have to endure all of that and more just so your blood can sustain the unending lives of a bunch of parasites who should have died a thousand lifetimes ago. You cling to life long after your time has come and gone, living off of us like a bunch of fleas, and then you expect me to feel *bad* about killing one of you? When have you ever felt bad about killing one of *us*?" I spat.

"Don't you understand? The Realms were created so that we wouldn't kill humans anymore. We don't feed from you directly so that we don't risk losing control. It's to protect you-"

"We only need protecting because *you* exist. You're forgetting that you need humans to survive but we don't need *you,*" I growled.

Clarice nodded as if she accepted what I was saying, or could at least see that I wasn't about to have a sudden change of heart, but if she really did understand any of it, then she wouldn't treat us the way she did. We were nothing but food to them, and they were nothing but monsters to me.

"There are things you don't understand, Callie. It's not as though we can just stop being what we are; my brothers and I were cursed a long time ago. And believe it or not, we don't *want* to be this way. But the only way to change it is to break the curse." Her eyes roamed over me like there was more to that declaration, but she said no more about it.

"What does that have to do with me?" I asked.

My foot was still burning painfully from the venom, but I gritted my teeth against it, refusing to complain about it to her.

"Possibly everything. The prophecy speaks of twins; we believe you and Montana could be a part of the answer we seek."

"So, this prophecy says I have to marry some asshole with pigtails and because I'm a twin, you think everything will just go *poof* and your curse will end?" I sneered.

"Not exactly..." Clarice looked away awkwardly.

"Oh right, I forgot the part where you want him to impregnate me with his twisted demon spawn."

Her eyes widened and she moved towards me, shaking her head as she dropped down to sit beside me on the couch.

"No, no, the children aren't twisted," she said, and she reached out as if she might touch me, but the look I gave her made her drop her hand before it made contact. "I promise, when you have your babies, you will love them unlike anything else in this world..."

"What aren't you saying?" I asked, sensing she was holding something back and ignoring the implication that I would be going through with some forced pregnancy.

"You're strong. The strongest we've ever had in fact. We've never had anyone who has actually taken their vow," she said reassuringly. "It won't matter for you."

"What won't?" I frowned, refusing to let the subject drop.

"Well, it's just that...not all of the wives have survived the births," she said gently.

I barked a laugh, but it held no humour. "Of course they haven't. And why would you care about that anyway? We're only humans, just things for you to use one way or another. So long as you get what you want from us."

"We do care," she protested. "It's why we turn you as soon as it's over. A vampire can heal. Those who are strong enough to hold on while the change takes place live a wonderful life here-"

"Oh yeah, it sounds great. You rip us away from our families, rape and murder us all before bringing us back from the dead and saying you *care*." I kept up my aggressive tone, but my heart was racing. This was the fate they had in store for Montana. This was what I'd come so far to stop, and yet I'd ended up in the same fucking net as her. There had to be a way out of this for both of us. The wedding was today. Tonight, they'd expect to consummate it and seal our fates. There was no way I'd let that happen.

"No one is raping anyone. If you don't want to take part in a natural conception, then we can use insemination-"

"Fuck you and your supposedly reasonable bullshit," I spat, because it was clear she didn't give a shit no matter what she said. She planned to use me and my sister for this regardless of our opinions on it, and nothing I said would sway her from it.

"I can see we aren't getting anywhere with this," Clarice said coolly. "So I may as well spell it out for you. You *are* getting married today. And one way or another, I will get you in that dress and have your hair and makeup styled to perfection. If it comes to it, I will shackle and gag you, then drag you down the aisle myself. Or you can be a good little girl and do as you're told. Either way, this *is* happening because it could end the curse. Then we'll all be free. Surely you want that too? So what's it to be?"

I glared at her as I turned over everything she'd said. It didn't seem like I had much chance of getting out of this while I was still cooped up in this place. If they shackled me, then it would only make escaping more difficult. I needed to be free to run. And I'd damn well need to run before this day was up. There was no way I was marrying a Belvedere. And I wouldn't let that fate fall on my sister either.

"When is Montana getting married?" I asked, knowing I had to get her out of this place. If her wedding was due to go ahead before mine, then I had to make some bargain to change it.

"It's a joint ceremony," Clarice replied. "You'll see her at the altar."

My mind spun with that knowledge. We'd be together, waiting for the brothers to arrive and claim us. But there were things Clarice didn't know about the wedding. Like the poisoned blood which would be served to their guests. It might just cause enough of a distraction for me to get Monty away from them once and for all.

"Fine," I replied bitterly, making sure I didn't show any of the excitement that was building in my chest. "I'll wear the stupid dress."

She beamed and took my elbow as she guided me through her room towards the ensuite at the far end. I left a bloody footprint every time I stepped on my right foot, and Clarice jerked me to a halt as she noticed.

"What happened to your foot?" she asked.

"I kicked one of your friends in the mouth."

"Which one?"

"I don't know, you all look the same to me," I replied dismissively.

She glared back at the five male vampires and one of them raised his hand sheepishly. "Craig? Did you taste her blood?"

"It was an accident, master, I swear it wasn't intentional-"

"Don't you know the punishment for biting a courtier?" She stared at him incredulously and he hung his head in shame. "Get out of my sight! All of you - just go!"

They fled the room, and I was left alone with her. Somehow that didn't make me feel any safer.

"I can't apologise enough. The water will clear the venom from your system, and you'll feel much better," she said, patting my arm.

I pulled away from her, not wanting her false apology or anything else from her at all. We continued into the ensuite, and I eyed the lavish decoration uneasily.

A huge rolltop bath with clawed feet sat in the centre of the pale pink room, and Clarice moved around me to set the water running. I watched as she poured a pink liquid into the water and bubbles began to foam on its surface.

"We'll have you fit for a prince in no time," she promised as she removed the rope which bound my arms at my back. "In you get."

I rubbed at the chafed skin on my wrists and hesitated a beat before dropping the robe and revealing my body. Clarice gave me an encouraging smile and I had to fight the urge to roll my eyes as I climbed into the water. My foot instantly began to feel better as the venom was washed away at least.

"Do you want to explain why you're even bothering with this marriage bullshit?" I asked as I sank into the bath and fought the urge to moan in pleasure. I'd never felt anything as good as the hot water which lapped around my skin. "You can force what you want without dressing it up in matrimony, so why fake it?"

Clarice frowned like she didn't much like my tone, but I didn't much like anything about any of the motherfuckers here and I wasn't going to apologise for it.

"If you're going to bear the children of a prince, then it's right that you should be honoured as his wife. The point is to show you respect and offer you a position of power within our court in thanks for what you are offering us in return."

"I'm not offering shit," I hissed.

Clarice cleared her throat, looking more than a little uncomfortable as she tried again.

"I know you haven't had the proper time to adjust to this choice. But I promise your husband will make the fertilization very pleasurable if you choose to accept him as your husband physically as well as in name…"

I frowned at that weird ass choice of wording, then cringed as I realised she'd meant me fucking Fabian so that he could stick his demon baby inside of me. The memory of his body pressing me down on the bed sent a shudder through me. I would never give myself to him like that.

"There's no fucking way that's happening," I commented.

"You know, swearing isn't particularly becoming for a wife of a prince-"

I glared at her, and she shrugged one shoulder as she let it drop.

"If you are certain you don't want to proceed physically with your new husband, then you can choose insemin-"

I ducked below the surface of the water and scrubbed at my hair, wanting to get the feel of vampires off of my body and the sound of her words out of my fucking head. It was so peaceful beneath the surface that I was tempted to stay there with nothing for company but my own thoughts, where I could pretend I was all alone in the world and not surrounded by parasites.

But unlike my undead fiancé, I had to breathe, and as my lungs began to burn, I pushed myself upright.

I pulled down a deep breath as I surfaced and swept my hair back off of my face.

Clarice reached out and started rubbing something into my hair, but I jerked away from her.

"What the fuck are you doing? I'm not a doll," I said as I snatched the bottle of shampoo from her and did it myself.

I wondered why the hell she was the one watching me anyway. She was one of the most powerful people in the country; didn't she have better things to do than babysit me? I could only imagine that she really thought I was important. Perhaps she truly believed I could play some part in ending their curse. But if that was the case, then why not just ask for my help? Either way, I wasn't going to be fucking any vampires, and I sure as shit wouldn't be allowing them to inseminate me either.

The moment I was clean, I stood up and exited the water. Clarice handed me a towel and I dried myself quickly, refusing to enjoy the sensation of the fluffy material against my skin. In the Realm the towels were rough and scratchy, but of course the vampires kept the best for themselves.

I tossed the towel at her feet when I was done, refusing to be intimidated by the fact that they'd taken my clothes from me.

Clarice approached me with a thick robe which fell past my knees when I shrugged it on. I guessed the ridiculously skimpy one I'd woken up in hadn't been her idea. Besides, it was covered in blood now, so I supposed wearing it again would have undone the work of the bath.

"What now?" I asked.

"Now I'm going to transform you into a princess." She beamed at me, and I scowled in return.

She led me back out into her room and directed me to sit on a stool before a huge dressing table. A mirror in an ornate gilded frame sat above it and I looked at myself for a moment, taking in the hardness in my expression, the grief colouring my eyes and the tightness of my jaw before turning away.

There was a knock at the door and Clarice moved away from me to open it. Three vampires filed into the room, and my gut prickled uncomfortably as I was surrounded by my enemies once more.

The male vampire reached out and lifted a lock of my long hair into his grasp. I flinched away from him, smacking his hand so he released it again and he frowned at Clarice in confusion.

"It's alright, Callie. These are my personal stylists; they're here to do our hair and makeup."

"What do you mean *do* my hair?" I asked with a frown as the vampire reached for me again.

"I'm Jacob," he said slowly, like he thought I might have trouble understanding plain English. "And I'll have this fixed before you know it."

"I was wondering, what you think of a bob?" Clarice said to him. "She has such strong cheekbones; I think she could really pull it off-"

"Who's Bob?" I asked, interrupting them. I wasn't going to sit by and let them talk about me as if I wasn't there. Bob could be some lost remnant in the afterlife for all I knew.

"It's a hairstyle," Clarice explained patiently. "It's quite short, but I think you could really-"

"You're not cutting my hair," I snarled, shoving to my feet, and pressing my back to the dressing table.

"Oh, but I really think you could pull it off, and there's nothing like a makeover to help you feel like a new woman." Clarice pouted, and I got the impression she was about to force this decision on me.

"No!" I snapped. My heart pounded in panic at the thought of them taking something so personal from me. It was bad enough that they were making me do everything they commanded, but cutting my hair would feel like losing the last thing which bound me to my missing family. "My hair is the only thing I have to remind me of my mother. I can't remember anything else about the way she looked. You're *not* taking it from me. And if you're stupid enough to bring a pair of scissors close to me, then I'll use them to kill every fucking one of you."

One of the female stylists gasped, covering her mouth in horror.

"What happened to your mother?" Clarice asked gently, and I bristled at the false pity in her tone.

"She got sick, so your people came and took her to the blood bank. You didn't even let her die with her family around her."

There was a ringing silence as the vampires looked between each other uncomfortably. I could see they didn't like to be faced with the reality of how their food was reared, and a dark hatred washed through my veins. How easy it must have been to convince themselves they weren't monsters when they could simply look away from the cost of their meals. Blood simply turned up in bottles for them, so why worry about the source of it? If suffering was caused along the way, they could just claim ignorance while filling their bellies.

Clarice reached towards me in some pretence of a comforting gesture, and I glared at her with enough intensity to set her alight.

"I'm so sorry." She released a sigh filled with regret, and my anger hardened to stone in my gut. "It shouldn't have been that way."

"Some bullshit apology won't bring her back. I guess you're sorry about murdering my father, too? And about kidnapping my sister? Just not quite sorry enough to stop your brothers from raping us," I spat.

Inside, my heart was breaking with grief as I laid out everything the vampires had done to my family, but I refused to let it show. If I allowed even a sliver of my anger to thaw, then I'd descend into a sobbing wreck. And I couldn't do that. Montana needed me. I had to be strong for her.

Clarice seemed like she wanted to say something else but perhaps she realised how pointless it would have been. Instead, she shook her head in defeat and glanced at Jacob. "We don't have to cut her hair. I'm sure we can do something exquisite with it as it is."

I looked between the two of them, searching for a lie, but it seemed like I'd actually won this battle, so I moved back to the stool and sat down.

One of the female vampires scurried away and returned with another stool for Clarice. We sat side by side in silence as the stylists got to work.

Jacob dried my hair with a strange machine which blew hot air at me, and I had to fight hard to sit still throughout the process. As much as I wanted to argue against this pampering bullshit, it wasn't doing me any harm, and I needed to make sure I wasn't bound in chains for the wedding. They had to believe I was giving up. If the price of that was being poked and prodded for a few hours, then I could tolerate it.

"I've had an idea, master," Jacob said as he switched off the machine and ran his fingers through my dry hair.

"Oh?" Clarice asked.

"What if we embraced her nature rather than trying to hide it? The marks on her skin won't be easily covered anyway, and it could be very symbolic. We could tell the world that you have a true slayer within your power. I can style her hair in a way inspired by her warrior heritage. Her makeup too." Jacob gazed at Clarice with a weird amount of trepidation as she considered the idea. He seemed way too keen to please her for it to be natural.

"What do you think, Callie?" she asked. "Shall we make you look like a warrior queen?"

I raised an eyebrow at her, surprised she was asking my opinion at all. "Better that than a vampire whore I suppose."

Clarice laughed as if I'd been joking, and Jacob got to work. He twisted the hair on the left side of my head into intricate braids and I was suddenly reminded of the way Magnar's mother had worn her hair in his dream.

Jacob left the rest of my hair free but styled it into loose curls which tumbled down my back to the base of my spine.

When he was done, one of the females moved in front of me and began painting my face. I had to grit my teeth to force myself to endure her cold touch on my skin, and I released a relieved breath when she finally stepped away.

I stared at the girl who looked back at me from the mirror in fascination. It was still me, but I looked...fierce. My lips had been painted a dark red and they appeared even fuller than usual. She'd outlined my eyes in deep black shadows and painted something on my lashes which made them seem longer. My cheekbones were more pronounced too and she'd deepened the warm colour of my skin, emphasising just how mortal I was in comparison to the undead who surrounded me.

"You look captivating," Clarice said almost smugly.

I noticed her hair and makeup had been finished as well, and I had to wonder why she'd bothered. Her face was beyond alluring without her needing to add to it. If anything, the touch of makeup dampened her beauty a little.

"Am I finished?" I asked, turning away from the mirror dismissively.

I didn't want her to know how much I liked what they'd done to me. I looked like a warrior. I just hoped I'd get the chance to prove that I was one.

"Just the dress. I've had several sent over for you to choose from." She ushered me to my feet and led me across the room into a huge walk-in closet.

There were six white dresses hanging in a line along the far wall. I eyed the swathes of chiffon, silk, and lace with my arms folded, but my gaze caught on the one at the far right of the room. It was simpler than the others; thin straps held a tight bodice of intricate lace which spilled to the floor and gathered into a long train.

"Do any of them stand out?" Clarice asked. "Is one of them *the one?*"

"Why would I care what my wedding dress looks like when I have absolutely no desire to marry the groom?" I deadpanned.

Clarice sighed like she found my continued objections tiring and crossed the room to grab the dress I'd been eyeing.

She laid it over a chaise lounge and passed me a box tied with a cream ribbon. I ripped it open and pulled out a handful of sheer lace. It took me a moment to realise it was underwear, and I tossed it back in the box before dropping it on the floor.

"No way," I snapped.

Clarice's gaze hardened and she shot towards me, spinning me around and shoving me down onto the chaise lounge. My heart leapt with surprise, and I reached for my gifts to defend myself as she loomed over me.

"I'm not going to keep arguing with you on this. Do you think I make a habit of dressing people?" she hissed. "I'm trying to help you adjust to what's going on here but let me make myself clear: you are going to wear this outfit. If I have to force it onto you, I *will* do it."

I longed to punch her too-beautiful face, but I ground my teeth as I drove the violent urges away from me. She was right. I didn't have a choice, and I had to play along to make sure they didn't shackle me.

Wearing a dress and some stupid underwear didn't mean anything. I still wouldn't be marrying a bloodsucker.

"Fine," I gave in, and she withdrew from my personal space.

I threw the robe off and pulled on the white underwear. It took me several minutes to figure out how to fix the suspenders in place, but I refused to ask Clarice for help, ignoring the way she watched me like a fly eyeing shit the entire time.

Finally, I stepped into the dress, and she fastened it for me before I could utter a word in protest, her unnatural speed making quick work of the buttons at my back. It fit like it had been made for me, clinging to my curves and hugging my body before sweeping out into a train which pooled around my feet.

"Why does this fit me so well?" I asked suspiciously.

"Well." She coughed awkwardly. "We measured you while you were sleeping."

"When I was unconscious because you drugged and kidnapped me," I corrected.

She made a non-committal noise and handed me a pair of shoes. They were white, inlaid with lace which matched the dress, and had stiletto heels that were about three inches tall. I opened my mouth to protest, wondering if I stood a chance of walking in them, but I stopped myself. Those heels could easily be transformed into a weapon if I needed one, so I'd figure the fuckers out.

I slid the shoes onto my feet and was pleased to find that after a few strides, my enhanced muscles adapted to them, allowing me to balance and hold myself upright without looking like a fool. I was soon striding across the room, confident in my steps as I went, two new weapons attached to my feet.

Another knock came at the door and Clarice shot away from me. She returned holding a small black box and held it out to me with a smile.

"What's that?" I asked.

"A gift from Fabian. I told you he wasn't all bad."

I rolled my eyes as I took it and flipped the lid open. A small card sat on top of a little black bag. The card was covered with swirling blue writing, and I lifted it out, shoving it towards Clarice.

"I can't read that."

"You can't read?" she balked.

"Maybe you should put schools in the Realms if you expect me to be educated. But that wouldn't really tie in with keeping us ignorant, would it? The dumber the humans are, the easier it is to control us, right?"

"I thought you did have schools in your Realm..."

I gave her a flat look. If that was true, then it didn't make it any better. It just meant that she cared so little about the way her food was raised that she'd never even bothered to look into it.

She cast her eyes down to the card and read it aloud for me. "To my beautiful bride, I hope you will receive this with joy and that it helps to convince you of my intentions. I promise that after tonight, when I take you to my bed and show you exactly how well I can...err, the rest of it really doesn't matter," she said clearing her throat. "Why don't you see what the gift is?"

I opened the little bag and tipped the contents into my hand with little enthusiasm. But I couldn't help the gasp that fell from my lips as I spotted my mother's wedding ring hanging from my father's chain. I lifted it up and noticed an addition to the necklace; hanging beside the ring was a diamond the size of a grape. I quickly unclasped the chain and pulled the diamond off of it, tossing it back into the box with disgust.

"Do you have any idea how valuable that is?" Clarice asked in surprise.

"It's not valuable to me at all. It's a shiny rock; I can't use it for anything, and I don't want it hanging beside my mother's ring." I fastened the necklace around my neck and released a breath as its weight fell against my skin. Something about the ring just felt calming to me, and my smile widened as I wrapped my fingers around it, relieved to be reunited with this one remaining relic from my past.

Clarice shot away from me, then sped back again, holding out a delicate silver bracelet. She threaded the diamond onto it and placed it on my wrist. "He'll be offended if you don't wear it."

I considered telling her that I didn't give a shit about offending Fabian Belvedere, but it wasn't worth it. My complaints were falling on deaf ears anyway, and if she hadn't gotten the hint about what I thought of her and her family, then there wasn't much point in bringing it up again.

"So what now?" I asked.

"Now, you get married." Clarice smiled and grabbed my arm, threading it through hers as she led me out of the room. I followed her willingly. I was more than ready to leave this place and head towards my sister.

I had no idea how Montana and I were going to get out of this mess, but I was sure that we'd find a way once we were together again. I just had to make sure I didn't end up married first.

MONTANA

CHAPTER TWENTY EIGHT

Two armed guards drove me to St Patrick's Cathedral in the city in a huge black vehicle with metal bars on the front of it. Two smaller cars drove ahead of us and two more behind. I guessed Erik wasn't taking any chances on me being kidnapped again. I'd be walking down that aisle one way or another, and I just had to hope he stuck to his word and kept his plan in place to help Callie. If he decided not to help her out of spite, I wouldn't be surprised, but luckily for me, I had a backup plan.

I hadn't seen Erik since he'd come to my room, and now I suspected the next time I did would be at the altar. Would Callie be there when I arrived? The possibility set my heart pounding and my gut spinning. For all the world, I wouldn't have wanted to be reunited in this way, but I couldn't deny that I was desperate to see her face.

The SUV pulled up outside an enormous cathedral and I gazed out at the heavily guarded street, taped off by two cordons. A horde of angry rebels were held back by a line of armed vampires, holding placards with their horrifying demands written across them.

We have the right to bite!
Let us hunt the human runts!

We'll riot 'til we die-et!

They made me sick to look at, so I returned my gaze to the gothic building which stretched up above me, tapering to three sharp points at the top of it. It looked ancient, the cream stone weathered and cracked, but besides that, it was breath-taking, a building that must have been in place long before the final war.

A group of photographers stood ready beside the arching entranceway, and white petals were scattered across the street, dancing in a gentle breeze. The sky was the lightest it could be without breaking through the clouds and I suspected Valentina had a hand in it. I wondered if she was a captor to the royals now, forced to wield the weather, or if they still had no idea she had come with Julius and I willingly.

My driver stepped out of the car and the photographers started clicking their cameras, readying for the moment I appeared. I shifted uncomfortably in my seat, taking a deep breath.

Find Callie. Wait for the slayers. Then run like hell when the chance comes.

Nightmare was concealed deep under the folds of my dress, strapped to my thigh with the use of my suspenders. I'd had to leave Valentina's phone behind because every time I'd tried to secure it to my leg, it kept pushing buttons, making noises I didn't know how to stop, and the damn thing kept sliding out of the suspenders anyway. But Julius had the information. If he could be here today and get inside, he would.

I feared how easy it would be for me to reach my blade beneath the swathes of material, but it sang a soft tune against my leg, sending a wave of comfort through me.

Time to rise, Moon Child.

I wondered what that meant but didn't have a moment to concentrate as the driver pulled my door open. Flashes exploded from the cameras, and I was half blinded as I exited the car, taking in the entourage awaiting me.

The driver gestured for me to go ahead, and I raised my chin as I walked toward the cathedral.

The rebels started jeering, calling out my name and begging for my blood, fangs bared and tongues slicking out with a hunger that made my skin crawl.

I shuddered, focusing my mind on the desperate situation I was in, being part of a wedding I'd never wanted to walk into, clutching onto an escape plan I couldn't be sure would work out.

Callie could be just beyond those huge wooden doors.

If she's here, I'm going to lose my mind.

If she's not, I'm going to scream.

As I made my way up the steps with surprising grace on my heels, two guards pulled the doors wide.

I stepped into a grand entranceway and found my view blocked by a large red curtain.

Two female vampires darted toward me wearing beautiful navy gowns. I eyed the white flowers in their hands as both of them took hold of my arms, their fingers tightening on me like manacles.

"What are you doing?" I tried to pull free, but they held on.

"Just walking you down the aisle," one of them said with a bright smile, like she wasn't manhandling me.

I scowled back at her, not liking this. I wanted to do this on my own terms, not dragged along like an animal to slaughter.

"That won't be necessary." I yanked my arms back and they released me, sharing a look of unease.

"The last one didn't go so easy," the brunette muttered, and my heart beat a little harder. Did she mean Callie?

"I'm good," I confirmed, plastering a false smile on my lips. "I'm here to marry the man I want above all others." Hell, I wished that didn't sound so much like the truth. "No need to force me down the aisle."

The vampires swooned, apparently buying my bullshit as their eyes glimmered with emotion. They pointed me toward the curtain, and I pressed my shoulders back, stepping that way. The women pulled the curtains aside and an incredible room opened up before me. Arching pillars led all the way up to an impossibly high ceiling, and a bright aisle swept away from me between long rows of pews which were crammed full of beautifully dressed vampires.

I blinked hard, my eyes tearing across the end of the aisle as I hunted for my twin. Two women stood there in white dresses with their backs to me and several guards stood around them in menacing stances. The girls were both blonde. And for a moment, my thoughts tumbled as I didn't recognise which one was my sister.

One of them glanced over her shoulder, and I realised Paige was the girl on the left. So, the one on the right was…

My heart drummed in my ears, and I strode up the aisle at a fierce pace, abandoning any etiquette as I broke into a run, hearing the click of heels hurrying after me. The surrounding audience rose from their seats, gasping and clapping as they spotted me.

"Oh look! She just can't wait to be married," a man cooed, clutching his heart as the woman beside him released a sob of joy.

Callie turned.

I ran faster.

My heart screamed.

My soul begged for its other half.

I reached the end of the aisle with a thousand words on my lips and tears burning the backs of my eyes.

Callie's bright green gaze locked with mine, and I was taken aback by her appearance. Her face was striking, painted as well as mine. Her dress was so beautiful and enhanced the curves of her body. She looked different. And not just because of the makeup. She looked like a warrior, despite what they'd done to her. Her gaze flared with strength, and even the muscles in her arms looked more defined.

"Monty?" she gasped, her eyes widening, a desperate hope filling her expression.

I was dragged back into a moment from our past. Two young girls playing in the street of our Realm. We'd brought sugar-water to a dying honeybee. It had lapped it all up and flown away out of the Realm, toward the life we'd always dreamed about. *"We saved him, Monty."*

"Callie!" I closed the distance between us, flinging myself at her.

She stumbled back on her heels, and we hit the floor in a tumble of white silk and netting, squeezing each other tight. A commotion broke out around us and hands dragged me off of her, pulling me to my feet. Callie was handled more roughly, forced upright and pulled away from me.

"Get off of her," I snarled, reaching out and grabbing her hand. Her fingers intertwined with mine for the briefest moment before I was hauled back and planted five feet away between her and Paige, my heart ripping apart at being separated from her.

"You can reunite properly the moment the ceremony is over, I promise." I turned to the woman holding me, finding Clarice there in a pale pink gown with a silver crown on her head. She turned to face the crowd with a bright smile.

"The girls are sisters!" she called to them. "They've been apart for quite some time."

Applause rang out, followed by several comments about how adorable we were.

My stomach knotted as I gazed at Callie, trying to shake off Clarice's iron grip to get to my twin.

"Wait until after the ceremony," Clarice whispered to me. "Just hold on."

Anger flared through me, and I turned back to my sister with an ache in my soul.

"Are you okay?" I asked, my heart squeezing hard with worry.

"I will be when this whole room is turned to dust," Callie growled, loud enough for people to hear. A guard drew his sword, glaring at her with a threat in his eyes.

Callie rolled her eyes and I laughed, delighted that she wasn't hurt. Or broken. And hadn't lost any of the spark that had always lived in her. But she didn't smile, her gaze trailing over me with pity.

"I'm so sorry I didn't get here sooner," she whispered.

I shook my head, sorrow burrowing into my heart. "I wish you hadn't come at all."

She opened her mouth to reply, but the closest guard snarled at her, baring his fangs.

"We'll move you further apart if you don't shut your mouths," he said in an icy tone.

Clarice waved a hand at him. "Oh, stop being so melodramatic, Jeffrey. The girls are pleased to see each other, that's all. Leave them be and think on how you present yourself. It's wholly unbecoming."

He bowed his head in shame, backing up a bit to give Callie some room. She didn't seem remotely fazed by his threat, and I had to admire her courage in the face of all this. At least I'd had some time to adjust to being in the company of so many vampires. She'd barely had a day and looked ready to take them all on.

Guilt ran through me as I thought of Erik and all that had passed between us. What would she think of me if she knew about my feelings for a vampire? Was I ever going to be able to tell her the truth about all this?

I glanced over at Paige, and she gave me a frown.

"Are you alright?" she mouthed, and I nodded, unable to conjure any more words.

The doors sounded again, and I looked back to find the red curtain fluttering in a breeze.

"Ladies and gentlemen!" Felicia called as she stepped up at the edge of the altar in an extravagant pink dress. "The Belvedere brothers have arrived."

The sound of music filled the air, and my heart stuttered as everyone in the room rose from their seats.

Miles appeared first, striding along the aisle with his chest puffed out. He wore a dark green suit with a white flower pinned to his breast pocket. He looked radiant...almost happy, but I swear I could see a few cracks in his facade. Especially when his eyes found someone in the crowd, and I spotted Warren gazing back at him with a painful intensity. Miles twitched a small smile of encouragement at him before schooling his expression, turning away from his true love as he reached the end of the aisle.

Miles threw me a wink before floating past me and moving to Paige's side.

She drew in a breath, then smiled shyly at him. "Hi," she whispered.

"Hey, are you ready for all the pizzazz and dazzlement, beautiful?"

She nodded, and I wondered what the last few days had held for her since the ceremony. I hoped Miles was treating her well, like he'd promised.

The curtain parted again, and my heart tumbled as Erik stepped through it in his ebony suit, looking more fit for a funeral than a wedding. He strode up the aisle as purposefully as if he were going into battle and was down it before anyone could take a decent photo of him.

He reached my side, and I heard Callie suck in a breath.

His presence sent an electric current coursing through my veins, but he didn't look my way. He simply clasped his hands behind his back where he stood on my left, and I was glad I was between him and Callie, feeling like she might sense what had passed between Erik and I if she looked too closely.

Erik leaned toward me, his breath skating over my ear as he spoke directly to me and no one else, sending a shiver down my spine. "I was wrong before."

"About?" I hissed, sensing he was about to insult me again. One last pot-shot for old time's sake.

"What I should have said is that you look radiant. Fucking bewitching. It's how I've felt every time I've called you passable and all the times in between. But you don't need this dress to steal my heart, rebel. You stole it with mascara running down your face, wearing nothing but tacky underwear."

My heart clenched like he had it in his grip, and I turned to him with a light growing in my soul that brightened up all the dark spaces inside me. His expression didn't hint at any of the sweet things he'd just whispered to me, his callous mask firmly in place, but his eyes burned with them.

He took my hand, pressing a small piece of paper into it before leaning away, and I turned it over, glimpsing the words on it before anyone could notice.

When I say run, you run.

CALLIE

CHAPTER TWENTY NINE

I stared at Montana as she stood beside Erik Belvedere, and something set the hairs rising along the back of my neck. She didn't recoil from him. There was no hint of fear or concern in her posture as he leaned close to her. It was almost as if she didn't mind him being near to her at all. In fact, I almost could have believed she wanted him to be.

My eyes narrowed as I tried to figure out what was going on. Something had changed in Montana since I'd last seen her and it had nothing to do with the extravagant clothes and makeup. Instead of the terrified girl I'd expected to find desperately in need of rescuing, I was looking at someone with such inner strength that it was like she was in control of her own fate. But if that was the case, then how the hell could it have led her here?

My heightened hearing picked up the sound of the final Belvedere brother approaching, and I turned away from my twin, forgetting about that particular mystery as my groom drew closer.

Fabian had chosen to wear a charcoal grey suit and it brought out the darkness in his colouring, the danger which clung to him like a second skin. His eyes widened as he looked at me and he held my gaze as he approached, sparing no attention for anyone else in the colossal room. I glared back at him, thinking of all the different ways I'd like to kill him and hoping he could tell.

"Callie," he breathed as he reached me. "Words cannot adequately describe how you look. You take my breath away." He took my hand, raising it towards his mouth, but I snatched it back before he could touch his lips to my skin.

"That's not exactly a compliment, seeing as you don't need to breathe," I replied, not bothering to lower my tone.

Miles let out a surprised laugh, and Montana turned to give me an approving look. Erik glanced my way too, a smile tugging at his lips as if we had shared a joke.

"What are you looking at, murderer?" I asked icily, and the smile fell from his face.

Montana reached out and placed a hand on Erik's arm as if she was reassuring him, and my scowl deepened. What the fuck was going on?

Fabian leaned close so he could whisper in my ear. "I'm going to have a lot of fun with that smart mouth later."

"In your dreams, bloodsucker," I hissed.

"And what filthy dreams they are." He slid his hand across the small of my back and I tried to jerk away from him, but to my utter horror, my body didn't do what I'd told it to.

A heavy pressure began to build around me, making it feel like I was being buffeted by a strong wind, but my hair didn't so much as flicker in response to it. I was trapped in a storm that no one could feel but me, and Idun's laughter resounded through my skull as panic gripped me.

As quickly as I'd felt her touch, it faded away again. I blinked up at Fabian, feeling totally disoriented and trying to remember what he'd just said to me.

My lips parted in confusion as I leaned towards him instead of away. My side pressed up against his until I could feel the firm pressure of his muscles beneath his suit. I looked up and found his mouth inches from mine as his gaze heated, nothing in his expression suggesting he knew what was happening, but inside my skull, I was screaming.

Out of the corner of my eye, I noticed a bald, male vampire stepping onto a podium, and his voice echoed out around the colossal cathedral as he began announcing the union which was about to take place.

My mind thrummed like a bird trapped in a cage as I fought to regain control of my body. The wedding was already beginning, and instead of finding a way to escape the clutches of this monster, I was gazing up at him like some love-sick puppy, unable to so much as turn my head.

"Callie?" Montana called, but I couldn't turn to look at her.

Fabian frowned at me slightly as if he'd noticed the difference too and didn't know what to make of it. Surely he knew that I wouldn't just change my mind about this? But then why would he care? They were forcing me into this either way and if I suddenly appeared willing, it didn't alter anything.

Because I wasn't willing. I was desperate to escape. My hand ached to hold Fury in my grasp, and it definitely shouldn't have been reaching out to caress this monster's chest.

Internally I was fighting, aching to be set free, but my fingertips were clasping his lapel and my mouth was curving in what I absolutely refused to accept was a motherfucking smile.

MONTANA

CHAPTER THIRTY

The priest gestured for Miles and Paige to approach him first and adrenaline poured through my veins. I glanced at Erik, wondering when exactly he was going to initiate his plan.

"We gather today to wed the Belvedere brothers to their beautiful brides," the priest announced. "They all enter into their partnerships joyfully and with the knowledge that love is both our destined path and life's most treasured gift."

Yeah, there's a real joyful bunch of ducks in this line-up.

I glanced at Callie, unsure why she was snuggling up to Fabian instead of kneeing him in the balls. It was probably the most disconcerting thing of everything going on right now, and that was saying something.

Erik didn't look at me, seeming totally transfixed by the priest, but I sensed a tension in his posture.

Maybe a heads up on the specifics of this plan would have been nice, asshole.

I could hardly listen to the words Miles and Paige were speaking, prompted by the priest. My heartbeat reverberated in my ears, and I stole a glance over my shoulder, wondering if anyone was going to rise to stop this. But everyone looked content, gazing back at me with light in their eyes. I spotted Hank in the front aisle, his face seeming entirely different somehow. Alluring, captivating-

Holy fuck.

The truth hit me like slap. Clarice had sired him. Made him one of *them*. And he was actually smiling as if it didn't bother him at all anymore. He raised a hand as he caught my eye and I shook my head in horror, turning away as shock sped through me.

I focused on the priest again as he addressed Miles and a moment later, Miles answered, "I do."

"Paige West, do you take this man as your chosen husband?" the priest asked. "To treasure and adore for all of time? To bear the fruit of his loins and join him in his eternal form?"

Paige hesitated a moment, taking a breath. "I do."

Clarice moved forward, holding out her hand to them and they each took a ring from her palm. The priest spoke as Clarice encouraged them to place the rings on one another. I turned to Erik, and he finally looked down at me with a terse smile. I knew what it meant. We were next.

Clarice placed a silver crown on Paige's head and applause broke out. She and Miles stepped away from the altar, hand in hand, giving the crowd bright smiles. They returned to the line-up, and I didn't have a moment to think before Erik guided me toward the priest.

Oh fuck, this is actually happening.

The priest smiled at us, but I couldn't find it in me to smile back, a weight dragging at my lungs. I felt Callie's eyes on me and wanted to turn and tell her I was okay. That we were going to get out of here. We might just have to do it married…

"Erik Belvedere, turn toward your beloved," the priest instructed, directing me to do the same.

I gazed at Erik with trepidation in my heart, and as his grey eyes met mine, I knew there was no backing out of this now.

"Erik Belvedere, do you take this woman as your chosen wife?" the priest asked. "To admire and protect for all of time?"

My lips pursed at his words, but Erik gave me one of his usual smirks. "I do."

My heart thumped fiercely. It was just words, they didn't matter, so why did it feel like they did? Like taking these vows would really mean something?

The priest turned to me. "Montana Ford, do you take this man as your chosen husband? To treasure and adore for all of time? To bear the fruits of his loins and join him in his eternal form?"

My lips parted, but no words came out. *The fruits of his fucking loins?? He can keep his goddamn mango dick away from me if it ever wants me to bear anything for it.*

Erik gave me a prompting look and my heart free fell in my chest. I had to answer. The crowd was waiting, the priest was getting sweaty. But still, the seconds ticked on until I gave in to the inevitable. *It's just words.*

"I do," I breathed, and a fire lit in Erik's eyes like he wasn't entirely hating this part of the plan. In fact, I had the suspicion he could have got his plan moving along well before this moment, but here we were. Fucking married. Husband and wife.

Clarice moved forward, offering us two gold rings, and tears glimmered in her eyes as she gazed at her brother.

Nightmare burned with expectant energy, making my back straighten.

Twins of sun and moon will rise. Rise, Moon Child.

I could barely process its words. Was I walking the path of the prophecy right now? Was doing this somehow a part of it?

I took courage in the possibility. If this was my fate, I'd dive into it with both feet. I'd do whatever I could to break the curse.

We each took a ring, and Erik lifted my hand as the priest spoke. "May you adore each other for all of time. May love flow between you as powerfully as the waters of Hvergelmir, with all the strength of Thor's Hammer and burn as brightly as the fires of Muspelheim. May the joy of your endless youth and the wisdom of a thousand ages bless your hearts until the final battle of Ragnarok is upon you."

Erik slid the ring onto my finger and held out his hand for me to the do the same. As I pushed it on, something burned within my left palm, and I gasped. Erik frowned, turning his right hand over and eyeing it too.

Power surged into me, dripping through my body and claiming my heart with a violence that made my knees tremor. A presence seemed to move closer to us, but its aura was light and beautiful, unlike Andvari's. I knew it was a god. It had to be.

I turned over my hand as the heat grew in my skin, the warmth of some unknown magic coursing through my veins. As I watched in fear, a silver X emerged across my palm, shimmering with some unearthly light.

"By the gods…" Clarice gasped, grabbing Erik's wrist. "It's the rune of partnership."

"The what?" I demanded, dragging my eyes away from the unsettling mark and finding Erik with the exact same X on his right palm.

My heart tugged and I had the immediate urge to be closer to Erik, like a burning need inside me I could never sate. He nudged Clarice aside, grabbing my arm and yanking me into a world-altering kiss before I could even draw a breath.

"Er- you may kiss the bride!" the priest announced a beat too late.

The mark on my palm came alive with power, sending flames skittering through my entire body. I moaned, gripping his jacket, and pulling him closer still, needing his body against mine. The potent magic danced though the centre of my being and made me feel bound to Erik in a way I could never have imagined. My heart was his. My soul. My blood. We were like one being in two bodies, and I couldn't get enough of him.

My senses felt so heightened, like his touch was a thousand times more compelling than it had been just moments ago.

"Fuck," Erik breathed against my lips, pulling away from me with a confounded expression.

Clarice moved toward me with a silver crown in her hand that was encrusted with diamonds. She placed it on my head and the weight of it took me by surprise, jolting me awake from the fierce energy spiralling through my blood.

"I now pronounce you husband and wife. Prince and Princess of the New Empire," the priest called, and applause rang in my ears.

My feet were rooted to the spot, my body weak from what had just happened, and my mind swirling with the new sensation settling into my bones.

Erik took my hand and as the marks on our palms met, a violent eruption of power took place inside my chest. I sucked in a breath, pulling my hand free and taking a step away from him, suddenly afraid of this new bond.

We took our places beside Fabian and Callie, and my sister's eyes drilled into mine with a question burning in them. *"What have you done?!"*

I gazed down at the X on my palm, feeling like I'd just taken much more than a wedding vow. That the words we'd spoken had truly linked us for all eternity, and no matter what happened today, I could never part from Erik. It left me with a terrifying realisation. Because if I could never be away from him, how was I ever going to escape?

CALLIE

CHAPTER THIRTY ONE

My sister had just married a monster and my heart slammed against my ribs as I realised I was next. How could this have happened to her? How could it be happening to *me*? I'd come so far to save her from this fate and yet I found myself joining her in it instead, my body an unwilling slave to the power of the deceitful gods.

I fought against the hold Idun had on me, crying, and raging in silence, trapped within my own skin while externally I smiled up at a monster as if he were the love of my goddamn life.

Fabian drew me closer to the priest and my body followed him willingly. I was anything but willing, but no one could see it, only I could hear my screams of protest, could feel the cries of panic.

Fabian turned me towards him, his hands gripping my hips as he stared down at me intently. His gaze was filled with a deep longing, and a part of me which wasn't really me at all ached to fulfil his every desire.

No, no, no, no.

My traitorous hands slid down his chest until my fingertips were resting just above his belt and a teasing smile found its way to my lips as lust burned in his dark eyes.

I wanted to scream, cry, and beg for my freedom, but if Idun could hear my thoughts, she wasn't interested in them. How could she be doing this to me? I thought she wanted us to destroy these creatures. What could she possibly gain from this?

Her amusement rattled through me again and I was filled with the knowledge that this wasn't about me. It was about Magnar. I was just a toy for her to torment him with.

As my mind fell on the warrior who had saved me in so many ways, my panic increased tenfold. What if I couldn't stop this from happening? The priest was already talking about love and commitment, and my feet hadn't moved a single inch. I should have been running as far from this place as I could get with Montana in tow, but I was rooted to the spot as if I'd never take another step again.

What would Magnar think if I married one of his greatest enemies? How could I betray the vow I'd made with him like that? Would he even try to come for me when he found out? Or would he abandon me to this fate the moment I succumbed to it?

As I battled my will against Idun's with everything I had, a single tear slipped from my eye and tracked its way down my cheek.

My fingers started trembling with the effort I was summoning to try and regain control of them, but I was still helplessly trapped within my own skin, a puppet for the gods to command.

Fabian frowned at me as he noticed the line of moisture rolling down my cheek. He raised a hand and brushed the tear from my face, his cold fingers lingering against my skin despite the way I thrashed within the confines of it, desperate to break free.

I wanted to jerk away from his touch. I didn't want his hands on any part of me, but I still couldn't move so much as an inch, and my heart was filling with dread as the seconds ticked away at my fate.

His palm stayed on my cheek, cupping my jaw as his thumb brushed over my bottom lip. It didn't feel comforting, it felt possessive, like he was laying claim to my emotions, my body, my fucking soul, and I couldn't even utter a single word against it.

"Fabian Belvedere, do you take this woman as your chosen wife?" the priest asked. "To admire and protect for all of time?"

"I do," Fabian replied loudly, his voice sending fear deep into my soul as he peered into my eyes. Panic rose in me like a tide as the priest turned his attention on me. I knew what I'd be forced to say when he asked, and I couldn't bear it, couldn't believe it had come to this, that the goddess had betrayed me so cruelly after I'd vowed to follow in the path she laid out for me.

"Callie Ford, do you take this man as your-"

A heavy bang rang out as the door to the cathedral flew open and every eye in the room swivelled towards it.

My chest swelled with hope as I turned too, expecting to see Magnar charging down the aisle with Tempest and Venom raised to destroy this monster who was going to chain me into wedlock.

A strong wind blew along the aisle, tossing my hair around my shoulders, but there was no one there to save me.

A tinkling laugh rang out, and my eyes swivelled to find Valentina sitting in the front row with a hand pressed to her mouth. "I'm so sorry, I lost control what with all the excitement and blasted the door open. It must have seemed like someone was coming to ruin the ceremony!" The wind swirled around the room before catching the door and slamming it shut again. The rest of the congregation began laughing too, and my hatred for her flared as they all mocked me.

My heart plummeted as Fabian chuckled, taking my chin between his fingers, and pulling me around to look up at him once more.

"No chance of that," he murmured. "There's no way I'd let you go so easily."

My pulse pounded in my ears as the priest cleared his throat and started again.

"Callie Ford, do you take this man as your chosen husband? To treasure and adore for all of time? To bear the fruit of his loins and join him in his eternal form?" he asked.

I looked up at Fabian and my treacherous arms slid around his fucking neck like I was some simpering fool, the panic in me rising beyond measure, my heart thrashing against my ribcage so hard it hurt.

I couldn't. I *wouldn't.*

My lips parted to speak the words, but I threw every ounce of my will against them as I fought off Idun's control with all I had, every ounce of strength that belonged to me. I wouldn't do it. I'd rather fucking die. I'd throw myself from the closest bridge or plunge a knife into my own heart before I'd bind myself to this monster-

"I do." My voice wasn't my own, but it didn't matter, it had spilled from my mouth, sealing my fate with a clap of laughter from Idun herself, the sound of it only apparent to me.

I couldn't breathe. My chest was locked in the space between breaths, horror spilling through every piece of my being as the truth of what had happened settled over me.

Clarice stepped forward, presenting two silver rings, and Fabian slid one onto my finger, but it felt more like a chain around my neck. I wouldn't be bound to him, I couldn't be. But I was already pushing a ring onto his finger in return, and he was smirking at me like he fucking owned me.

The priest was talking again, but my gaze had slipped beyond Fabian, rising above the heads of the congregation of vampires until I was looking up into the rafters. A shadow moved above me, and I stared at it as my gifts allowed me to pick out Magnar's face where he gazed down at me, a chilling darkness clinging to his expression which cut me to my core.

My heart cracked right down the middle. I could only imagine what he was thinking, the fury, the hatred, the betrayal. I wasn't chained and forced to speak under duress so far as he could see. I stood with my body pressed against Fabian's and a smile on my traitorous lips.

I ached to cry out to him and tell him what was happening, but I couldn't make a single sound, the goddess's hold on me still as tight as a fist around my soul.

There was a resounding boom which seemed to echo from the centre of the universe itself, and a deep power slammed into me with such force that I stumbled forward a step. Fabian caught me in his arms, holding me upright as his eyes burned with confusion, the power lashing against him too.

Something was weaving its way between us like a thread which tugged and pulled, a needle burying its way into my skin born of the sickly power of the gods, and a flare of heat shot across my left palm, causing a curse to spill from my lips.

Fabian gasped too, holding his right hand out and revealing a shining silver cross as it formed on his palm. I uncurled my fist, terror inching through me as I found my left hand branded with the same mark, and I recoiled internally. A bond had been formed between us with the power of the deity who was toying with my destiny.

I hated Fabian. He was an undead, soulless monster who deserved nothing but the swiftest of executions. I never wanted anything to link us to each other, and yet I was beginning to feel the strangest pull towards him. It went beyond Idun's control over me; like a piece of my soul ached to be with his.

I stared at Fabian in horror as the coldly beautiful features which had repelled me so viscerally began to call to me instead, desire forming in the footsteps of the contempt I'd held for him so fully.

"I now pronounce you husband and wife. Prince and Princess of the New Empire."

Clarice stepped towards me with a glittering silver crown held ready. She reached out to place it on my head, and its weight felt like a ton of bricks crushing down on my soul.

"You may kiss the bride," the priest announced.

Fabian moved towards me with undisguised heat, and my traitorous body pushed up onto my tiptoes as my hands tangled with his hair, gripping the back of his head as I pulled him closer. Inside I was begging, pleading, and offering any bargain I might be able to make to halt this. More tears fell from my eyes, the only sign at all that my mind was my own even if my body clearly wasn't, but they couldn't do anything to stop what was happening.

I looked beyond Fabian and found Magnar's golden eyes once more. My heart shattered as if I could feel the pain my betrayal was causing him, feel the hurt, the hate, the fury.

Fabian's mouth met mine and my eyes fell shut against my will, blocking out Magnar and the aching loss which pierced my heart so brutally at the press of those ice-cold lips against my own.

Fabian's kiss was fierce and demanding, his hands gripping my hair as he forced me to yield to his desires. My body continued to betray me as I kissed him back, his tongue burying itself in my mouth, his fangs grazing my lower lip, his growl of pleasure echoing through my soul. And a piece of me, which I refused to accept was me at all, *liked* it.

The mark on my palm burned with excited energy in response to Fabian's touch and I couldn't deny the desire pooling in my stomach. It was like my soul had been severed in two and he was claiming the part of it which I couldn't control, making it his own and forming it into something which wasn't me at all. I was bound to this creature of the night. I was his. And he was mine.

His kiss grew hungrier as he felt it too, and I met his passion with my own, tasting the desire on his tongue and aching to give in to the full call of it.

But my heart pounded in fear and longing for a warrior with golden eyes who should have been mine instead. I was losing him in that moment, and there was nothing I could do to stop it.

Somewhere deep inside of me, something fractured. And I wasn't sure I'd ever be able to fix it.

MONTANA

CHAPTER THIRTY TWO

Igazed at Callie, unable to believe she'd just gone through with the marriage so willingly. And not just willingly, she'd looked like she'd enjoyed the whole thing. When they'd kissed, she'd practically been melting against Fabian, pulling him closer instead of shoving him away.

Something wasn't right. But for the life of me, I couldn't figure out what the fuck was going on. My mind was still spinning from the bond placed on me and Erik, like grains of stardust were crashing through me, each one lashing me to the Belvedere Prince. And it was making it impossible to think straight.

I ground my teeth, focusing on why I was here, what this was all for. *My sister.*

I glanced at Erik, hoping he was about to set his plan into motion because I needed to get Callie out of here. Right now.

The priest raised his arms in the air. "Let us toast to the love of these three partners and wish them all the happiness in their futures together." He stepped aside to reveal a huge font, and as he approached it, blood gushed into the basin from a tap, making my stomach roil.

A ring of silver chalices circled the bottom of it and the priest stooped down, picking one up. Three guards rushed forward, filling the remaining chalices, and hurrying into the crowd, handing a cup to the vampire on the end of each of the aisles. The guards ran back and forth until all of the chalices were handed out, preparing for whatever fucked-up ritual was in order next.

"Drink the modest blood of Realm G in thanks to the humans of the world, without whom we would be nothing. Once you have taken a sip of their godly sacrifice, pass the cup to the person beside you," the priest encouraged, lifting his own cup to his lips and smiling serenely.

I grimaced as he took a drink, the blood of my people passing down his throat. He smacked his lips together, then handed the chalice to Fabian. Callie gazed at the cup with a strange sort of hope as Fabian drank, then handed it to Erik. What was she thinking?

Erik gave me a dark look, lifting the chalice to his lips and taking a sip before handing it to Miles.

As Miles gulped down the last of it with a grin, the priest raised another chalice into the air. "To the never-ending rule of the Belvederes!"

His words were echoed from the congregation, and I glanced over my shoulder, spotting the chalices reaching the centre of the aisles.

Callie threw me an excited glance, seeming ready for something to happen. I frowned, trying to figure out what she meant, but before she could give me any more indication, the priest in front of us screamed.

He held his throat, eyeing the chalice in alarm, spluttering as he tried to speak.

"Are you alright?" Clarice darted to his side in alarm.

The priest took a slow breath, seeming to regain his composure, patting Clarice's arm.

"Yes, my apologies, your highness." He turned to face the congregation. "Right. Back to the ceremo-ah!" His entire body exploded into dust, and I stumbled back in shock as Erik shielded me from the falling ash.

Screams rang out behind us, and I turned, finding half of the congregation bursting into dust. Their beautiful clothes fell to the ground, glittering dresses and fine suits fluttering onto the pews, and those still standing started screaming at the sight.

Confusion and fear coursed through me as the vampires holding chalices gazed down at the blood in horror.

I turned to Erik, panic scorching through me as I realised what had caused their deaths. "Erik – the blood!"

I clutched his arms, waiting for something terrible to happen. I couldn't lose him. I couldn't see him die.

"I didn't drink. I never do in front of you," he said, and relief ran through me, but then he looked to his family in terror.

My pulse quickened as I glanced from Clarice to Miles and Fabian, fear passing through their eyes. Though Miles broke away from them, searching the crowd in desperation. "Warren!"

"I'm here – I didn't drink," his partner called back, and my heart lifted as they shared a look of relief.

Another tense moment passed, but the royals remained standing, glancing between each other like the thought of losing each other was too awful to consider.

A battle cry filled my ears, and a huge warrior with long dark hair leapt from the rafters above us, landing among the crowd and slicing a vampire in two with his sword. My breath snagged in my throat as dust plumed around him, settling at his feet alongside the shorn pieces of a grey suit. Panic broke out as the wild man started killing anyone who hadn't drunk the blood, swinging his golden sword with a furious malice.

"Magnar!" Erik roared and their eyes met for the briefest second before ten guards blocked the path between them.

A weight slammed into my back, and I found Julius there, tearing me from Erik's arms.

"No!" I gasped, the bond snapping tight between us.

Erik's fist hit Julius's face so hard that the slayer wheeled backwards and lost his grip on me. Before Julius could lunge at us again, Erik's hand surrounded mine and he dragged me away with a burst of speed. The Xs on our palms met, lighting a fire of need in me, and defying all plans of escape.

I must stay with him.

I gritted my teeth, forcing out the thought in place of my truth.

No, I have to run.

Nightmare hummed on my thigh as I searched for Callie, desperate to get her out of here.

Sun Child is close.

Erik forced me through the surging bodies, dragging me away from the fight.

"No- wait!" I gazed around to try and spot Callie in the room, but she was no longer at the altar with Fabian, and my heart splintered in fear. "My sister!" I demanded as Erik tugged me behind an enormous pillar.

He slammed his hands either side of my head, pinning me in place with his fangs bared. "Stay here. I'll find her."

"No," I snarled, dragging up the folds of my dress and snatching Nightmare from my leg. I raised it and Erik's eyes flashed at the slayer blade. "I'm coming with you."

His jaw pulsed and I could tell he was about to refuse, but I ducked under his arm and fled back into the mayhem, not waiting on some pointless permission from him. He wasn't my ruler.

The congregation were fleeing for their lives, running for the exit and wailing as they went.

Vampires fell at Magnar's feet again and again. No one could get close to him. He was like a savage animal, killing without mercy, without any hesitation, terrifying in his brutality. His eyes swept across the crowd as if he was searching for someone, and I was sure it was Callie.

I spotted a flash of blonde hair and my heart soared as I shouldered through the crowd, crossing the cathedral. No one paid me any attention as I forged a path towards my sister, everyone either trying to escape or get close enough to engage Magnar in battle.

I'm coming, Callie. We won't ever be parted again.

CALLIE

CHAPTER THIRTY THREE

Magnar moved among the vampires, leaving a trail of swirling ash in his wake as he killed time and again. Most of them were unarmed and had nothing available to defend themselves with aside from their teeth. But none of them could get close enough to bite him, his swords moving so fast they were little more than a flash of gold between the bodies he was carving a path through.

Idun suddenly released her grip on me, and I sagged with relief, dropping to my knees as I regained control of my muscles, heaving down a breath which I felt I might choke on. I swiped the back of my hand across my mouth to remove the taste of Fabian's kiss from my lips.

Fabian knelt down beside me, cupping my face in his hands, his dark eyes lighting with concern.

"It's alright, love," he breathed. "I'll never let him take you from me."

Anger surged in my gut, and I shoved his hands off of me.

"Don't touch me," I snarled, though the traitorous half of my soul yearned for the opposite, urging me closer, making my mind rebel against its own desires.

Fabian's gaze swam with confusion, a frown lowering his brow. "You can't tell me you don't feel this," he said as he reached for me with his right hand, the silver cross glimmering on his palm, the magic which had been knitted between us flaring powerfully.

I tried to slap his hand away, but he caught me instead, pressing his palm against mine and joining our marks.

I inhaled sharply as power flooded beneath my skin and every inch of my body throbbed with desire for him. I needed him. I had to have him, make him mine in every way that counted.

I grabbed the front of his shirt with my free hand, ignoring the commotion surrounding us as I dragged him towards me, so our lips met again.

Fabian groaned with pleasure, pulling me to my feet and tugging my body flush to his, the hard ridge of his cock driving against me, the need to have every inch of him overwhelming all else.

His hands bunched in the fabric of my skirt, tugging at my dress as if he might rip it from me right here, in front of every person gathered in the cathedral just to take me the way he was clearly desperate to.

He gripped my ass in his free hand, lifting me off of my feet and sprinted through the cathedral, carrying me away from the panicking congregation while kissing me with the ravenous hunger of a demon the entire time.

Fabian slammed me against a heavy pillar, his teeth dragging against my bottom lip, fangs almost breaking the skin.

I moaned as my need for him sharpened, my ankles hooking tight around his waist, my spine arching as I ground myself against him and he breathed my name like a curse and a prayer.

Fabian released my hand so he could push his fingers through my hair, deepening our kiss, but as our marks disconnected, I felt like a surge of cold water had been thrown over me, reality crashing back in and reminding me of who I was and what I wanted.

I remembered all of it, every moment of my will being toyed with by that fucking goddess. I pulled away from him sharply, breaking our kiss and bringing my fist up to meet his jaw in place of my mouth.

Fabian staggered back at the impact, dropping me to my feet and

I punched him again, splitting his lip open while he blinked at me in confusion, his shirt hanging open where I'd been clawing at it just moments before.

"Don't fucking touch me!" I snapped, advancing on him with my hands curled into fists, fury eating at me. But I found myself caught between the two warring halves of my soul. The half that yearned for him and the half which hated him unable to come to terms with one another.

Fabian frowned at me as he backed away, holding his hand up between us so the mark on his palm stood out starkly.

"What have you done to me?" I demanded. "What the fuck is this?"

"I don't know," he replied, and my heart raced faster because I could see he was telling the truth. "But I *need* you, Callie. We're meant to be together. Can't you feel it?"

"I can feel it," I admitted.

I couldn't deny the lust, need, and desire which were stirring inside me, but they weren't mine. He was a vampire. And even if he wasn't, I didn't know him at all. I had no reason to feel *anything* for him and whatever this was, it wasn't real. It wasn't me.

"Then come with me," Fabian urged, not seeming to care where these feelings had come from or even if they were his own. "I'll take you home and we can be together-"

"No," I growled. "I don't know what this is, but I do know who I am. And I'm not going anywhere with you."

I started to back away from him and his expression darkened, a feral look passing through his eyes as he took a step after me.

"Callie don't leave me," he growled, the plea a warning, panic showing in the whites of his eyes.

My lips parted in fear. I had no weapon. No way to defend myself, and it was clear he wasn't going to let me go.

"I'm begging you," he said, his voice low. "Don't go. Don't make me do something I'll regret."

The threat was there, the monster in him shifting to the surface of his skin, but it was the desperation in that demand which had my pulse spiking. Fabian Belvedere was begging at my feet, and to make it worse, a part of me wanted nothing more than to do what he was asking.

I wished I still had Fury. With my blade in my hand, I could have put us both out of this misery with one swift blow. But even as the thought crossed my mind, the horror of the idea consumed me.

How can I live in a world without Fabian?

I shook my head violently, refusing to accept those thoughts as my own. "If you really care about me, then don't follow me." I turned and ran from him before I ended up running towards him instead, shoving between a crush of vampires as they sprinted for the exit, buying myself a few moments to steal a head start.

I'd lost sight of Magnar, but it didn't matter. I only had to head in the opposite direction to the fleeing vampires and I knew I'd find him.

Someone stepped on the train of my dress, and I stumbled as it tore. Reaching down, I ripped the remaining length of excess material off as well, forcing a slit up the side of my leg too so that I could lengthen my stride and run.

I instantly moved faster, putting more vampires between myself and Fabian, racing towards the sound of a battle cry in the centre of the cathedral. If I could just get to Magnar then I knew I'd be alright. He'd find a way to undo whatever the fuck had happened to me. He knew all of the vampires' tricks. He'd fix this.

I shoved my way between two fleeing females and stumbled to a halt as Venom cut through the air in front of me, narrowly missing my chest, the flash of gold and brilliant red chased by a billowing cloud of ash.

Magnar's eyes were filled with rage as they fell on me, but they deepened with recognition when he took me in, a snarl twisting his mouth at the sight of my torn wedding dress.

I leapt at him as fresh tears spilled from my eyes, forcing every inch of my will against Idun's rules so I could fling my arms around his neck and hold him close for half a heartbeat.

Magnar fought her off too. and for the briefest moment, he pulled me against him and everything in the world seemed right again. The stubble of his jaw grazed my neck and he inhaled deeply, growling against my skin.

"I thought I'd lost you, drakaina hjarta," he breathed.

"Never," I replied, clinging to him as Idun tried to make me let go, her power forcing me to part from him.

"Magnar Elioson!" Fabian roared from somewhere behind me, and a tremor of fear rolled down my spine. "You will unhand my wife."

MONTANA

CHAPTER THIRTY FOUR

I pushed through a line of guards but was slowed by their immovable strength. A clamour of noise rang out as they surged toward Magnar and a gap allowed me to slip past them.

Julius called my name and I turned, spotting him driving Menace through the chest of a guard. She scattered to ash in front of him, and he strode toward me at a fierce pace.

I shook my head in refusal of his intentions.

"Get Callie!" I yelled, but two more guards turned at my voice, spotting Julius behind me. They pushed me aside to engage him and I slammed into a pew, catching myself before I was knocked to the ground.

"Fuck," I hissed.

Julius roared as he intercepted them, and my heart leapt at his ferocious expression. I wasn't worried for him; I wouldn't have wanted to be a vampire standing against his wrath.

I climbed up onto the bench, gazing across the madness, ignoring the sting of my freshly acquired bruises. My heart lifted as I spotted Callie in Magnar's arms, but Fabian was closing in on them at a terrifying speed.

"Callie!" I roared, but she couldn't hear me over the commotion.

"Rebel!" Erik bellowed, and I spotted him throwing guards out of his way like sacks of shit as he made a beeline for me. My stomach fluttered as I started scrambling over the pews, jumping from bench to bench as I headed away from him, knowing if he caught me, he'd take me from here. Away from my sister. And with this new bond playing havoc with me, I just might let him.

My heart tore apart as I was tugged in two opposing directions, the mark on my palm aching, telling me to turn back, but I fought it with all my might.

I have to get to Callie. She's all that matters.

I spotted a whip of dark hair at the back of the hall. Valentina was by the doors, wrenching them open and letting vampires flood away onto the street.

"Hey!" I called, quickening my pace towards her.

She could help. She could bring a storm down on this place and get Callie out of here.

A severed arm came spinning through the air, slamming into my back, and I cursed as it knocked me forward a step. I slipped on the netting of my dress and my knees crashed into the floor, my chin colliding with the bench so hard I tasted blood. The crown fell from my head, clattering to the flagstones with a ringing of metal.

I groaned, crawling along the cold stone and forcing my way out of the aisle.

Blonde hair spilled in front of me and soft hands grabbed my arms. I looked up, my heart lifting as I prayed it was Callie, but my shoulders sagged in disappointment.

Paige stood there, her cheeks drained of blood and her eyes wide. "Are you okay?"

"Yes. Listen, I can get you out of the city. You have to trust me," I said.

"What do you mean?" she asked in shock, but I didn't have time to explain.

"Where's my sister?" I demanded, trying to peer past her head. She pushed me toward the doors, ignoring my question.

"Come on, we have to move."

I spotted Valentina hurrying outside and quickened my pace to catch her. "Hey! Wait! Help us!" I turned to Paige. "Follow me," I commanded, and she nodded, fear dancing in her eyes.

I sprinted to the doorway, gazing out at the street where rain was pummelling the ground like bullets.

Run, Moon Child! Nightmare screamed, scorching the inside of my hand.

A shadow fell over me, and I didn't react fast enough. I was shoved hard, thrown down to the floor on my back as an impossible weight fell on me.

Panic seized me and I clawed at the vampire who held me in place, his hands pushing my hair from my throat.

"We have the right to bite," he growled with a manic grin, then dug his fangs into my neck. Pain flared through me and white stars exploded before my eyes, a scream pitching from my throat.

The rebels were here.

My fist tightened around Nightmare, and I plunged it into the vampire's side, once, twice, three times. Rage guided my actions, and Nightmare cried out a beautiful song in my mind, praising my vicious work.

The vampire choked, coughing blood over my dress as he reared backwards in pain. Nightmare guided my next movements, and I forced the blade into his chest with a shout of defiance tearing from my lungs.

He crumbled to dust before my eyes and I threw his clothes from me, taking a breath as I regained my feet. I touched the wound on my neck to make sure it wasn't life threatening. Adrenaline kept the pain at bay, and there wasn't too much blood, so I guessed I'd survive.

Terrorised cries caught my ear, and I spotted Paige pinned to a pillar, thrashing as a female vampire drank from her neck.

More of the rebels poured into the hall, falling upon the guards in droves, their attacks savage and reckless.

I sprinted toward Paige, Nightmare raised with a deadly promise, but before I reached her, strong arms surrounded me, yanking me back.

I wriggled desperately as my captor caught my wrist and ripped

Nightmare from my grip. "I'll have that."

I recognised Valentina's voice and my stomach clenched. She turned me in her arms, grabbing hold of my throat and lifting me of off the ground, her fangs bared in victory.

Confusion riddled my mind and fear scratched at my heart. I raked my nails up her arms, desperate for her to release me as my air supply was cut off.

"Rise biters! Take the humans! Drink the blood you are owed!" Valentina cried to the room, and horror flooded me. I kicked the bitch who had hold of me, trying to force her to let go as I struggled for air, but she was immovable.

A group of salivating vampires ran towards us, and Valentina dangled me before them like a hunk of meat.

"They're going to rip you apart, Montana. I've been looking forward to this moment." She smiled wickedly, then threw me away from her, and my arms flailed wildly above me as if I could grab onto the nothingness between my outstretched fingers.

I screamed as I crashed to the ground, the air leaving my lungs in a hard whoosh from the impact. All four of the biters leapt on top of me, searching for flesh to bite, teeth gnashing and hands clawing at me. They tore at my dress, slicing the lace apart with desperate fingers like starving beasts.

My cries were lost to the tumult of noise around me, and as I kicked and fought, throwing punches that cracked against cheeks as tough as stone, a terrifying reality fell over me.

Without Nightmare, I couldn't fight. Without Nightmare, I was dead.

Panic burst through me as the first set of teeth sank into my arm and I threw a hard punch, kicking and flailing so that they had to take hold of my limbs to hold me still. Pain tore through me as venom sailed into my veins and I was pinned between the monsters, firm, cold hands shoving me down. Teeth sank into me from every direction, and a scream tore from my lungs.

One of them crawled up me like a wraith, her eyes like the pits of hell as she took in her prize.

Terror flooded me, my fate closing in on all sides, and if the gods were watching now, it was clear they had no inclination to step in. I was just a feast for hungry mouths. It was a more horrifying truth than any other. That I had never claimed the freedom I'd dreamed of, never had even a taste of liberation with my family.

The female dipped her head toward my neck, but before her teeth reached me, she was wrenched back by her hair.

Erik stood there, holding her head between his hands, his face a picture of wrath built by the gods themselves. With a roar of monstrous rage, he tore her head from her shoulders with impossible ease. Scarlet blood splattered over him, and he kicked her body to the floor, stamping on her chest so hard, her heart was crushed, and she turned to ash.

The biters released me in an instant, cowering beneath him in terror.

"Wait!" a male cried, but Erik caught him by the collar, plunging his hand straight into his chest and ripping out his heart, tossing the bloody lump of flesh to the floor and crushing it beneath his heel with a cold brutality, the body bursting to dust in the next moment.

Erik grabbed another biter, tearing out her throat with his fangs before slamming his fist into her heart and dropping her body beside me. She twitched once before turning to dust, and the final biter fled. Erik gazed after him as he darted out of the door into the rain, fangs bared and murder in his eyes.

I stared up at his snarling expression, shock keeping me frozen on the floor.

He bent down, dragging me up by the hand and checking me over with a fierce intensity. When he spotted the bite marks, his eyes darkened with a need for vengeance, his lips twitching with purest ire.

Pain sizzled through the wounds, but I tried not to focus on them even though the venom burned like a bitch.

I turned to find Paige, and shock jarred me to a despairing halt as I spotted her broken body on the floor, her lifeless eyes glazed over.

A sob caught in my throat and Erik pressed a hand to my back, drawing me close.

"I couldn't get to her," I choked.

"It's not your fault," Erik said firmly, but I couldn't turn away from

419

her. She deserved more than this. "Look at me, rebel."

I dragged my attention to him and found a sea of resolve in his eyes.

"You didn't do this," he growled, and I nodded, accepting that even though it didn't lessen the pain of her loss.

"Valentina let them in," I growled, my grief turning to fury. "She's one of them."

He searched the crowd behind us with a snarl, and I spotted Valentina using Nightmare to kill guard after guard, proving her betrayal.

"Traitor," Erik growled, keeping my hand in his as he stormed toward her with death in his eyes.

Valentina gasped as she spotted him, forcing her way between the guards to get away.

A bellow filled my ears, and I was knocked sideways as Julius collided with us, trying to drag me away. He aimed his sword at Erik to keep him back, and I cried out in fright, catching his arm as I tried to stop him advancing.

"You promised," I hissed at Julius.

"I'm keeping my promise, now let's go."

"Not happening," Erik said icily, stepping menacingly toward him. His eyes swung to me momentarily, realisation blazing in them. "You invited him here?"

"I had to," I breathed, and Erik's gaze flickered with that betrayal.

He growled, advancing on Julius. "You're not taking her. I will kill you before you make it a single step out of this cathedral."

Erik lunged forward and Julius swung Menace in a deadly arc.

"No!" I screamed as Erik darted aside, missing the blow by inches. I leapt onto Julius's back as he swung Menace again.

"Stop!" I commanded, pulling on Julius's neck.

The slayer wheeled around, trying to shake me off, but I clamped my hands over his eyes so he couldn't see.

Erik gazed at me in alarm, then bared his fangs at Julius, like he was about to take the advantage I'd just given him.

"Don't you dare!" I shouted at Erik.

Julius grabbed my legs, pulling sharply so I fell backwards and hit the floor. I swore, kicking the back of his knee, and he buckled as he swung the sword at Erik again, missing him by inches.

"It's self-defence," Julius snapped, but I was sure he wouldn't hesitate to kill Erik if he got too close.

Clarice dove over Erik's head like an angel of death, colliding with Julius and taking him to the floor beside me with an echoing bang. She straddled him, kneeling on his arms and grasping his neck as he flailed, trying to turn Menace toward her, but she had him pinned down.

I rolled onto my knees as Clarice's nails dug into his throat.

"Don't hurt him!" I cried in panic, dropping down beside Julius and shoving Clarice to try and stop her.

Erik stepped on Julius's wrist, and he cursed in pain, releasing Menace from his grip. Erik kicked it away from him and snarled at Julius, looking ready to rip him apart.

"Clarice, please don't kill him," I begged.

She gazed down at me in dismay, then looked to Erik for direction.

"He's a slayer," Clarice implored. "He's killed countless of our kind."

Erik glanced at me, at war with his decision, and I glared right back, letting him see what it would cost him if he killed this man. I would never forgive it.

Julius suddenly yanked an arm free from where it was pinned down by Clarice's right knee and he punched her square in the face. She was thrown off of him, slamming onto her back. He was on his feet in seconds, dragging me up with him and pulling me against him like a shield.

"Sword," he commanded, and Erik released a noise like a feral animal.

"You're dead," Erik promised.

"Not before she is," Julius bluffed, and I hoped Erik distrusted him enough to believe him.

Erik glanced at Clarice, his jaw ticking angrily. He kicked the sword to Julius, and he snatched it up with a low noise of contentment.

"Go," I hissed at Julius, prising his fingers from my neck.

"I won't leave y-"

"Go!" I shoved him, and Clarice darted forward, forcing Julius to run. She chased after him and they sprinted out onto the rain-swept street, disappearing into the storm.

"We need to get out of here," Erik demanded, still seething as he gazed after Julius and his sister.

"Not without Callie," I said darkly, hunting the room for her.

A heated trickle ran down my neck, and I lifted a hand to the blood there, wincing as the throbbing pain sharpened. Erik growled at the sight, my wounds sparking a fury in him that knew no limits.

I pushed past Erik, not caring what lay ahead as I searched for my twin. Because there was no way in hell I was going anywhere without her.

CALLIE

CHAPTER THIRTY FIVE

The rest of the vampires nearby had fled, leaving a ring of space surrounding us, the floor stained with the bright blood of those who had escaped with their lives and a solid inch of ash from those who had met their end.

I surveyed the area carefully, looking for any other vampires who might try to move against us, but they'd all headed to the far end of the cathedral in a desperate bid to escape.

Fabian stood at the other end of the aisle, his gaze flitting between me and Magnar as if he couldn't decide which one of us to fix his attention on, his polished shoes crunching over broken decorations as he stalked closer. Tension spiralled in the space dividing us, thick with the promise of violence.

I tore my eyes away from him, scouring the panicking crowd for any sign of Montana, but I couldn't spot her among the fleeing vampires. Fear gripped me. I'd come so far to rescue her, and I couldn't fail her now.

"I need to get to my sister," I breathed as Magnar slowly rotated his swords in his grip, ready for battle.

"Julius is getting her," he replied confidently. "We'll meet them outside once I'm finished here."

Relief flooded me and I nodded, looking around once more in case I could spot them heading for an exit. Julius had gotten her away from the Belvederes once already, I was sure he could do it again.

I stepped aside as Magnar moved towards Fabian, and my heart pounded with terror for both of them. I tried to force the concern I felt for Fabian out of my skull, knowing it wasn't real, but it wouldn't budge. It was like a seed that had burrowed under my skin and wouldn't leave. It had taken root and had no intention of releasing me, its grip on me only tightening with every moment that passed.

But perhaps his death would free me. If I could only force myself to stand back and watch, then maybe Magnar would break the chain that bound me to my enemy. The thought alone sent terror racing through me, and I gritted my teeth, reminding myself of all the reasons I had to hate him.

Fabian's eyes fell on me, and he raised a hand, beckoning me towards him. He'd removed his jacket and pushed up the sleeves of his white shirt in preparation for his fight with Magnar, the dishevelled look all kinds of working for him.

Fuck.

I bit my tongue against that thought, but my gaze was drawn to the swell of his biceps despite my efforts to force the lust aside, so I closed my eyes before any more unwelcome thoughts found their way in.

"I swore I'd always protect you, Callie," Fabian called, and I opened my eyes again at the sound of his voice, unable to fight off the pull I felt towards him. "Come here, *please.*"

I took a step in his direction, then forced myself to stop, shaking my head in a firm refusal. "Get out of my head!"

I looked to Magnar so I could remind myself of who I truly was. He was my kin, my anchor. I'd sworn an oath to stand by his side, and I had no intention of abandoning him. His brows were pinched together in confusion as he watched me struggling against the urge to join Fabian, and there was a violence building in his gaze which promised nothing but bloodshed.

"What have you done to her?" Magnar growled, returning his

attention to the royal vampire before us.

"She is my wife," Fabian hissed as he stooped to retrieve a silver sword from the ground beside the uniform of a dead guard. "And she loves me."

Magnar's gaze flicked back to me for a moment before returning to Fabian.

"She is a slayer," he replied defiantly. "She was born to destroy you. She could never love you."

I opened my mouth to agree with him, but something stopped me, some horrifying reality born solely from the mark on my palm which wouldn't be denied.

Magnar lifted Venom higher, pointing it at Fabian's chest before tossing Tempest to me. I caught the heavy blade automatically, surprise flooding me as its presence swept through me.

Hello, Dream Walker. Shall we dance?

The blade's energy was darker and more forbidding than Fury's, but it hungered for the blood of the vampires in just the same way, its power sinking into me, helping me ground myself in the truth of who I was.

"Come, Callie, let's show this creature just how much you love him," Magnar scoffed as he began to advance on my husband.

I hesitated for a moment, and Fabian's gaze met mine, his eyes full of longing. But his feelings couldn't be any more real than my own. We'd been placed under some spell of the gods, and I refused to let them drive my fate anymore.

I locked my jaw and pushed my consciousness towards Tempest's thirst for blood. I could trust the blade to guide me back to the path I'd chosen even if I wasn't sure if I could trust myself. It would never falter in its hatred of the vampires.

I called on my gifts, and my ancestors' memories rose in me. They knew all about Fabian; he'd killed many of them, and some had seen weaknesses in his fighting techniques before their end came. I could use that knowledge against him. And my rage at their deaths helped to remind me of what he truly was. With Magnar by my side, we were sure to succeed where they'd failed.

Magnar released a warrior's cry as he charged into battle. I mimicked his stance, holding Tempest high and digging my heels into the solid flagstones beneath me while I watched him charge into battle.

Fabian lunged beneath Venom and brought his own sword around so quickly that I was sure Magnar was about to lose an arm. The clash of steel rang out as he managed to block the blow just in time, and the two of them instantly fell into a ferocious battle.

Their swords met again and again before Magnar's boot suddenly collided with Fabian's chest. He was thrown backwards, skidding across the concrete floor on his polished shoes until he came to a halt right before me.

Fabian's eyes met mine and he lowered his sword a fraction just before I swung Tempest over my head at him with a cry of effort.

Aim true, Sun Child.

Fabian flinched back in surprise, barely parrying the blow before I spun aside and swung at him again.

My movements weren't as fluid as they should have been because whatever it was that bound me to him fought against my actions. He blocked my blows, and I was sure he could have countered them easily, but he didn't attempt to. His face was taut with barely contained emotion, and I could tell he had no intention of harming me.

"Why?" he breathed but I had no answer to his question.

I didn't know why I couldn't force myself to fight him with my full strength. And I didn't know why I even wanted to. The warring halves of my soul confused me enough that my attacks grew sloppy.

I swung at Fabian again and he caught my arm, using my own motion to spin me away from him just as Magnar raced back towards us.

Fabian shoved me away from the fight and I fell against one of the pews, tumbling over it and falling to the other side.

I pushed myself upright, wincing as pain flared through my side. It was enough to realign my thoughts, and my lip pulled back as I set my gaze on Fabian once more.

I will break this bond.

Magnar and Fabian moved away from me, their battle growing in intensity as neither of them could gain the upper hand, and the clash of furious metal echoed through the enormous space that surrounded us.

I vaulted over the pew and ran towards them, my heels clicking on the stone floor as I raised Tempest again.

Magnar glanced at me, and Fabian slammed into him, taking full advantage of his distraction. Magnar was thrown back, soaring through the air until he slammed into a huge stained-glass window which shattered as he fell through it, disappearing outside.

My heart leapt into my throat, and I released a furious cry, raising my blade as I faced off against my husband.

"I know you feel it," Fabian growled, bright red blood trickling from his hairline to stain his jaw, the sight of it setting my pulse spiking with panic. "I know you can't hurt me."

My lips parted on a denial, but he was right, I felt it in my bones. I wouldn't be able to land a death blow against him which meant there was no point in me fighting him at all.

"I know," I admitted, my gaze meeting his as the urge to throw myself into his arms and taste his lips against mine almost overwhelmed me. "But I can run."

I turned from him before I had to see his response to that, my heart aching with the desperate desire to turn back, but I blocked it out with all I had, focusing on the thought of Magnar lying hurt somewhere outside the cathedral. Then I ran for the door as fast as my legs could fucking carry me.

MONTANA

CHAPTER THIRTY SIX

I ploughed through the mass of bodies before me. Every time the biters got near, they turned into a frenzy, trying to grab me, but Erik crushed their necks, broke bones, and flung them from me with a frightening disregard for their lives, carving a path through them like they were no more than stalks of grass.

I caught sight of Valentina up ahead, and my eyes fell on Nightmare in her grasp. My upper lip curled back as I took a step toward her, longing to reunite with my blade and get some vengeance on her while I was at it.

Erik sprinted past me in a blur, knocking the blade from her hand and grabbing hold of her throat as simple as that.

"Mas-ter," she begged. "Don't hurt me."

His eyes blazed with a destructive power that would see her crushed in moments, and I willed him to follow through. "Give me one reason why I shouldn't end you."

I ducked down, grabbing Nightmare from the floor and calming a little as it purred in my hand. I pointed it at Valentina with an ache of revenge in my heart. She'd caused Paige's death. She'd let those monsters in here and thrown me to them, happy to see me die.

"If only you'd try our ways," Valentina rasped, glancing at me with hatred, the truth of her exposed. "Drink from her, then you'll see the delights we can claim from them. The hunt is what we're made for."

A group of biters descended on us, and strong hands snatched my shoulders, pulling me back. I didn't think, didn't feel as I turned and slammed Nightmare between a vampire's ribs. She dissolved into dust but another one pounced on me in seconds. I slashed out as Nightmare whispered encouragements in my mind, urging my movements, telling me to strike this way and that, though my blows weren't precise and deadly as I needed them to be.

In moments, I was overwhelmed, and a male pulled me around to face Erik, his hand locked tight around my jaw.

"Unhand the one true queen!" my captor demanded, and Erik glared at him, squeezing Valentina's throat tighter.

"Release my wife or I will kill you all. And I shall make it torturous beyond all measure."

My heart clenched at Erik's words and the mark on my palm burned as if a sunbeam was etched into my skin.

"Let Valentina go," a female biter cried, taking hold of my wrist and bringing it to her mouth. Her fangs brushed my skin, and Erik's eyes flared with fury. He threw Valentina to the floor, her head cracking against the tiles before he shot toward me.

The biters intercepted him, but his strength was pure and wild. He ripped them to pieces as if they were nothing more than dolls, their screams falling silent as their bodies burst apart and ash swirled around Erik's feet. It had all happened so fast, I'd barely blinked before it was done, the ash of my captor swirling around me.

Erik turned to find Valentina, but she was no longer on the floor where he'd left her, the bitch having made a run for it.

"Gods be damned," he snarled, taking my arm and tugging me close.

Biters circled around us once more, taking the place of those he'd killed, and Erik rolled his shoulders, his fine clothes stained with ash, warning them of the deaths he'd already delivered.

I knew I had to find Callie, but there was no way through the onslaught without fighting our way forward.

I readied Nightmare in my palm and Erik snarled a warning at our enemies.

"Remember what she said," a male announced to the group. "Detain the prince, but the girl is ours."

As one, they surged toward us, immediately breaking me away from Erik. Adrenaline bolted through me as I stabbed with Nightmare, gasping as I managed to bury it in a female's side and yanking it free again. My heart lurched as she grabbed my hair, ripping my head back and throwing me to the floor. I rolled fast as she tried to leap on me, crawling through the sea of legs, then springing upright.

Erik collided with me as four biters took him on, and I stumbled in alarm, grabbing onto his jacket to stay upright. With a shriek of anger, I slashed Nightmare across the face of a biter holding his arm, and he reared away, screaming as blood poured from his eye.

Erik tossed a female to the floor, caving in her head with a violent kick. His next victim was cleaved apart by his hands alone and left in a bloody heap.

I finished off any biters who lay crumpled in his wake, clinging to their immortal lives beneath him, stabbing their hearts and laying waste to their bodies as ash collected at our feet, energy clashing through my blood and awakening a part of me that thrived on the fight.

Destroy them all, Moon Child.

Nightmare was alight with the battle, each death making it purr and sigh. This was what Julius had been talking about, my slayer blood making me built for this fight, and I knew the vow he spoke of could only make me stronger.

Erik finished the final two with a monstrous brutality, beheading one and snapping the other's spine like it was nothing more than a branch in his grip. Blood coated him from head to foot, dripping from his hands in a steady stream and plinking against the tiles, a severed head hanging from his fist.

I walked toward the twitching body of the vampire he had beheaded, driving my blade into its chest, and he turned to ash. The blood soaking Erik turned black as night, falling to dust along with the head in his hand, and a swirl of debris scattered from his clothes.

He turned to me with a fervent look, striding forward and pointing over my shoulder.

Miles was on the ground, apprehended by nearly twenty biters who had managed to lock him in chains and were piling on top of him to hold him down. Erik rolled up his sleeves, dragging me with him as he bounded towards his brother.

Valentina pushed through the biters, pressing her six-inch heel onto Miles's spine. "Stay back or I'll end him, Erik." She pressed her foot down and Miles cursed. "I'm taking over the New Empire. You and your family need to yield, or we'll destroy you all."

Out of nowhere, Warren appeared, swinging the huge stone font and smashing it into Valentina's face. I gasped as she hit the floor with blood pouring from her obliterated nose. The biters looked to her in horror, but Warren was upon them in seconds, ripping off limbs as he dragged Miles upright.

The moment Miles had enough room, his muscles bulged against the chains and they broke with a wrenching of metal, the pieces falling around him.

The golden-haired prince leapt upright and rolled his shoulders back, advancing on Valentina with deadly intent. "I despise traitors."

"Make it hurt," Warren urged him, and Miles smiled wickedly.

Valentina gained her feet, glancing around in fright with a storm flaring in her eyes. Erik took a threatening stance, ready to take her on alongside Miles and Warren, and I was right there with them.

An almighty crash sounded, and a blinding light sent us stumbling backwards.

The entire roof tore apart as lightning scored through it and sent a cascade of bricks plunging toward us.

Erik slammed into me, and the breath was knocked from my lungs as I hit the floor. He arched over me, grunting as bricks crashed into his body, taking the brunt of the impact. My pulse thundered violently, and I squeezed my eyes shut from the dust and debris whipping up around us.

Screams rang through the air and another flare of lightning hit the pews across from us. A fire roared in its wake, and Erik rolled, pulling me between two of the pews and shielding my body with his.

"We have to run," he said fiercely. "Hold on to me."

I wrapped my arms around his neck in answer, praying Callie was okay. That she'd survived the collapsing roof and the rampant biters. Because there was nothing I could do for her now, and that thought terrified me.

Erik scooped me upright and started running, diving over pews and tearing toward the exit at a furious speed.

As we neared it, a well-dressed vampire staggered into us. "Sire, are you okay!?" she yelled in fear.

A piece of the roof fell onto her so hard that she was crushed in an instant. I gasped in horror, clinging to Erik as he leapt over the wreckage and darted out into the rain. I was immediately soaked as he kept running and the wind battered every inch of us.

Nightmare flared in my hand. *Sun Child needs help.*

"Stop!" I cried, and Erik skidded to a halt, leaning back to look at me with raindrops clinging to his cheeks.

"We've got to go, rebel," he urged.

"Callie," I gasped as Nightmare sent a rush of energy through me. It could sense her around the next corner. She was achingly close. "She's not far."

"Where?"

"That way!" I pointed and Erik resisted for half a second longer before following my command.

CALLIE

CHAPTER THIRTY SEVEN

I raced towards the doors at the far end of the cathedral and wrenched them open as the roof began to fall in lumps around me. Torrential rain poured from the sky and battered me, carried on a freezing wind. I took a step into it, but a cold hand landed on my arm, spinning me around.

I flinched away from Fabian, raising Tempest a fraction higher but unable to convince myself to strike him.

"Don't go after him," he breathed, his hand gripping my waist, his gaze boring into mine. "Stay with me."

For a moment, I longed to give in to his request, the magic that was driving me towards him begging me to do so. Heat flared along my skin where his hands met my flesh, desire driving me close to madness as my focus dropped to his mouth, the way his shirt was clinging to his body in the rain...

I shook my head hard, pushing off those thoughts and shoving him back so he was forced to release me. I raised Tempest between us, the tip of the blade pressing to his chest right over his unbeating heart.

"This is madness," I told him over the roar of the rain. "You have to see that. You don't know me. You can't love me."

"If this is madness, then I'd gladly choose insanity," Fabian replied, his voice rough as he held his ground, Tempest burning a hole through his shirt and scorching his skin where I kept it pressed to him. "I can feel more while I stand here looking at you than I have felt in centuries. I haven't wanted anything like this in so long that I can't remember ever feeling desire like it. You've awoken something in me, Callie, something that won't rest until I make you mine entirely."

"This wasn't awoken, it was planted," I spat.

My chest ached from this distance I was maintaining between us, my need for him sharpening to the point of pain. I wanted his mouth on mine again. I needed to feel the weight of his body pinning me down and the bite of his teeth against my-

I jerked back as that invasive thought pressed its way through my mind and was joined by another; a memory of Wolfe lunging for my throat, his eyes feral with the need for my blood, the scream ripping from me when I realised he'd taken my father instead.

Dad.

The grief I felt for him overrode all else. He had been stolen from me by the monsters this man ruled over. Our entire lives had been dictated by this creature and the vampires he called siblings. I didn't lust over him, and I sure as shit didn't *love* him. He was my enemy, plain and simple.

My grip tightened on Tempest, the urge to thrust it forward spinning through me as the blade roared for the death of a Revenant. But even with the blade helping me clear my thoughts and the sharpness of my grief anchoring me inside my own skin, I still couldn't bring myself to do it. The pain I felt at the idea of a world without Fabian in it was too much to bear. But that didn't mean I was going to let him drag me back to his castle either.

"You're mine, Callie," Fabian called over the rain. "Every piece of you feels the truth of that. I know you do. Lower the blade. Let me hold you. Let me kiss those-"

A cry escaped me as I launched myself at him, Tempest swinging wide, giving me room to twist closer. I threw a kick at his side, knocking him off balance, the element of surprise buying me a couple of seconds which would have to be enough.

I used the momentum to continue my spin, whipping Tempest around with as much strength as I could muster before cracking the hilt of the blade against Fabian's temple hard enough to crack bone.

A choked sob caught in my throat at the thought of hurting him, but he was falling, stumbling to one knee with bright red blood spilling from the wound to his skull.

I met his dark eyes as he stared up at me in shock, an apology clawing its way up the back of my throat which I refused to let pass my lips.

"This is how it is," I breathed before launching myself away from him and racing out into the rain.

"Elder?!" I cried as I sprinted through the storm.

The rain saturated me, plastering my hair to my scalp and my wedding dress to my body.

The clash of steel drew me further into the darkness and I charged towards it, needing to get far away from Fabian and the unnatural pull I felt towards him. I should have plunged Tempest into his chest. Why the fuck had I left him breathing?

I ran down the rain-soaked alley, following the sounds of fighting, Magnar's battle cry leading me closer.

"Callie!" Fabian roared behind me, and I upped my pace.

I needed to get away from him, and I absolutely wasn't slowing down in the hopes that he might catch me and take me away from here. *Fuck.*

I tightened my grip on Tempest, absorbing as much of its hatred for the Belvederes as I could, increasing my speed again. It urged me onwards, and I made it around the corner of the enormous cathedral.

I staggered backwards as Magnar crashed onto the ground in front of me. No, not Magnar; Julius. They were so alike in their battle leathers that I'd mistaken him for his brother. He tumbled over and over before pushing himself upright and raising his sword.

"Julius?" I gasped. "Have you seen-"

"Not right now, beautiful," he grunted as he sprinted back into battle, Clarice racing to meet him with fangs bared and fury etched into her stunning features.

I wanted to help him somehow, but the two of them were like a force of nature. They collided with enough impact to rattle the ground beneath my feet, and I was certain I would only get in his way if I tried to assist him.

I looked around wildly. Julius should have had my sister with him, but she was nowhere to be seen.

"Montana?" I called, frantically searching the shadows for any sign of my twin.

There was no answer.

The rain slammed down so violently that it was hard to see anything more than a few feet away, but I was sure if she was near, she would have answered my call.

Panic built in my chest and my heartbeat thundered in my ears. I had to find her. We couldn't have gone through all of this for nothing. If I couldn't get her away from here now, then Erik Belvedere would take her to his bed and force her to have his demon children.

I turned back towards the cathedral and started running even faster than before. My stilettos weren't made for sprinting, but with the use of my gifts, I managed it.

"There you are!" Fabian caught up with me, the wound to his temple already healed, the blood washed away by the storm and his abs incredibly visible through his saturated white shirt. I raised Tempest, warning him back.

"Please stop chasing me," I begged.

I knew I should be plunging the blade into his chest, but my muscles wouldn't obey the command. It was all I could do to keep myself from leaping into his arms and ripping that shirt right off of him.

"I can't." He stared at me like I held the world in the palm of my hand and it was mine to offer.

"Try harder," I growled, because this wasn't fair, I was trying as hard as I could to keep on hating him, but when he looked at me like that, it chipped away at my resolve.

Fabian stepped closer, the tip of my blade touching his chest right above his heart once again as he held his arms wide.

"If you don't want me, then you might as well kill me," he breathed, his voice barely carrying over the storm. "My life is yours, Callie. I don't know why, but it's true. I can't bear to be without you. If you don't end me, I won't stop coming for you. I need you to be mine."

I gritted my teeth as the part of me who had been born to end the vampires battled against the part which lit with joy at his words. I wanted to drop my sword and rip his clothes from his body and... stab him, stab him, stab him!

I screamed as I pressed Tempest forward and a line of blood stained his white shirt. He didn't move to stop me, but I couldn't force my arm to continue.

We stared at each other, neither of us understanding what we were now. Neither of us able to move away.

A tremendous roar made me turn my head half a second before Magnar collided with Fabian, knocking him away from me and sending the two of them crashing into the street.

Venom was strapped across his back, and he fought Fabian with nothing but his bare hands. Magnar's fist slammed into his face, and I winced as the impact was followed by a horrible snapping sound.

Fabian struggled beneath the bulk of the enormous warrior, and I almost wanted to step in and help him. I shook my head angrily. I didn't want to help Fabian, I wanted to help *Magnar*.

As I hesitated, Fabian managed to get his legs up between them, kicking Magnar off of him with enough force to send him rolling across the concrete.

Magnar was on his feet again in moments, charging at Fabian again, death written into his features.

My heart tumbled over. I wanted to join the fight, but I didn't think I could trust myself to help. What if my involvement caused Magnar's death? Or Fabian's? I wasn't sure I could bear that either.

"There she is!" a female voice cried.

I turned at the sound of excited shouts behind me and found Valentina pointing me out. She gave me a dazzling smile and my eyes widened in horror as a horde of vampires swarmed for me, salivating like I was a freshly baked pie.

I swallowed thickly, raising Tempest between us and reaching for my gifts. Valentina was lost to the swell of the crowd, but I couldn't spare any attention for her with the swarm of bloodthirsty monsters coming for me.

I had half a second to prepare myself before the hungry crowd fell on me, but that was all I needed. Maybe the gods had fucked me up and made it impossible to strike at Fabian, but I had no reservation at all about cutting through these beasts.

Tempest burned with pleasure in my palms, hungry for the battle, and I swung it before him as the first of them made it close enough to me. Blood flew, splattering my white dress, and I hefted the blade again, ending three of them in a ferocious strike that carved through blood and bone.

More piled into their place, surrounding me as they tried to get close enough to bite, every one of them feral with the desire to sink their teeth into me. I smiled like a savage at the vampires who thirsted for my blood, Tempest purring hungrily in my hands.

Let's carve them from this earth, little warrior, it cooed. *Give me a taste of their demise.*

They came at me in a rush, but I didn't falter, my grip on the blade unyielding, my need for survival undeniable.

I refused to let them have me. My blood was my own, and I'd carve through a thousand of them before they would ever take it.

MONTANA

CHAPTER THIRTY EIGHT

We circled the cathedral, and I knew with every speeding footstep Erik took, we were getting closer to my sister. I clung to him as he carried me, willing him to move like the wind and bring me to her.

An ear-splitting noise sounded from above, and one of the spires toppled from the building, smashing into the ground before us. I gasped as Erik leapt onto the crumbled mess with impossible agility, avoiding lumps of jagged rock and shards of glass. Leaping from one place to the other until somehow, we made it to the other side without a single scratch.

My heart was in my throat as we rounded into a wide street and chaos spread out before us.

Magnar and Fabian were locked in a fierce battle, the rain pouring over them in a never-ending torrent. I couldn't tell who was winning; they were too evenly matched, blocking every blow, clashing with the wildness of beasts.

I hunted for Callie urgently, my mouth dry as I climbed out of Erik's arms and my heels hit the pavement, my wedding dress weighing me down. The rain was so thick that I could hardly see a hundred paces ahead. A dark shadow loomed beyond the fight, and the sound of snarls reached my ears, sending my gut spiralling.

A scream tore through the air and Clarice flew over our heads, smashing into the wall of the cathedral before collapsing on the ground. She regained her footing in seconds, the sound of bones fusing back together as she snarled. Julius approached her at a terrifying pace, sword raised and hatred in his dark eyes.

"By the gods, you've got a fire in that undead body of yours," Julius called to her.

Erik stepped into his path, shoving me back a few paces, and Julius took him in with an assessing gaze, slowing to a halt.

"You've got a free pass today, parasite," Julius spoke to him, offering me a nod. "But only because of her."

"He's *mine*!" Clarice rose to her feet, leaping over Erik and launching herself at Julius with nothing but her bare hands. She slammed into him, the two of them hitting the concrete and rolling away from us as each of them fought to get the upper hand.

Erik gazed after his sister, seeming unsure if he should follow them, but it didn't look like Clarice needed any assistance. I just prayed Julius survived the wrath of her fangs, because she looked fit to rip him apart.

"Callie!" I called, turning my attention back to finding her, the sheeting rain making it hard to see much ahead of us. But she had to be out here. I couldn't let myself consider the possibility that she hadn't made it out of the cathedral.

I started running, and Erik swore through his teeth as we closed in on Fabian and Magnar.

"Brother!" Erik called to him, and both he and Magnar turned.

Magnar's eyes burned as they locked on Erik, and an endless moment hung between them, filled with a thousand years of hatred. Fabian collided with Magnar and the tension was broken, the two of them locked in their fight once again.

A scream cut through the air, and Erik's head snapped toward the source of the cry.

My heart stalled as the shadow in the mist came into view, the rain easing just enough to see what it was. At least twenty biters surrounded

Callie and it was clear she'd taken even more out before our arrival. She moved like a warrior, tearing through their bodies with a huge sword, scattering the vampires to the rain. I didn't know how it was possible that she was so strong. So fearless. I almost didn't recognise her.

"Erik, help her!" I ordered, running forward with Nightmare raised, readying to dive into battle right at her side where I belonged.

He sped toward the biters and threw a fist that sent a female flying to the ground with a vile crack. Callie was fighting furiously, but she was nearly overwhelmed. She panted heavily, and I could see she was tiring, no matter how hard she fought it.

Fear clutched my heart as Erik battled his way through the biters, forging a path for us, and I wielded Nightmare at his back, slashing at them as hard as I could. The rebels were so intent on reaching Callie that I managed to bury my blade in several of their chests before they knew what was happening.

Erik was ruthless in his attacks, cleaving out the biters' hearts without mercy while I powered through the throng of wet, cold bodies, keeping close to him. My gaze fixed on my twin, Nightmare guiding my movements to block any blows that came my way while I advanced with Erik. I had to reach her. I had to stand at her side in her hour of need.

As we finally broke through the circle, I leapt to Callie's side, panting and slick with sodden ash. She gasped her joy, then cursed, ramming her golden blade into the heart of a snarling vampire coming up behind me. Dust exploded around us, and the wind and rain stole it away just as quickly. Callie grabbed a male's arm, ramming the sword into his chest and half-spearing another female behind him too. With a surge of adrenaline, I darted forward and pushed her further onto Callie's blade. The female's shriek was cut off as she turned to dust around us, the rain washing it away like she had never existed.

Erik tore through a line of biters ahead of us, keeping them back as they tried to overwhelm us. Every one of them who got close met the wrath of his hands and teeth. The rain gushed around our feet, washing away the remains of the dead, and the onslaught slowed.

Callie released a choked noise, and I stole a glance at her. Her eyes were pinned on something behind me, and she started running before I could stop her.

"No!" she cried, her voice laced with fear.

I spun to watch, my heart in my throat as Magnar's golden blade sliced across Fabian's arm and he lost his grip on his weapon. Fabian stumbled back, lifting a hand to stop Magnar advancing, snarling a warning.

Magnar smiled keenly, cornering him against the wall and slamming his blade into Fabian's stomach. My mind spun at the sight, the brutality of the strike, the promise of death in the air.

"Erik!" I called as the final biters ringed around him and we were forced to fight once more.

But while we were stuck here, Fabian's last moments on earth were ticking down, and I could see the terror in Erik's eyes over that fact, his love for his brother stark in the face of his impending death. And there was nothing he could do to stop it.

CALLIE

CHAPTER THIRTY NINE

Fabian's cry of pain drew all of my attention as I ran, racing away from my sister and Erik Belvedere. I was compelled by the mark on my palm, driving me toward my husband, forcing me away from my sister no matter how desperately I wanted to remain by her side.

My heart clenched in panic as I sprinted towards Magnar and Fabian.

I saw the blood first, and my pulse pounded violently as I charged closer. So much blood, too much blood.

Please be alright, please, please.

Fabian staggered sideways with a hand pressed to the gaping wound on his stomach, his shoes sliding in the rain as he fell back against a wall, barely remaining upright. Magnar swung Venom over his head, preparing to finish what he'd started, death written into his features and challenging the entire world to defy him.

Terror threatened to overwhelm me, and I threw myself between them without a single moment of hesitation, raising Tempest to take the force of the blow which was intended to rip Fabian from this world.

Venom crashed against my blade so hard that my bones shook, the brute force of Magnar's strike almost toppling me before him.

I stared up at Magnar in shock, unable to believe what I'd done. I'd leapt between a Belvedere and death, my blade still ringing with the force of the collision.

My arms started to tremble with the strength required to hold Magnar off, and he wrenched Venom back, staring down at me in wild confusion, and as Fabian sagged to the ground at my back, he readied another blow.

"Please don't," I begged, catching Magnar's arm as he lifted his blade above Fabian's heart, my husband bleeding out on the street beneath him, unable to so much as regain his feet. Tears burst from my eyes, mixing with the rain that continued to drench us as they scored acidic lines down my cheeks.

"What the fuck is this, Callie? What the hell has he done to you?" Magnar demanded, pausing long enough to look into my eyes, his golden gaze searching mine, disgust and betrayal swimming in their depths.

"It wasn't Fabian." I held my left hand out and showed him the cross on my palm. "It was Idun. She doesn't want me to love you."

"And do you?" he asked, his eyes burning with an intensity that carved its way through me, past every wall I'd ever constructed to shield myself from men with black hearts and smiles gifted by the devil.

My breath caught in my throat as I stared up at him, the rain slicking across his skin, highlighting the strength of his features, the ruin I could so easily find in his arms. My tongue stuck to the roof of my mouth as the goddess tried to seal my lips, but I wouldn't let her. Not this time.

"I've been falling for you since the moment you pinned me against that wall." It broke my heart to admit it because I knew I didn't deserve his love. I was offering him a fractured version of myself. I was tied to a monster he'd sworn to kill.

Magnar slowly lowered his sword. His eyes filled with a burning desire as something shifted within his expression, and he took a step towards me before halting again. Idun still wouldn't let him move closer, but I knew he wanted to.

Fabian released a groan filled with pain, and Magnar's gaze hardened instantly, whatever he'd been going to say lost as his focus returned to the Belvedere who lay at my back. "Step aside, Callie. I have to do this."

Magnar's command slammed into me, and I was forced to do as he said, despite the unwanted portion of my soul crying out in alarm as he raised Venom over Fabian's heart.

"No," I gasped, a sob escaping my lips as I looked down at the vampire I wanted to hate but found myself longing for instead.

Fabian was slumped against the wall, his skin even paler than usual, his white shirt stained bright red. His hand pressed down on a wound which would have been more than enough to kill a mortal but wouldn't ever be enough to end a vampire.

His eyes were on me, and he reached out, brushing his fingers against the hem of my dress, his sword laying forgotten and out of reach. "You shouldn't have put yourself in danger for me."

I wanted to pull him into my arms and take away his pain...or maybe I wanted to end it myself, drive my blade through his blackened heart and save the world from the burden of his existence. My grip tightened on Tempest, but I couldn't raise it. I was so confused, I didn't know what *I* wanted anymore, but as I looked down at the immortal monster with eyes so deep I could lose myself in them, I knew that his death would tear me in two.

"Please," I whispered, knowing I couldn't stop him if he chose to act now, the power of his control over me keeping me back, his skill outmatching my own even if it wasn't. "If he dies, I think a part of me will die too."

Magnar released an angry growl, but he stayed his blade for a moment, though the tip of it hovered over Fabian's chest.

"I will tear Idun from the heavens in payment for this curse," he snarled, indecision halting him as he weighed my words, none of us knowing how much truth they held.

"I propose a trade!" Clarice's voice startled me, and we turned to find her at our backs, her dress bloody and torn, her hair plastered to her cheeks, but victory clinging to her just as fiercely. Julius was kneeling on the floor in front of her and she held a thin blade pressed to his throat while fisting his hair in her grip to expose his throat to it. "My brother for yours."

The silence around us was pregnant with violence. Even the rain began to slow as the world held its breath for Magnar's answer.

"Tell her to get fucked, Magnar," Julius called into the space between raindrops. "I took my vow, same as you. I'd give my life to end his, and you know it."

Magnar's gaze was locked on his brother, and I could tell the strength of his belief in the vow he lived by was battling against the unending love he felt for his brother. Of course he wouldn't give Julius's life for Fabian's, but Idun wanted him to. I could feel her watching us, testing his devotion to her cause yet again, despite how often she toyed with him and betrayed his loyalty.

I needed more than just this trade though. I had to get as far from Fabian as possible. Whatever the goddess had done to me was growing stronger with every second that passed, and I couldn't bear to think about what that might mean for me. What it might make me do. My legs were already shaking with the desire to bend, to drop me down beside my fallen husband so that I might take him in my arms, press my mouth to his and-

"*Please*, Magnar," I begged, his name falling from my lips as I forced my tongue to follow *my* commands instead of Idun's. He stilled as he realised what I'd managed to do, and his eyes glimmered with some deep emotion, his resolve hardening as he made his choice. "I don't know what's happened to me, but I need to get away from here. Away from *him*." I pointed at the bleeding vampire at our feet. "Please, just make the trade and take me far away."

My heart thumped painfully at the thought of leaving Fabian behind, but I knew I had to do it. The closer I was to him, the more I ached to be with him, the more I yearned to feel his flesh against mine, his mouth on my skin, more and more until I couldn't breathe with the need for it. It wasn't right. It wasn't *me*. And I needed to get away from him to make certain that I wouldn't give in.

"You would leave me for him?" Fabian asked quietly, his voice laced with raw pain, the power of this spell which had captivated the two of us ripping something open in him.

I fought hard against the part of me which yearned to be his and spoke what I knew in my heart was the truth as I looked down into his dark eyes. "Yes. I belong with him."

The heat in Magnar's gaze burned a little brighter and his shoulders sagged as he drew Venom back an inch.

MONTANA

CHAPTER FORTY

My heart wouldn't settle as I watched the madness unfolding before me, the last of the biters now turned to dust around us. Erik stood at my side, assessing the situation in stony silence, looking from Fabian to Clarice like he was measuring every outcome of each decision he could make from here.

"Trade!" Clarice commanded, her golden hair plastered to her cheeks and a look of desperation in her eyes.

Magnar stiffened, glaring at her, then turning his gaze to Erik.

The Belvederes' love for one another was undeniable, their bond defying all else.

Miles and Warren appeared, running over to join us. "Sorry we're late to the party, we were off hunting biters," Miles commented, then his eyes fell on Fabian at Magnar's feet, terror brightening his blue eyes. "No - brother!"

Erik didn't reply, watching Fabian intently, his jaw tight and his eyes as black as night.

Magnar's face contorted as he weighed his odds. The slayers were outnumbered. And fear struck a chord in my heart at the idea of this descending into another fight. Of more blood being shed.

I took a step toward Callie, my heart hurting over what the gods had done to her, twisting her mind and binding her to Fabian. It was sick.

Magnar turned his gaze to Julius, his chin raising with a firm decision. "Release him."

I let out a breath of relief as Magnar took the trade, praying we could all still walk away from this with our lives.

Clarice nodded, lifting her knife from Julius's throat, the tension in the air easing just a little. Magnar kept his sword aimed at Fabian until Julius was at his side, then reluctantly drew it away. Callie pushed Magnar back a few steps, keeping close to him, her features fraught with confliction.

The moment they moved, Clarice darted forward and dropped to her knees beside Fabian. She hugged him to her chest, but he seemed to have fallen unconscious, lying in an ever-growing pool of bright red blood.

Erik advanced, his shoulders tensing as he stared Magnar down.

Magnar snarled in response, lifting his huge sword, seeming ready to fight Erik to the end. "Come and face me, monster. I will give you the slow and drawn-out death you deserve for what you did to my father."

"No- *please*," Callie begged Magnar. "I have to get away from here."

Erik didn't slow, his fists curling in preparation of a fight, and my heart lurched into my throat.

I raced into his path, turning my back to Magnar and planting a hand on Erik's chest.

"Stop. Let them go," I commanded.

Erik's eyes slid down to mine and the darkness in them lifted a fraction. "I cannot let the slayers leave. They'll never stop hunting us. I have to finish this."

He took my arm to push me aside and fear tangled with my blood.

"No!" I yelled, pressing my full weight against him even though I knew it was pointless. If he insisted on this, I couldn't stop him. But I couldn't let that happen. I wouldn't let him dismiss me.

"Erik," I growled. "You will let them go. If you hurt them, I'll never forgive you."

I could hear Callie begging Magnar to leave, and he looked tempted to give in. If I was able to convince Erik to stay his hand, maybe I could give them a chance to run at least.

Miles and Warren shared a glance, seeming willing to follow Erik's lead.

"Rebel..." Erik took hold of my chin, his expression torn. "You don't understand."

"I do." I took his hand, pressing my mark to his so a hungry energy flowed between us. "And I'm still asking you to let them go."

I glanced over my shoulder, spotting Callie, Magnar, and Julius grouping closer together with their golden weapons raised.

"Monty?" Callie called.

She wanted to run, but she wouldn't leave without me. I could see it in her eyes.

My heart was tugged in two directions, the new bond demanding I stay with Erik and my heart wanting that too, but my choice would always be my sister.

"Leave him - let's go," Callie insisted, her cheeks ashen and her eyes glimmering.

"Please," I begged Erik. "Stand down."

Erik released a low growl, slowly turning to Miles with his fangs bared. "We'll fight another day," he commanded, and Miles opened his mouth in surprise.

Tears pricked my eyes as I backed up, relief spilling through me, but it was quickly drowned away as I realised what came next. I couldn't part from Callie again. We'd been away from each other too long. We were owed a free life, away from the vampires, far away from this city and any fences that were built to cage us.

"She needs me," I breathed as the rain battered my cheeks. "And I need her."

Erik's posture stiffened as he stared at me in anguish, realising what I was saying.

"You're leaving," he stated with so much pain it was as if he was announcing my death.

He wasn't going to keep me, no more cages or possession. He was finally taking the shackles off.

"I have to," I said, my words choked as emotion threatened to overwhelm me. Because we both knew, the moment I walked away, we'd never see each other again. I may have had plans to help with the curse, but now I'd seen the carnage caused by the slayers and vampires colliding, how could we ever return here? And with Callie bound to Fabian, I couldn't risk him getting his hands on her. Maybe we could help from afar, maybe there was something yet to be done. But right now, there was only one option available to us. We had to run and never come back. Leaving Erik behind was a pain I couldn't bear to endure, but it was one I had to choose for myself as much as my sister.

"My whole life has been dictated by your kind," I said, the truth of what Erik and I were, vampire and human, too stark to ignore anymore. "I'm done living in cages."

He raised a hand, carving his thumb along the line of my cheek. "And I'm done caging you, Montana."

"You mean it?" I whispered.

He looked ready to argue, to demand I stay or even take me into his arms and refuse to let me go. But he did none of those things. Erik was letting me make my own choice for once. As his arms fell to his sides and defeat took root in his eyes, I knew his decision was made.

"If it's what you truly want," he said tightly, staring at me like he could see the part of me that wanted to stay.

"It is," I said, ignoring the agony those words caused me, the way the mark on my palm seared.

"Then I won't stop you."

I moved closer to him, tears burning the backs of my eyes as I stared up at this creature who had claimed some piece of my heart, if not all of it entirely.

"Thank you," I whispered, my soul shattering at the weight of this goodbye.

"I won't look for you," he said darkly, and the mark on my hand screamed, demanding I take back what I was saying and let Erik steal me away. But I knew my own mind, and my decision had been made long before the gods tried to decide it for me. "Even when the demons in me demand it."

I leaned into him, his cypress scent surrounding me, and I felt the burning stares of the slayers at my back. The judgement they must have been casting on me. But I couldn't waste my final moments with Erik Belvedere pretending I didn't care about him. Leaving him felt like tearing out a piece of my heart and abandoning it here. It would hurt like hell, and perhaps I'd never really recover from it, but it had to be done. I couldn't abandon my sister. Not now. Not after everything we'd been through to find each other.

"They're waiting for you," he said coldly, his eyes slipping to the slayers with unmasked hatred, but there was envy in his gaze too now. "Perhaps you will come back for me one day, and you will raise a blade against me at their side."

"Never," I said through my teeth. I wanted him, no matter what the world thought of that, but that didn't mean we could be together.

"It's in your blood," he said. "We're made to destroy each other."

"I don't care what the gods made us for. I'm not their pawn."

"Always the rebel." He smiled but there was no light in it, a sea of darkness clouding his gaze. "But I fear your blood will out. Though perhaps that fate isn't so unbearable if it means I will see you once again."

"Stop it," I begged, gripping his arms and fighting against the jagged lump in my throat. Our seconds were counting down, each one fractured and lost.

"*Montana*," Julius barked, but I didn't look back.

Erik's gaze slid over my head, arrowing in on the slayer who had called my name, and his hand curled around mine, latching tight.

I backed away, knowing I was crushing him by doing this, and I was breaking myself in the process.

I turned to leave, unable to bear this goodbye a second longer, but Erik yanked me back to him, crushing his lips to mine. Rainwater sailed between our mouths, the taste of unfulfilled promises making a sob crack through my chest.

His lips were icily cold and sent a shiver through to my heart, but as he held me, the cold ebbed away and a fire coursed through my veins in its place. I knew with a suddenness that frightened me that I had fallen in love with him, and this love was condemned to die.

I pulled away and heated tears rolled down my cheeks, mixing with the rain. His hand still gripped mine as I backed up, like he was regretting agreeing to this, like he might just change his mind and seize me once again.

But then he let me go, his brow lowering as the rain cascaded over him and he became a broken creature accepting his fate.

My feet stopped moving, but Callie ran to me, taking my hand and dragging me away. I kept looking over my shoulder as I forced myself to run with her, and Erik's gaze burrowed into mine, a ceaseless want passing between us. A want that had been doomed the moment we'd first felt it.

The rain swept around Erik and his family, making them appear like statues in the mist, so still they defied nature.

I fell into step with Julius and Magnar as they raced away from the royals, my soul crushing with every step I took, the mark on my hand burning, begging me to go back.

We turned a corner and my heart shattered into a million pieces, even though I was sure I'd done the right thing. I had to stay with Callie, the last of my family. But doing so sent a shudder of finality through me, the agony of it slicing through my veins.

There was one thought I held onto in the wake of my choice. It was more than a promise, it was a vow. One I committed to with my entire being.

I'll find a way to break the curse, Erik.

I swear it.

AUTHOR NOTE

Hey, how are you doing after that one? Full of joy at the twins finally escaping the evil clutches of those bastard vampires, never to return again? Are you shouting 'good riddance to bad rubbish' at the top of your lungs and hoping the sun shines down on those immortal dicks and makes them cower inside for the rest of time while Callie and Montana head off to live out their lives on a desert island far away, never to think of the bitey butt holes ever again?

Well…that might be the outline of book four, orrr there might be a whole world of pain and consequences headed your way.

This series holds a very special place in our hearts because it was the very first one Caroline and I wrote together. It was where we learned how to build a story in harmony with each other and create a world and characters together too. It was the beginning of our writing journey in many ways and it's crazy to think that a little idea of us giving co-writing a go one Christmas spiralled into the twisted beast it is now, but none of it could have been possible without you. We can never stop trying to express our gratitude to you as our readers for stepping into the worlds we create together and falling in love with them the way we have.

So thank you, we love you, and we promise to keep torturing characters and creating hateful antagonists in your honour for as long as we possibly can,

Love, Susanne and Caroline XOXO

WANT MORE?

To find out more, grab yourself some freebies and to join our reader group, scan the QR code below.

Made in United States
North Haven, CT
08 April 2024

51028235R10278